THE COLLECTED [illegible]

The Collected Martin Millar includes *The Good* [illegible] *York*, *Ruby & The Stone Age Diet* and *Lux the Poet*. Martin Millar is also the author of *Milk, Sulphate & Alby Starvation* and *Dreams of Sex & Stage Diving*. His homepage can be located on the internet and he can be contacted on kbh38@dial.pipex.com.

THE COLLECTED MARTIN MILLAR

The Good Fairies of New York

Ruby & The Stone Age Diet

Lux the Poet

Martin Millar

FOURTH ESTATE • *London*

This edition first published in 1998 by
Fourth Estate Limited
6 Salem Road
London W2 4BU

10 9 8 7 6 5 4 3 2 1

A catalogue record for this book is available from the British Library.

ISBN 1 85702 910 0

Printed in Great Britain by Cox & Wyman Ltd, Reading, Berkshire

Contents

The Good Fairies of New York 1

Ruby & The Stone Age Diet 223

Lux the Poet 377

The Good Fairies of New York

'My main concern in life,' said Kerry, 'is collecting my flower alphabet. This is a difficult task, as some of the flowers involved are rare and obscure, particularly in New York. Once I have my flower alphabet, however, all sorts of good things will follow.

'For one thing, it will look beautiful. For another, it may well benefit me with regard to the strange wasting disease I suffer from, because an Ancient Celtic flower alphabet is bound to be very powerful. Also it will be a devastating weapon against Cal, a man who, by going back on his promise to teach me every New York Dolls guitar solo, proved himself to be one of the lowest forms of life. Once my flower alphabet wins the East 4th Street Community Arts Association Prize his life will be in ruins.'

The nurse smiled at Kerry, placed a thermometer gently in her mouth, and busied herself with the preparations for the operation.

ONE

Dinnie, an overweight enemy of humanity, was the worst violinist in New York, but was practising gamely when two cute little fairies stumbled through his fourth-floor window and vomited on the carpet.

'Sorry,' said one.

'Don't worry,' said the other. 'Fairy vomit is no doubt sweet-smelling to humans.'

By this time, however, Dinnie was halfway down the stairs, and still accelerating.

'Two fairies just came though my window and were sick on the carpet!' he screamed on reaching 4th Street, not fully realising the effect that this would have on the passers-by till the men sweating with sacks round a garbage truck stopped to laugh at him.

'What d'you say?'

'Upstairs,' gasped Dinnie. 'Two fairies, with kilts and violins and little swords . . . green kilts . . . '

The men stared at him. Dinnie's monologue ground to a halt.

'Hey,' called the foreman, 'leave that dumb homo alone and get back to work. C'mon, let's get busy!'

'No, really,' protested Dinnie, but his audience was gone. Dinnie stared hopelessly after them.

They didn't believe me, he thought. No wonder. I don't believe myself.

On the corner, four Puerto Ricans kicked a tennis ball back

and forth. They looked pityingly at Dinnie. Chastened by public ridicule, Dinnie slunk back into the old theatre on the ground floor of his building. His room was right at the top, four flights up, but Dinnie was unsure whether he wanted to climb them or not.

'I like my privacy,' he grumbled. 'And my sanity.'

He decided to buy some beer from the deli across the street.

'But if I find two fairies in my room when I get back, there's going to be trouble.'

Five more fairies, all suffering from massive confusion due to beer, whisky and magic mushrooms, were at that moment fleeing in drunken terror from the chaos of Park Avenue to the comparative shelter of Central Park.

'What part of Cornwall is this?' wailed Padraig, narrowly escaping the wheels of a honey-roasted-peanut vendor's trailer.

'The Goddess only knows,' replied Brannoc, and tried to help Tulip, who had become entangled in the dangling reins of a sightseer's horse and trap.

'I think I'm still hallucinating,' whimpered Padraig as a tidal wave of joggers trundled down the path towards him. He was saved by Maeve, who hurried them on, deep into the undergrowth.

They flopped down to rest on a quiet patch of land.

'Are we safe?'

Noise still surrounded them, but no people were in sight. This was a relief. They were invisible to most humans, but so many hurrying feet were a terrible danger.

'I think so,' replied Brannoc, oldest fairy present and something of a leader. 'But I'm beginning to suspect we're not in Cornwall any more.'

A squirrel hopped over to join them.

'Hello,' said Brannoc politely, despite his terrible hangover.

'What the hell are you?' demanded the squirrel.

'We are fairies,' answered Brannoc, and the squirrel fell on the grass laughing, because New York squirrels are cynical creatures and do not believe in fairies.

Meanwhile back on 4th Street, Dinnie swallowed a mouthful of Mexican beer, scratched his plump chin and strode confidently into his room, convinced that he had imagined the whole thing.

Two fairies were sleeping peacefully on his bed. Dinnie was immediately depressed. He knew that he did not have enough money to see a therapist.

TWO

Across the street, Kerry was just waking up in her soft bed of old cushions. Kerry, as well as being wondrously lovely, could pick up some tattered old piece of material and make it into a beautiful cushion, or maybe a hat or a waistcoat, with ease.

She was also a talented painter, sculptor, singer and writer, a dedicated shoplifter, and a serious collector of flowers. And she was a keen guitarist, but her technique was dreadful.

Most people loved her but despite this she was not happy this morning. Her unhappiness stemmed from four main sources. The first was a news report on television about terrible floods in Bangladesh with pictures of bodies which upset her badly, and the second was the chronic wasting disease she was suffering from. The third was her lack of skill on the guitar. Despite hours of practising, she still could not play Johnny Thunders' guitar solo from 'Pirate Love'.

The fourth, far outweighing these at the moment, was her complete inability to make up her mind as to what looked best pinned in her hair: carnations or roses. Kerry's hair was based loosely on a painting by Botticelli and the right flowers were essential.

She sat gloomily in front of the mirror, trying first one then the other, reflecting bitterly that it was no use at all dyeing your hair to a beautiful silvery blue when you still had problems like this to face up to.

The flower alphabet was coming on well and she now had fifteen out of the twenty-seven flowers she required.

Across the street the fairies were waking up.

'Where are our friends?' muttered Heather, brushing her golden hair away from her beautiful eyes.

Dinnie stared balefully at her.

'I don't know what you are,' he said, 'and I don't care. But whatever you are, get the hell out of my room and leave me alone.'

Dinnie MacKintosh was not noted for his politeness. He was not really noted for anything except his rudeness, intolerance and large appetite.

'My name is Heather. I am a thistle fairy. And this is Morag. Could I have a glass of water please?'

'No!' thundered Dinnie. 'You can't. Get out of here!'

'What sort of way is that to speak to us?' demanded Heather, propping herself up on a tiny elbow. 'Where we come from anyone would be honoured to bring us a glass of water. They'd talk about it for years if we so much as appeared to them. We only appeared to you because we heard you playing a Scottish violin tune.'

'Extremely badly,' interjected Morag, wakening slightly.

'Yes,' agreed Heather, 'extremely badly. The violin had an

interesting tone, but frankly it was the worst rendition of the "Reel of Tulloch" I have ever heard, and that is saying something. It was worse than the playing of the blacksmith's son back home in the village of Cruickshank, and I wouldn't have thought that was possible.'

'My playing is not that bad,' protested Dinnie.

'Oh, it is. Really terrible.'

'Well no one invited you here to listen to it,' said Dinnie angrily.

'But don't worry,' continued Morag, fingering her tiny violin. 'We will show you how to do it properly. We are good fairies, and always happy to help. Now kindly bring us some water.'

'Hi,' purred a naked woman on the TV, rubbing her breasts with a phone. 'We're the Cream Team and we give ass, head and pussy so well it's a fucking crime. Phone us on 970 T–W–A–T.'

'I must still be hallucinating,' said Morag. 'I swear I will never touch another magic mushroom. Except possibly for medicinal purposes.'

Dinnie strode up to the bed and loudly requested that Heather and Morag leave immediately as he did not believe in fairies. The fairies burst out laughing.

'You are funny,' chortled Heather, but the action of laughing upset her precarious hangover and she threw up again, all over Dinnie's arm.

'Well he certainly believes in us now!' screamed Morag.

'Don't worry,' said Heather. 'Fairy vomit is no doubt sweet-smelling to humans.'

They both went back to sleep and no amount of abuse from Dinnie could wake them.

THREE

The homeless clustered everywhere in New York. Every street corner had its own beggar with dull eyes who asked passers-by for change with little hope of a response. Every park was laced and ribboned with makeshift plastic tents and stinking blankets rolled up as sleeping bags. These homeless had the most hopeless of lives. No government scheme would ever give them a fresh start. No charity would ever be rich enough to house them. No employer would ever give them work without their having a place to live, or at least some clean clothes, and clean clothes were never going to appear to anyone who sweated all day in a swelteringly hot park. All they could do was get by the best they could until they died, and this did not happen nearly quickly enough as far as the decent citizens of New York were concerned.

One homeless old man sat down for a rest on 4th Street, sighed, closed his eyes, and died.

'Another one dead,' muttered Magenta, arriving on the scene. Magenta herself was a homeless beggar, though a fairly young one.

'At this rate I'll have no troops left.'

She saluted the fallen warrior and toiled her way along to Broadway, keeping a wary eye out for Persian cavalry divisions. Even though she was still some way from the army of Antaxerxes and was not expecting trouble, she knew that being this deep inside enemy territory she had to be careful.

Back in England, in Cornwall, Tala the King was most upset at the flight of Petal and Tulip. As his children and rightful heirs they were already being whispered of by rebels as suitable replacements for himself.

'Find them,' he instructed Magris, his Chief Technician, 'and bring them back.'

Of course, the Fairy King of Cornwall could not know that at this moment two of the fugitives were waking in an empty room on 4th Street.

They immediately began to argue.

'I feel terrible.'

'Well, it's your own fault,'said Morag. 'The way you were throwing back mushrooms and whisky.'

'What do you mean? You were the one who vomited over your new kilt.'

'I did not. It was you. You can't take your drink. Just like the well-known saying, never trust a MacKintosh with a glass of whisky or a fiddle.'

'That's not a well-known saying.'

'It is in my clan.'

'Morag MacPherson, you will be the death of me. And if you insult the MacKintoshs' fiddle playing one more time, I will be the death of you.'

'There is no fiddle playing to insult.'

They glared at each other.

'What happened to the others?'

'I don't know. We lost them after you fell unconscious and I had to help you.'

'I did not fall unconscious, you did. No MacPherson fairy can hold her whisky.'

'Any MacPherson can hold it better than a MacKintosh,'

The argument intensified until it became too much for their hangovers. Heather swore an obscure Scottish oath and stumbled off the bed, rubbing her temples. She approached the window. The wings of a thistle fairy are useful only for short flights at the best of times and now, weakened by mushrooms, whisky, beer and jet-lag, Heather had a hard time fluttering up to the window-sill.

She finally made it and looked down on East 4th Street. She gasped. To a Scottish thistle fairy, used only to hills, glens and the quiet village of Cruickshank, it was an amazing sight. Cars and people everywhere, children, dogs, noise, and at least ten shops within twenty yards. In Cruickshank there was only one shop, and very few cars.

'What is this place? Where are we?'

Morag joined her. Her first sober sight of their new environment made her forget the argument and she clutched Heather's hand.

'I think it must be a city.'

'What's a city?'

'Like a big town. Like lots of villages put together. I think we must be in Glasgow.'

'But we were in Cornwall,' protested Morag. 'Cornwall isn't close to Glasgow, is it?'

Heather shook her head. She did not think so, but her geography was as shaky as Morag's. Since leaving Scotland neither of them had had much idea of where they were most of the time.

They peered down at the street where a ragged man with a shopping bag tramped forcefully along the sidewalk, spilling small children out of the way.

This ragged man was Joshua. He was in pursuit of Magenta who had made off with his recipe for Fitzroy cocktail, a drink consisting of shoe polish, methylated spirits, fruit juice and a secret concoction of herbs.

After pursuing her down First Avenue he had lost sight of her when she dodged down the subway. She was a cunning adversary but he would never give up the hunt for his recipe, the most precious thing he had ever had in his possession.

'What happened to our friends? Where are Brannoc and Maeve and Padraig and Petal and Tulip?'

It was impossible to say. They could be anywhere in this city. Neither of them could remember much except waking up in a huge bumpy machine and being tossed into the street in a beer crate. Their friends had presumably been carried off by the machine. They started to argue again about whose fault it was.

'Right, you two,' said Dinnie, stomping back into the room. 'Get out of here immediately and don't come back.'

'What is the matter with you?' demanded Heather, shaking her golden hair. 'Humans are supposed to be pleased, delighted and honoured when they meet a fairy. They jump about going "A fairy, a fairy!" and laugh with pleasure. They don't demand they get out of their room immediately and don't come back.'

'Well, welcome to New York,' snarled Dinnie. 'Now beat it.'

'Fine,' said Heather. 'We'll go. But don't come crying to us if your lineage is cursed to the seventh generation.'

'Or even the thirteenth.'

They stared at each other. A cockroach peered out from behind the cooker, then went about its business.

Morag, generally the more rational of the two fairies, tried to calm the situation.

'Allow me to introduce myself. I am Morag MacPherson, thistle fairy, from Scotland.'

'And I am Heather MacKintosh, thistle fairy. And greatest fiddler in Scotland.'

'What?' protested Morag. 'I am the greatest fiddler in Scotland.'

Heather fell about laughing.

'How dare you laugh at my fiddle playing. I am Morag MacPherson, champion of champions,' continued the dark-haired fairy.

'Well I'm Dinnie MacKintosh and you two can just beat it.'

Now Morag burst out laughing.

'What's so funny?'

'He's a MacKintosh,' chortled Morag. 'No wonder his fiddle-playing is so bad. The MacKintoshes never could carry a tune.'

Heather looked uncomfortable.

'He's only a beginner,' she said, but Morag continued to laugh uncontrollably. She was greatly amused at this turn of events. In her eyes she had won the argument.

'How dare you laugh at a fellow MacKintosh,' raged Heather, who could not bear to see her clan belittled in any way. 'Even a human MacKintosh is worth more than a lying, cheating MacPherson.'

'How dare you call the MacPhersons lying and cheating,' screamed Morag.

The fairies' green eyes blazed.

'Look— ' said Dinnie, but he was ignored.

'You are lying and cheating. Lying, cheating, thieving, no good— '

'Heather MacKintosh, I hope I never see you again!' shouted Morag, and hopped out the window.

There was a silence.

Heather looked glum. Shouts drifted up from the footballers on the corner below.

'Phone 970 C–L–I–T for the hottest phone sex in New York,' whispered a naked woman on the television screen.

'I'm lost in a strange city and now my friend's gone away and it's all the fault of your stupid violin playing,' said Heather, and began to cry.

FOUR

'Yes,' admitted Kerry, tucking a pair of gloves underneath her waistcoat. 'I do shoplift compulsively.'

'Why is this?' enquired Morag. 'Is it kleptomania, which I once read about in a human newspaper?'

'No, it just burns me up the way there are nice things everywhere and I can't afford to buy them.'

'Are you poor?'

Kerry was.

'And often depressed. But I have been much more cheerful since you appeared.' Outside in the street, Kerry tried on her new gloves with satisfaction.

The fairy, after arguing with Heather, had flown across the street and there had the good fortune to meet Kerry, one of the very few human beings in New York who could see fairies.

Anyone who knew Kerry, with her long silvery blue hair, her hippy clothing, her flower alphabet and her quixotic quest to play New York Dolls guitar solos, would not have been surprised to learn that she could see fairies. They would only have been surprised that she had never seen one before.

She had made friends with Morag immediately and now they regularly went shoplifting together. Kerry fed Morag, found her whisky, and listened to her fiddle-playing and her stories. She also explained the intricacies of her flower alphabet and the reasons why she loved the New York Dolls and why she was determined to be revenged on Cal, a faithless and treacherous lead guitarist who rehearsed with his band across the street in the old theatre.

'My revenge on Cal will be terrible and complete,' she told the fairy. 'He will bitterly regret ever promising to teach me all the guitar solos on the first New York Dolls album, then letting me down so disgracefully. Particularly as I fucked some dreadful, boring roadie merely so he would give me a guitar.'

'Excellent,' agreed Morag. 'Give him hell.'

Kerry had several methods of revenge in mind, but mainly she planned to defeat his entry for the East 4th Street Community Arts Association Prize.

'They are producing a version of *A Midsummer Night's Dream* at the theatre,' she explained. 'Cal is directing it. They imagine that they will win this year's prize. But they won't. I will. My radical new version of the ancient Celtic flower alphabet, assembled afresh for the first time in centuries, will win the prize. And this is good, because I am very fond of flowers. I used to take flowers to bed with me when I was little.'

'So did I,' said Morag.

On 4th Street a beggar asked for money.

'I'm sorry, I don't have any,' said Kerry. 'But have this instead.'

'What was that?' asked Morag.

'A postcard of Botticelli's *Venus and Mars*,' Kerry told her. 'A most beautiful picture.'

Morag was unclear as to how this would help a starving beggar, but Kerry said it would do him the world of good.

'If more people had nice pictures by Botticelli there would be much less trouble everywhere. I base the flower arrangements in my hair on *Primavera*, the world's greatest painting.'

'Now let me get this straight,' said Spiro, chief squirrel of Central Park who, alerted by reports from his subordinates, was paying the strange new creatures a visit.

'You call yourselves fairies. You are invisible to almost all humans. You come from a place called Cornwall. You lived happily there until some technically minded fairy called Magris invented the steam engine and precipitated an industrial revolution in your fairy society. Consequently Tala, your king, started moving previously well-contented fairies out of the fields and gardens and into workhouses, thereby producing a miserable and oppressed fairy kingdom almost overnight, complete with security police and travel permits. Am I right so far?'

Brannoc and the other fairies nodded.

'Whereupon you, being mainly concerned with playing music and eating mushrooms and having no interest in working twelve hours a day in a factory, decamped for Ireland, aided by two Irish fairies. On the way you met two Scottish fairies who claimed first to have been run out of their home town for playing Ramones songs on their fiddles, and second to have been run out of Scotland for some other offence they would not admit, and then you found a field of magic mushrooms and ate them all. Instead of carrying on fleeing.'

'We were tired.'

'Right. Subsequently you drank more whisky and beer than you can remember, then you got bundled on to a truck somehow and next thing you knew you were being driven up Fifth Avenue, after presumably being loaded on to some sort of cargo-carrying airplane. Is that it?'

The fairies nodded miserably. Central Park was better than the furious streets beyond, but it was not like home.

'Well, cheer up,' said Spiro. 'It's not too bad. At least you ended up in America. You speak the language, more or less. You can rest here a while, and what's to stop you sneaking out to JFK and boarding a plane home?'

'We can't go back. Tala the King wants us dead.'

'Looks like you're stuck here then. But what's so bad about that? New York is a good place, you'll like it.'

Somewhere around City Hall Magenta halted for lunch, unwrapping a half-eaten pizza she had picked up on a bench along the way. She ate it warily.

She was sure that Tissaphernes was in the area. Tissaphernes was head of the Persian cavalry. Magenta's force consisted mainly of Hoplites and Pelasts, so she had to be careful not to be outmanoeuvred. She rose and carried on up Broadway.

Outside, the sun shone. Inside, Kerry and Morag got drunk. This was not good for Kerry as her wasting disease left her short of energy, but it made her mind feel better.

'Two in two days,' she mused, referring to another tramp who had lain down and died on the sidewalk outside. Kerry and Morag placed some flowers around the corpse and called an ambulance. Tired now, she lay down to rest and asked Morag the reason for her continuing argument with Heather.

'It is partly because I am a MacPherson and she is a MacKintosh,' explained Morag. 'And there is a very ancient and bitter feud between the MacPhersons and the MacKintoshes. I will tell you all about this later. But even apart from that, Heather showed herself to be of dubious character right from the start.

'It was way back when we were children, or bairns as we might say in Scotland. Both our mothers had taken us, along with our clans, to a great fairy piping and fiddling contest. The gathering was held near Tomnahurich Hill, which is close to a town called Inverness.

'My mother told me that the gathering used to be held on the hill itself back in the old days, when the Fairy Queen lived right inside it, but now humans have built a cemetery there. Thomas the Rhymer is buried there. He was a famous Scottish prophet and fairy friend, some time in the tenth century. Or eleventh or twelfth. Or some time, I forget. Anyway, with a cemetery there we couldn't use the hill any more. There are many places we can't go any more because of humans. But we still like the area.

It is beautiful, and convenient for all the fairy clans to come and play.

'I remember on the way there we passed by Culloden. There are many stories about Culloden but they are all very painful for the Scots, so I will not tell them just now. Anyway, the festival was a wonderful event. All the great pipers and fiddlers were there, and singers and jugglers and acrobats and story-tellers and horse-racers and everything you could imagine, everyone bright and happy and colourful.'

Morag smiled at the memory.

'I was very excited because my mother had entered me for the junior fiddle competition. It was the first time I would ever have played in front of anyone else but my own clan. I had been practising all year. I was going to play "Tullochgorum". That is the tune I was playing outside your window a while ago. I don't wish to be immodest, but these days I am famous throughout Scottish fairydom for my playing of "Tullochgorum". It is a famous strathspey, which is a kind of Scottish reel, but it is very difficult to play well. A Scottish fiddler can build a reputation just by the way she performs it. Rabbie Burns, who is the most famous poet in the world, called it the Queen of Songs.'

She laughed.

'My mother wanted me to play something less difficult but I was a very determined bairn, if rather quiet. And in fact, though all the great fiddlers were there, playing in competitions during the day and for fun all night, and I heard the tune played by some of them, I did not really think that any of them did it better than me.

'Well, come the day of the junior contest, I was a bundle of nerves. My mother, who despite many faults did understand the fiddle, poured a dram of whisky down my throat and told me to get on with it. The whisky calmed me down and when I heard the other young competitors I realised that I was a better fiddler than any of them. It was my turn next and I was just starting to feel confident when a pale, sickly-looking little fairy with unusual golden hair got up and played. She played "Tullochgorum" and it was the best version anyone had heard at that festival. The audience went wild. Naturally I was furious.'

'Naturally,' agreed Kerry. 'It was a mean trick.'

'It certainly was. And I might have been put off except I could see from the blonde fairy's kilt that she was a MacKintosh and I certainly was not going to let a MacKintosh fairy get the better of me. I had the pride of my clan to think of. Also, my mother would have been mad as hell.

'So I stepped up, closed my eyes and played. And was I good?'

'Were you?'

'I was sensational. The best version of "Tullochgorum" heard this century, according to independent witnesses.'

'So did you win?'

'No, it was a draw between me and Heather. She got the sympathy vote because she was such a sickly-looking child. Also it was rumoured that the MacKintoshes had bribed the jury. But I wouldn't have minded being first equal except – and I know you will find this hard to believe – Heather and her mother started complaining that Heather's rendition had obviously been superior and suggesting the MacPhersons had bribed the jury on my behalf! Can you imagine?'

'So what happened?'

'I attacked Heather and tried to kill her. Unfortunately she was tougher than she looked and we had a terrible fight. We both had cuts and bruises and missing teeth before we were pulled apart. And then after that we made friends.'

'Just like that?'

'Yes. After all, we were the best two fiddlers there. And when the wise fairy woman was bandaging us up, we started to like each other better. That's how me and Heather met. And also how we got our excellent fiddles. They were our prizes. But she will never admit that my version of "Tullochgorum" was better than hers.'

'And this underlying tension makes you argue?'

Morag was not sure what 'underlying tension' meant, but agreed that that was probably it.

'Also, she claims it was her idea to form a radical Celtic band, but it was mine. I heard the Ramones first. The blacksmith's son had their first three records.'

Morag mused.

'And now I have ended up in New York, where they come from. This is obviously fate, as one reason Heather and I left Cruickshank in the first place was because all the other fairies ganged up on us for playing garage-punk versions of Scottish reels and wearing ripped kilts. They didn't like us dyeing our hair either.'

She picked up her fiddle, played a majestically traditional version of 'Tullochgorum', then got down to the business of working out the notes of the guitar solo on the New York Dolls' 'Bad Girl'. Once she had it worked out she could try to show Kerry how to play it, although as Morag was not a guitarist and Kerry had little musical knowledge, this was proving to be an arduous business.

'That miserable motherfucker Cal could play this solo,' grumbled Kerry, eyes shining with hatred.

Across the street Dinnie looked out of his window.

'That's funny,' he muttered. 'I'm sure I heard someone playing the violin over there.'

'Ignore it,' said Heather. 'It was just some cat in heat. Now, are you sure you don't have a wee drop of whisky anywhere?'

FIVE

After Morag's departure, Heather stayed with Dinnie. Dinnie was enormously unenthusiastic about this.

'Go live somewhere else,' he told her.

Heather replied that she could not desert a fellow MacKintosh in trouble.

'I'm not in trouble.'

'Yes you are.'

In reality, Heather had nowhere else to go. But as it seemed like an obvious stroke of fate that the first person she had met in this vast metropolis was a fellow MacKintosh, she was content to stay. With her ability to make herself invisible, Dinnie was powerless to chase her out, much as he would have liked to.

She sat now eating his cookies and working his TV remote control. Only dimly familiar with the small choice of programmes available back in Britain, she was fascinated by the fifty channels that beamed and cabled their way to Dinnie's TV.

Dinnie was out, trying to earn some money. He had snarled at Heather that he was behind with his rent and was in danger of being evicted.

'Fine, fine,' said Heather, unaware of what this meant.

He had spent a miserable morning hanging around the courier office waiting for work. As a cycle courier, Dinnie was a disaster. Too fat to ride quickly enough and too argumentative to accept less than good work, he was lucky to earn anything at all, and served mainly as a figure of fun for the other riders.

Today, like all other days, had proved unrewarding and Dinnie rode home in a foul temper, wondering where he was to find money for his rent.

Turning on to East 4th he cycled past Kerry. Dinnie frowned his deepest frown. He saw Kerry often, and he detested her.

'You cheap tart,' he would mutter to himself as she waltzed by.

'You faggot guitarist,' he would hiss quietly after whatever lithe and attractive young man was trooping along beside her.

'You slut,' he would mumble, when peering out of his window at four one lonely morning to see Kerry being off-loaded by a cab driver and helped, drunk and giggling, up the steps and into her apartment.

Dinnie was deeply attracted to Kerry.

Heather greeted him brightly as he appeared.

'Don't speak to me,' he grunted. 'I've decided not to believe in you in the hope you'll disappear.'

'Why are you so rude to me?'

'Because I am a sensible human being and I have no time for nasty little fairies.'

Dinnie opened a tin of corned-beef hash, heated it in a frying pan, ate it and piled the dishes in the sink. He was fastidiously untidy. In his two large rooms there was nothing clean or in its proper place. He had an unusually large living space for the rent he paid, as the rooms he occupied above the theatre were not meant to be lived in. He rented them illegally from the caretaker. Because of this he lived in constant fear of eviction, even when he was not behind with his rent.

'I saw an incredible programme,' said Heather, 'about a big family who own oil wells in Texas. Would you believe that one of them had a car crash and couldn't breathe because of his injuries, so his secretary, who had trained as a medical student, jabbed a knife into his throat, stuck a pen into his windpipe and blew into it until an ambulance arrived, thus saving his life? An emergency tracheotomy, I think they called it. When he held her hand in the ambulance and told her he loved her I was moved to tears.'

Ignoring her, Dinnie picked up his violin and left, bicycling determinedly up Second Avenue.

'Where are we going?' said a disembodied voice from the handlebars.

Dinnie wailed and fell off the bike.

'I'm not surprised you don't make any money as a courier,' said Heather, brushing the dirt off her kilt. 'You keep crashing.'

Dinnie coughed and spluttered.

'Do you need a tracheotomy?' asked Heather hopefully, unsheathing her tiny sword.

'What the hell are you doing here?'

'I wanted an outing.'

Dinnie was going busking, something he did only in times of dire need.

He chained his bike at St Mark's Place. Three separate ragged and homeless young men begged dimes from him, but he ignored them and began to play.

Heather shook her head in disbelief. Dinnie's playing was bad beyond description. Passers-by crossed the street to avoid him, and shouted insults. The small-time coke dealer on the corner left for his lunch break. The ragged homeless people, who had suffered too much to be driven away by a violin, just turned the other way.

After half an hour of painful wailing Dinnie had earned nothing whatsoever. He sadly unchained his bike and made to leave.

Heather was appalled to see a MacKintosh musician so defeated.

'Don't go,' she whispered.

'What's the point of staying?'

'Play again,' instructed Heather, and she leapt on to Dinnie's violin, deadening the strings. Unseen by the rest of the world, she played her fiddle while Dinnie mimed. She played her way through some thrilling Scottish reels – 'The Salamanca', 'Miss

Campbell of Monzie', 'Torry Burn' and various others, each linked with some of her favourite Ramones riffs – before plunging into a stirring version of 'Tullochgorum'.

The crowd burst into loud applause. Coins rained into Dinnie's fiddle case. Dinnie scooped them up and made a triumphant exit. He was so pleased with the money and the applause that he was moved to say thank you to Heather, and all in all it would have been a memorable occasion had he not found that his bike had been stolen.

'You stupid fairy,' he raged. 'Why did you make me play after I'd unchained my bike?'

'Well I didn't know it would be stolen,' protested Heather. 'Bikes don't get stolen in Cruickshank.'

'Damn Cruickshank!' shouted Dinnie, and stormed off.

Magenta cycled serenely down First Avenue. Joshua, some way behind, shook his fist in frustration. He had almost caught her when Magenta, showing great tactical skill, had leapt on an unchained bicycle and made off.

Unable to run far, Joshua soon abandoned the chase and flopped down on the sidewalk.

He started to shake. Without regular doses of his Fitzroy cocktail he got withdrawal symptoms, but his mind was so addled by it he could not remember the recipe without the piece of paper Magenta had stolen.

A homeless acquaintance of his ambled by and offered him a drink of wine, which helped, though only a little.

'Damn that Magenta,' snarled Joshua. 'And her stupid classical fantasies.'

'I always knew it was a mistake to take her drinking in the library,' said his friend. 'Who does she think she is now?'

'Some ancient Greek general,' grumbled Joshua.

'It is not my fault if you live in a city populated by thieves and criminals,' said Heather, fluttering after Dinnie. 'I earned money for you, didn't I?'

'Twenty-three dollars. Where am I going to get a bike for twenty-three dollars?'

'At a bike shop?' suggested Heather, but this seemed to enrage Dinnie even more.

When an old woman with three worn and filthy coats hanging round her shoulders asked him for some change he swore at her quite violently.

Back at the theatre he stepped over a body at the foot of the stairs without so much as a glance. Heather did stop to look. It was another dead tramp. Too far gone for a tracheotomy.

It is just awful the way these people die on the street here, she thought. Why is there no one to look after them?

Downstairs at the theatre, rehearsals for Cal's production of *A Midsummer Night's Dream* were under way. When Dinnie heard the actors' booming voices, he would scream abuse through the floorboards. He was not a fan of Shakespeare.

'Never speak to me again,' said Dinnie to Heather, who thought he was being most ungrateful.

She was used to ingratitude, however. After she and Morag had spent countless hours in Scotland developing their new fiddle techniques, dyeing their hair and experimenting with inhaling the vapours of fairy glue, neither of their clans had been very pleased. Both their mothers had in fact threatened them with expulsion from their clans if they did not stop trying to subvert the youth of the Scottish fairydom. When they later enquired politely of Callum MacHardie, famous fairy instrument maker, whether he could make them an electric amplifier, he had actually reported them to their Clan Chiefs, thereby subjecting them to long lectures on what was and was not suitable behaviour for fairies.

'Tripping around in meadows is fine,' their chiefs had told them. 'And helping lost human children home again. Also, increasing the milk supply of friendly farmers' cows. But a large-scale youth rebellion is quite out of the question. So go home and behave yourselves.'

Right after this Heather and Morag had fluttered around the valley wearing hand-painted T-shirts saying 'First Mohican Fairy on the Block', but as no one else knew what a block was, the joke fell flat.

Morag stole what small pieces of food she could carry, loose cookies and bagels, and fed them to the homeless. She had not appreciated it before in her village, but here she could see that being human could involve some very unpleasant things. Despite this, she was still marvelling at the wonders of New York.

Kerry was twenty-five and had lived in New York since she was fifteen, so she did not marvel any more, but she liked it.

They sat in a bar in Houston Street, drinking beer from a bottle. The fairy enthused about some South American musicians they had seen busking in Broadway.

'What good players they were. And lovely rhythms.'

'Mmmm,' replied Kerry.

'And all the young people walking up and down the pavement right next to them just to show off their new clothes. What a pleasant occupation.'

'Mmmm,' replied Kerry.

'And weren't those two boys romantic, sitting kissing on the fire escape?'

Morag was keen on the fire escapes that snaked down the fronts of buildings and she frequently hopped up and down them, looking in the windows.

'Mmmm,' said Kerry.

'I am sure I am having a better time with you than Heather is with that lump of a MacKintosh. I can tell that he is much too mean to give Botticelli postcards to beggars, or flowers.'

Kerry was silent.

A cheerful young barman gathered up the bottles from their table, giving Kerry a hopeful grin. Kerry stared into space.

'It is nice the way people smile at you all the time, Kerry.'

A tear trickled down Kerry's face.

'Let's go home,' she said.

They walked home, noticing as they did a worried-looking bag lady slinking her way up 3rd Street, taking cover behind cars and lamp-posts.

'Another madwoman. There are a lot of them here.'

Magenta was not exactly mad, but after plunging over the handlebars of the bicycle due to too much alcohol, she was not feeling very well. She retired to a doorway, fished out her stolen copy of Xenophon's *Expedition to Persia* and thumbed through it for a hangover cure.

The birds and animals gossiped in Central Park.

'I heard from a blackbird,' said a pigeon to a squirrel, 'who heard from a seagull, that the albatrosses are looking for some creatures who sound a lot like these fairies.'

The pigeons and squirrels looked at the fairies and wondered if there was going to be trouble.

'I miss Heather and Morag,' said Brannoc.

'Well I don't,' answered Padraig, tuning his fiddle. 'I never met such argumentative fairies in my life. I'm not surprised they were run out of Scotland. If they ever made it to Ireland, they'd be run out of there as well.'

Violin tuned, Padraig started to play. He played 'The Miltdown Jig' slowly, then a little faster, then broke into a dazzling version of 'Jenny's Welcome to Charley', a long and complicated reel. Maeve joined in on her pipes. Fairy musicians have magical control over the volume of their instruments and the two blended perfectly.

The animals stopped gossiping to watch and listen. Maeve and Padraig were the best fairy musicians in Ireland, and this is almost the same as saying they were the best musicians in the world, although Heather and Morag might well have had something to say about that.

Kerry's apartment consisted of two small rooms. The bed was raised on a platform and underneath she stored her clothes. She lay on the bed. Morag sat beside her.

'Back in Scotland,' said the fairy, 'I am well known for my astute psychic insights. And it strikes me that since I have been here you have never really been happy. Am I right?'

Kerry burst into tears.

'I was unhappy long before you arrived,' she said.

'Why? Your life seems good. Braw even. Everyone likes you. You have lovers queuing up at your door, though you turn them all away.'

Kerry stared at her poster of the New York Dolls. They stared back at her, pouting.

'I turn them away because of my disease,' explained Kerry.

Kerry had Crohn's disease, a most unpleasant ailment which rots away the intestines.

'After a while doctors have to cut out the diseased parts.'

Morag shuddered. This was beyond her imagination.

Kerry undid her shirt. On her left side she had a bag taped to her skin.

The meaning and function of a colostomy bag were not obvious to Morag until Kerry explained.

Morag stared gloomily out the window. Life streamed past but she was not entertained. She was imagining what it would be like to have a hole cut in your side for your excreta to empty into a bag.

The sun was particularly strong today. The heat was overpowering. Pedestrians sweated their way along the sidewalks and drivers cursed and sounded their horns.

Kerry patted her triple-bloomed Welsh poppy, an almost unimaginably rare flower and the pride of her collection. It was finding it growing wild in a ruined building which had set her off on her quest for the flower alphabet. She kissed it, stroked it and spoke to it nicely.

Next she checked her new *Mimulus cardinalus*, a pretty red and yellow flower, the newest addition to her alphabet. The cut flower hung upside-down to dry. Once it was dry she would spray it with hairspray to preserve it and add it to the other fifteen preserved blooms covering her floor.

Cal had stopped going out with her when he learned about her colostomy, saying that he could not see himself having a relationship with someone whose excreta emptied into a bag at her side. This made Kerry feel very bad.

Morag sighed. Being human did seem to involve some very unpleasant things.

SIX

'I don't want a violin lesson,' declared Dinnie. 'And I don't want you here. Go and join your friend.'

'She isn't my friend,' protested Heather. 'Just someone I had the misfortune to meet. I took pity on her. To tell you the truth, she annoyed the hell out of me.'

Heather settled down with a thimbleful of whisky, skilfully removed from the bar on the corner.

'Brag, brag, brag, all the time. Just because she's got a few psychic powers. So what? Psychic powers are ten-a-penny among fairies. Common as muck. I wouldn't take them as a gift. Of course, her basic problem is that she is insanely jealous of my spectacular golden hair which made all the male fairies in Scotland fancy me like nobody's business. Drove her crazy. Gentlemen prefer blondes, as we used to say in the Highlands.'

'You both dye your hair,' Dinnie pointed out, eyeing the crimson ends of Heather's blonde tresses with disapproval.

'But mine always looked better,' chuckled Heather. 'Morag's is too dark to dye properly.'

Dinnie stared glumly at the wall. If he had believed in fairies, he wouldn't have expected them to spend all their time bitching about each other's hairstyles.

He eyed his violin. A defeated expression settled on his large pink face. It was too difficult for him. He would not make any progress. He did not even genuinely like the instrument any more, although when he had first seen it in the junk shop, lying under a pile of broken trumpets, it had seemed to mean something to him.

At school he had learned to play for a short while before giving up. He had bought the violin and music book because they reminded him of school, which was the last time he had had any friends.

'Pick it up,' instructed Heather.

'No.'

This was all very frustrating to Heather. If Dinnie did not learn the fiddle she would lose face in front of Morag. Heather had unwisely boasted to her that with her superior fiddling skills it would be no trouble to teach Dinnie to play.

Now she realised that Morag had trapped her into this rash statement by deliberately laughing at the MacKintoshes.

'When you can play well you'll earn money busking.'

'Not soon enough to prevent me getting evicted,' grunted Dinnie. After the theft of his bike, busking was a sore subject.

Heather ran her fingers through her golden hair, admired herself in the mirror, and thought desperately. She would die before admitting failure in front of Morag MacPherson.

'Well how about this,' she suggested. 'I will try and teach you the fiddle. If you make progress, you will be pleased. If you fail to make progress, I promise to go away and leave you in peace. Then you will also be pleased.'

The notion of Heather disappearing into the depths of Manhattan was indeed pleasing to Dinnie.

'Okay,' he agreed, 'teach me something.'

'I'll make you lick my snatch you filthy worm,' snarled a woman's voice. 'Phone 970 D–O–M–M now!'

'Please turn off channel twenty-three,' said Heather. 'It is not conducive to fiddle teaching.'

Dinnie laughed.

'I might have known you fairies would be prudes.'

'I am not a prude. In the Highlands I was widely regarded as the hottest lover since the great fairy piper Mavis MacKintosh, who once lay with eighteen men, twelve women and the chief of the MacAuly fairies in one night, leaving all of them pleased but exhausted. I just don't like phone domination. Kindly turn it off.'

In Central Park, Brannoc was moodily eyeing Petal and Tulip who were holding hands under a bush. As they were brother and sister they had every right to hold hands, but it made Brannoc jealous. Brannoc had been infatuated with Petal since the day he arrived in Cornwall, a wandering minstrel from the cold, unknown shires of northern England.

Maeve and Padraig were asking the squirrels where they might find a drop of Guinness.

'In many bars,' one of the squirrels told them. 'This place is full of Irish people who love to drink Guinness and their bars have shamrocks outside them. But it would mean going on to the streets which are full of humans. And though you claim that back in Ireland any human would have been delighted to stop whatever they were doing and bring you some beer, here I am not so sure.'

Maeve declared that she would go right that minute and find some because she was Maeve O'Brien from Galway and not afraid of humans or anything else, but Padraig was cautious and said they should wait.

Petal and Tulip were lost in a dream. They frequently disappeared into the trance-like fairy dream state to forget about their father. They were the children of Tala the King and they knew he would never stop pursuing them.

‘Wow,’ said Spiro when he learned of this. ‘You’re the King’s children. Imagine! Royalty! Right here in Central Park!’

But Maeve poured scorn on this because she detested English royalty. She dismissed Petal and Tulip’s arguments with their father as standard English aristocratic stupidity.

‘Never did a day’s work in their lives,’ she muttered, and played a fierce jig on her pipes.

Brannoc strummed his mandolin lightly. He was teaching Petal and her brother mandolin and flute. When they were not dreaming, they were quick to learn.

Dinnie was not quick to learn.

‘Use the bow delicately. You are not trying to saw the fiddle in half.’

Heather, five minutes into her first lesson, was beginning to regret it. So was Dinnie. He stood up, tall, fat and awkward.

‘I’ve changed my mind,’ he said. ‘I’ll learn some other time.’

Heather clenched her teeth.

‘Dinnie, you are trying my patience. A fairy teaching you music is a big honour. Enjoy it.’

‘Big fucking honour, you dumb elf,’ rasped Dinnie.

‘Eat shit, you fat sonofabitch,’ rasped Heather. She had already picked up a few useful expressions in the bar on the corner.

They glared at each other.

‘Pick up the fiddle.’

‘I’ve got other things to do.’

‘Like what? What do you have planned for this evening? Visiting a few friends perhaps?’

Dinnie narrowed his pudgy eyes uncomfortably.

‘You don’t have any friends, do you?’

‘So what?’

‘So this: despite your incredible rudeness to me, really you are pleased to have me around because otherwise you would have no one at all to talk to. In this enormous city you do not have so much as one friend. Is this not true?'

Dinnie picked up the remote control and switched on the TV. Heather nimbly leapt on to the control and switched it off.

'Do not feel bad about it, Dinnie. I have been busy learning about this place. Apparently loneliness is not uncommon. I know this because I read an article about it in a young women's magazine that an old man was reading in the bar. In Cruickshank, everyone is friendly with everyone else. How it is that with so many people here some people aren't friendly with anyone at all is beyond me, but I can fix it for you.'

'Don't bother,' grunted Dinnie.

'It is no bother. Among Scottish fairies I am famous for my ability to win friends. Of course, with my golden hair and other-worldly beauty, everyone generally wanted to make friends with me anyway – something, incidentally, that used to drive Morag crazy – but even so, I could always win over the unfriendliest troll or Red Cap.'

'Fine. If you meet any trolls down 4th Street, you won't have any problems.'

'I am the best fiddle player in the world. And you will soon be good as well, with a MacKintosh fairy helping you. You should have heard Neil Gow before my mother showed him a few tricks.'

'Who's Neil Gow?'

'Who's Neil Gow? He was the most famous Scottish fiddler ever. He was born in Inver, which is close to where I come from. He is buried in the churchyard of Little Dunkeld, a very pretty place, although we fairies are not too keen on churchyards as a rule. I could tell you many interesting stories about Neil Gow.'

'And no doubt you will.'

'Later. Anyway, his technique was appalling till my mother took him in hand. My family taught all the best Scottish violinists, and I'm sure I can teach you. So stop eyeing up the TV control and let's go.

'Lesson one. "The Bridge of Balater", a slow strathspey, but stirring in the hands of a master.'

Heather played 'The Bridge of Balater'. It was a slow strathspey, but stirring in her hands. Each Scottish Snap snapped in a way rarely heard since the time of Neil Gow. On the windowsill, birds settled down to listen. Outside on the street, Rachel, an old bag lady, hearing Heather's beautiful playing, rested her weak legs on the theatre steps.

'I'm glad I heard something worthwhile before I die,' she murmured to herself, and warmed her insides on the good fairy's aura.

Upstairs, Heather beamed at Dinnie.

'Now you try.'

Dinnie, his battered copy of *The Gow Collection of Scottish Dance Music* balanced uncomfortably on his knee, struggled his way through 'The Bridge of Balater'. The birds departed and Rachel was jerked unwillingly back to the land of the living.

'Appalling,' said Heather, truthfully. 'But you will be better in no time. Now look. This symbol on the music means a turn, played like this . . . And that symbol means tremolo, played like this . . . Try it.'

Dinnie tried. He still produced a horrible noise. Heather sighed. She had far less patience as a teacher than she imagined.

'Dinnie, I can see that desperate measures are called for. And you had better believe that this is a rare honour, granted to you only because you are a MacKintosh in trouble. Also because my ears won't stand much more. Hold out your hand.'

She touched his fingers. Dinnie felt them go slightly warm.

'Now try again.'

Dinnie looked at his warm fingers, and tried again. For the first time ever, he managed to produce a sound which was tolerably close to being musical.

Aelric squatted under a bush. It was deepest night, and all of Cornwall was quiet. His five followers sat behind him, tense and ready. At Aelric's sign, they fluttered into the air, flew over the shed containing the spinning looms, magicked fire into their hands, and set it alight.

The shed burned brightly, but before the alarm was even raised Aelric and his followers had fled safely away into the night.

Aelric was the leader of the Cornish Fairy Resistance Movement, and the one ray of hope for the fairies under their oppressive leaders. However, as his resistance movement consisted of just him and five others, and Tala was by far the most powerful ruler the kingdom had ever seen, his task seemed a hopeless one.

Still, the burning of the weaving shed was a useful piece of economic sabotage. Aelric had learned about economic sabotage from a book on terrorist tactics he had found in a human library, and so far it seemed to be working well.

Dinnie made some progress, but soon complained of sore fingers.

'Play it again,' instructed Heather.

'My fingers are sore.'

'Haud your wheesht, you fat lump,' cried the fairy eventually.

'Don't try your obscure Scottish expressions on me,' said Dinnie. 'And I would rather be a fat lump than an eighteen-inch freak in a tacky kilt.'

'How dare you. And after me actually teaching you a tune.'

'I would have learned it anyway.'

Heather was outraged.

'You have the natural talent of a haggis,' she said, and departed into the night.

A very few people, like Kerry, are born with the natural ability to see fairies. Others, like Magenta, develop the ability through drinking strange potions like meths, boot polish and fruit juice.

'I take it you are an other-worldly servant of Tissaphernes, Persian satrap of the region?' said Magenta.

'No, I am Heather, a Scottish thistle fairy.'

Magenta was not convinced, and gripped her sword.

'Well I am Xenophon. I am leading the Greek mercenaries in aid of Cyrus, brother of King Antaxerxes, against that same Antaxerxes. And if you are a servant of his, tell him his end is nigh.'

A car with speakers built into the back trundled past, vibrating the area with its music.

I'd like to play my fiddle through a system like that, thought Heather, which made her think of her and Morag's plans for their band. This made her sad.

Magenta marched off, firmly and happily fixed in her fantasy.

SEVEN

'Everyone's yellow,' said Morag.

'We're in Chinatown,' Kerry told her.

They were taking their daily walk. While in Chinatown Kerry was on the look-out for a flower of the Ginka Biloba, a Chinese tree.

'How did the flower from a Chinese tree end up in the ancient Celtic flower alphabet?' Morag enquired.

Kerry did not know. She supposed that the Celts were well travelled.

'Or else it used to grow in other places. Anyway, it is one of the rarities that makes my flower alphabet difficult to collect.'

Morag scanned the horizon for Ginka Bilobas. She had supposed, on first hearing of the project, that a flower alphabet meant one flower beginning with A, another with B, another with C and so on, but apparently it was more complicated than that. The flowers required corresponded to ancient Celtic symbols rather than modern English letters, and not only did they have to be the right species, but the right colour as well.

No Ginka Bilobas being in sight, Morag studied the people.

'What a place this New York is. Black people, brown people, white people, yellow people and people sort of in between. I love it.'

'So do I,' said Kerry. 'But sometimes the people fight.'

'Why?'

'Because they are different colours.'

Morag had a good laugh.

'Humans are so dumb. If fairies were all different colours, they wouldn't fight about it.'

Today Kerry had woken up cheerful, and even dealing with her colostomy bag had not depressed her. Morag knew that it would later, however, and was still grappling with the problem of what to do about it. Being a fairy she had some magical healing powers, but these did not extend to complicated surgical matters.

A small brooch in the form of an eight-sided mirror caught Kerry's eye and she walked into the shop to look at it. It was an unusual shop, a second-hand place full of clothes and jewellery, with a few books and cards on the counter. Behind the counter were some old instruments. Morag examined them while Kerry asked the Chinese owner about the brooch. It was not for sale.

'Why not?' said Morag, outside.

Kerry shrugged.

'I don't know. He just said it wasn't for sale.'

They carried on along the street and Kerry took the brooch from her pocket.

'You are an excellent shoplifter,' said Morag, admiringly. 'I didn't notice a thing.'

Morag spotted some lobsters in a large tank at the front of a restaurant.

'Why are those lobsters living in that shop?' she asked.

'They stay in that tank till a customer wants to eat them. Then they get cooked.'

'What?!'

Morag was appalled. Back in Scotland, while wandering round the east coast, she had had many pleasant conversations with lobsters. She had no idea that people ate them. When they went home later for Kerry to eat and take part of the daily dosage of steroids that controlled her Crohn's disease, Morag felt rather depressed about it.

She unwrapped her violin from its green cloth and placed it gently under her chin.

'That is a lovely tune,' said Kerry.

'Thank you. It is a well-known Scottish lament. Although to tell you the truth I am a little bored with this sort of thing. If Heather hadn't been such an ignorant little besom and got us thrown out of Scotland in disgrace, our radical Celtic thrash band would have been rousing the nation at this very moment.'

The sight and sound of Morag gloomily toying with a mournful lament made Kerry sad as well and by the time twilight came they both agreed that the only thing to do was go to bed depressed with the phone muffled by a pillow.

Kerry said goodnight to her flowers, kissed the fabulous Welsh poppy, and lay down to sleep.

Downstairs in the theatre across the road Cal was auditioning young actresses for the part of Titania in *A Midsummer Night's Dream*.

Heather looked on with some annoyance.

'None of them was anything like a fairy queen,' she complained later to Dinnie, but Dinnie was too busy smearing extra peanut butter on his chocolate cookies to take much notice.

'I followed a bag lady yesterday,' continued Heather. 'She

was under the illusion that she was Xenophon, an Athenian mercenary in the year 401 BC, going to fight for Cyrus, the pretender to the Persian throne, against his brother Antaxerxes.'

'I hate the way you make up these stupid stories,' said Dinnie. 'Leave me in peace.'

Unable to sleep, Morag rose and determined to free the lobsters.

'Poor little things.'

She hopped on a car heading downtown, feeling adventurous.

'Rather like James MacPherson,' she muttered. James MacPherson was a famous robber and fiddler in seventeenth-century Scotland and a good friend to the fairies, before he was hanged.

On the next street a firecracker went off, and a few folk were out on the sidewalk, but it was mainly quiet.

She found the restaurant and waved a cheery hello to the lobsters. Setting them free was not difficult. Most locks are no trouble for a fairy to pick and soon she had sent them swimming to safety down the sewers.

A spectacular success! thought Morag. A triumph in fact. A smooth operation, entirely without hitch. MacPherson the Robber himself could not have done better.

'And what exactly do you think you're doing robbing a restaurant on our patch?' demanded a voice behind her. Morag whirled round, and found to her great surprise that there was a very angry-looking fairy with yellow skin and slanting eyes glowering at her.

Morag fled.

On the corner of Canal Street she hopped on a passing motorcycle which raced away much faster than she could fly and she hung on for dear life. Behind her an angry horde of Chinese fairies waved their fists at her and looked for vehicles to mount to pursue her.

'White devil!' they screamed. 'Raiding our restaurants.'

As the motorbike reached 4th Street Morag risked injury with a spectacular leap on to the ground, then ran for home. A quick glance over her shoulder showed no one in pursuit. She prayed that she had shaken them off. Fortunately for her the motorcyclist had been drunk and had driven like a madman.

Aha! thought Magenta, creeping up Broadway and seeing the Chinese fairies in unsuccessful pursuit of Morag. Early skirmishes. Antaxerxes has sent out his captain Tissaphernes and a host of oriental soldiers. She realised that battle was near and, to steady her nerves, had a good pull at her bottle of Fitzroy cocktail. The boot polish stained her lips a grim purple colour but she was much heartened.

Thinking that she should take cover she headed for East 4th Street and ducked into the theatre.

Inside, Cal was giving instructions to the actor playing Theseus, Duke of Athens.

'You're a duke. Be regal.'

'Preposterous,' announced Magenta, appearing in the wings. 'Theseus was never Duke of Athens.'

'What?'

'Theseus was never Duke of Athens. The rank of duke was unknown in Athens for one thing.'

'Well, how the hell do you know?' demanded Cal.

Magenta drew herself up. Magenta had not been weakened by her life on the streets. Thirty-five years old and muscular, with short cropped iron-grey hair, she could be an intimidating sight when roused.

'How do I know?' I was born there.'

'Beat it, bag lady,' said the performer.

Magenta dealt him a dismissive blow on the ear.

'I resign,' said the actor, from the floor. 'Serious performers cannot work in these conditions.'

Morag sped into Kerry's room, safe home. Kerry had woken up and was sitting on a cushion making a hat to match her light blue hair, drinking beer and listening to the radio.

'Devilish yellow fairies— ' began Morag, but Kerry interrupted her.

'Morag, I was just thinking about you. Listen to the news.'

The newscaster was describing the day's events in Brooklyn, where there had been serious trouble between Koreans and Dominicans after a fight in a deli. The incident had developed into a major disturbance, and the deli was now surrounded by pickets.

'Another race row,' said Kerry. 'What a pity humans cannot be like fairies, as you mentioned this morning.'

'Right,' said Morag, looking at the ceiling.

Kerry switched off the radio and looked thoughtful.

'What does "devilish yellow fairies" mean?'

'Nothing. Nothing at all. Just a pleasant Scots blessing. We often say it on meeting an old friend.'

Morag hunted out her whisky supply and made for the bed.

'I think I'll go to sleep now. If anyone calls, tell them I'm not in.'

'Do you have to sit on my shoulder?' complained Dinnie.

'Why not? It's a good fat shoulder. Lots of room.'

'My shoulder is not fat.'

'Yes, it is.'

They stopped on the corner to argue. This heated discussion between a violinist and an invisible fairy would have drawn attention in some places. On a corner of East 4th Street, no one took any notice.

They walked on, Dinnie more grumpy than usual but Heather completely unaffected by the argument. Dinnie was on his way to the supermarket on Second Avenue where he could shop cheaply and buy his favourite cookies.

'Any change?' asked a beggar. Dinnie ignored her. Dinnie's

meanness saddened Heather. She did not think it was fitting for a MacKintosh to refuse to help the poor.

'She doesn't have a home. It is terrible not to have a home.'

'I couldn't care less. If you're so bothered about it, go and build her one. It'll get you out of my hair.'

'I've never been in your hair. It is too dirty.'

Dinnie had thick black hair, bushy and uncombed. Along with his height, this sometimes gave him a wild-man look, particularly when he had not shaved – either because he could not be bothered or because he could not get the hot water to work.

He did not appreciate personal criticism from a fairy and endeavoured to walk on in silence. This was not possible with Heather on his shoulder.

'Why does steam rise from the pavement?'

'I've no idea. And they're called sidewalks.'

'Really? Are we almost there yet?'

'No.'

'Fine. I'll tell you a story while we're travelling. I'll tell the sad tale of why I was expelled from the lovely lochs and glens of Scotland. Why I can never go back to see the beautiful heather-covered hills and the snow-tipped peaks of Glencoe. How I am for ever denied the pleasure of heather ale and whisky, as expertly brewed and distilled by the MacKintosh fairies, and will never again see the bonnie wee churchyard of Inver.'

Dinnie gritted his teeth. 'Get on with it.'

'I was just setting the atmosphere. Anyway, one night, dark, stormy and lashing with rain, Morag and I were travelling in Skye, which is an island off the west coast of Scotland. We were on our way to the grand MacLeod fairy fiddling competition. Conditions were terrible, but being a MacKintosh I was not too bothered. Morag, however, was whining and complaining even more than usual about being cold and wet. The MacPhersons never did have any true mettle. She was about to lie down somewhere and give up when I took matters in hand and found us a castle to shelter in.'

'You found a castle? Just like that?'

'Castles are not uncommon in Scotland. In fact, Scotland is full of castles. We found a room that was nice and dry. There wasn't any sign of a bed but there was a comfy-looking casket on the floor so we climbed in. There was nothing inside it except a large piece of green cloth.'

A cab crawled past, blaring its horn at the truck in front, which was blaring its horn at the car in front of it, which was temporarily blocked by another car which had stalled. The vehicles behind the cab joined in, sounding their horns in a huge impatient chorus, although there was nothing any of the drivers could do except wait. Dinnie threaded his way across the street.

'Morag was still complaining about being cold of course, so to shut her up I got out my sword and cut a few pieces of this material for some blankets. And very good blankets they were too. We had an excellent sleep. But guess what the cloth turned out to be?'

'I don't care.'

'It was the famous MacLeod Fairy Banner!'

Heather waited for a gasp of astonishment for Dinnie. None came.

'Aren't you amazed?'

'No.'

'Haven't you heard of the famous MacLeod Fairy Banner?'

'No.'

Heather was surprised. She assumed that everyone had heard of it.

'It is one of the most famous fairy artefacts in Scotland, as famous and important to Scottish fairies as the MacPherson Fiddle and the MacKintosh Sword.

'It was given to the human MacLeod clan by the fairies some time in the eleventh century and they keep it in their ancestral home, Dunvegan Castle. It saved the clan and must only be unfurled in an emergency. You can't play around with the MacLeod Fairy Banner. No one is meant to even touch it. Cutting it up for blankets is completely out of the question.

'Anyway, next day, ignorant of what we'd done, we went on

our way. We used the blankets to wrap our fiddles in, thinking that they might come in useful later. But when we reached the sight of the competition and unwrapped our fiddles, there was uproar. The MacLeod fairies were going to kill us there and then for mutilating the banner. I told them it was an accident and I hadn't even realised we were in Dunvegan Castle, let alone that I was cutting up the Fairy Banner, but they seemed to think we'd done it deliberately. MacLeod fairies are noted for their low intelligence. Unfortunately there are an awful lot of them and we had to flee back to the mainland on a porpoise.

'And after that they wouldn't let up. They chased us everywhere. Even the fact that we are good fairies and are known for never committing malicious deeds didn't make any difference. Hence Morag's and my flight from Scotland. Now we can never go back and it's all because that dumb bitch Morag kept complaining about the cold. She has ruined my life.'

'Well,' said Dinnie, sensing an opportunity to discomfort Heather. 'It was you who cut up the banner.'

'Only to help a weaker creature. And I wasn't to know it was the famous MacLeod Banner. What did they leave it lying around in a casket for?'

Dinnie by this time was tired. The walk from 4th Street to the supermarket had made him pant and he concentrated on shopping quickly and returning home.

'You might at least express some sympathy,' said Heather, as he loaded up with cookies and tins of corned-beef hash.

'Why? I don't care about you being chased out of Scotland.'

'But it is a terrible thing to be homeless.'

'Bah!'

Dinnie had a brief argument with the woman at the checkout when he mistakenly thought she had overcharged him, then headed home.

'Just the man I was looking for,' said the caretaker, meeting Dinnie on the steps. 'I'm evicting you.'

Dinnie stamped his way up to his rooms and flung his shopping bag on the floor.

'I am sorry,' said Heather. 'It is a terrible thing— '

'Don't say it,' snarled Dinnie, and savagely opened a tin of corned-beef hash.

The albatross landed heavily on the shore of Cornwall. Magris was there to greet her. He was the King's Chief Wizard, although he now liked to be known as Chief Technician, and his wings were neatly folded under a long grey cloak.

'Have you any news for me?'

The albatross shook her head.

'There is no sign of them in any of the kingdoms we fly over. We have seen wars, famines and plagues, ships, trains and cars, ants, camels and lizards, Spriggans, Church Grims and Mer-women, but we have not seen your two fairies, or their friends.'

Magris frowned. He was annoyed, but knew better than to criticise the albatrosses.

'Please continue your search.'

The bird nodded and flew off. Albatrosses are not given to idle chatter, as a rule. Nor was Magris. He was too furious about the rebel Aelric and his economic sabotage. Warehouses and factories were burning all over the kingdom.

It was being whispered by the rebels that if Petal and Tulip were to rule instead of Tala, things would be well in the kingdom.

Petal and Tulip were resting in a peaceful little clearing surrounded by the thick undergrowth of Central Park, listening to Maeve and Padraig playing their tin whistles. They played 'Ballydesmond' and 'Maggie in the Woods', and Petal and Tulip tapped their feet to the cheerful polka rhythm.

'And when will we see Doolin again, I wonder?!' said Maeve. Doolin in Ireland was famous for its tin whistlers and the two fairies had spent much time there, listening and playing. They thought for a little while about the good times they had had in County Clare.

Magenta had never been keen on the twentieth century. When her father died, electrocuted by his word processor after washing his hands and not drying them properly, she had gone off it entirely. She was not too keen on washing either.

The Xenophon fantasy she sank into was a pleasant escape and a good way of keeping her spirits up while hiding from Joshua. She and Joshua had been lovers once, before Magenta caught him with another bag lady and stole his cocktail recipe in retaliation, knowing that he could not live without it.

Now, however, prowling along the sidewalk, she considered giving it up. The fierce alcoholic potion was wearing off and she was blearily aware that she actually bore little resemblance to the legendary Greek hero.

A fairy shape flickered in the distance.

'Must still be hallucinating.'

Heather was looking sadly at another corpse, another old tramp who had died of illness, exhaustion and hopelessness. That made three in three days. She hated the way these people just expired on the streets and stayed there. People would walk right past and not even look. This would never have happened in Cruickshank.

A fairy will put a flower on a corpse as a sign of respect, and Heather went to look for one. Inside the theatre, next to Cal's guitar, she found a glorious poppy with red, yellow and orange blooms and scooped it up to lay on the corpse.

She played a sad lament, then departed.

Magenta reached the corpse and was appalled to see that it was someone she knew well, a woman Magenta had begged with and been friends with for fifteen years.

She sat down gloomily and took a long drink from her Fitzroy cocktail. The city seemed like an unpleasant place to be.

'To hell with this,' muttered Magenta's subconscious. She rose to her feet majestically.

'Cyrus is dead,' she announced to the waiting troops. 'My dear friend and benefactor, killed in battle. Now how will we

Greeks ever find our way home across thousands of miles of hostile territory?'

She picked up the flower that Heather had left and marched away purposefully.

The albatross made a heavy landing on the Cornish beach.

'We have found them,' she told Magris.

'Where?'

'One of them was spotted by a sparrow in New York, talking to an old woman.'

'Thank you,' said Magris, and gave the albatross a golden reward.

EIGHT

The loss of Kerry's triple-headed Welsh poppy was a mind-numbing blow.

Kerry stared at the space where it should have been, trembling with shock and fury. Morag, perched on top of a speaker and listening to Suicide, flew over to ask her what was the matter.

'My poppy is gone.'

In Kerry's book of Celtic myths the Welsh poppy was the centre-piece of the mystic alphabet. Furthermore, it had to be one with three blooms and this was so rare as to be practically unobtainable.

'I found it after the police bulldozed a crack factory,' wailed Kerry. 'There isn't another one in America!'

How it could have vanished was a mystery.

Cal buzzed the apartment. When he came up he brightly thanked Kerry for the loan of her flower.

'My Titania was panicked by a strange bag lady who attacked the theatre. I had to get her something to calm her down. I let myself in with your key and took a flower. I knew you wouldn't mind. I'm afraid someone took it though. Wasn't important, was it?'

The Chinese fairies were not at all happy that a restaurant in their area had been robbed by an interloper, but this was as nothing compared to their horror on discovering that their Bhat Gwa mirror was missing. A Bhat Gwa mirror is specially designed to reflect bad Fung Shui, which means various forms of misfortune, and was most precious to the Chinese fairies. This mirror, a small octagon, had been left in the shop of their human friend Hwui-Yin.

Without it to reflect away misfortune all sorts of calamities would occur, particularly as it was nearing the time of the Festival of Hungry Ghosts, when dissatisfied spirits roamed the earth.

They sniffed around the shop, scenting out clues as to where it had gone.

'The strange white fairy with multicoloured hair has been here,' they cried, picking up Morag's aura, as fairies can do. They assumed that she had stolen it – a reasonable assumption, although really it had been Kerry, and the mirror was now pinned to one of her Indian waistcoats as a pleasant decoration.

'That was a braw punch,' said Morag. 'Reminded me of the time I had to fight off the MacDougal clan single-handedly.'

'Thank you,' said Kerry, nursing her bruised hand.

'Do you think Cal's nose was actually broken? He ran away so quickly I couldn't see.'

Kerry said she hoped it was, and muttered about the further dire revenge she would now take. She was deeply depressed by the loss of her flower, and presumed that it was deliberate sabotage by Cal.

Right now she was busy untaping her colostomy bag before disposing of it. She hated the noises it sometimes made.

Morag perched on her shoulder.

'How will we replace the flower?'

'It can't be replaced.'

'Nonsense,' replied Morag. 'Am I not here to help you? I will scour the city.'

Kerry took her sterilised saline preparation and a swab to clean the hole in her side. Morag flitted down on to a pile of Velvet Underground bootlegs, peering briefly at a photo of a young and sad Nico.

'Would you like me to steal you some cocaine from the dealer on the next block? It might give you inspiration.'

Kerry laughed.

'How do you know that?'

'Another psychic insight.'

Kerry did not think stealing cocaine for her was a very good idea. She carefully taped a ring of cardboard on to her side for today's bag to fit on.

'Well, how can I cheer you up?' asked Morag, slightly frustrated. She never had these problems cheering up the unhappy women in Cruickshank.

'Tell me a story.'

Morag was pleased.

'What an excellent idea. I will tell you the story of the feud between the MacPhersons and the MacKintoshes, a tale which will enlighten you about the glories of Scottish culture and also help you understand how Heather turned out to be the total bitch she is today.'

And she settled down comfortably on the Velvet Underground bootlegs to do just that.

'From around the twelfth century, there was a powerful confederation of clans in Scotland, the Clan Chattan. This was made up of the MacPhersons, with whom my tribe of fairies is associated, the MacGillivrays, the MacBeans and the Davidsons. And the accursed MacKintoshes— '

'Please don't spit on the floor again,' said Kerry.

'Very well. Anyway, the MacPhersons were the natural leaders of this federation. For one thing they were braver and smarter than anyone else. They were also stronger and more beautiful than anyone else. And their pipers were the finest in the land, naturally enough, as my family was around to teach them, and we are famous pipers, as well as fiddlers.

'In addition to this, the MacPhersons were descended from Muireach, the Parson of Kingussie in 1173, and he was the father of Gillechattan Mor, who was the undisputed leader of the Chattans, and of Ewan Mor, who started the MacPherson line. So the MacPhersons were descended from the man who started the Chattan line, and were their natural leaders. But when leadership of the Chattans passed to Eva, daughter of Dougall Dall, in 1291, Angus, Sixth Laird of the accursed MacKintoshes, kidnapped her, forced her to marry him and stole the leadership.'

Kerry was meanwhile taping on a clean plastic bag to collect the excreta which would today ooze out of her side.

'Of course, the MacPhersons never accepted this but down through the centuries the MacKintoshes used every dirty trick and subterfuge imaginable to hang on to their ill-gotten position. Nothing was too base for them. They cheated, connived, sold out to the French, English or anyone else who would pay them, and generally disgraced the good name of the clans by their shocking behaviour. I believe they are still doing it.

'So you see,' concluded Morag, now flushed with emotion, 'with a background like that it was inevitable that Heather would turn out bad. Thieving, cheating and ratting on her former lover comes naturally to her. It's in her blood.'

'Oh, come on,' protested Kerry. 'Surely she can't be that bad?'

The small fairy snorted derisively.

'Ha! Never a day went past in Cruickshank without Heather committing some disgraceful act. If the farmer's milk went missing, they sent out search parties for Heather. If a villager's cottage burned down, "Where's Heather?" was the cry. Honestly, it's a wonder she wasn't lynched from a hawthorn bush long before she was drummed out of the country. I tell you, she may be a thistle fairy but she is the most miserable, cheating, unscrupulous scunner— '

'Oh dear,' said Kerry kindly. 'You are desperately in love with her, aren't you?'

'Certainly not. All she ever did was brag that she could dye her hair brighter than mine. That was before you introduced me to the art of pre-colour bleaching of course. If I never see her again, it will be fine with me. She has ruined my life. It was her stupid idea to cut up the MacLeod Fairy Banner for blankets. I was perfectly comfortable without a blanket. Now I'm exiled from Scotland all because of her. And even before that she had her mother on to me, accusing me of being a bad influence because she learned to play the whole of the first Anthrax album on her fiddle. The suffering she has caused me is appalling.'

Kerry, having completed the process of changing the colostomy bag, was now dressing. Because of the bag's location on her body, she could not wear anything which was tight round the waist, and the colourful leggings which she tried to put on proved to be too constricting. She gave a deep sigh and hunted for something looser. Morag studied her while she dressed.

'On the other hand,' said the fairy, 'compared to some things, I have not really had a lot of suffering.'

Kerry took a small bottle from the shelf for the dose of steroids that would prevent the disease from flaring up.

'Maybe not,' she said. 'But your story is sad. Let's go and buy an enormous pizza and wallow in it. Then we will try and think of a way to replace the poppy. I will win the East 4th Street Community Arts Prize or die in the attempt.'

NINE

Dinnie tried to persuade the caretaker not to evict him but the caretaker was adamant. He was risking his job by letting anyone rent the top-floor rooms as it was illegal, and if Dinnie could not pay, he had to go.

'But I am the only respectable presence here. Without me the entire building will be taken over by faggots. I am a good tenant, quiet, no trouble to anyone. I'll have the money tomorrow.'

The caretaker wavered. Unfortunately Heather at that moment succumbed to an irresistible urge to perch invisibly on his shoulder and play a series of fast jigs.

'Leave tomorrow,' said the caretaker, and departed.

'What the hell did you do that for?' screamed Dinnie. The fairy could offer no reasonable explanation. The outraged Dinnie threw both of his sandals at her and she departed in a huff.

Dinnie slumped in front of his TV.

'I should have swatted her with the fiddle,' he muttered.

Under Heather's tuition, Dinnie had learned to play 'The Bridge of Alar' and 'The Miller o' Drone', another well-known Scottish strathspey. His practising had become more enthusiastic. He could still not play well, by human standards, and by fairy standards he was quite abominable, but it was definite progress. Dinnie had almost been moved to show some gratitude to Heather, but had restrained himself.

'Make a thousand-dollar pledge to God now,' said a handsome TV evangelist. 'Break your cycle of poverty and misfortune. Pledge me a thousand dollars now and your troubles will melt away with the help of the Lord.'

Dinnie swore out loud at the evangelist and switched over.

'We're here waiting for your call,' said a naked woman soothingly, rubbing her body with a red telephone. 'Nice, pink, warm, young, juicy pussy, on 970 C–U–N–T.'

'What are you watching?' said Heather, hopping in the window with a satisfied whisky grin on her face.

'None of your damn business.'

'What does nice, pink, warm, young, juicy pussy mean?'

'How dare you show your face back here.'

'Do not worry,' said Heather. 'I have forgiven you for throwing your sandals at me.'

On the outskirts of Heaven there was great activity. Bodies went to and fro, talking excitedly to one another and looking earthwards.

'What's happening?' said Johnny to his friend Billy.

'Coming up to the Festival of Hungry Ghosts,' Billy told him. Billy had died some years before Johnny and knew more of what went on here. 'All the Chinese spirits with things on their minds, maybe some affair that didn't go too well or some other unfinished business, get the chance to go down and look around, maybe finish a few things off.'

'Well, that is interesting,' murmured Johnny. 'And I would sure like to know what happened to my guitar.'

Aelric left his followers to fly into town. Once there he headed straight for the reference section of the public library. It was a struggle for a small fairy to take a book from the shelves and read it, and liable to cause panic among the customers, but Aelric was badly in need of information.

He was stuck for inspiration as to what to do next in his guerrilla war against King Tala. Guerrilla warfare did not come naturally to peaceful Cornish fairies, and he and his small band of followers had to fight continually against the urge to walk up to Tala and say something like, 'Look, we're all fairies here. Let's be reasonable about this.' Tala was a new type of oppressive fairy, and not to be reasoned with.

Aelric hunted out the political philosophy section and dragged out a summary of the works of Chairman Mao.

'Hi, I'm Linda, and me and my friend do the hottest two-girl phone sex in town— '

'Why do you spend your time watching this ridiculous sex channel?'

'I do not spend time watching it. I was just flicking through the channels and it came on.'

Heather laughed.

'I have an urge to hear some Scottish music. Let us go and find some musicians.'

'No one plays Scottish music in New York. Only Irish.'

'Really? I am surprised. But never mind, it's much the same. We taught them everything they know. Where can we hear some?'

Dinnie knew of a bar on 14th and Ninth where there were regular sessions, but he had no enthusiasm for the journey. Heather nagged him.

'It's all very well you burbling on about jigs and reels,' said Dinnie crossly. 'But how am I to enjoy listening to music when I am going to be evicted tomorrow? No thanks to you.'

Heather frowned.

'Let me get this straight, Dinnie, because I am not sure that I quite understand it. You have to give that man money every week to live here. You have failed to do this for five weeks. Consequently he has told you to leave. Am I right so far?'

'Dead on.'

'So,' continued Heather, 'all that is required is for you to get a bundle of these dollar things and give it to the man. Then everything will be all right.'

'Yes, you dumb fairy, but I don't have any of these dollar things.'

'What about when you went to the cycle courier place? Didn't you earn enough to pay the rent?'

Dinnie snorted.

'I didn't earn enough to buy a pizza.'

'Would a pizza do instead of the rent?'

Dinnie clutched his brow.

'Please leave me alone. I can't stand any fairy stupidity right now.'

Heather took out her sword and posed briefly in front of the mirror. She made a minor adjustment to her kilt, and smiled.

'Well, as you will realise by now, there is no limit to the ingenuity and resourcefulness of a thistle fairy. Take me to hear the music and I will find money for the rent.'

Heather still did not fully understand why you had to pay dollars to live in a dirty room – a very strange business it seemed to her – but she was willing to help.

Heather enjoyed herself at the session. She sneered only occasionally at the human musicians, who were really very skilful, as they sat round a table at one end of the bar, wreathed in cigarette smoke. It was delightful to hear the pipes, whistles, violins, mandolins, banjos and bodrans, and she stamped her bare feet on the table in time to the jigs and reels. Though she and Morag were bent on radicalising Scottish fairy music, she was still fond of tradition.

When the musicians played some hornpipes, 'The Boys of Bluehill' and 'Harvest Home', young and old Irish descendants and expatriates left their Guinness and Jamesons to get up and dance in formation.

'I'm touched,' said Heather, watching them go round.

'Why?'

'Because they're thinking of home.'

Italian fairies are friends with the wind, and skilful at riding on its back.

Three of them rode now on the breeze over Houston Street, just north of their home in Little Italy. They studied the streets to the north, and waited.

'There,' said the youngest, and pointed. 'There she is. Sitting on the shoulder of that large round person.'

Dinnie was trudging down Broadway with his eyes fixed firmly on the ground. He was depressed, humiliated and angry.

'I'm sorry,' said Heather, for the twentieth time. Dinnie ignored her. He also ignored the beggars, lovers and partygoers who walked beside them in the dark.

'It was a brave attempt,' continued the fairy. 'It was worth trying. Next time will be better.'

Dinnie said that there was not going to be a next time. There would not have been a first time if Heather had not blackmailed him into playing by threatening to make herself visible to the whole audience and create a scene. After a few whiskies she had decided it would be a very good thing if Dinnie showed off his new skill at the fiddle, but it had been a complete disaster. Fingers stiffened by nerves, he had scraped and scratched his way through two strathspeys in the most amateurish way imaginable, all the time surrounded by experienced musicians who did not know whether to grin or look away in embarrassment.

When his dreadful rendition of the tunes finished, there had been a deathly hush. Even the uncontrollable drunk at the next table was quietened. No one in the audience had ever heard such bad playing in public; the session had never seen anything like it. Generally thick-skinned, Dinnie had never before realised that such humiliation was possible.

Dinnie told Heather that there would not be a next time

because he was never going to play the violin again, either in public or private. Furthermore, he would appreciate it if she would now find somewhere else to live and leave him alone. For the rest of his life.

When he tramped past a honey-roasted-peanut vendor's stall without even a hungry glance, Heather knew that things were serious.

'Do not be so down-hearted,' she pleaded. 'Everyone has to start somewhere. I'm sorry I made you play before you were ready. I know it was a mistake. I understand that you are embarrassed. But all these good players were once beginners too. They know what it is like.'

'They didn't have a fairy blackmailing them into playing before they were ready and making a fool of themselves in public.'

Heather had to admit that this was probably true.

'But I can make it up to you. I have the money for the rent.' She brought a bundle of tightly folded dollars out of her sporran and handed it to Dinnie.

He took it in silence. Even rescue from eviction could not cheer him up after his embarrassment.

'Where did you get this?' he asked, back in his room.

'Fairy magic,' lied Heather.

Dinnie switched on the TV.

'I'll lick your asshole and you can bang mine,' crooned a naked woman with long dark hair, kneeling over a couch. 'Only twelve dollars for three minutes.'

'I did not entirely understand that,' said Heather, trying to start a conversation. 'Is it connected with the nice, young, pink, warm, juicy pussies?'

Dinnie ignored her completely.

The Italian fairies made their way home.

'She handed him the stolen money.'

'What does it mean? Who is she?'

The Italian fairies did not know. They had heard rumours of some disturbance with the Chinese fairies who lived not far away, and wondered if it was something to do with them. It was a long time since there had been any contact with them, but some distant suspicion, born of old, still lingered.

Whatever it meant, they were most unhappy that a strange fairy had boldly gone into an Italian bank, picked the lock of the vault and made off with a sporran full of money.

TEN

Kerry and Morag hunted the Lower East Side for the poppy with no success. After Cal's criminal act of removing it from her apartment then leaving it in the theatre, it had vanished.

Morag made efforts to lighten Kerry's mood by working out the guitar parts on 'Born to Lose', a Johnny Thunders classic, but neither Kerry's heart nor her fingers were in it. All she felt like doing was drinking beer.

Heather was most perturbed at Dinnie's refusal to play his fiddle. If she failed in her attempt to teach him, then Morag would subject her to terrible ridicule. Terrible ridicule from Morag was more than Heather could bear. She was already dreading that her rival might learn of the débâcle at the session.

'Why did I ever brag to that foul MacPherson that I would

teach this useless lump to play? I was taken in by the beauty of his fiddle. It has the most exquisite tone, but I have staked my clan pride on an imbecile.'

'Come on Dinnie, practise.'

'No.'

'If you don't practise, Morag MacPherson will mock me and all the MacKintoshes,' cried the fairy in frustration.

'Aha!' said Dinnie. 'So that's why you're so keen for me to learn. I might have known you had an ulterior motive. Well, I don't give a shit about the MacKintoshes, or the MacPhersons.'

Heather swallowed her outrage and spoke sweetly. She pleaded, persuaded, whined, nagged, flattered and cajoled him, finally appealing to his vanity by telling him that with his fiddle under his chin, he really was a fine figure of a man.

'Do you really think so?'

Heather nodded. 'Most attractive.'

Dinnie grinned, and Heather knew that she had found a weak spot. One of Dinnie's most profound desires was to be attractive.

'I shouldn't doubt,' she continued, 'that if you learn a few more tunes and go back to that session, the young Irish colleens will be clustering round you in no time. Even last week I noticed a few of them eyeing you up.'

Dinnie picked up his fiddle.

I have excelled myself, thought Heather. I have finally made him love the fiddle. She tripped happily downstairs on her way to the bar. Cal was on the steps, talking to a young woman.

'You will be a great Titania,' he said. 'Come and audition. You'll love it. You get to be the Fairy Queen on a stage strewn with flowers.'

The mention of flowers made Heather think of her estranged friend Morag. They had both been very friendly with flowers in Scotland. She decided to fly across the road and see what she was up to.

Across the road, Morag and Kerry were listening to old Lydia Lunch tapes and drinking beer. Kerry told Morag about her childhood in Maine and her parents, who had died when she was young, leaving her nothing but a large health-insurance policy, which turned out to be very fortunate.

'And since then I have been poor. I have tried making money from my art here in New York but without much success. It is very dispiriting.'

Kerry's last artistic effort had been a commission from friends of Cal to draw an album cover for them for a record they were putting out with their own money.

'I drew a beautiful woman, based on Botticelli's Venus – similar to me in fact – lying on a bed of rose petals. It was lovely, but the band said it didn't go with the album's title.'

'What was that?'

'*Rock Me, Fuck Me, Kill Me*. Lousy record.'

This had been Kerry's last commercial enterprise, since when she had been living on virtually no money. Now Morag was here to help with the shoplifting and rob tills for the rent, things were a little easier.

'Now, Morag, where am I going to find a red, yellow and orange Welsh poppy? Without that flower the alphabet will not be complete and it must be complete if I am going to beat Cal in the competition.'

At the mention of Cal, Kerry threw down her Indian headband in fury. Not only had he rejected her because of her colostomy bag, he had also sabotaged her flowers.

Magenta arrived at a small park in Houston Street and sat down to consult her copy of Xenophon. A few pigeons meandered round, picking up crumbs. Before she could begin reading she was interrupted by a tramp who knew her well. He took some time off from washing windscreens at the traffic lights and sauntered over.

'What you got there? Xenophon?' He burst out laughing.

'Xenophon is a pile of crap. All the most recent literary–archeological authorities show that he was not as important in the expedition as he made out.'

Magenta did not stop to listen to any more. She checked that her new booty, a priceless triple-bloomed flower, was safely tucked in her shopping bag and marched off.

'Wait till Joshua catches up with you!' he shouted after her.

'I see a sewage spill closed three Long Island beaches yesterday. Also Nassau County health authority received a flurry of calls from people who became ill after eating contaminated clams.'

Morag was reading a newspaper after a Kerry attempt at a guitar solo had ended in defeat. She was persistent in her love of the New York Dolls, though, and would never entirely give up.

'And a Brooklyn teenager was stabbed to death in Sunset Park after an argument.'

'Mmmm.'

'And two muggers went on a crime spree in Midtown, doing three knife-point robberies in five minutes.'

Kerry grimaced.

'Perhaps you should tell me a tale about Scotland instead.'

'If you absolutely insist.'

Morag swallowed an oatcake, washed it down with a little beer, and began.

'James MacPherson was a famous Scottish robber and a great fiddle player. He was afraid of no one and his exploits were legendary, but eventually he was captured by treachery in Keith market. This was around 1700, I think. MacPherson was a good friend of the fairies and even had a happy relationship with a mermaid, which is a sort of fairy.

'Now, the most famous fiddle-maker of the MacPherson fairies, Red Dougal MacPherson, lived around then, and he was very fond of MacPherson the Robber. They used to drink and play music together in the hills around Banff. Red Dougal taught James many fairy fiddling techniques and it is said that no fiddling duo before or since could match them. In return for this, MacPherson the Robber used to bring Red Dougal and the other MacPherson fairies muckle great skins full of whisky and choice jewels from his robbing.

'Eventually they were such good friends that Red Dougal made a violin with all his skill and craft and took it to the great Annie MacPherson, who was head of the MacPherson fairy clan. She gave the fiddle shape-changing powers so it could become big enough for a human to play, and Red Dougal presented it to James.

'The instrument had a matchless tone. In the right hands it could hypnotise an audience. It could make you laugh or cry. It could send warriors marching through the glens or send a baby to sleep. It was famous throughout Scotland, and although MacPherson carried it with him, it was counted as one of the three great Scottish fairy artefacts, and belonged to the clan as a whole.

'Then MacPherson the Robber was betrayed and captured and sentenced to death by the sherriff. He was locked up in prison in Banff. The fairies tried to free him but the sherriff was too strong with English magic and we could do nothing. MacPherson sat in his cell and composed one last tune, the famous "MacPherson's Lament".

'Annie MacPherson did manage, through her great power, to secure a pardon for the robber, and this would have pleased all the Scottish folk, for he never robbed the poor, only the rich. But the sherriff knew the reprieve was on its way and cunningly moved the town clock on an hour. So the execution went ahead an hour early, and the reprieve arrived too late.

'When James MacPherson stood on the gallows he played the tune he'd composed in his cell, the "MacPherson's Lament". MacPherson fairies were watching and they remembered the tune, which is how it still survives. Then the robber smashed his fiddle to bits over his knee in anger and cried his defiance to the world. After that he was hanged.

'And that was the end of the famous MacPherson Fiddle. No one even knew what happened to the pieces.'

Heather crouched outside Kerry's second-floor window, listening.

'A terrible shame it was lost,' Morag was saying, 'because Red Dougal was the best fairy violin maker that ever graced the country, and by all accounts the MacPherson Fiddle was the finest instrument he ever made.'

Outside the window Heather clutched her brow. She was awestruck. She raced back to Dinnie's rooms.

It had been a puzzle to Heather why Dinnie's fiddle had such a stirring tone even in the hands of such a bad player, and she had just had a startling psychic insight, which she was not at all famous for.

'Dinnie! This is none other than the legendary fairy instrument, the MacPherson Fiddle.'

Dinnie lounged in front of the TV and paid Heather no attention.

'Oh baby, I'd love to suck your hard cock,' cooed a woman in a bikini down a red phone. Phone 970 S–U–C–K for the hottest phone sex in town.'

I might have to kill this person some time, thought Heather.

Morag rode, walked and fluttered through the city, but failed to find any trace of Kerry's missing flower. The competition was less than three weeks away. There was only one thing to do. She climbed a fire escape, looked up at the sky, and prayed to Dianna, Goddess of the Fairies.

When she glided back down to street level, there was Magenta, marching towards her, and poking out of her shopping bag was the preserved bloom.

'Thank you, Dianna,' said Morag, and materialised.

She briefly explained about the flower and asked for it back.

Magenta fled, calling orders for her troops to form a square, archers and horsemen at the rear.

'Could we possibly find another one somewhere?' asked Morag, back at Kerry's.

'No,' said Dinnie. 'No, no, no. You can't have it.'

He grabbed hold of the violin.

'But you don't even like it.'

'Yes I do. It makes me attractive. Young Irish girls will soon be flocking round. You said so yourself.'

Heather glowered in hopeless frustration. She had made Dinnie love his instrument, and now she needed it.

'Anyway,' protested Dinnie. 'I don't believe you. How can this be the famous MacPherson Fiddle, whatever that is?'

'It's one of Scotland's most famous fairy icons. I don't know how it ended up in New York, but it has. I recognise its tone. Any Scottish fairy would. Except we all thought it was lost centuries ago. I must have it. If I go back to Scotland with the MacPherson Fiddle, I will be forgiven for the damage I did to the MacLeod Banner.'

'How could it be a fairy instrument? It's too big.'

'It's a shape-changing instrument.'

'It would be.'

Dinnie and Heather glared at each other.

'I could steal it.'

'No you couldn't,' said Dinnie triumphantly. 'You're a good fairy. You're not allowed to steal a human's favourite thing. Especially a fellow MacKintosh's.'

Heather thought frantically. What did fairies do when they needed something from a human and were unable to steal it? Of course. They bargained.

'I'll trade you for it.'

Cal was suffering from stress. Trying to put on a production of *A Midsummer Night's Dream* on a minimal budget was proving to be extremely difficult. To make things worse, he seemed to have landed himself with a highly strung group of performers, and interruptions from mad bag ladies were more than they could cope with.

He plugged in his guitar to relax. Cal was a good guitarist. He could play almost anything; he could play along to the noise of the traffic, or the rattle from his air-conditioner.

He played through some riffs and chord sequences, then his fingers slid easily over some of his favourite guitar solos.

He frowned. Playing old New York Dolls guitar solos made him feel slightly guilty, since he had promised to teach them to Kerry, then left her before doing so.

'Listen,' said Johnny, up in Heaven.

'What?' said Billy.

'Somewhere down there. They're still playing my stuff.'

Johnny Thunders and Billy Murcia, deceased members of the New York Dolls, picked up the vague vibrations of the lead break from 'Rock and Roll Nurse'.

'I really wish I knew what happened to my guitar,' repeated Johnny. 'I miss that Gibson Tiger Top. There was never another one like it. Even here I can't find a replacement.'

Across the blessed heavenly field from them, Chinese spirits were still making their preparations to visit earth for the Festival of Hungry Ghosts.

'A thistle fairy engaged in a trade is empowered to offer anything,' claimed Heather. 'Just name it.'

Dinnie looked at Heather suspiciously.

'Okay,' he said, 'I'll give you it for a million dollars.'

'Eh, well, I can't really do that.'

'Ha! I knew you were lying.'

Heather fluttered around in agitation.

'I was not lying. I can trade you anything. Except money. We are not allowed to bargain with wealth. Sorry.'

'You paid my rent.'

'That was helping a human in need, not a bargain.'

'Well, to hell with you. I'll keep the violin.'

'Oh, come on, there must be something else you want. I can get you your heart's desire.'

Dinnie wandered over to the window. He couldn't think what his heart desired and he had no wish to give up his fiddle.

'I don't want anything. So you can't have it. Now excuse me, I'm off to buy some beer. And let this be a lesson to you. You fairies might think you're smart, but compared to a human like me, you're nowhere.'

Dinnie, vastly pleased at putting one over on Heather, whom he regarded as altogether too pushy for her own good, hummed a tune as he waddled down the stairs.

In Cornwall, Magris was not pleased. King Tala had instructed him to bring back Petal and Tulip. In Magris's eyes, this was a waste of time. They were far away and could do no harm.

Magris was more interested in his restructuring of Cornish fairy society. Already, under his guidance, the fairies no longer lived free in the woods but were concentrated in workhouses under the rule of barons. As a consequence of this, production had soared and trade with the fairies in France and elsewhere was booming. As far as he could see, the only problem facing them was Aelric and his band, and he had every confidence that they would soon be apprehended by the security forces.

'I have moved you overnight from being the nominal lord of a hunter–gatherer society into the king of a well-ordered feudal realm,' he told Tala. 'And now that I have invented the steam engine, there is no limit to our progress. We will make as many goods as the humans. Forget Tulip and Petal, they are not important.'

Tala, however, was set in his ways and would not accept their flight. He ordered Magris to bring them back. So Magris sent messengers with gold to gather a band of mercenaries, and thought about the most efficient way of sending them to America.

Kerry and Morag were buying coffee and beer in the deli.

'What's that noise?'

There was a distant hum which grew quickly into a loud bustle of shouting and marching as a large procession turned into 4th Street and tramped their way along.

'It's a protest march.'

'What's it about?'

'We're here, we're queer, get used to it!' chanted the procession.

The marchers stretched out their arms through the ranks of the surrounding police to give out leaflets detailing their grievances. Kerry took a leaflet and read it to Morag. It said that in recent weeks there had been an increase in attacks on gays in the city. Men were waiting outside gay nightclubs and bars and harassing anyone who came out. This had led to serious injuries and the gay community was protesting that they were not receiving enough protection from the police.

'We're here, we're queer, get used to it!'

The men and women marching were mainly young and they were grim faced. Scores of police officers surrounded them and roughly shepherded them along. Not far away, in Tomkins Square, there had been a series of disturbances and as the demonstration was heading that way there was an added tension in the way the police were handling the crowd.

Kerry saw faces she recognised and waved to the marchers. She told Morag that only last week two friends of hers had been beaten up after leaving a gay bar in the West Village.

Morag was perplexed by the whole thing. Kerry did her best to explain it to her but she was a little disconcerted when Morag burst out laughing.

'What's funny?'

'You humans,' shrieked Morag, and laughed uproariously. 'You make such silly problems for yourselves. We fairies have no such difficulties. Even the MacKintoshes, who are thiefs, cheats and liars, have more sense than to take any notice of two men fairies rolling round in the glens.'

'These glens are sounding more and more interesting,' said Kerry. 'You must take me there some time.'

'Get out of my way, you damned faggots,' sounded a rough voice nearby. 'Can't a man go out for a beer these days without being apprehended by a bunch of pansy radicals?'

It was Dinnie, elbowing his way to the deli.

'Hello, Dinnie,' said Kerry. Dinnie seemed taken aback, and spluttered. He walked off without replying.

'We're going in the wrong direction,' said Heather, on his shoulder. 'And why are you blushing?'

Back in his apartment Dinnie poured beer down his throat and Heather sniggered.

'You are in love with Kerry.'

'Don't be ridiculous,' snorted Dinnie.

'I'm not being ridiculous. I saw you blush, stammer and walk away in the wrong direction after she said hello. You can't fool a fairy about this sort of thing.

'Well, Dinnie, this is your lucky day. Bringing lovers together is a particular speciality of mine. No case too hopeless. And this can be our bargain. You give me the MacPherson Fiddle, and I will get you Kerry.'

Dinnie was more than dubious about Heather's proposal. He dismissed it as preposterous.

'There's nothing preposterous about it. It is a braw scheme. The best I ever had. You give me the fiddle and I give you Kerry.

'Think of the advantages. Once you are going out with Kerry, everybody will want to be your friend because she is immensely popular and any man she chooses to go out with must be a fairly desirable specimen. Virtually overnight you will be transformed from a lonely and pathetic creature, despised by all, into a hip young man about town with a cool girlfriend. Instead of wallowing about in an armchair every night watching baseball and sex programmes you will be able to turn up at gigs and nightclubs with Kerry on your arm, making everyone jealous. She is a most attractive young woman, and highly desirable. Your happiness will be unbounded.

'As for me, once I have the MacPherson Fiddle, I will be changed from a wanted outlaw into Scotland's most popular fairy. Returning home with such a famous and long-lost item will stun and amaze the whole of fairydom and more than make up for the accident with the banner. It will sink into the heads of even the ignorant MacLeods that I am a fairy to be fêted and honoured, rather than chased with knives and claymores over Ben Lomond.'

Heather shuddered at the memory of this particularly unpleasant incident.

'And even it if doesn't sink into their heads, such a heroic act would place me under the protection of Mavis, the Scottish Fairy Queen. I would be safe and welcome everywhere.'

Heather glowed at the thought of returning in triumph to her clan lands round Tomatin. If the famous and revered MacPherson Fiddle was returned to Scotland by her, a MacKintosh, it would shut the MacPhersons up in a spectacular manner, and keep them in their proper place for ages to come. She might even be able to get the judges' decision at the junior fiddling contest re-examined, forcing them to admit that her version of 'Tullochgorum' was better than Morag's.

And for another thing, Dinnie dating Kerry would upset Morag no end. The way Morag had been able to brag that her human friend was popular, attractive and a bundle of fun while Heather's was a sort of human slug had been most annoying. What would Morag say when her popular attractive friend fell hopelessly for the majestic Dinnie MacKintosh, pride of his clan?

Dinnie agreed to the bargain; Heather chuckled in anticipation.

Kerry crossed the road to the theatre. Morag picked the lock and they sneaked in. Once inside Kerry destroyed all the props for *A Midsummer Night's Dream*. She sliced up the costumes with a knife and broke all the scenery with a hammer.

'Feeling better?' asked Morag, back at the flat.

'A little,' replied Kerry. 'Now, what should I pin in my hair? A rose or a carnation?'

Morag gave this her deepest consideration, but it was a tough question.

'What flower do you need next?'

They were pressing on with the alphabet in the hope that they would somehow recover the most important flower.

Kerry consulted her book.

'A bright orange Eschscholzia. Grows in California. That shouldn't be too difficult.'

Heather journeyed down to the small park in Houston Street to give the matter of Dinnie's romance her best consideration.

Below her on the street groups of young people wandered by on their way to a gig at the Knitting Factory. Studying them, Heather appreciated that they were not really the same as the young people she had been acquainted with in her small village.

Perhaps I should do a little background research before deciding on how to bring them together, she thought. I am in a strange city and I do not want to waste my time getting Dinnie to do all the wrong things. For instance, a gift of oatcakes, while guaranteed to win over a Highland fairy, may not have the same potency in New York. I will need to plan carefully.

Pleased with her astute reasoning, she fluttered into the air and headed off to do a little research.

Dinnie, unusually, never ate out. He did not like to waste money in restaurants but bought the cheapest things he could fry easily on his little cooker. He passed a quiet evening eating corned-beef hash and watching quiz shows and wondered if

Heather could indeed do as she promised. Although he had no intention of admitting it to Heather, he had never had a girlfriend. It did not seem possible that his first one would be the much sought-after Kerry.

In the happy aura created by Heather and Morag's presence, the two tramps on the stairs passed into deep dreams of pleasant places, places so wondrous that they did not want to come back.

'Hi, Dinnie,' said Heather, performing a happy somersault on the window-sill. 'I'm back. I have considered the matter and I have it well in hand.'

Dinnie blushed.

'And,' said Heather, bounding on to Dinnie's shoulder, 'I have worked out a complete plan of action. Guaranteed to make Kerry fall in love with you.'

Dinnie sneered.

'Don't sneer. I can do it. I made you play a difficult strathspey, didn't I? A next-to-impossible task, your playing being what it was. Well, I can get you Kerry.'

Heather hopped right on to Dinnie's head, which he particularly hated, and peered down over his forehead.

'Now do not think, Dinnie, that I am underestimating the problem. I am well aware that the chances of you capturing Kerry's heart would seem to be extremely slim. Possibly non-existent. She is, after all, a highly desirable young lady with practically everything going for her, while you are a fat lump without any notably attractive features.'

'Thanks a lot,' muttered Dinnie.

'Also, do not think that I am unaware of the social mores of New York. I am. I know that a gift of oatcakes is not going to have the profound effect here that it might among the fairies of my village. I had one of my most pleasant ever experiences in Cruickshank after taking a fellow fairy four oatcakes and a jar of honey. Three weeks of uninterrupted sex and debauchery in a quiet cave. Wonderful. However, things are different here. Kerry is a young rock and roller and we have to act accordingly.'

She leapt down on to the table, red and golden hair streaming, face beaming.

'And how do I know all this?' she demanded. 'I'll tell you how I know all this. I have spent all afternoon spying on Kerry and her dumb friend Morag, and all evening in the hip cafés of Avenue A listening to the fashionable young people and reading rock and roll magazines. I know what she likes and I know how to make you into it. All that is required is for you to do as I say.'

Dinnie remained silent. He was unwilling to believe it. Heather exchanged a few words of gossip with a cockroach that was scuttling its way past the cooker, picking up scraps. The cooker, uncleaned for years and utterly filthy, was a fertile hunting ground.

'So, Dinnie, here is the bargain. I promise to make Kerry fall in love with you. In return you give me the MacPherson Fiddle. Do you agree?'

Dinnie agreed, even when Heather further informed him that from now on he must do precisely as she instructed, or she would regard the bargain as broken and depart with the fiddle.

'Anyone breaking a bargain with a fairy renders themselves liable to almost anything.'

The fairy peered out the window.

'Oh, no,' she cried. 'I can't believe it. Two more tramps have died on the steps.'

Dinnie did not react.

'Do something, Dinnie.'

'What?'

'Phone up whoever you phone in New York when someone dies. I hate the way they just lie there.'

Dinnie grunted that it was fine with him if they lay there all year.

'Dinnie. Listen well. From what I have seen of Kerry, apart from being a friend to the accursed MacPherson, she is a kind, warm human being. No doubt she will like men who are also kind, warm human beings. It therefore follows that you are going to become a kind, warm human being. Failing that, you are going to pretend to be one. So get on the phone.'

Dinnie did as he was told.

ELEVEN

Morag hopped in Kerry's window with an Eschscholzia bloom and a troubled look.

'Found this on a flower stall in Midtown,' she muttered, then proceeded to tell Kerry a sorry tale.

'I saw a young child crying after dropping her lollipop in the gutter. Naturally I materialised in front of her to cheer her up. In Scotland this would have met with total approval, shouts of glee from the child and suchlike. Unfortunately in New York it didn't. She got a fright and jumped backwards into the street.'

Morag frowned.

'It takes a terrible long time for an ambulance to arrive in this city.'

Kerry sympathised, and said at least she had meant well, but Morag could not be easily consoled. She had caused a serious accident which was bad enough, but she was convinced something terrible would happen to her in return. According to Morag, fairy karma was notoriously powerful.

Still, there was nothing to do but press on with today's programme, which was to track down the young bag lady in possession of the triple-bloomed Welsh poppy.

The afternoon was uncomfortably hot. Magenta sat down to rest at the corner of Avenue C and 4th. Today, by her reckoning, she had marched forty parsangs under continued harassment from Tissaphernes. This lieutenant of Antaxerxes was a crafty opponent, content at this stage to harry her troops while avoiding a direct frontal attack. This was just as well for both sides really, as Xenophon's Greek Hoplites were immeasurably more disciplined that the Persians' and would inflict dreadful casualties if attacked, but this deep inside enemy territory the Persians' greater numbers would tell in the end.

A fire truck wailed by. Magenta ignored it and scanned the rooftops for hidden archers. Finding none, she took a swig of her drink and allowed herself a short sleep outside a little hall with a banner over the door.

Kerry busied herself with the bag at her side. There is no known cause for Crohn's disease, and no known cure, so when Morag asked Kerry if she would one day get better, Kerry could only reply that she might.

'I might heal up inside and then the doctors could give me a reversal operation and I wouldn't have to have a colostomy bag any more. Or I might stay just the same for a long time, which would still not be well enough to be fixed. Or I might have more attacks and have to get more of my intestines removed and then I would never be able to have the reversal operation.'

This was always enough to bring a tear to Kerry's eye and Morag would generally have to change the subject.

Kerry hunted among the bundles on the floor for all her brightest garments – her long ragged yellow skirt, her sweatshirt dyed red, blue, pink and purple, her green Indian waistcoat covered with embroidery and mirror fragments, her beads and headband, round sunglasses tinted blue, fringed suede bag with more embroidery, baseball boots splashed with the entire contents of a junior painting kit, and a carnation to pin in her hair.

'Would the rose be better?'

'I still can't make up my mind,' said Morag. 'Have you considered daisies?'

'Let's go.'

Outside, Kerry, who was regularly whistled and shouted at by men in the street, suffered a prolonged stream of unpleasant cat-calls when she passed by a gang of construction workers. She did not like this but did not answer back.

'I'd like to get between the cheeks of your tight ass!'

'How depressing,' said Morag, on her shoulder. 'Perhaps this is the start of my bad karma.'

Kerry assured her that it was not, as it happened to her all the time.

In the hot sun pedestrians toiled along unhappily and the traffic was everywhere tangled and congested. It did not feel like a good day.

As Kerry and Morag reached Avenue B, scene of Morag's sighting of Magenta, a cab made a violent manoeuvre on to the sidewalk in an attempt to break free of a traffic jam and Kerry was forced to leap for her life. Morag tumbled into a doorway and landed heavily.

'My karma.' she wailed.

'I'm sure it is just a coincidence,' said Kerry, and brushed the dirt off the fairy's kilt. Morag was not convinced, and when on the next corner two crazed skateboarders forced Kerry to leap briskly for cover, sending Morag once more plummeting groundwards, the fairy declared that she would be doing well if she was still alive at the end of the day.

'Change, any change?'

Kerry brought out some change, gave it to the beggar, apologised for not having any Botticelli postcards on her, and scanned the horizon. A flowerpot tumbled from somewhere above and missed her by inches.

Kerry was shaken.

'Can't you do anything about this, Morag?'

'There is only one possibility. I shall have to perform some immense good deed and work off the bad karma.'

They looked around for some good deed to do but none was in view.

'I'll just have to wait it out,' whispered Morag, 'and hope I get the chance before some more terrible occurrence overwhelms me.'

Dinnie and Heather met Cal as they left the theatre. Cal's arms were full of flowers. He nodded to Dinnie pleasantly.

'Coming to see *A Midsummer Night's Dream*?'

'Damned fairy rubbish,' replied Dinnie, pointedly. 'And how about not making so much noise when you rehearse.'

'Who was that?' asked Heather, following Dinnie on his mission to buy beer.

'Cal. Big mouth big shot of the community theatre downstairs. He's got some stupid idea to put on a show and play all the music on his guitar. The whole thing will be a disaster. He only wants to meet young actresses and fuck them.'

Magenta woke, sensing danger.

'There she is,' cried Morag.

Magenta bolted into the hall behind her.

Kerry and Morag hurried after her, but inside what turned out to be a small gallery there were so many people it was difficult to move and their quarry was nowhere in sight.

This was a fund-raising event with many local artists exhibiting their work and local poets doing readings. It was meant to be fun, but as today was intolerably hot it seemed more like an ordeal for everyone.

Trapped in the crowd, Magenta nowhere in sight, Kerry and Morag could only stand and strain their necks to see what was going on.

A young red-haired woman mounted the stage.

'I know her,' whispered Kerry.

It was Gail, a friend of hers, about to read her poems.

Unfortunately by this time no one was paying attention to anything any more, except sweating and wondering whether to leave.

'Oh, dear,' muttered Kerry. 'Everyone is fed up with the heat and the crush and will not listen to Gail, even though she is a great poet.'

As Kerry had predicted, few people paid attention. It was just too uncomfortable to listen to poetry, or anything. Morag saw her chance to undo her bad karma. She unwrapped her fiddle and played, just on the threshold of human hearing. The effect was immediate. The audience were hypnotised by Gail's words and the fairy music. They quietened down and listened, transfixed.

When Gail read a poem of sadness Morag played a lament and it was as much as anyone could do to stop from crying. Gail read a fierce poem about property developers moving into the area and chasing out the poor and Morag played a stirring strathspey. When this was over the audience was on the point of storming the property developers' offices and running them out of town. Gail finished with a love poem and Morag played 'My Love is Like a Red, Red Rose', and the entire crowd felt that they were definitely in love with someone, and it was going to work out well.

As she finished there was wild uncontrollable applause. Gail smiled. She had been a huge success. Morag smiled as well. This successful good deed would surely have worked off her bad karma.

'There she is,' cried Kerry, sighting Magenta in the distance, and hurried off. Morag made to follow but the man next to her, clapping his hands furiously, knocked the fiddle on to the floor. It was invisible to him and he stamped on it.

Kerry found Magenta as she was about to make her getaway and retrieved her flower with a determined frontal assault. Later she placed the bloom back in its place as pride of her collection. She was happy now, but Morag was inconsolable.

They looked at the shattered violin.

'This is the worst day of my life,' said Morag.

TWELVE

Spiro the squirrel ceased chewing a nut to peer at Maeve.

'Why are you sad?'

'I miss Ireland,' she replied, and Padraig nodded agreement. They regretted the day they had ever hopped on the ferry to England just to find out what it was like.

'And why are you sad, Petal and Tulip?'

'We are scared that our father the King will find us even here and make us go back,' they said.

'Does he know how to get on a jumbo jet?'

'Magris knows everything,' said Brannoc, and thought about killing him.

In the distance some joggers panted their way through a long circuit of the park.

'Play us some music,' said Spiro. 'The whole park has seemed more peaceful since you've been here. Play some music and I will show you where to find the largest mushrooms this side of the Atlantic.'

So the fairies played in Central Park and the animals and humans stopped to listen. Radios were turned down and children stopped screaming. The joggers, cyclists and baseball players took a rest. Everyone who heard went home happy and stayed happy for the whole day. No one fought or argued and no crimes were ever committed while the park fairies played.

Cornwall was less happy.

'I cannot have my son and daughter escaping the country,' said Tala the King. 'It will give encouragement to the resistance groups.'

Magris shrugged. He was more interested in inventing new and efficient machines for producing goods.

'I could try opening up a moonbow between here and New York. But generating enough power to send a full host will take time.'

Tala was impatient with this. He wanted his children back now.

'Do you have enough power to send over a smaller force?'

Magris nodded.

'Very well. Assemble some mercenaries.'

Tala had a gold crown of the finest workmanship. He also had twelve powerful barons controlling his Cornish fairy population. This meant that his crown was not quite as powerful as it used to be. However, with his mind concentrated on the greatly increased production which Magris's reorganisation of their society had brought, he did not yet realise this.

Due now at a meeting with the barons, he walked through a corridor of small trees but was halted on the way by a messenger with the shocking news that Aelric and his band of resistance fighters had set fire to the royal granary, thereby destroying the King's food store and that of his court. This grain would have to be replaced by one of the barons, which would cause hardship in his territory.

Magris held a propaganda leaflet, distributed by Aelric. It urged Cornish fairies everywhere to throw off their chains and support the beloved Petal and Tulip as new rulers of the kingdom.

'The rebels tried to distribute them,' Magris told the King. 'Fortunately our troops prevented it.'

'This Aelric must be caught,' raged the King, and he gave instructions that the strongest flyers among his army must be sent to guard his installations from the air, so that the harmful propaganda leaflets could not be dropped.

'I must have some whisky,' said Padraig, laying down his fiddle, and no one disagreed with him. It was a long time since any of the Central Park fairies had had a drink. The squirrels, friendly though they were, could not be persuaded to bring them any. They said it was too dangerous an endeavour. This particularly disgusted Maeve.

'Back in Ireland,' she told the others, 'a squirrel would go out of its way to bring a fairy some poteen. Although normally the problem would not arise as the humans there are good, friendly folk and generally leave it lying around for us.'

There was nothing for it but to mount an expedition to the streets beyond the park.

'We'll hit the first bar we see.'

The loss of the triple-bloomed Welsh poppy, so soon after its dramatic recovery, was a shattering blow to Kerry. She stared furiously at the ransom note from the Chinese fairies.

'How dare they hold my flower hostage!'

Kerry saw her ambitions crumbling into nothing. Without the Welsh poppy she could not win the East 4th Street Community Arts Prize and without Morag's fiddle she could not learn any Johnny Thunders guitar solos.

'I have made up my mind,' said Johnny Thunders. 'I can never be satisfied, even here in Heaven, until I know what happened to my 1958 Gibson Tiger Top. I just laid it down on a barstool for a minute in CBGB's and when I looked round it was gone. And there never was another guitar like it.'

Billy Murcia nodded sympathetically.

'And I sure could do with my best guitar right now,' added Johnny. 'Because as far as I can find out, there is an acute shortage of good rock bands around here. Plenty hippies and plenty gospel choirs, but nothing gritty. So when these Chinese spirits head on out for the Festival of Hungry Ghosts, I'm going with them.'

The fairies from Central Park ventured warily into the streets.

'That looks like a bar,' hissed Brannoc after a while, although they found it difficult to tell. The buildings were all so different from the small Cornish and Irish dwellings they were used to. Because of this uncertainty they had travelled further into Harlem than they intended and were now well out of sight of the park.

People were everywhere on these streets and traffic belched fumes that made the fairies' eyes sting. They were all nervous, though both Brannoc and Maeve refused to show it. Pausing to let four small children with a huge radio scurry past, they made ready to invade the bar.

'Fill your bottles with whisky and pouches with tobacco as fast as you can, then get out of there. The sooner we're back in the park the better.'

'Harlem's Friendliest Bar' said a newly painted sign outside. They hurried in. The bar was quiet. A few customers sat with beers, watching the television up on the wall. Unseen, the fairies set to work. They pressed their wine skins to the whisky optics and gathered up tobacco from behind the bar.

'Just like the time we raided O'Shaugnessy's in Dublin,' whispered Maeve, and Padraig managed a nervous grin.

'And did we not get ruined that night!'

It was a smooth operation. Within minutes the five of them were gathered at the door ready to return to their sanctuary.

'Everyone ready?' said Brannoc. 'Okay, let's go.'

'Correct me if I'm wrong,' said a voice behind them, 'but have you just been robbing this bar?'

They spun round, shocked. Standing there were two black fairies, and they did not seem at all pleased.

Unaware of the other-worldly drama on the sidewalk, humans walked back and forth. A group of three men, fresh from a meeting concerning the setting up of a fund to help destitute former baseball players, strolled into the bar to discuss the day's progress. Two construction workers walked in to spend the rest of the afternoon eking out one beer each, because these days the construction business was terrible.

'Construction spending fell 2.6 per cent last year', it said in their trade paper. No one seemed to have any money to give them work.

The barman sympathised with their troubles. His trade was not good either.

Outside, the fairies fled.

Forty-two mercenaries gathered at nightfall on Bodmin Moor in Cornwall. Magris looked down at them and up at the clouds. Muttering a few words of the old tongue he magicked up a light fall of rain. As a scientist Magris disliked magic, but it had its uses. He waited for the moon to appear.

The mercenaries were homeless fairies from around the British Isles – Scottish Red Caps, English Spriggans, Welsh Bwbachods, and Irish Firbolgs. They stood, silent and grim, and waited. Twenty-one of the mercenaries would begin a determined search-and-destroy mission against Aelric, while the other twenty-one were to cross over to America on the moonbow and capture the fugitives.

Back in Central Park, Tulip was gloomy.

'That was very unfortunate.'

'Yes,' agreed Petal. 'It should have been nice meeting other fairies. I'd no idea there were any here.'

'I tried my best to be friendly.'

'So did I.'

'I hated it when they threatened us with death.'

They all looked accusingly at Maeve.

'It would have been fine if you had not acted in such a hot-headed manner,' said Brannoc, angrily.

Maeve tossed her red hair.

'They threatened us. No one threatens an O'Brien fairy.'

'Well, it was completely unnecessary to threaten him back with tearing his head off. Is that the way you act in Ireland?'

'Yes.'

Brannoc turned away in disgust. The episode had been a disaster. They had succeeded in gathering supplies but, thanks to Maeve's temper, they had alienated a previously unsuspected clan of black fairies.

'They could have been helpful, you know. Now we'll have to avoid them.'

Maeve would not give in. She said she did not care how helpful they could have been, no one threatened an O'Brien fairy and got away with it. She drank some whisky and told Brannoc he could go back and make peace if he wanted.

'Though I hope you make a better job of it than the English have done in Ireland so far.'

She donned her uillen pipes and started up a jaunty jig to demonstrate her lack of concern. Padraig joined in on his tin whistle, but the tune he introduced was 'Banish Misfortune'. Although he would not speak against Maeve, he felt that she had not handled things very well. After all, the black fairies did have reason to object. Maeve and he would not have been very pleased had they found one of their local bars in Galway being raided by a bunch of strangers.

'Banish Misfortune' is a very lucky jig. Generations of Celts have played it with optimism, which has given it a magical power to make things go well. Since ending up in New York, Padraig had found himself playing it more and more.

The barman in Harlem noticed how empty the whisky bottles had become.

'We sure sold a lot of Scotch this week,' he told the construction workers. 'Maybe trade's on the increase after all.'

This seemed like heartening news and the workers were cheered. In the pleasant afterglow of the fairies' presence, they felt that better times were bound to come soon.

THIRTEEN

'Dinnie, I have been reading the magazines that were lying in the gutter outside.'

'So?'

'Focus your mind carefully on our bargain.'

'Why?'

'Because it's time for you to lose weight.'

Dinnie gave a yelp. The last thing Dinnie wanted to do was lose weight. Heather knew that this was going to be an awkward beginning to her plan to transform Dinnie, but she was insistent.

'A recent survey in *Cosmopolitan* gave excess weight as the number one turn-off for American women. Kerry is an American woman. It therefore follows that to win her heart you have to lose weight. To put it another way, she is not going to fall for a fat lump like you. So you're going on a diet.'

Dinnie spluttered.

'You said you'd make her fall in love with me. You never said anything about making me suffer.'

'I said if you did exactly as I said I'd make her fall for you. And I say you have to lose weight.'

Dinnie immediately refused, but Heather countered by informing him that this would be breaking their bargain and she would now shrink the fiddle to fairy size and remove it.

Dinnie was cornered. He clutched his packet of cookies, panic stricken. He could feel himself going faint as the awful prospect of dieting loomed in front of him.

Heather, not averse to putting one over on Dinnie, smirked maliciously.

'But do not despair, my fat friend. The magazine promised that it is easy to fill yourself up with nourishing and appetising meals and still lose weight. I have memorised the recipes and you are starting today.'

Wails of passion from a rehearsal came up through the floorboards, as Lysander, Demetrius, Hermia and Helena struggled there way through their difficult romance. Dinnie screamed abuse at the performers.

'Now, now,' Heather chided him. 'Remember that you are also becoming a pleasant and civilised human being. Pleasant and civilised human beings do not scream out to strangers that they are guilty of having sex with their mothers.

'Today's recipe will be nuts and tomatoes. Also Chinese cabbage leaves, because you need green vegetables. You take a walk to the health food shop on First Avenue for the nuts and buy some tomatoes from the corner shop. Tomatoes are these round red things. I will find the Chinese cabbage leaves because I could do with a little fresh air. While you are at it, keep a look out for a triple-bloomed Welsh poppy. I have learned that it is most important to Kerry.'

Heather hopped on to the window-sill.

'If you get back before me, practise the new jig I showed you, "The Atholl Highlanders". It is an extremely fine jig and it is in your book if you can't remember it. Take care not to confuse it with "The Atholl Volunteers", "The Atholl Volunteers' March", "Atholl Brose" or "The Braes of Atholl". A popular place for songs, Atholl. Cheerio.'

The ransom note from the Chinese fairies was a terrible blow to Kerry and Morag.

'GIVE US BACK THE MIRROR OR YOU'LL NEVER SEE YOUR WELSH POPPY AGAIN.'

Kerry gazed at it. It seemed to imply magic forces beyond belief.

'How did they get hold of my Welsh poppy? How did they know where it was? How did they know it was important? And how did they know I had stolen the mirror?'

Morag made a small loop in the air before settling on Kerry's shoulder.

'Fairies can know lots of things by intuition,' she explained. 'I expect that after they chased me following the regrettable lobster incident, they sensed that I'd been in the shop where the mirror had been. Probably they've been looking for me ever since and when they spotted me they took the first opportunity to burgle your apartment.

'You were wearing your waistcoat today so they couldn't find the mirror, but they took something else. They might have known the Welsh poppy was important to you due to cunning psychic insights. There again, it might have been because you wrote a sign in red ink above it saying "This is my most prized possession." '

Morag volunteered to make the exchange.

'I am sure it will not be too risky. We fairies are reasonable creatures and I will simply explain the whole thing away as a misunderstanding. If that doesn't work, I'll claim you are a kleptomaniac currently undergoing treatment.'

'That was the most unpleasant customer I've ever encountered,' said an assistant in the health food shop to her fellow worker. 'You'd think I was twisting his arm to buy a bag of mixed nuts.'

'What was it he accused you of?'

'I don't know. It was something about collaborating with fairies to poison the city.'

'What a weirdo. Did you notice his coat?'

They shuddered.

Dinnie tramped home. The slight satisfaction of having

subjected the sales assistants to some good solid abuse had not made him any happier about the day's events.

He flung the nuts on a shelf and settled down for his afternoon nap.

Morag hovered over Canal Street, slightly uncomfortable at the prospect of facing an entire Chinese fairy clan, but confident that things would work out well enough and she would be able to return with Kerry's dried flower. It was desperately important to Morag that Kerry won the Community Arts Prize because this would make her immensely happy, and Morag had read in a medical directory in a bookshop on Second Avenue that being happy was very important to Crohn's disease sufferers. An unhappy Kerry was likely to be a sick Kerry, and a sick Kerry was likely to get more of her insides removed by a surgeon.

Heather, meanwhile, was travelling the short distance to Chinatown to find some Chinese cabbage leaves.

'This is extremely good of me,' she thought, idly combing her long hair as a delivery truck took her down Broadway to Canal Street. 'I could get him any old cabbage leaves. He'd never know the difference. But the recipe said Chinese, and I am willing to expend effort for a fellow MacKintosh.'

She looked up into the dazzling blue sky, and started in surprise. Up above was Morag, surrounded by strange yellow fairies. Heather was not particularly psychic as fairies go, but she easily sensed the hostility of the strangers towards Morag. As she watched, they seemed to be in the process of robbing her of a shining brooch.

Unsheathing her sword and her skian dhu, she flew up into the air.

'Unhand my friend,' she screamed, plunging into the floating host, slashing wildly.

Dinnie slumbered peacefully, undisturbed by the four Puerto Rican footballers on the street below kicking around their tennis ball.

'Raise the clans!' screamed Heather, to Dinnie's immense distress, as she thundered in the window, Morag in tow.

'We're being invaded by a host of yellow fairies!'

'What?'

'Get your sword out. They're attacking over the hills!'

'Will you stop shouting.'

'Barricade the doors!' screamed Heather. 'Sound the warpipes!'

'Will you shut up, you imbecile!' demanded Dinnie. 'What's the idea of bursting in here shouting and screaming. You know I need my afternoon sleep.'

'Never mind your sleep. There's yellow fairies with strange weapons massing on the borders.'

'Oh, for God's sake, you're not in the Highlands now.'

'I had to fight my way out of Canal Street. Only a master swordswoman like myself could have done it. Then we escaped on a police car but they'll be after us. Come on, Morag.' She turned to her friend. 'Get your sword out.'

Heather's mood changed to one of open defiance. She leapt on to the window-sill and began marching up and down.

'Wha daur meddle wi me!' she yelled out the window. 'Touch not the cat bot a glove!'

This was the motto of the MacKintosh clan, and obscure even by Scottish standards.

She leaned out to check for the enemy. None were in sight.

'Well,' she said. 'It seems like I shook them off. Hah! It takes more than a few odd-coloured fairies to capture one of the fighting MacKintoshes.'

She brandished her sword one last time at the world in general, then hopped back inside.

'Well, Morag, we may have our differences, but never let it be said I was not willing to intervene in a crisis.'

Morag, seemingly dazed by recent events, shook her head.

'Heather,' she said. 'You are a profound idiot.'

Magenta marched on, grinning with satisfaction. The Gods were obviously with her. And she had every right to expect that they would be, for she was assiduously consulting Zeus, Apollo and Athena at every opportunity, and she always followed their advice.

Only yesterday she had lost the poppy to the young hippy girl. Shaken by this defeat, Magenta had sat down to consult an oracle, the insides of a dead pigeon. A commotion in the sky made her look up, and there was a battle between various Persian winged demons.

Cyrus might be dead, but she was not returning home without some profit. The triple-bloomed Welsh poppy and a small and gleaming octagonal mirror had plummeted down into her lap from the sky. Recognising valuable booty when she saw it, Xenophon gathered them up and hurried off.

'Well, I wasn't to know you were involved in some shady dealing on behalf of that dumb woman Kerry,' protested Heather. 'I thought you were being mugged.'

Heather was indignant. She had risked her life to save a fellow Scot from the enemy and all she got was abuse.

'Now we don't have the mirror any more and neither do we have the flower. You have ruined everything. Why do you have to leap into everything feet first? Or sword first?'

'We MacKintoshes are used to fighting,' replied Heather,

stiffly. 'Remember, we had to hold off the filthy Camerons for generations.'

'I thought it was the MacPhersons,' said Dinnie.

'We had a feud with the Camerons as well. A desperate affair, though not as bad as the one we had with the disgusting Comyns. Now that was a feud. Bloody deaths everywhere.'

Dinnie shook his head in despair. Morag departed in disgust.

'To hell with it,' sneered Heather. 'Last time I risk my life for her. Still, I am interested to learn that Kerry wants to win the East 4th Street Community Arts Prize. That piece of information is bound to come in useful to us.'

She returned to the subject of Dinnie's diet.

'For the meantime you will have to make do without the Chinese cabbage leaves.'

'What? You expect me to eat these nuts on their own? You promised me green vegetables.'

'Well you can hardly expect me to come back with an armful of Chinese cabbage leaves when the entire market was filled with yellow fairies hacking at me with curved swords and axes, can you? You'll just have to make do. Now excuse me, I am off for a well-earned dram.'

FOURTEEN

'Surely it can be repaired?'

'No, it can't.'

Morag was lying face down on a cushion, her head resting heavily on a cassette of L 7's new album. In normal times she liked the way these women screamed and hit their guitars, but now she was in the depths of incurable depression. Her rescue mission had gone disastrously wrong and her fiddle was still in ruins.

'This fiddle is the product of Callum MacHardie and he is the finest fiddle maker in Scotland. The MacHardies, fairies and humans, have always made the best fiddles. This one took Callum three years to make and another's year's wait before varnishing. It's made of maple and pine and ebony and box-wood, and the amber varnish Callum uses is a secret only he knows. Now it's in bits. I don't even know if Callum himself could fix it if he had it in his workshop under the Sacred Ash Tree. Who could repair it here?'

'New York must have skilled violin makers.'

'Would they work on a fiddle four inches long?'

Kerry sprawled on the cushion beside Morag. Her most precious flower was missing. It could not be replaced. After Morag fell from the sky during the fiasco with the Chinese fairies, the original had again disappeared, and she had already scoured the wasteland where it had grown. There was nothing else there like it.

Kerry played a listless version of the New York Dolls' 'Lonely Planet Boy', but without Morag playing along it didn't feel the same and they soon lapsed into listening to gloomy Swans records instead.

There were three weeks left before the closing date for entries to the Arts competition. Kerry, who would have had her work cut out gathering the remaining flowers even without the recent setbacks, seemed to be defeated. Cal and his version of *A Midsummer Night's Dream* seemed destined to win the prize, no matter how terrible his version might turn out to be. The only other entrants Kerry knew of were poets, and poets were not fashionable right now.

Unexpectedly, Heather flew in the window. She felt that some sort of apology was in order and, having drunk enough whisky, had come to make it. She said she was sorry about the mix-up and volunteered to do all she could to help rectify the situation.

In this she was quite sincere, although it was at the back of her mind that the more she knew about Kerry's flower alphabet the more likely it was that she could make something out of it to benefit Dinnie. She was careful to give no hint of this, knowing that Morag would be irate at the thought of a match between her pleasant friend and the unlovely Dinnie.

It was a beautiful day in Cornwall, the sort of day when fairies should be out playing music and sniffing flowers. Most of them were toiling in workhouses, however, and the few that weren't were hiding in a barn, plotting revolution.

'So, Aelric, what's the next step?'

'Further economic disruption,' said Aelric.

'But there are not enough of us to ruin the King's economy as you say we must.'

Aelric admitted that this was true and told them the next stage was to spread the revolt.

'A peasants' revolution is what we need, although how we manage this I am not sure. From the subject index in the library, Chairman Mao seems to be the acknowledged expert on the subject, but there are an awful lot of books by him and I haven't quite mastered his tactics yet.'

They all prayed to Dianna, Goddess of the Fairies, for help because it would have been quite shocking for them not to, even if, as Aelric had discovered, Chairman Mao had decidedly strong views against this sort of thing.

Morag sat with Heather on the fire escape outside Dinnie's.

'Don't worry,' Heather comforted her. 'Your hair is looking beautiful with all its colours and the beads Kerry gave you suit you really well. And when we get back to Scotland you can get a new fiddle. You are such a great player that Callum MacHardie will be happy to make you a bonnie new one, even if he does disapprove of you playing Ramones tunes on it. And in the meantime, you can share mine.'

Morag's spirits rose slightly. It was good at least to be friends with Heather again.

'Having a nice rest?' came Dinnie's voice from behind.

Dinnie was scowling. Something he would not admit even to himself was that he was jealous of the relationship between Heather and Morag. He did not wish them to be friends again in case Heather left him alone.

'You're meant to be giving me a violin lesson.'

'Hold your wheesht,' said Heather, brusquely.

'What?'

'Be quiet,'

'Oh, fine,' said Dinnie. 'Abuse me. I don't remember that being part of our bargain.'

'What bargain?' asked Morag.

'Nothing, nothing,' chirped Heather.

They began to talk together in Gaelic, which made Dinnie more frustrated. A pleasantly malicious thought entered his head. He could think of one very easy way to get rid of Morag and put one over on Heather, whom he still resented for making him diet.

'When you've quite finished, Heather, could you get on with teaching me how to play my fine MacPherson Fiddle?'

There was a brief silence.

'Fine what?' said Morag.

Heather paled slightly.

'Nothing, nothing.'

'He said fine MacPherson Fiddle,' stated Morag. 'And I am beginning to have one of those psychic insights which . . . '

She sped across the room and climbed right on to the instrument to study it. Heather placed her tiny hand across her brow and rested her head against the filthy cooker. She knew what was coming.

Morag shrieked with delight.

'It's the MacPherson Fiddle! The real MacPherson Fiddle. You found it!'

She danced around happily.

'What a wonderful coincidence. The treasure of my clan, right here in East 4th Street. And the only fiddle I would rather play than my own! Everything is turning out well. Heather, help me shrink it to our size so I can play!'

'She will do no such thing,' declared Dinnie, smugly. 'It's mine until I hand it over to Heather. That's our bargain. So beat it.'

'What does he mean?' asked Morag. 'It obviously should be mine. I'm a MacPherson.'

'She has a bargain with me,' repeated Dinnie, 'which cannot be broken.'

'Is this true?'

'Well . . . ' said Heather, who could neither deny nor break the bargain.

'But my fiddle is broken. I need it.'

'Tough,' said Dinnie, who was enjoying himself greatly.

Morag erupted in a terrible fury. Heather had never seen her in such a state. Morag claimed the fiddle as hers by right of being a MacPherson and called Heather a thief, a cheat and a liar.

Dinnie chuckled to himself. He had known very well what would happen if Morag found out about the bargain.

'I can't help it,' protested Heather. 'I made the bargain with the human and a good thistle fairy is not allowed to break a bargain.'

Morag's pale skin was scarlet with rage.

'The violin belongs to my clan, you lizard.'

'Please, Morag . . . '

'And you are a goblin fucker and a disgrace to Scotland.'

This was too much, even for a contrite Heather.

'Well, you ignorant MacPhersons shouldn't have lost it in the first place.'

'You MacKintoshes are all scum,' yelled Morag. 'I spit in your mother's milk!'

With this approximation of an insult she'd picked up in a Mexican restaurant, Morag stormed out of the window.

Heather hung her head. What a disaster. Thank the Goddess Morag had not thought to ask what the other half of the bargain was. If she discovered that Heather was intending to pair off Dinnie and Kerry, things might have got violent.

'Dear, dear,' said Dinnie. 'What a terrible argument. How tactless of me.'

Heather gave him a ferocious glower but did not argue.

'Next lesson. Holding the bow. And this time try not to saw the damn thing in half.'

FIFTEEN

Everywhere there were dissatisfied fairies. While Heather and Morag had their own various problems, they had caused problems for others as well.

'Where does this money come from?' asked both Dinnie and Kerry, noticing that both Heather and Morag liked to keep the houses well stocked with provisions.

'Standard fairy magic,' lied Heather and Morag.

But in Grand Street the Italian fairies were most unhappy. Unknown strangers kept robbing their human allies' banks.

'Four times this month,' they grumbled. 'We cannot let our Italian friends' businesses be ruined by these thieves.'

On Canal Street the Chinese fairies were still fuming over the theft of their Bhat Gwa mirror. This important icon had been given to the Chinese fairies two thousand years ago by the blessed Lao Tzu before he departed the Earth. It was their greatest treasure and was housed in the shop of Hwui-Yin as a symbol of friendship between fairies and humans.

Now, on the verge of seeing it returned, they had been frustrated by another unknown fairy who had brandished a sword at them and screamed abuse in a horrible barbaric accent.

'We are a peaceable tribe. But we cannot tolerate this.'

They wondered who was responsible. It could be the Italian fairies, whom they had known in the past but had no contact with now, even though they lived only a few blocks away.

In Harlem there was great upset over the incident in the bar. It was most impolite for strangers to come and rob a place in their territory and the violent threats from the red-haired stranger caused great concern.

'We have not seen any other fairies here for generations,' they said. 'And now they come like thieves. We must prepare for the worst.'

In Central Park, Brannoc was extremely dissatisfied. He had just found Tulip and Petal making love enthusiastically under a rose bush. It was not taboo for a fairy brother and sister to have sex, but it annoyed the hell out of Brannoc. He burned with jealousy.

Maeve and Padraig were drunk and maudlin. They sat in a tree playing their tin whistles. Brannoc had to admit he was impressed at the way these Irish musicians could still play so well after drinking so much, but he was not in the mood to be appreciative.

Petal and Tulip were nowhere in sight. Presumably they were still practising their youthful fairy sex techniques, although from what Brannoc had seen they seemed fairly advanced already.

Brannoc felt lonely. It struck him that only a little way to the north were a whole new tribe of fairies he could be friendly with. If he was to go back he was sure he could make good the argument. He was a reasonable fairy. He saw no reason why they should not be. It was not good to make enemies in this strange place.

'Where are you going?' called Padraig.

'To make peace with the black fairies,' he replied.

'Good luck. Bring us some whisky.'

In Cornwall also there was great dissatisfaction. The fairies of the land were no longer allowed to pay tribute to their Goddess Dianna. Her festivals had been replaced by ceremonies dedicated to a strong new god who would defeat their enemies.

The moon appeared from behind the clouds. Magris spoke a few more words of the old tongue and a moonbow in seven shades of grey slid out of the sky.

Half of the mercenary band climbed the moonbow and made their way up into the night. They climbed without a sound till they disappeared from view. Magris turned and muttered to the remaining mercenaries. They marched off into the night on the track of the rebel Aelric.

The light wind that always followed the production of a moonbow tugged at Magris's cloak as he too left.

Magenta was tense, though not dissatisfied. She eyed the skyscrapers that stretched up First Avenue and her soldierly instinct told her that here would be a good place for an ambush. Joshua, now merged in her mind with Tissaphernes, might be waiting round any corner. She took a drink from her cocktail, made a mental note to buy more methylated spirits and boot polish, and flicked through her copy of Xenophon.

One of the most impressive parts of the book was the Greeks' trust in the Gods. Even in the most dangerous circumstances, when quick action was imperative, they would do nothing until they had made the proper sacrifices and consulted the omens.

Magenta looked round for a likely sacrifice. A squashed pigeon lay in the gutter. Magenta spied it and hurried over to inspect its entrails. They were a little hard to read, having been run over by numerous cars, but on the whole Magenta thought they looked favourable.

'Right, men,' she called. 'Advance.'

There were more dissatisfied fairies in Cornwall. In a corner of Bodmin Moor behind an ancient standing stone, a corner as cold and grey as the Atlantic over which the mercenaries strode, the moonbow was about to fade in the dawn. Out of the dark bushes crept four silent figures, scanning the area warily.

'Where is it leading?' whispered one, eyeing the seven bands of grey.

'Who knows?' said another. 'But Heather MacKintosh and Morag MacPherson will be on the end of it. Let us go before it fades.'

Without another word they began to ascend. They were four female warrior fairies from the MacLeod clan. Each of them was tall, lithe and strong, and heavily armed. They intended to recover the stolen pieces of their banner and none of them had the manner of one to be trifled with.

A small child dropped a dime on the sidewalk. Brannoc kindly stopped to pick it up and return it.

'I don't believe it,' came a voice. 'Not content with robbing the bars, they're stealing dimes off children now.'

Brannoc was confronted by an angry group of black fairies.

'These whites are even meaner than they used to be.'

'You don't understand,' protested Brannoc.

'Someone's stolen my dime,' wailed the child.

Brannoc made a hurried departure, learning with great speed the technique, already well known to Heather and Morag, of making an emergency exit on the fender of a speeding cab.

'What happened?' cried Tulip and Petal as he stumbled into the safety of their bushes. Brannoc refused to talk about it, although he did mention that cab drivers in New York were appallingly reckless, luckily for him.

SIXTEEN

'I saw an awful lot of police outside,' said Morag, as Kerry took her lunchtime steroids.

Kerry told her that they were probably on their way to Tomkins Square, where today there was a free festival.

'I hate to see so many police.'

'Why?' enquired Morag. 'Police are nice. In Cruickshank our village policeman, Constable MacBain, is a braw man. Every afternoon after he has his dinner and a few drinks in the pub he comes for a sleep behind the bushes near where we live and he often leaves some tobacco for the fairies. All the children like him because he gives them rides on his bicycle. And he is not a bad piper either. Now I think about it, I'm sure I heard him say one day that he has an Irish cousin who is a policeman in America. I'm sure he is a braw man too.'

Kerry said that this did not sound like any policeman she had ever come across, and the chances of any member of the New York Police Department leaving tobacco out for the fairies were pretty slim, but Morag did not really understand what she meant.

'So, what are we going to do today?'

'The festival in Tomkins Square. Cal is playing guitar with a friend's band so we can scream abuse.'

'Sounds good to me.'

Kerry struggled into her pink and green dungarees because today she would need lots of pockets for beer. After a long and detailed discussion with Morag about what to put in their hair, involving much study of Botticelli's *Primavera* and associated works, they left.

In Chinatown the Chinese fairies were making final preparations for the Festival of Hungry Ghosts, making sure they had enough food and drink for celebration and for offerings, and the correct incense and paper money for burning. This active time would normally have been a happy one, but the community was instead gripped with apprehension due to the loss of their prized Bhat Gwa mirror. What new and terrible dissatisfied spirit might appear among them without the mirror to reflect away bad Fung Shui?

Lu-Tang, their sage and wise woman, sent envoys all over looking for it, but where it had got to since last seen falling from the skies into Canal Street, no one could tell.

Further inspection of Kerry's apartment showed that it was no longer there, although the Chinese fairies who staked out East 4th Street were interested to see Heather sneaking into the apartment for a good look round.

Heather was taking this opportunity to break in to Kerry's apartment and gather more information about her. The more she knew about Kerry's tastes, the easier it would be to change Dinnie into the sort of person she would like.

She wondered where they had gone.

'To have fun somewhere, no doubt,' she muttered wistfully, rummaging through Kerry's huge collection of cassettes, and wishing again that she had ended up with a human friend who liked to have fun, instead of one who sat around all day watching dubious programmes on television.

It took Kerry some time to persuade Morag that they had not actually been responsible for the riot in Tomkins Square and that it was merely a coincidence that it had erupted after they lobbed a bottle on-stage at Cal's band.

'I'm sure there would have been trouble anyway,' proclaimed Kerry, as they fled from the chaos. 'It had little or nothing to do with us drinking too much. The police were just waiting for an opportunity to wade in with their truncheons.'

Bloodied victims of the riot streamed past them, much to Morag's distress.

'These police here are very heavy-handed,' she said, wincing at the sight of the injuries. 'I will have some strong words to say to Constable MacBain when I get back to Scotland.'

As soon as they were out of the immediate area they plunged into a deli to buy beer.

'Why do they sell beer in brown bags here?' enquired Morag.

'Something to do with the law.'

'Oh. I thought it made it taste better. Still, we'd better obey the law unless we want to get a truncheon over the head.'

Magenta hurried past on the other side of the street, escaping after the vicious mêlée with the Persians. Morag spotted her and gave pursuit.

'Well,' mused Johnny Thunders, gently floating down through the Nether Worlds. 'I can hear screaming guitars and a riot going on. Sounds like New York to me.'

He was right. It was.

'Now, how am I to find my 1958 Gibson Tiger Top?'

In the mad pursuit into the mountainous regions Magenta, badly harassed by Persian mounted archers, New York motorcycle police and a Scottish fairy, was forced to abandon some of the booty picked up on the campaign so far.

This was regrettable because, as with all mercenaries, booty was one of her main motivations. Mercenary pay was not really sufficient to justify the dangers and rigours of the life. However, they were too heavily laden and something had to go. She dropped the triple-bloomed Welsh poppy and carried on with her flight.

She was protecting the rear. Up in front Chirisophus the Spartan led the way. Xenophon did not trust Chirisophus one bit.

'That bag lady is madder than the rest of them,' Morag told Kerry. 'Younger and fitter, though. It took me fourteen blocks to catch up with her.'

'What happened?'

'I asked her for the flower. She shouted to some imaginary followers to form a square because they were under attack. Then she threw down the poppy.

'Did you get it?'

Morag shook her head.

'Three fire trucks arrived at that very minute. By the time I'd made my way round them it was gone.'

She gazed at her knee, which was red.

'When I tried running round the fire trucks I fell over and skinned my knee. I think the beer may have slightly affected my balance.'

Kerry trudged home with Morag in her pocket. She needed this flower and it was high time it stopped circulating round the city, but who could say where it was now?

SEVENTEEN

'Your waistline is definitely getting smaller,' announced Heather. 'Have you done your exercises today?'

Dinnie nodded. He had never exercised before and he ached.

'Good. Soon you will be a fine strapping MacKintosh, fit for anything. Now, who do you like best, the Velvet Underground or Sonic Youth?'

Dinnie shook his head blankly, one of the many habits of his which annoyed the fairy.

'The Velvet Underground? Sonic Youth? What are you on about?'

'I have made an important discovery.'

'You have to leave?'

'No, I don't have to leave. To fulfil our bargain, I am prepared to hang around indefinitely. The important discovery I made, during a daring commando raid on Kerry's, is that she is very fond of music. There are these things – what are they called – cassettes? Right? Cassettes. All over the place. She is almost as untidy as you, though not so dirty. Now, of course I had not heard of any of the bands that played on these cassettes, but I picked out the one she plays most often— '

'And how did you find that out?' said Dinnie, with some sarcasm. 'Asked a cockroach, I suppose?'

'No, I did not ask a cockroach. I asked the cassettes.'

Heather picked something out of her sporran.

'And here it is.'

Dinnie glared woefully at the tape. 'A New York Compilation', it was called: Sonic Youth, the Ramones, the New York Dolls, Lydia Lunch, Richard Hell, the Swans, Nine Inch Nails, Television and many others.

'Well, so what?'

Heather scowled in frustration.

'Dinnie, stop havering. If you want to be the sort of boyfriend Kerry will like you have to at least pretend to like the same sort of music as her. Haven't you seen her going out to hear bands at night? It is obviously important to her.'

Dinnie was appalled.

'Is there no end to these impositions?' he barked. Only yesterday Heather had lectured him for refusing to give money to a beggar and right after that she had forbidden him to call the assistant at the deli a Mexican whore, even in private.

'This is not the sort of thing Kerry will want to hear. And you are not to mutter bad things under your breath when black people come on television either.'

Heather waved aside his protests and inserted the cassette in Dinnie's tape recorder. 'Now, you listen to this and memorise it. I am away for a few drams and I'll test you when I get back.'

Dinnie, however, had not finished protesting.

'What use will it be liking the same sort of music as her when I'll probably never even get the chance to talk to her?'

Heather slapped her thigh triumphantly.

'I was hoping you'd ask that. Because I have that angle covered as well. When you make a bargain with a MacKintosh fairy you get the full service.

'Kerry, as I have told you, is very fond of flowers. She seems to collect them, in dried form at least. And today, while having my afternoon flutter along the rooftops, I happened to spot a very unusual flower lying on the pavement.'

She handed the triple-bloomed poppy to Dinnie.

'I feel that once you give this to her she will be very favourably disposed towards you.'

Heather stood on the play button of Dinnie's cassette deck.

Dinnie winced as Lydia Lunch began to blast through his rooms.

'But I hate this sort of stuff.'

'So what? You can pretend. You don't think you're going to win Kerry by being sincere, do you?'

Aelric's guerrilla campaign in Cornwall suffered a reverse when he fell in love with the King's stepdaughter.

He sat in a barn, musing on this misfortune.

'Are you sure you are in love with her?' asked Aelis, one of his trusted companions.

'Yes. When I saw her drawing her sword and preparing to give chase after we set fire to Tala's Royal Mint, I knew immediately.'

Aelis shook her head in sympathy. She knew that when a fairy falls in love at first sight it is practically impossible to get over it, but she also knew that as a romance it was doomed from the start. With Marion being the stepdaughter of the King there seemed little chance of her falling for Aelric, a rebel who kept burning down the King's most important buildings.

Barn owls nestled in the shade beside them.

Aelric looked thoughtfully at the ceiling.

'Of course,' he mused, 'she is his stepdaughter and for all I know she might hate her father. Stepdaughters have a notoriously bad time of it in fairy royal families.'

Aelis agreed that this was possible and promised to find out from one of her contacts, a handmaiden at the royal palace, the precise standing of the King's stepdaughter.

The rest of the guerrilla unit stole silently into the barn in preparation for the night's raid.

On the problem of how Morag was to obtain the MacPherson Fiddle from Dinnie, Kerry had a useful suggestion.

'Offer Dinnie something better than Heather has. Then he would give you the fiddle.'

Morag considered this. It seemed like a good idea.

'Except I don't know what that scumbag of a MacKintosh has offered,' complained the fairy, and spat on the floor.

'In that case you will have to offer him what he wants most in all the world. And as he seems like a lonely soul, I imagine what he would most like is a nice girlfriend. Unless he is gay, in which case he would like a nice boyfriend.'

Morag fluttered across the road.

'Dinnie,' she asked. 'Are you gay or straight?'

'How dare you!' roared Dinnie, and threw a cup at her.

She fluttered back.

'That probably means he is straight, though somewhat prejudiced,' explained Kerry.

'Then I will bargain with him for a girlfriend,' declared Morag. 'Although finding anyone who would want to go out with that abusive lump will be a sore test.'

Heather stared sadly at the corpse in the doorway. Two policemen were attending to it.

'I can't understand why these tramps keep dying in East 4th,' said one, and the other shook his head. This made eight in the past few weeks.

'Phone Linda at 970 F–U–C–K for the hottest two-girl sex in town.'

Dinnie was watching television.

'I presume you are now fully expert in New York music?' said Heather, appearing in the sudden way which was so distressing to Dinnie. She switched off the TV and worked the cassette.

'Who's this?'

'The Velvet Underground.'

'Wrong. It is the Ramones. What about this one?'

'Band of Susans.'

'Wrong. It is Suicide. You have failed. Listen to the tape again. I am going to sleep, but do not worry about disturbing me. I am becoming fonder of that funny sweet American whisky and am now able to drink more of it.'

'You mean you're drunk.'

'Drunk? Me? A MacKintosh fairy?' Heather laughed, and slumped on the bed.

Kerry was enormously depressed about everything. Her flower alphabet, while growing steadily, was missing its most important component. Her disease did not seem to be getting any better, which made her drink more, which made her more depressed afterwards. And seeing Cal on stage with his band had been a sore trial.

Kerry wished that he had stayed with her and carried out his promise to teach her all the New York Dolls guitar solos.

'I miss Cal,' she told Morag. 'And even throwing a bottle at him and ruining his gig has not driven him out of my mind.'

'Find a new man,' suggested Morag. 'While I'm finding a new woman for Dinnie.'

Kerry said that this was not so easy.

Morag stared at the adverts on the back page of *Village Voice*.

'Transvestites, Singles, Bi's, Gays, all welcome, Club Edelweiss, West 29th St.'

'Young man on Brooklyn bound 'B' train, Thursday 6/21, light jeans, got off Dekalb Ave, I was too shy to talk, would like to hear from you.'

'I see that it can be difficult to make relationships here.'

When Dinnie once more failed to identify any of the bands correctly, both he and Heather were frustrated. Dinnie had come round to agreeing that it was a good idea, but he could not manage a single right answer.

'They all sound the same to me. I'll never be able to tell Cop

Shoot Cop from the Swans. Kerry will never fall in love with me.'

Heather pursed her lips. This was proving to be more difficult than she had imagined.

She fingered her kilt. Back in Scotland Heather had ripped it deliberately to outrage her mother, but now, after so much travelling, it was in danger of disintegrating completely. She took out her dirk, and cut a little piece from one of Dinnie's cushion covers to make a bright patch. Perhaps while sewing she would find some inspiration. If she had known what Morag across the street was thinking she would have agreed. This city was a difficult place to make relationships. The way things were going, Dinnie might as well phone up 970 C–U–N–T and get on with it.

Still, she thought, there was always the flower. This poppy with its three blooms seemed like a very special sort of flower. She was sure that once Dinnie presented it to Kerry she would look on him favourably.

EIGHTEEN

It rained – a strange warm rain that was unfamiliar to Morag. In Scotland the rain had been cold, cheerless and grey. This warm summer rain disquieted her, though she could not say why.

'Kerry, I have just had a good idea.'

'Yes?'

'About Dinnie and the fiddle. The idea that he might swap it for love is very sound. However, what are the chances of any woman falling in love with him?'

Slim, they both agreed.

'So,' continued Morag, 'I will be unable to make a true bargain with him. There is only one thing to do.'

'What?'

'Be deceitful.'

'You mean lie?'

'Not exactly. If I were able to lie to humans I could simply steal the fiddle, but if I did that, terrible things would follow. As you have already observed, fairy karma is a bitch. Me and my clan might be cursed for generations.

'So I will merely bend the truth a little. Bending the truth a little is a respectable fairy tradition.

'I will gain the instrument and return to Scotland in triumph. I will be forgiven everything. My clan will no longer shun me for playing Ramones riffs on my fiddle. The MacLeods will not bother me any more as I will be a Scottish hero. Quite possibly I will be made sole recipient of the junior fiddling prize. Evil MacKintosh objections will wither away in the face of such a mighty feat. Yes, I am sure that deceit is the best way forward.'

'So what do you plan to do?'

'I will pretend to Dinnie that I could convince you to be his girlfriend. He is bound to go for it. You would be a girlfriend away and beyond his wildest dreams. Whatever that raghead Heather has offered him will look paltry by comparison. All it will require is for you to lead him on a little. Once I have the fiddle, you can tell him to go boil his head.'

Dinnie, in addition to listening to rock music, was under standing instructions to keep an eye on the street below in case Kerry appeared. Once she did he was to hurry down and present her with the Welsh poppy.

'It will be an excellent introduction,' Heather assured him.

Unfortunately when Kerry did appear in the street, hurrying between her apartment and the deli for some beer, Dinnie's nerve failed him and she returned home before he could work up the nerve to accost her.

'You fat useless lump,' said Heather, and roundly criticised him as a disgrace to the fighting MacKintoshes.

'Give me the flower!' she said, seeing that she would have to start the process herself. 'I will take it to her and tell her it is a present from you. Now I think about it, this will be even better. Any young woman receiving a present of a flower from a fairy can hardly fail to be impressed. She will fall into your arms.'

This decided, she placed the poppy in her bag, slung it over her shoulder and departed, promising as she did to bring some money home for the rent.

Back in Cornwall, Aelis had bad news for Aelric.

Marion, the King's stepdaughter, apparently got on unusually well with Tala, and also with her mother. They were a notably happy family.

'How depressing,' said Aelric. 'And Tala such a monster as well. Still, I remember seeing in the library that Hitler was a good family man so perhaps it is not so surprising. It just goes to show that step-parents get a bad press. What am I going to do now? I have twelve followers, not nearly enough to disrupt the Cornish fairy economy, and a hopeless passion for the King's stepdaughter.'

Aelis took a swig of mead for her flask and considered the matter.

'Well, Aelric, you must find some way to win her heart. Of course, burning down her father's property will always put a bit of a damper on the relationship, but maybe something will turn up. My contact at court tells me she is very fond of flowers so perhaps you could do something in that direction. As for recruiting more followers, we must get on with distributing our propaganda leaflets.'

This, while a good idea, was proving to be a problem. With the strongest flyers from Tala's army guarding the airspace above all his most vital institutions and population centres, the rebels had been unable to distribute a single one.

Heather's day had started off well after a few drams and a visit to the West Village to look round the expensive art galleries and shops. After that it had gone seriously downhill. She now hung on grimly to the rear mud-guard of a speeding motorbike as it thundered round the corner at Delancy and Allen. Behind her, twenty Italian fairies hung on to the roof of a wailing ambulance in hot pursuit.

'What sort of motorbike courier are you?' she yelled furiously as the bike stopped at an intersection. 'Jump the lights!'

Behind her the ambulance had also halted, but the Italian fairies, using their unusual affinity with the wind currents, swept forward through the air from one vehicle to the next. When the lights changed and Heather's bike took off they were no more than four vehicles behind.

Heather had robbed the Bank d'Italia one time too many. They had been waiting for her outside and she had been caught red-handed with a sporran full of dollars.

Racing up Allen Street and over Houston, Heather began to despair. The Italian fairies had transferred themselves on to a fire truck and were gaining fast.

At the last moment, as the fire truck drew level and her pursuers prepared to leap across, Heather, in desperation, jumped blindly out into 2nd Street. She was then extremely fortunate. A small and fast foreign sports car, which at that moment was being pursued by the police, screeched by and she caught hold of the aerial. The car carried her along 2nd Street and into Avenue A while her pursuers, taken by surprise, disappeared from view on the fire truck.

Heather's car was brought to a halt by police gun-fire at the end of 4th Street and she slipped off to hurry home.

Morag was out taking the air and saw her frantic arrival.

'What on earth have you been doing?' she said. 'Why are the police shooting at you?'

'They're not shooting at me, you idiot,' exclaimed Heather. 'Oh no!'

The Italian fairies reappeared, cruising their way along on a Ford with music blasting out of the huge speakers built into the rear of the chassis.

'Get her!' they screamed.

The two Scottish fairies leapt on to a cab and fled.

The moonbow stretched from Cornwall to Manhattan and on it marched the mercenaries. At their head was Werferth, a ferocious Red Cap from the Northern borders of England. Behind him marched three red-haired Pechs from Scotland and at their sides trotted three Cu Sidth dogs with green fur and malevolent eyes.

The company contained more of the frightening border Red Caps along with Bwbachods from Wales, Spriggans from Cornwall and various other fierce creatures. They had gold in their pockets, a half-payment from Magris, and they did not anticipate any difficulty in earning the rest. The moonbow bent and warped space and distance, making the journey between Britain and America no more than a day's march. America was now in sight and they quickened their pace.

'Well, if you continually rob banks you have to expect this sort of thing!' whispered Morag.

They were hiding on a fire escape at the bottom of Orchard Street.

'Maybe,' whispered Heather. 'But I swear that when they were screaming abuse at me from the fire truck they said something about being continually plundered by *two* fairies in kilts.'

'Was that a firecracker?' muttered Morag. 'I did not quite see which way the cab took us. Are we anywhere near Chinatown?'

There was a sudden shout from above.

'It's them!'

They looked up and groaned. Swarming down the fire escape was an army of Chinese fairies, yelling in triumph.

Some way behind the mercenaries, the warriors from the MacLeod clan strode easily over the moonbow. They were clad in dark leather tunics and their kilts were green with stripes of yellow and red.

The four were sisters; their names were Ailsa, Seonaìd, Mairi and Rhona and their home was on the banks of Loch Dunvegan in the west of the Isle of Skye. They lived in sight of Dunvegan Castle, ancestral home of the MacLeods of MacLeod, leaders of the human branch of the clan.

The MacLeods had fought many fierce battles in the distant past. There had been a time when the human MacLeods had waged continual war on the MacDonalds of Eigg, their hereditary enemies, and the MacLeod fairies had done likewise with the MacDonald fairies.

The MacLeod fairies and humans had been closely allied since the far distant time when Malcolm MacLeod, chief of the human clan, married a shape-changing fairy wife. They had a son before she went back to her own folk, and the legendary MacLeod Fairy Banner was a gift to the son. It was a thing of great power and could never be unfurled except in times of dire need.

On one occasion during battle with the MacDonalds, the MacLeods were on the point of defeat. Their chief unfurled the green Fairy Banner and immediately the fairies came to his aid and won the day. For Heather and Morag to cut two pieces from it was the most sacrilegious thing they could possibly have done. It was no surprise that the MacLeods had sent their most feared fighters to regain the pieces.

'This is as bad as the time the MacLeods chased us from Loch Morar to Loch Ness,' groaned Morag.

'It sure is,' agreed Heather, and winced at the memory. After an extremely long chase they had been on the very point of capture when they fortunately ran into a group of MacAndrew fairies. As the MacAndrews were associates of the MacKintoshes they had been willing to protect Morag and also her companion, enabling them to escape.

Later, though, there had been no protection anywhere from the powerful MacLeods and their allies. Heather and Morag's clans could not go to war on their behalf when they were so obviously in the wrong.

Now they were sat atop another fire truck which was racing north, sirens wailing.

Behind them the Chinese fairies were pursuing on motor cars.

'Lucky for us there's lots of fires in New York.'

Heather declared that she was definitely innocent of angering the Chinese fairies and demanded to know what Morag had been doing to them.

'Nothing. I only freed a few lobsters. And it wasn't me that stole their brooch, I was just an accessory after the fact. Obviously these New York fairies have no manners.'

Heather nodded.

'You're right there. I mean, what's wrong with taking dollars from a bank to buy food? Nothing to get upset about. There's millions of spare dollars in that bank. Nobody will miss a few. If everybody took some then there wouldn't be all these poor people begging on the streets.'

They seemed to be outdistancing their pursuers.

'We're losing them.'

The fire truck came to a halt outside a burning apartment

building. The two Scots jumped down. Another fire truck roared up alongside. Seemingly hanging off every available handhold were white-clad Italian fairies.

Heather and Morag fled.

Ailsa was the oldest MacLeod sister and the leader. They were descended from Gara, the original fairy who married the human chief, and all four of them were hardened warriors. They had high cheekbones, large dark eyes and jagged black hair cut short. Their claymores were keen and hung over their backs and the sharpened dirks strapped to their legs had been handed down through generations of warriors.

'When we find the MacPherson and the MacKintosh, are we to kill them?' asked Mairi.

'If need be,' replied Ailsa. 'Although I have a sleep spell with me. We will try that first. How much further have we to go, Mairi?'

Mairi had the second sight.

'Not much further. I can sense a very strange land only a little way away.'

'Where are we?'

Heather shrugged. Neither she nor Morag had been this far north before.

'Have we shaken them off?'

'I think so.'

'How are we ever going to get back to 4th Street?'

The cab sped all the way up to East 106th before turning left. Heather and Morag dismounted in Fifth Avenue and looked around them.

'That was a long journey. And we're still in the city. What a massive place.'

'Look. There is some countryside!'

In front of them Central Park was green and appealing.

'At least we can rest for a while.'

They bounded into the park.

'We've found the thieves!' yelled the leader of a hunting party from the black fairies. 'After them.'

The mercenaries were over Manhattan. Werferth halted the company and they stared down at the alien land. It was dusk but the city was lit up brighter than anything they had seen before. The huge array of human buildings was off-putting, but the moonbow stretched down into what appeared to be a large wooded field.

'Right, lads,' said Werferth. 'Down we go.'

They began their descent into the foreign land.

'I absolutely did not do anything to offend any black fairies,' said Morag, perched on the back of a mountain bike. 'I never even met a black fairy before.'

'Me, neither,' said Heather. 'They are obviously paranoid about strangers.'

The bicycle raced round the north edge of the park.

'Lucky for us this cyclist has good powerful legs.'

Heather and Morag flew from the cycle on to a passing horse and trap carrying tourists, and from there made their way to Broadway via a busking juggler riding a unicycle.

'This way,' yelled Morag, and leapt on to a car going south.

The car took them steadily down Broadway.

'I think we've finally shaken everybody off.'

They began to relax a little. They were now near Union Square, far away from the black fairies.

A stretch limo drew up along side of them. On top of it, to Heather and Morag's horrified amazement, were four figures from their nightmares. Brandishing claymores and preparing to board their car were the dreaded MacLeod sisters.

NINETEEN

Kerry lay on the floor drawing her comic. This was one of numerous artistic enterprises she carried out mainly for her own amusement. The comic was causing her problems. Inspired by Morag and Heather it was meant to be about fairies, but as Kerry mainly liked to write about fairies, or people, being kind to one another, it was short on action. Morag hobbled painfully into her room.

'Morag? What's wrong?'

The fairy slumped on to a yellow cushion. She was so stiff and sore she could barely move.

Kerry did her best to make a good cup of tea. Morag loved tea but Kerry, along with the rest of New York, was lamentable at making it.

Morag told Kerry about the day's terrible events: her pursuit by the Italians, Chinese, black fairies in Central Park, and finally the MacLeods.

'How did you escape?'

'We leapt off the car and started running when suddenly we were scooped up by a person who hid us in her shopping bag. Some time later when we poked our heads out the MacLeods were nowhere in sight. Strangely enough, our rescuer was none other than the funny lady who had your Welsh poppy.

'She told us not to worry because she had rescued us from Carduchan tribesmen, whoever they are, and to remember that Xenophon was the best leader of the army, in case it ever came to a vote between her and Chirisophus the Spartan. What this means, I am unclear.'

Morag hung her head a little.

'Unfortunately she then took the poppy again.'

'What? Where from?'

'From Heather. She was bringing it for you from Dinnie.'

'How did Dinnie get it?'

Morag shrugged.

'Anyway, the stupid wee midden took it out of her sporran and started waving it about. The bag lady said that it was not fitting for mere Pelasts to be in charge of so much valuable booty and claimed it was hers by right of conquest.'

Kerry was aghast.

'It certainly gets around, this flower.'

'Oh, well,' said Kerry. 'At least you escaped.'

'Well, sort of. Except we were just turning into East 4th Street when I remarked to Heather that if any of the Italian fairies were like me, that is, well known for psychic insights, they might well be waiting for us. They were. They took the money back. What a terrible day. I ache all over. My Indian headband is ruined. Have we got any whisky?'

Morag sipped her drink.

'It was nice seeing Heather, though. Till we argued.'

' "Tullochgorum" again?'

Morag shook her head.

'Not at first. She accused me of deliberately putting my feet in her face in Magenta's shopping bag. Stupid besom. I was only trying to get comfy. Then she said no wonder the MacPhersons couldn't play strathspeys properly if they all had such big feet to worry about. Completely uncalled for. After that we argued about "Tullochgorum". Then the incident with the poppy happened and I threatened to kill her for losing your flower. It really was a terrible day.'

Magenta trundled on. She was satisfied with the day's events. She had rescued her men from a serious attack and begged enough money to replenish her cocktail. Best of all, she had regained her booty. The Welsh poppy was now dear to her heart, as dear as the guitar fragments she carried in her shopping bag, and she would fight to the death to keep hold of it.

Kerry hurried down to the deli to buy more whisky for Morag. Inside she met Dinnie.

'Hello, Kerry,' said Dinnie, summoning up his courage. 'I had a really nice flower for you except that stupid fairy Heather lost it somewhere.'

'How dare you meddle with my flower alphabet!' shouted Kerry, and gave him a good solid punch in the face.

TWENTY

Kerry and Morag harvested a fine crop of daisies from a scrubby patch of grass in Houston Street.

They had gathered enough both for the collection and to wear in their hair. Morag also left some on the corpse of the tramp who lay dead on 4th Street.

'How many's that now? Nine?'

Inside, Kerry studied her flower book.

'*Bellis perennis*,' she said. 'One of the easier parts of my flower alphabet.'

'Mmmm,' said Morag, studying herself in the mirror. 'I am almost convinced that daisies are the ideal adornment.'

'Possibly,' agreed Kerry. 'But it's always hard to tell right away. When I first put a ring of tulips round my forehead I thought I would never be unhappy again, but I soon got tired of them. Tulips are not profound.'

Suddenly angry she picked up her guitar and plugged it into her tiny practice amp.

'How an I going to replace my lost poppy? There's only two weeks left!'

She ran awkwardly through 'Babylon'. Morag stared glumly at her shattered violin and wished she could help.

Johnny Thunders, in celestial form, floated around Queens, where he was born, before visiting some old East Village haunts, musing on the subject of his lost guitar. He had a definite feeling that if he could not locate it he would never be entirely satisfied, even in Heaven. Furthermore, if he ever faced any awkward questions from one of the numerous saints in Heaven about aspects of his behaviour while on Earth, he hoped to be able to play himself out of trouble. He always had before.

As he trailed down to East 4th Street a semi-familiar tune caught his ear.

'Dear, dear,' thought Johnny. 'It's nice to know people still play my stuff, but that is a terrible attempt at "Babylon".'

Dinnie peered out of his window. The four young Puerto Ricans were still kicking a ball about on the corner. Naturally, Dinnie did not approve. He regarded all games as stupid and soccer was an especially stupid one. It was not even American.

At school games had been a nightmare for the unfit Dinnie.

His father used to encourage him to play basketball. Dinnie would have been happy to see basketball made illegal, along with his father.

He kicked around his room. Heather was meant to be giving him a music lesson, but the famous MacPherson Fiddle lay silent on the bed. She had not reappeared from her mid-morning visit to the bar. No doubt she was lying drunk in some gutter.

From downstairs the same lines of Shakespeare had been echoing up through his floor all morning. Today there was another audition and performers were trooping in and out, repeating the same unintelligible things over and over. Dinnie's hatred for community theatre was reaching new heights.

Feeling at a loose end, he wondered if he should clean the cooker. He restrained the urge and diverted his attention to the television instead.

'This beautiful fourteen-carat gold chain can be yours for only sixty-three dollars!'

The jewellery in question rotated on a small turntable.

Dinnie found the sales channel particularly upsetting. He hated it when people phoned in to say how happy their new gold chain had made them.

'And you sell them so cheap! You've made my whole year feel just great!'

Dinnie changed channels.

'Any of you boys out there dream about being dressed up like a dirty little slut? Phone 970 D–O I–T, where all your fantasies come true.'

The man in the advert was dressed in a white corset. It was a nice corset. It suited him. Dinnie did not approve.

The heat pounded into his room from outside. Today it was almost too hot and humid to bear. He wished he could afford air-conditioning. He wished he could afford anything. He also wished that Kerry had not punched him in the face. Dinnie might be inexperienced but he knew that this was a poor start to a relationship. It had not made him like her any less.

Morag fluttered through the window, a pleasant sight with her eighteen-inch figure covered in bright hippy garments and her multicoloured hair layered with daisies.

'Kerry, I have potentially a great bit of news.'

'Yes?'

'Yes. The ghost of Johnny Thunders, New York Dolls guitar virtuoso, was outside your window when you were playing "Babylon". He sympathises with your difficulties in hitting all the notes and is scandalised than an ex-boyfriend of yours promised to teach you and then ratted on his promise. So Johnny has offered to help you play it properly.

'In addition he is going to give a thought to where I might get my fiddle repaired. He naturally knows about these things, having himself one time been poor, with only broken instruments to play.

'This Johnny Thunders is a splendid person, or ghost. He told me some funny stories about a place called Queens where he was born and showed me his tattoos. Even said he would keep a lookout for your poppy. In return I will help him look for his 1958 Gibson Tiger Top, which apparently was a wonderful guitar. It is called a Tiger Top because it has stripes.'

Kerry burst out laughing.

'It's true,' protested the fairy. 'You can't see him because he's a spirit, but I can. He is very handsome. I can see now why he was such a hit with women.'

Kerry laughed some more. She still did not believe Morag, but it was a good story.

She threaded a few more daisies in her hair, checking the arrangement against her poster of *Primavera*. She was pleased with the way the yellow and white of the daisies stood out against her blue hair. To please Morag and advance her plan, she was going to visit Dinnie and apologise for hitting him.

Dinnie pulled at the back of his hair. Heather was making him grow a pony-tail.

'A pony-tail? Are you completely out of your mind? Why the hell would I want to grow a pony-tail?'

'Because Kerry likes boys with radical hairstyles,' explained the fairy. 'The last man she liked was Cal. Cal has a pony-tail. I am sure you can grow an excellent one. I will dye it green for you.'

Dinnie almost choked. The thought of him, Dinnie MacKintosh, parading round the streets with a green pony-tail was so bizarre he could barely comprehend it.

'You stupid fairy. Just because she liked some jerk with a pony-tail doesn't mean she's going to fall for anyone else who has one, does it?'

'Well, no, I suppose not. But it will help. I tell you, an unusual hairstyle is a must. That's the sort of boy she likes. And me and Morag, for that matter.'

Dinnie, seeing that she was quite serious, became desperate.

'It will take years to grow.'

'No, it won't.' Heather was smug. 'Because it just so happens that growing hair is one of the magics available to a thistle fairy. You can have a braw pony-tail in no time.'

She flew up behind him and touched the back of his head.

Dinnie waved his hands angrily in the air.

'Are you forgetting that this woman punched me in the eye only yesterday?'

'A mere lovers' tiff,' said Heather, and departed for her mid-morning dram.

On Bodmin Moor Aelric and his band carried out a daring raid, setting fire to Tala's main cloth factory, the one which manufactured clothing for export to European fairies.

'This'll upset his balance of trade,' mused Aelric, hurling his torch into the building.

But when Aelis tried to drop her propaganda leaflets she was chased off by the strong flyers posted as guards. Aelis, who was Magris's daughter, and very clever with her hands, had made the printing press, the first one ever in the land of British fairies. The propaganda leaflets had seemed like a master stroke and it was enormously frustrating that they could not be distributed.

They were then nearly trapped by the mercenary band sent out to hunt them down. They made their getaway only by the hand of Aelis, who magicked up a thunderstorm to cover their retreat.

Afterwards there was some criticism of Aelric, and it was murmured among the band that he had not planned the raid carefully enough due to being distracted by his love for Marion. It was even whispered that he was wasting his time hunting for rare flowers to send her as gifts.

Dinnie picked up his fiddle. He could now play seven Scottish tunes fairly well. He would go and busk. He'd show Heather that she was not the only one round here who could get hold of money.

At the bottom of the stairs he was assailed by actors' voices.

'Stay, gentle Helena; hear my excuse

My love, my life, my soul, fair Helena!'

Before Dinnie could shout any abuse, Cal appeared wearing a gold crown and holding a copy of *A Midsummer Night's Dream*. Dinnie ignored his greeting.

'Busking again?' said Cal, spying the violin.

Dinnie knew that Cal was laughing at him.

'I'll show him,' thought Dinnie, and unslung the fiddle.

'Yes,' replied Dinnie. 'I have been perfecting my technique with the help of a famous teacher. Listen to this.'

He burst into what was meant to be a fierce rendition of 'The Miller of Drone'. Unfortunately under Cal's gaze his fingers would not seem to work properly. They felt like sausages, too big and clumsy to hold down a string. He ground to a painful halt on the fourth bar.

'You must introduce me to your teacher,' said Cal.

'Music, ho, music, such as charmeth sleep,' came an actress's voice from the next room.

'Shut the fuck up!' screamed Dinnie, assuming he was being made fun of, although it was in fact a line from the play. Humiliated by his performance in front of Cal he stormed blindly out of the building.

Immediately outside the door he crashed into another pedestrian and they both tumbled down the steps into the street.

Dinnie, enraged beyond endurance, picked up his fiddle and prepared to physically abuse whoever it was.

'Why can't you watch where you're going, you ignorant bitch,' he screamed.

He paused. He recognised that jewelled waistcoat.

A bruised and distressed Kerry struggled to her feet, having come off much the worse in the collision.

Dinnie felt faint. He had just bowled his heart-throb into the gutter.

'I guess he was still mad about the punch in the face,' Kerry told Morag, checking to see that her colostomy bag had not suffered any damage.

She felt unwell after this collision and slept for the rest of the day.

Morag studied her sleeping form carefully. In her opinion Kerry's disease was getting worse. Morag had no great healing skills, apart from the normal run-of-the-mill ones possessed by all fairies, but she was sure that Kerry's health aura was starting to dim, and wondered if another major attack was on the way.

TWENTY-ONE

It was midnight in Central Park and the fairies were lying around smoking their pipes and drinking whisky. Brannoc sat with Petal, teaching her 'The Liverpool Hornpipe', which he had learned long ago from a travelling Northern piper fairy. Petal struggled to get her fingers round the notes. So did Tulip, though Brannoc was not teaching him.

'That is not a bad tune at all,' said Maeve from behind her tree, and ran through it gently on her whistle. She had entirely forgotten her argument with Brannoc, although he had not.

Padraig took up the tune on his whistle. Both he and Maeve had quick ears and could play anything after the briefest of hearings. Petal and Tulip were slower, but it did not take them too long to learn, and soon the jaunty sound of 'The Liverpool Hornpipe' was filling their grove. When they had played it through a few times Maeve started in with another hornpipe they all knew, 'The Boys of Bluehill', and the nocturnal animals danced their way around the clearing as they went about their business.

'Now, what is that?' said Spiro, looking upwards. A curve of grey in seven shades was descending from the sky to the ground.

'You ever seen any thing like that?'

'Of course,' said Brannoc. 'It's a moonbow. From the rain at night.'

'Well, what's it doing here? It hasn't been raining.'

Brannoc shrugged.

‘Oh, no,’ said sharp-eyed Tulip. ‘They’re coming down the moonbow.’

Out of the sky came twenty-one Cornish mercenaries, marching in good order.

The black fairies lived, unseen by any humans apart from a few old wise women, in a small park on 114th Street. The park was in disrepair, uncared for by the city authorities, but it was well known for its air of peace and very rarely did anything unpleasant happen there.

They were holding a council meeting after learning that there had been a further incursion into their territory, presumably hostile.

‘They both had swords. We pursued them but they escaped on a bike.’

The piece of news prompted a stormy discussion. Some were in favour of marching down through the city and teaching the Italian fairies a lesson. Others felt they should let the matter pass in the interests of peace.

Their sage took note of their counsel and considered the matter. Her name was Okailey, and she was a direct descendant of the fairies who flourished in the powerful African empire of Ghana, as long ago as the fourth century.

A troop of young girls wound their way through the park, all in blue uniforms on an outing from school. They caught the fairies’ aura and laughed as they passed.

‘These happy school children would have more sense than to march off and wage war,’ said their sage. ‘And so should we. But I don’t think we should ignore the matter entirely. I will lead a delegation down south to visit the Italians— ’

‘They might have been agents of the Chinese.’

‘—Or Chinese. And we will sort things out in a reasonable manner.’

This decided, they made ready to leave. For the community

of Ghanaian fairies this was a major event. They had never in living memory been south of Central Park.

'Who are they?' hissed Padraig, shrinking back into the arms of his lover Maeve.

'English mercenaries,' whimpered Tulip, who recognised several of the band from Cornwall. 'Paid by Tala the King.'

The five stared in alarm as the mercenaries strode down the moonbow. So accurate was Magris's conjuring that they were coming to ground less than a hundred yards away and had already spotted the fugitives.

'Right,' said Maeve, standing up and drawing her sword. 'I'll teach them to come chasing me over the water.'

'Are you mad?' protested Tulip. 'They'll cut us to pieces. We'll have to flee.'

'An O'Brien fairy does not flee from anything,' said the Irish piper. 'Particularly Maeve O'Brien, finest sword in Galway.'

Tulip burst into tears. She was far from being the finest sword in Cornwall and she did not want to be cut into pieces.

Brannoc was of a mind to fight himself, being generally so depressed about his futile passion for Tulip that going down in a last desperate battle did not seem to be a bad thing. The sight of Tulip in tears changed his mind.

'We are too outnumbered,' he said. 'We'll have to run.'

Padraig agreed, to the extreme displeasure of Maeve.

'No O'Brien fairy has ever fled from danger before. Padraig, I am ashamed of you.'

This brief disagreement almost lost the fairies their chance to flee. The Cu Sidth dogs were loosed from their chains and bounded towards them. Maeve stepped forward and killed two of them with two thrusts of her sword. The third fled in confusion.

How about that, thought Brannoc. She really can use her sword.

They fled through the undergrowth, running, hopping,

climbing and fluttering their way south as far down the park as they could go before stumbling to an exhausted halt near the exit at East 59th. There they collapsed on the ground, unable to go any further.

Some way behind the mercenaries on the moonbow had been the MacLeod sisters. When the warriors in front of them had marched down to the ground the MacLeods had leapt from the moonbow high in the air and floated to the ground, unseen by anyone.

They had been aware of events below them, and had seen Maeve killing the dogs, but hurried on to the far edge of the park, for there they had seen something far more interesting to them – Heather and Morag, their prey, busy escaping from an angry mob of black fairies by riding on the back of a bike.

The MacLeods had almost caught them by following suit. Had it not been for the intervention of their strange ally with the shopping bag they would have succeeded. They sat now in Union Square, acclimatising themselves to this bizarre new city and preparing to continue the hunt.

Back in Central Park the mercenaries, prepared only to face a few fugitives, were surprised to find themselves completely surrounded by a large tribe of black fairies.

Too outnumbered to fight, they were taken prisoner by their equally puzzled adversaries, who could not quite understand who these interlopers were.

TWENTY-TWO

The day quickly grew hot and damp. Morag, awake as usual hours before Kerry, mopped her brow and wondered if she could reasonably remove several thousand dollars from a bank to buy Kerry air-conditioning.

Feeling just too hot to lie around she went out to see what she could find. She found Heather in the corner deli, eyeing up a bottle of whisky, unsure how to open it.

'Your drinking is getting out of control,' said Morag.

'A MacKintosh's drinking is never out of control,' replied Heather, stiffly. 'Not that it is any of your damned business. No doubt you are here for the same reason.'

'I am not. I am here to get some bagels.'

'What are bagels?'

'Bready things. I rip bits off them for breakfast sometimes and then the people in the delis think they're damaged and they give them to tramps outside. Have you noticed how many people here just live on the streets?'

'Of course. I spend half my time finding food and change for them. Have you noticed how they keep dying on 4th Street?'

Morag had. Around ten since she arrived.

'What will we do about the MacLeods?'

It was frightening to be in the same city as the sisters. They were bound to be caught.

It was a time for shared thought and concerted action. So, naturally, they began to argue about whose fault it all was.

Morag ripped some pieces from the bagels and departed haughtily.

Heather was unsure what to do with herself. It was not safe to linger in the street with so many enemies everywhere, but it was equally unsafe in Dinnie's rooms. He had been upset to the point of violence ever since Heather had walked in unannounced while he was masturbating in front of the television.

'Get out of here, you disgusting little spy!' he screamed.

'I was not spying. I was exhibiting the natural curiosity of a thistle fairy in alien surroundings.'

Dinnie was not placated by this and carried out a savage attack with his bicycle pump. Heather fluttered to the other side of the room.

'You are risking tragedy, you know. A roused fairy is a dangerous thing.'

'I'll rouse this bicycle pump right up your ass.'

'You are breaking the bargain.'

'I'll break your neck.'

Heather regretted purloining enough dollars for Dinnie to buy a new bike. She decided that she'd better not go back for a while and departed to the bar to watch baseball. Inside she was pleased to discover that the Yankees were two up at the top of the seventh and next up was their best left-handed hitter.

Morag and Kerry had been visiting friends of Kerry's, all of whom were unwell. Kerry talked brightly to them while the unseen Morag used her fairy powers to help them.

They called in on a friend who had a terrible toothache and Morag touched his jaw and cured it, which was just as well as he had no money to go to a dentist. They visited a friend who had hurt his back moving an amplifier and could not get out of bed. Morag gently massaged his spine, producing a miracle cure, which was good as he had no money to go to a doctor.

They called in on a young woman who was perpetually nervous and agoraphobic after being attacked in the street and

Morag played soothing Highland airs into her subconscious, thereby bringing her great comfort, which was a relief as she had no money to go to a therapist.

After this Kerry was abnormally tired and went home to bed while Morag hung around on the rooftops.

On the fire escape Morag had a sudden insight that something was wrong. She rushed upstairs to find Kerry being sick on the bedclothes. She was vomiting continually and had already developed a high fever. Morag knew that this was beyond her powers of healing and phoned for an ambulance.

Kerry was taken away to hospital where they diagnosed an abscess in her intestines brought on by the Crohn's disease. This had poisoned her system and would kill her if not treated immediately. Surgeons re-opened the twelve-inch scar in her stomach and removed another small piece of her digestive system.

Sitting next to her in hospital, Morag was sad. She hated to see Kerry as pale as death with a drip in her arm and a tube running up her nose, a catheter attached to her urethra and another tube coming out of her stomach, draining away the poison.

She reflected that it was fortunate Kerry had such comprehensive health insurance; what happened to people without health insurance if they got Crohn's disease, Morag could not imagine.

TWENTY-THREE

Friendly birds told the Chinese fairies of widespread troubles; strange fairies were marching and fighting in New York.

Lu-Tang, their sage, a dignified fairy whose white and yellow wings folded neatly over her blue silk tunic, was worried. Neither she nor any of her community knew what to make of it all.

'But it is all the more reason for us to recover the mirror.'

With troubles around it was most unfortunate for the Bhat Gwa to be lost. It was time for the Festival of the Hungry Ghosts when malevolent spirits were liable to appear. The Chinese fairies did not want to be facing malevolent spirits without the protection of their Bhat Gwa mirror.

The mirror was at present hidden safely in Magenta's bag and Magenta was marching through the foothills of Fourth Avenue, keeping an eye out for Joshua and his Persian hordes, and also the Armenians, fierce local tribesmen.

There were a great deal of fierce local tribesmen on the streets of New York and Magenta was continually harassed. The worst ones had blue shirts and guns and they never seemed to leave her alone.

Joshua was some streets behind, still searching for her. He asked every tramp he met if they had seen her. Some of them gave him drinks from their bottles, sympathetic to his poor state of health now he no longer had his Fitzroy cocktail to rely on.

The Cornish mercenaries were meanwhile marching back over the Atlantic to England, having failed in their mission. The Ghanaian tribe were too peaceable to be interested in taking prisoners and were happy to just send them back. They assumed that they had now rid their city of hostile elements and were pleased that they were not facing trouble from their fellow New York fairies.

Unfortunately, the Cu Sidth dog which escaped Maeve's blade was not captured but bolted through Central Park and followed the scent of the fleeing Scots fairies. Somewhere around 16th Street it came upon two young Italian fairies who had separated from the scouting party to romance in peace on a fire escape. Crazed in the city the dog mauled them before help arrived and the beast ran off.

The Italians were furious. They assumed that their shadowy enemies had sent the dog to attack them. Scenting that it came from the north, they gathered their tribe and prepared to march.

Morag tried to make Kerry as comfortable as possible by feeding her soup and chattering away brightly. She told her tales of Scotland's history and great fairies of the past. She told her what was happening on the street outside, and what was in the newspapers – but as what was in the newspapers was generally more trouble in the Middle East or Texas abortion clinics being bombed by fanatics, this was not a great success.

'On the positive side,' continued Morag, reading the paper, 'Delta airlines are offering special cheap tickets if you want to fly round America with a friend.'

Morag put the paper down.

'Let's talk about sex,' she said. 'I know you like talking about sex.'

'You're right,' said Kerry. 'You start.'

Morag said she saw a strange thing while visiting Dinnie's room.

'An advert came on his television where a naked woman was being pissed over. You had to phone up a special number – 970 P–I–S–S, I think – to hear more about it.'

Kerry said she hoped the young fairy was not shocked by seeing such a thing.

'It's all right,' said Morag, not wanting Kerry to think she was backward in any way. 'Urine fetishism is not unknown among fairies. I believe that among the MacKintoshes it is quite popular.

'But I did see a book in a shop, the exact meaning of which eludes me. It was called *Lesbian Foot Fetishists – The Movie*. What exactly does this entail?'

Kerry explained, making Morag laugh. She said that men in Scotland would not be so stupid as to read such things, and Kerry answered she had no doubt they would be if given the chance.

'Where did you see such a book?'

'I went into a sex shop for a look around. I didn't like the sex books at all but I was interested to learn that humans did oral sex.'

She had imagined they would be too clumsy and might hurt each other with their big teeth.

'I suppose fairies are good at it?'

'Of course. I am a noted expert.'

'What a little goldmine of talent you are, Morag.'

Kerry struggled out of bed.

'Nine days left,' she said. 'I must have my poppy back. Where is it?'

'With Magenta, who is walking the streets hiding from the Persian army. You are not well enough to look for her.'

'I will tear them apart for this,' growled Ailsa, eldest of the MacLeod sisters. She glared balefully around her at the hateful city landscape. They were now stranded on a tree in Washington Square Park and they did not like it at all.

'This place is a nightmare,' said Seonaìd.

'How will we get home?'

'Where are the MacKintosh and the MacPherson?'

Ailsa shook her head. She did not know. Having lived most of their life on the Isle of Skye they were even less used to cities than Heather and Morag. The confusion of the place interfered with Mairi's second sight and she could not yet locate their prey. When crossing the moonbow they had not been prepared for such a place. Now they were tired and hungry. Their MacLeod kilts were mud-stained and torn from the chase through the park and the streets.

Ailsa, like her sisters a most beautiful fairy with a proud face under her jagged hair, unsheathed her claymore and slid from the tree to the ground.

'We need food and drink. Follow me.'

Seonaìd, Mairi and Rhona followed. They were wary, though not afraid. Mairi sniffed the air.

'That woman who helped Heather and Morag is close. I can sense it.' She sniffed the air again. 'And that man over the road is following her.'

The MacLeods fluttered across the road and floated gently behind Joshua.

Aelric picked some tulips, some daffodils and a bunch of wild thyme.

'Very pretty,' said Aelis, knowing they were for the King's stepdaughter. 'I'm sure she'll love them. However, aren't you meant to be hard at work in the library, learning how to carry out the next stage of the peasants' revolution?'

'It was half-day closing.'

'Fine,' said Aelis. 'But I imagine Chairman Mao still did something useful even on half-day closing. Come and help me print leaflets.'

Today, Aelric's heart was not in the revolution, even though his band of followers had grown to twenty. He spent all his time thinking about Marion, and passing secret messages to her via their contact at court.

TWENTY-FOUR

Dinnie's pony-tail grew extraordinarily quickly, to his great distress. When Heather struggled in one day with a tube of blue hair dye he locked himself in the bathroom.

'Go away,' he shouted through the door. 'I have already suffered enough today.'

'How?'

'I memorised all the tracks on the first two Slayer albums.'

'I quite liked them,' replied Heather, and proceeded to bully and blackmail Dinnie into letting her in.

'There,' she said afterwards. 'What a braw colour.'

Dinnie was horrified.

'It's awful. You never said anything about blue pony-tails when we made this agreement.'

'I said I would take all steps necessary. It's not my fault you chose to fall in love with a fan of bright clothes, psychedelia and hair dye. If you'd fallen for a young executive I'd have dressed you up in a suit. As it is, let's go and try you out on the world.'

They trooped downstairs. If Cal appeared and laughed at him, Dinnie swore he would beat him round the head, probably with Heather.

They walked to the health food shop. Heather ignored Dinnie's customary complaints about the horrors of alfalfa and veggie burgers and concentrated on studying the reactions of suitable young women as Dinnie passed. Did those two young punks on the corner show just a flicker of interest as he strode by? Possibly.

Although still overweight he had lost most of his double chin. His posture was better and, clean-shaven, he looked years younger. She had forbidden him to wear his old brown trousers and though she had still not come up with a suitable replacement for his voluminous brown coat, he was undoubtedly looking more attractive. Heather was pleased. At least this part of her plan was working.

'Do you have a nickel, sir?' a tramp pleaded as they passed.

'Fuck you,' muttered Dinnie.

Heather coughed.

Dinnie dropped some change into his cup.

'Doesn't that make you feel good?' asked Heather, to which Dinnie grunted an unintelligible reply.

Cornwall was wet and very cold, but in the workhouses the fairies were well wrapped up. Although they no longer had freedom, the new spinning machines had greatly increased production and there was more cloth for cloaks and blankets.

Tala the King was in council with Magris and his barons, discussing trade. The French fairies across the Channel in Breton were keen to import Tala's cloth and had placed a large order. Unfortunately this order could no longer be met due to Aelric destroying the cloth factory. The discussion was interrupted by news of the return of the mercenaries from America.

Tala was furious at the failure. He abandoned discussion of exchange rates and insisted that new plans were laid to recapture the fugitives.

This was frustrating for Magris, who had been anxious to put before the King his plan for a large fairy township which he saw as the logical next step in their society's development.

Tala would not listen to this now and demanded that Magris immediately devise a strategy for a general invasion of New

York. If necessary he would send the entire English fairy host across the Atlantic.

'Look at this propaganda leaflet!' he thundered. 'It proclaims Petal and Tulip as the rightful rulers of the Cornish fairy kingdom! What will happen if these leaflets are successfully distributed? While that pair are still alive, the rebel Aelric will always be able to make trouble.'

The assistant in the health food shop fumbled with Dinnie's change. Dinnie opened his mouth to complain but noticing Heather's warning look he smiled instead, and waited patiently.

'Did you recognise him?' the assistant asked her fellow worker as Dinnie left. 'He seemed to remind me of someone, but I can't think who.'

'Nice-looking guy anyway. Great pony-tail.'

As they walked back down First Avenue Heather announced that perhaps it was no bad thing that Dinnie had knocked Kerry down the stairs. After all, it now gave him an excellent reason to strike up a conversation.

'You can apologise for being such a clumsy oaf and then subtly work the conversation round to the first two Slayer albums. While you're doing it, be sure she gets a good view of your hip new hairstyle. You'll start to impress her right away.'

Dinnie thought that this was all a little simplistic and began to wonder if the fairy had ever matched up a pair of lovers in her life. Possibly some village idiots in Cruickshank.

As they turned on to 4th Street they saw Kerry and Morag coming out of the deli.

'Now is your chance,' whispered Heather.

They met on the sidewalk.

'Hello, Kerry,' said Dinnie. 'I'm real sorry I bounced you down the stairs. It was an accident.'

'That's all right. I'm sorry I punched you in the face.'

There was a short silence.

'I've just been listening to the first two Slayer albums. Fine stuff.'

Kerry smiled encouragingly. Unfortunately Dinnie's conversation then ground to a halt. He could not think of what to say next. Kerry's smiling put him off completely, because it was a lovely smile.

They faced each other in awkward silence.

'Well, good,' saia Kerry finally. 'I like them as well.'

'Right,' said Dinnie. 'Excellent records.'

'Yes,' agreed Kerry.

'I must be off,' said Dinnie, and departed quickly.

'Why did you run away?' protested Heather, back indoors.

'I felt stupid. I didn't know what to say. I was drowning in my own sweat.'

Heather told Dinnie off from force of habit, but she did not really mind that he had not made much of the conversation. She knew that prospective lovers often found each other's company a little awkward at first. Quite possibly Kerry would prefer a man who was a little shy to one who was too full of himself. The important thing was that he had made a start.

She reassured Dinnie that this had been a reasonable beginning.

'My plan is working fine. I got the distinct feeling she likes you.'

Heather looked forward to fulfilling her part of the bargain and gaining the fiddle.

Across the road Kerry was slightly shaky after her first trip outside since her illness. She drank tea with Morag.

'I'm sorry I couldn't do better with Dinnie,' she said, 'But I was feeling a little weak. Also he seemed difficult to talk to.'

'That's all right, Kerry. I thought you did fine. If I'm going to convince Dinnie that you've fallen in love with him it wouldn't do for you to be too enthusiastic at first. He might be suspicious. He will know from experience that women do not fall in love with him right away. Just keep smiling at him and we'll fool him easily. I am already looking forward to fulfilling my part of the bargain and gaining the fiddle.'

The MacLeod sisters sat in Joshua's shopping trolley as he pursued Magenta along West 23rd and down Sixth Avenue.

'Hurry,' hissed Ailsa. 'You're catching up.'

Joshua stepped up his pace. He did not really understand why four Scottish fairies had come to his aid in his pursuit of Magenta, but as they were liberal with their whisky and cunning in obtaining food, they were welcome to trail along.

TWENTY-FIVE

Morag was also out hunting for Magenta, but in the large city she could not find her.

She sat, dispirited, watching some squirrels in Madison Square.

'Hello, fairy.'

It was Johnny Thunders.

Morag repressed an urge to giggle. She found Johnny Thunders unusually attractive and regretted that he was four times as tall as her, and a ghost.

'You look sad.'

Morag explained all the latest developments. Johnny sympathised.

'I'm having a hard time myself. I can't see any sign of my guitar. If I even passed the building it was in I'd know, but it's gone. Still, I think I can help you. I remember down in Chinatown there was an instrument maker could fix anything. Hwui-Yin. To look at him you wouldn't think he knew what an electric guitar was, but one time he fixed one of my favourites when it was just about totally destroyed after a Dolls gig at the Mercer Arts Centre.

Morag shook her head. She remembered the name.

'I can't go there without being lynched by Chinese fairies.'

'Nonsense. Hwui-Yin was a good friend of mine. I'll see you're all right. Hop on my shoulder and we'll float on down.'

With the aid of the MacLeods, Joshua was able to cunningly corner Magenta at West 14th.

'Okay, Magenta. Hand it over.'

'Never, Tissaphernes.'

'Stop being crazy and hand it over.'

The MacLeods meanwhile dived into Magenta's shopping bag, hoping that it still contained Heather and Morag, but emerged looking frustrated.

'Where are they?'

'An Athenian nobleman does not rat on his associates,' replied Magenta, stiffly.

'Oh yeah?' sneered Joshua. 'Xenophon would have. For an Athenian he was very fond of the Spartans.'

'That is entirely beside the point. He was brought up fully in line with the high standard of conduct expected of an Athenian.'

Bored with this, the MacLeod sisters began to drift off.

'Hey,' said Joshua. 'Where are you going?'

Xenophon, a general renowned for his military cunning, saw his chance. While Tissaphernes talked with his allies, she sprinted for a cab, wrenched open the door and disappeared at speed.

'So where are Heather and Morag?' muttered Seonaid as they floated up to the sixth floor of a handy fire escape.

None of them knew. They would have to start their hunt anew.

'What is that, Rhona?'

'A flower,' replied the youngest sister, who was not always so serious as the others. 'I found it in the old lady's shopping bag. I feel that it is a powerful thing.'

She looked happily at the triple bloom, the most pleasant thing she had seen since arriving in New York.

Heather was in a bad humour. She had just seen Morag returning from what seemed to have been a wild drunken celebration with a group of Chinese fairies.

'I can't understand it,' she complained to Dinnie. 'Back in Scotland she was the quiet one. Now, not content with being the girl about town with Kerry, she is out partying with the Chinese. How did she manage that? Last week they were trying to kill us. How come she is having fun all the time while I'm stuck here with you?'

'I expect it's her pleasant manner,' said Dinnie. 'No doubt she treats her friends well instead of forcing them to eat vegetables and listen to endless tapes of Sonic Youth.'

Heather was not at all pleased. She had not liked the way some of these Chinese fairies were looking at Morag.

'Hello, Kerry,' shrieked Morag, and fell on the floor drunk. 'Guess what. My fiddle is being fixed by a clever man in Chinatown. He is a friend of Johnny Thunders. He is also a friend of the fairies and I explained everything away and now they like me. I have four dates for next week.

'Furthermore, I have brought you a bloom from the *Polygonum multiflorum* which I cleverly remembered appears in your alphabet. It grows in China, but the Chinese fairies had lots of them. And not only that,' – she raised herself on her elbow – 'Johnny Thunders played me the guitar solo from "Bad Girl". Slowly. I now have it in my head and will teach you it when I'm sober. He is a wonderful guitarist. Have you seen a 1958 Gibson Tiger Top guitar anywhere? No?'

Morag folded her wings untidily behind her and dropped into unconsciousness.

'I am sick of being stuck here alone,' declared Heather. 'I am going to make some fairy friends of my own.'

'Oh, yeah? Who?'

'The Italians.'

Dinnie laughed.

'You told me they were after you for robbing their banks.'

'I shall rectify the situation.'

Heather sat down in front of the mirror, spat on it to clean away the dust, and took a tiny ivory comb out of her sporran. She got to work on her hair, combing it out till it hung down golden and crimson almost to her waist.

'What are you going to do? Grovel and apologise?'

'No', replied Heather. 'A MacKintosh fairy does not need to grovel and apologise to put right a little misunderstanding. I shall find out who is important in the Italian tribe, then I'll flirt with them.'

'Flirt with them?'

'That's right. Works every time.'

TWENTY-SIX

In Central Park Petal and Tulip were receiving instruction in swordplay from Maeve.

'Parry. Lunge. Parry. Lunge.'

The young English fairies parried and lunged.

Brannoc and Padraig shared a pipe under a tree. Their new home at the south end of Central Park beside the pond was noisier than their last, but they were getting used to the humans everywhere around.

'It's no use moping about Petal all day,' said Padraig. 'Have you told her you're in love with her?'

Brannoc had not. Nor did he intend to.

'You can't spend the rest of your life hiding up a tree playing sad tunes on the flute, can you?'

Brannoc did not see why not. He was stuck in a foreign country pining over a fairy who spent half her time having sex with her brother. What else was there to do? He looked on at the sword practice, feeling vaguely that he could teach Petal just as well, but somehow never got the chance.

Maeve hit Tulip on the head with the flat of her blade after he made a particularly feeble attempt at parrying her attack.

'No good at all,' she cried. 'Hopeless. If I'd tried parrying like that the time three Firbolgs attacked me in Connacht they wouldn't have known whether to cut my head off or fall about laughing.'

'Why did they attack you?' panted Tulip, trying to catch his breath.

Maeve shrugged. 'Firbolgs are unpredictable creatures.'

'Especially when you cheat them at dice,' called Padraig.

'Yes,' laughed Maeve. 'Especially when you cheat them at dice. But they cheated first. And it was still a mighty battle, even if it was only over a game of dice. I fought them with swords, knives, bits of magic and bits of wood over three counties before they gave up and fled. My hands were so sore and bloodied it was weeks before I could play music again.

'Which is how I got together with Padraig, really, as he told me afterwards that he'd been trying to catch my attention for months but could never make himself heard over the sound of my pipes.'

Sword practice ended and Maeve came over to play music with Padraig. Petal and Tulip departed into the bushes. Brannoc felt left out as usual and flew off to wander on his own. Petal's white wings had looked particularly attractive while she was fencing, but this only depressed him further.

He was not, however, as depressed as the fairies across the ocean in Cornwall. They were all being drafted into the army. Tala was preparing a vast fairy host to march across the Atlantic, defeat whatever foreign fairies he found, and recapture his children.

Everywhere there was misery. Red Caps with dogs policed the invisible kingdom and any resistance was quickly put down.

Magris always made a point of saying that it was not compulsory for the fairies to work in his workhouses. This was true, but as it was forbidden to leave Cornwall, and as all the fairies' land was now in the hands of the landowners, there was no way of growing or gathering food, and the choice was between working for wages or starving.

Now, as the army mustered, the looms ceased and production came to a halt.

Brannoc, fluttering north through the park, would have been aware that things were bad in England had he thought about it, but he was too involved in thinking about Petal to notice much else. He had a fierce desire to wrap his wings around her and carry her off to a lonely tree-top somewhere. However, he would never do this. He was too polite. Also, Petal would strongly object.

He settled down disconsolately on a tree and there, on the ground below him, were four black fairies asleep on the grass. Brannoc's first impulse was to flee.

No, he thought. I won't. It is stupid for us to be enemies. I will go and talk to them.

Maeve and Padraig, as was customary with fairies, slept through the latter part of the day to awaken at dusk and play music.

They woke, kissed, and poured out a little whisky to set the night in motion. Petal and Tulip emerged from behind a bush to join them.

'Where's Brannoc?'

No one knew.

A furtive bag lady trundled her shopping trolley through the bushes, looking carefully to the left and right. The fairies were interested in this. They had seen her several times, and each time she passed, an equally strange-looking man followed after her.

A fairy-like shape plummeted through the branches above, hovered for a second, then plunged to the earth with a thud.

'Brannoc! What happened?'

Brannoc raised himself weakly on his elbows.

'I met the black fairies,' he mumbled.

'Did they hurt you badly?'

'No,' gasped Brannoc. 'We made friends. But they have some terrible potent alcohol.'

He slumped back to the ground, and began to snore.

A slight breeze stirred in the park.

TWENTY-SEVEN

Dinnie pulled on his ragged leather jacket in his clumsy manner and looked in the mirror with disgust. This jacket, the source of yet another bitter argument between him and Heather, had been picked out specially for him by the fairy at a second-hand clothes shop just opposite the Canal Street post office.

While there, Heather had been interested to see that on the walls of the post office were posters from the FBI giving details of wanted criminals.

'Well, I never,' she mused, studying the hardened faces staring out at her. 'This country is in a serious condition. What you need is PC MacBain from Cruickshank. He would soon sort them out. He'd give them a guid scone on the lug.'

'A brilliant solution,' said Dinnie, sarcastically.

Dinnie did not want a leather jacket, but Heather briskly bullied him into it. The fairy's patience was today even thinner than usual as she was still rather hungover from the party with her new Italian friends. She had been sick all morning, although she insisted to Dinnie that this was only because she was not used to pasta. They argued briefly, bought the jacket and returned home.

Tonight Dinnie had his first date with Kerry. It had not been difficult to arrange, although Dinnie went through a nightmare of nerves verging on complete panic when Heather manoeuvred him into it. She had led him to the deli when Kerry was there, then whispered in his ear that either he asked her out this very minute or she was leaving immediately with the fiddle.

'And I can fly to your room quicker than you can climb the stairs.'

To Dinnie's surprise, even after he had stuttered what must have been one of the most graceless and uninviting requests for a date in human history, Kerry happily agreed.

They were to meet that night at ten and go to hear some music in a club. Dinnie was extremely pleased, and very anxious.

Across the road, Morag was also pleased.

'Thank you, Kerry,' she said. 'I regard this as a great favour. Are you sure you don't mind going out with him too much?'

Kerry shook her head.

'It's okay, Morag. There'll be lots of my friends at the club anyway, so I won't be bored.'

'It won't make you very unhappy turning up at some hip place with that big lump trailing after you? I wouldn't want to ruin your credibility.'

'No, it's fine,' promised Kerry. 'Anyway, he doesn't look too bad these days. He seems to have lost a lot of weight.'

'And grown a nice pony-tail.'

While Kerry was out with Dinnie, Morag was going to pick up her fiddle from Hwui-Yin. Then she intended to show the Chinese fairies what a Scottish fiddler could do.

Tala the King's palace was made of trees grown together to form rooms and courtyards. Formerly a pleasant and open place, it was now dark and heavily guarded.

Aelric crept silently past the guards. He was coated in a substance which made his aura dim to other fairies and his scent undetectable to guard dogs.

He climbed swiftly up a solid oak to where he knew the bedroom of Marion was and peered through the leaf-covered window space.

Marion had long black hair covered in light-blue beads. This stretched like a cape down to her thighs. She was busy in her bedroom singing a preserving song to a cut flower. Aelric muttered a brief prayer to the Goddess and hopped inside.

Heather spent the first part of the evening feeling elated because her plan was working so well and she would soon have the MacPherson Fiddle in her hands, and the second part in dejection because she realised that Dinnie would probably ruin everything.

It was all very well getting him a date with Kerry, but after that it was up to him, and he was not a man to inspire confidence. She shuddered to think of the awful things Dinnie might do on a date with Kerry. He might get drunk and when he got drunk he tended to dribble beer down his chin. This was not a pleasant sight. He might suddenly lose control of his appetite and be overwhelmed by the urge to immediately buy and eat a family-sized bag of peanut and pistachio cookies. He had done this before, and it was not a pleasant sight either.

He could do worse things. He might insult Kerry's friends. He might swear at a beggar in the street. He might shout abuse at the band, even though Kerry liked them. He might be too mean to share a cab home. Kerry would not like any of these things.

Worst of all, he might try to grope her, something Heather had expressly forbidden as he went out of the door but still worried about terribly.

'If you grope this young woman on your first date, it's the end of everything,' she said to his departing figure. 'Do not grope her. She'll hate it. Have a nice time.'

Oh well. There was nothing she could do about it now except wait. She flew down to the bar to drink and watch the baseball.

Warmed by a few drams, things did not seem so bad. She knew that Dinnie would not be perfect, but his failings were essential to her plan. She was aware that a perfect Dinnie would be a bore, and this would be almost as bad as an appallingly badly behaved Dinnie. Heather was counting on the recent behavioural changes she had worked in Dinnie making enough of a difference to make him attractive, without the rough edges entirely disappearing.

'Which is a damn subtle plan, when you come to think of it,' she said to herself, meanwhile applauding a fine Yankees grounder that advanced the man on first right round to third. 'And well worthy of success.'

'Yes,' agreed the numerous Chinese fairies who surrounded Morag, plying her with drinks. 'Your friend's plan to win the East 4th Street Community Arts Prize sounds worthy of success. Of course we will try and help. Just bring us a list of the flowers you still need and we'll find them for you. And we will keep a look out for this Magenta woman who thinks she is Xenophon and see if we can retrieve the poppy.'

Attracted by this brilliantly coloured visitor from across the ocean, they were eager to please.

'You are very kind,' said Morag, pouring down a few more Chinese beers. 'Possibly while you're at it you could keep an eye open for a 1958 Gibson Tiger Top with "Johnny Thunders" stencilled on the back.'

'We already are,' said the Chinese. 'When Johnny Thunders' ghost brought you here he asked us to help, and we will. We have been fans of his ever since he recorded "Chinese Rocks", although we know that Dee Dee Ramone claims to have written it.'

Aelric joined his rebel band, now numbering thirty, just in time for the night's raid. Half of them were to stage a phoney attack on a grain barn to distract the mercenary band who were hunting them, while the other half were to carry out the real attack on Magris's new weapon factory, where swords, shields and spears were now being produced at a frightening rate.

'So,' asked Aelis, buckling on her breastplate, 'how was the King's stepdaughter?'

'Wonderful. I told her I love her.'

'What did she say?'

'She said I was a disgusting rebel who was ruining her beloved father's kingdom and I ought to have my head cut off. Then she pulled a knife and attacked me while simultaneously screaming out for the guards. She is a very resourceful young fairy.'

The two groups prepared to move out.

'So is this the end of the romance?'

Aelric looked pained.

'Of course not. A passionate young fairy like myself does not let a little thing like a knife attack put him off. I shall just have to find some way of winning her heart. Her huge collection of preserved flowers for instance. I could steal them and refuse to give them back until she falls in love with me.'

Aelis shook her head.

'Aelric, that is really dumb. You are a good rebel leader but a terrible romancer. What you should do is melt her heart by appearing with a spectacular addition to her collection.'

Heather had told Dinnie that to all practical purposes he could presume that Kerry was in love with him when she took him in her arms and kissed him passionately, without being asked. This seemed to her a reasonable yardstick and Dinnie, for want of anything better, agreed.

She heard him clumping up the stairs. Terror welled up in her chest. He had done something dreadful and Kerry never wanted to see him again.

'Well?' she demanded.

'It was fine,' said Dinnie. He was obviously pleased with himself.

'Fine?'

'Yes, fine.'

They had had a pleasant evening drinking with Kerry's friends before going to hear a band at a tiny club in Avenue C. He had pretended to like the band as they were Kerry's friends, and the two of them had got on very well the whole night.

'No arguments?'

'No.'

'No signs of disgust on her part?'

'No.'

'Any hint of possible sexual excitement between you?'

'Yes, I think so. And we've arranged another date.'

Heather clapped him heartily on the shoulder. Dinnie was equally delighted. As he took off his leather jacket he remarked that really it was a fairly good jacket as leather jackets go, and Kerry had complimented his pony-tail. For the first time ever he thanked Heather, then slumped into bed to dream happily of his next date.

'It was okay,' Kerry told Morag. 'No problem at all really.

Dinnie was all right to be with. I don't think he liked the band much, but he was polite about it. He even made me laugh sometimes. I quite liked him.'

TWENTY-EIGHT

Magenta sat down to rest in Stuyvesant Square. Not for the first time, she wished that she had more archers in her army. These winged demons who flew with the Persians were a dreadful menace.

A large family had gathered on the benches in front of her and were having heated discussions about something or other.

One thin middle-aged man, left out of the discussions, tried to encourage a young nephew to box. He continually pulled at his sleeve to gain his attention, then threw pretend punches and put up a guard, but the nephew was not interested and turned away. The uncle would not be put off and persisted in trying to show the uninterested child how to box. Eventually the child scurried off to his mother. His mother absent-mindedly spat on a handkerchief and scrubbed his face. The uncle looked faintly disgusted and hunted around for someone else to bother.

Magenta had a vague memory of her parents trying to get her to do things she did not want to do, then hunted about in her shopping trolley. Supplies were low. She had no money to replenish her Fitzroy cocktail and during the last engagement she had lost the precious triple-bloomed flower. This was a source of immense annoyance. Back in Greece the rare flower would have fetched a great price, thereby enabling her to pay her fellow mercenaries a decent bonus. Already they were grumbling about not being paid.

Now the army had hardly anything left. All there was in her shopping trolley was the recipe for the cocktail, a supply of old newspapers, the Bhat Gwa mirror and the two pieces of the guitar she had picked up after the riot at the festival in Tomkins Square.

With one week left till judgement day, Cal's production of *A Midsummer Night's Dream* was coming along reasonably well. The four lovers wandered the imaginary woods, lost in their confused emotional affairs. Puck danced this way and that, casting around bewilderment, while Oberon and Titania, the Fairy King and Queen, quarrelled mightily over the Indian boy.

Cal was particularly pleased with the new actress who was playing Titania. A young woman from Texas, currently serving meals in a diner, she was radiant and charismatic in her costume, and seemed to Cal every inch the Fairy Queen.

'She is rubbish,' thought Heather crossly, watching from the wings. 'More like a plate of porridge than a Fairy Queen.'

Heather regarded this actress, and all the other clumsy humans playing fairy parts, as something of an insult.

The Chinese fairies, well into the swing of their festival – that is to say, drunk – received heartening news from some scouts.

'We have located the old woman Magenta. Or rather, the fairly young muscular woman who looks old because she is so dirty. We tried to examine her shopping bag but in this we were not entirely successful because so much exposure to fairies has rendered her capable of seeing us.

'However, before she attacked us with rocks, we did see a glint of our precious mirror in her bag. She must have found it at the same time as she found the poppy. What is more, in her bag are two pieces of an old guitar.'

Morag wiped beer from her lips.

'Could this guitar possibly be— '

'Who knows? This woman is obviously a person of great cosmic importance. The way she draws all these vital artefacts to her is clearly part of some greater plan.'

Morag leapt up and drew her sword.

'Well, let's go and take them.'

The Chinese were a little shocked at this. They pointed out that they were good fairies and could not just go around robbing humans when it suited them. Morag was chastened. She had forgotten this. The pressures of the big city had got to her.

'We will have to go and bargain for them.'

TWENTY-NINE

Morag had a date with three Chinese and Heather had a date with four Italians and Dinnie was booked to go shopping with Kerry.

'Shopping?' he said, rather weakly, as she appeared at his door.

'Don't you like shopping?'

'I love it,' said Dinnie, lying so convincingly that even Heather was moved to give him a firm nod of approval.

'Okay. Let's shop.'

They went first to the psychedelic clothes shop in Ludlow Street. This had been a great success with Morag who, after visiting, had asked Kerry if she could possibly make her a fringed shoulder bag, a multicoloured waistcoat, pink and red sunglasses, tartan tights, and a headband with the Southern States flag on it. Kerry said she would do her best, and did. With Dinnie it was not such a success, but he pretended nobly.

Morag was meanwhile out with the Chinese fairies, searching for Magenta.

They laughed good-humouredly at her tales of Scotland and were sympathetic about her being forced to flee. They knew what it was like to be a fugitive; back in China their families had suffered hard times, and the humans they had joined to cross the oceans had been fleeing from terrible oppression.

'Still,' said Shau-Ju, 'I do not understand why you did not simply hand back the pieces of the banner to the MacLeods right away. Then they would surely not have pursued you.'

Morag shrugged, and said that the MacLeods were just not that reasonable.

Heather, now feeling fairly confident that Dinnie would not commit any outrages with Kerry, was settling into having a good time with the Italians. Her four prospective lovers showed her round the crowded streets of Little Italy, where the pavements outside the restaurants were jammed full of tables, and the quieter streets a few blocks north, where for some reason there was a series of shops selling guns.

Heather peered through the metal-clad windows and shuddered.

'If the MacLeods ever invent such things I'm done for.'

'Why did you not simply hand back the pieces of the banner?' asked Cesare, but Heather could not give a convincing reason, save that the MacLeods were most unreasonable and would have chased them anyway.

Kerry took Dinnie to all her favourite clothes shops in the East Village. Afterwards they made their way home via the health food shop.

'He sure is a good-looking guy,' said the assistant after they left.

'Looks like he's got a nice girl now.'

The assistants were slightly disappointed at this.

'Got a nickel?' asked a beggar down the street.

Dinnie gave him five quarters, four nickels and eight dimes, and apologised for not having any more change.

'No,' said Morag. 'I promise we are not Persian cavalry. Nor are we hostile Carduchian tribesmen. Neither are we enemies from the country of the Drilae, or a force of Macrone warriors. We are not any of these things. We are Scottish and Chinese fairies.'

'Ha, ha, ha,' said Magenta. 'Don't be ridiculous.'

'Isn't it wonderful having fairies visiting us?' said Kerry.

'Truly wonderful,' answered Dinnie, figuring that one more lie couldn't make any difference.

'But I'm so sorry for Morag and Heather having to flee from Scotland.'

Dinnie shrugged. He had never understood why they had not just given the pieces of the flag back, and said so to Kerry.

'Well,' said Kerry. 'I think the pieces have too much sentimental value for them. They can't bear to part with them.'

'Sentimental value?'

'The bargaining did not go well,' Morag informed Kerry, later in the evening. 'Magenta refused utterly to give up the guitar, which we suspect of being Johnny Thunders' 1958 Gibson. However, after much hard negotiating, during which time she referred to me continually as an agent of Tissaphernes and threatened to set her Hoplites on me and to hell with the consequences, she eventually agreed to trade the Bhat Gwa mirror for a tin of shoe polish, a bottle of methylated spirits and a bag of assorted herbs and spices.'

'And the poppy?'

'She lost it.'

Kerry was not surprised to hear this.

Heather rolled into Dinnie's rooms spectacularly drunk. It had taken her four attempts to mount the fire escape and a long time after that to climb in the window.

Dinnie was watching television. She lurched over to him and clapped him heartily on the shoulder.

'Hey, Dinnie old buddy,' she enthused. 'These Italians certainly know how to show a girl a good time. How'd it go with Kerry?'

Dinnie seemed to shrink in his chair and did not reply.

'Well?'

'She stormed away in a bad mood. I don't think she wants to see me again,' he replied finally.

Heather was aghast.

'But you were getting on so well. What went wrong?'

It took some time for Heather to drag the story out of him. Apparently Kerry had told Dinnie that she believed the reason Morag and Heather refused to let go of the fragments of the banner was because they had used them as blankets the first time they had had sex.

The sentimentality of this story left Kerry dewy-eyed. Unfortunately Dinnie had thrown back his head and guffawed heartily before saying he had always known they were a pair of goddamn lesbian pervert fairies and no wonder they had been chased out of Scotland. Probably they'd end up being chased out of the USA as well.

'And after that Kerry seemed to be upset.'

Heather abused Dinnie for abusing Kerry's sensibilities in the strongest possible terms, for a very long time.

'You have now well and truly fucked the whole thing up. Good night.'

THIRTY

Heather woke up with a sickening hangover. She tried to rise but could only make it to her hands and knees.

'My head feels as big as a tennis ball,' she moaned, and crawled slowly along the carpet to the bathroom, her wings trailing down limply around her. She promised herself she would stick to whisky in future, and avoid wine completely.

Dinnie was woken up by a series of groans and gurgling noises.

'Good morning, Dinnie,' said Heather, crawling back into his room. 'I have just been sick in your shower stall.'

'I hope you cleaned it up.'

'I was too weak to reach the tap. Don't worry, fairy vomit is no doubt sweet-smelling to humans. Make me some coffee.'

The thistle fairy was in a foul mood, partly because she was so hungover and partly because her hair was in such a state.

'The air here is filthy. It is ruining my looks.'

'It helps if you don't crawl home in the gutter,' commented Dinnie.

Heather sharply told him to shut up.

'If I'm going to think of a way for you to win your way back into Kerry's affections it will need total concentration. And let me say it is a difficult problem, enough even to tax the mind of a specialist like myself. Not only have you insulted Kerry's friend Morag, you have insulted all her other friends who are lesbians by calling them perverts. Furthermore, you have mocked her for being sentimental and she will hate that.

'Worst of all, you let your true self shine through, and no woman is going to want to risk that happening a second time.

'It will require much thought. In other words, you keep your big mouth shut for the entire morning and leave me in peace.'

Aelis and Aelric stood shoulder to shoulder, battling with Tala's mercenaries. Aelric had a sophisticated twin-sword-fighting technique and could hold his own even against the experienced mercenaries, as could Aelis, but the rebels were outnumbered and hard pressed.

After being surprised on a cattle raid they were now trying to reach the relative safety of Tintagel Castle.

Aelric slashed at his adversary, forcing him to retreat.

'I refuse to die without receiving a kiss from Marion,' he moaned, breathing heavily.

'For the Goddess's sake,' complained Aelis, 'will you shut up about that bimbo and concentrate on fighting while I conjure a mist.'

Aelric and the others gathered around Aelis to protect her while she magicked up a mist to help them escape.

Things were considerably more peaceful in Central Park now that Brannoc had made friends with the Ghanaian fairies. He had successfully explained who they were and where they came from and why, and apologised for any past misunderstandings.

The Ghanaians accepted these explanations and apologies like the gracious folk they were, and now the three English and two Irish fairies were welcome to come and go as they pleased. Maeve, Padraig, Petal and Tulip were now frequent visitors in Harlem. Brannoc visited too, but his most favoured destination was underneath a bush with his new girlfriend Ocarco, a fairy with black skin, black wings, black eyes and an excellent gift for cheering up poor lonely homesick strangers.

Everyone was happy apart from Okailey, wise woman of the tribe. When she sniffed the air she did not like it. She could smell some strange scent coming from somewhere. There was a light breeze from the west which troubled her. Though they had dealt easily enough with the mercenaries, she did not think that their worries were over.

She told the park fairies of her forebodings and asked them to tell her everything they could about Tala, King of Cornwall.

'Do you really think he might invade?'

No one knew for sure, but it seemed possible. His wizard, or technician as he now liked to be known, could send any amount of moonbows over the ocean if he wished, enough for an entire army.

There were one hundred and fifty Ghanaian fairies. Not enough to withstand such an invasion.

'What about the Italians and the Chinese?'

Okailey admitted that she did not know how many of them there were, but she doubted if either tribe numbered any more than hers. Living in the city parks did not seem to encourage much growth among their peoples. There was no room for their numbers to expand.

'I do not see how we could possibly match the numbers you say Tala can muster.'

They contemplated the prospect of the entire English fairy host marching into Central Park. It was a grim thought.

'Well, anyway,' said Okailey, 'we must decide what to do if it does happen. It may be that we shall just have to flee. But I think it would be as well to know what the other New York fairies think. Normally we have no contact, but I have now decided to go to their territory and speak with them.'

'It is odd,' said Padraig, 'that some fairies came here with humans from Ghana, and from China, and from Italy, but none seem to have journeyed from Ireland. I know that many Irish came to New York. I wonder why no Irish fairies accompanied them?'

'Perhaps they could not be induced to leave the beautiful green woods and meadows,' suggested Maeve.

'Perhaps they were too drunk to get on the boat,' suggested Brannoc.

'And what do you mean by that?' demanded Maeve belligerently. Okailey stopped the argument before it started. Her aura was both powerful and soothing and it was hard to lose your temper in front of her.

She departed to make arrangements for her journey south to Little Italy and Chinatown. Maeve, not pleased by Brannoc's remark, announced that she was going to look for some Irish fairies.

'If there are any more O'Briens here, we won't have to worry about a Cornish army.'

Heather spent the entire day either grumbling at Dinnie or trying to think of some way for him to win back Kerry's affections. When Dinnie played his fiddle she abused his lack of skill, saying that Morag was right, he was a disgrace to the MacKintoshes, and if that tune was meant to be the 'De'il Amang the Taliors', then she was a bowl of porridge.

When Dinnie listened to his tape of Bad Brains she said that if he didn't like it, it was because the merits of the music were far beyond the comprehension of his small brain and why didn't he get on and practise his fiddle.

All in all, it was a tense day. Heather switched on the baseball and switched it off in frustration as the Yankees' manager came off worse in a fierce argument with the umpire. She moaned loudly about not being able to find a drop of proper malt whisky anywhere and more or less accused Dinnie of being personally responsible for the production of Jack Daniels.

She switched on the baseball again, just in time to see the Red Sox hit a home run.

'Oh, to hell with it. This is a bleak day. And I cannot think what you should do next. You are an idiot, Dinnie, and you will never win Kerry now.'

Dinnie slouched in his armchair, too depressed himself to reply to Heather's tirade of insults.

There was a knock on the door.

'Hello, Dinnie,' said Kerry, flowers in her hair, bright smile on her face. 'You want to come out with me tonight?'

After she left, Heather was perplexed to the point of amazement. Was it possible that Dinnie had actually become so attractive that Kerry liked him even after his vile behaviour?

'Ha, ha, you dumb elf,' sniggered Dinnie. 'So much for all your plans and worries. She wasn't insulted at all, she's practically beating the door down for another date.

'Yes, sir.' Dinnie beamed at his mirror. 'That girl recognises a fine catch when she sees one.'

Across the road Morag was struggling through the window with a bag of candy and a beautiful yellow forsythia bloom.

'I couldn't have blamed you if you'd decided never to see him again,' she said happily, and gave Kerry her presents.

'It's nothing,' replied Kerry. 'I promised to help you get the fiddle back, didn't I?'

Kerry was tired, and not very strong, so Morag went about the business of preserving the forsythia and fitting it into the alphabet. The flower alphabet, laid out on the floor surrounded by Kerry's favourite possessions, now looked so beautiful that it was bound to win the prize if it could only be completed.

THIRTY-ONE

Cesare, Luigi, Mario, Pierro and Benito sat with Heather in her favourite bar, perched on top of the TV. There was not a lot of room for six fairies even on a large television set, but the Italians were happy at being close to Heather, although each wished that he were the only one. As each suitor for Heather was as keen as the next, finding a moment alone with her was proving to be impossible.

They drank whisky, which the Italians did not really like but tolerated because Heather promised they would soon acquire a taste for it. And when she apologised that the bar did not have a bottle of good Scottish malt, they said that they would see to it the next day, because their fairy family was good friends with the family who delivered drinks to this bar.

'Where have they gone on their date?' asked Mario, a pleasant, dark fairy who liked to show off his well-defined arm muscles.

'To a gallery in the West Village, then Kerry wants to do some shopping. They're going to eat at whatever restaurant takes their fancy, then on to a gig at the 13th Street Squat.'

'Sounds like a nice day.'

Heather nodded. She was full of expectations for this day. If at the end of it Kerry were to throw her arms around Dinnie and declare love for him, or at least give him an appropriately passionate kiss, she would not be at all surprised.

It had been, she told her friends, a not inconsiderable feat.

'Of course he is a MacKintosh, which is a good start, but even so, if you'd seen that slob when I first took him in hand you would not have believed it was possible to make him attractive. But once we thistle fairies get on the case, the job's as good as done.'

She bragged on happily like this for a while, and her suitors listened with intense interest, as suitors will.

Almost exactly paralleling this scene, at another bar a few blocks along 4th Street, Morag sat with five young Chinese, drinking, laughing and awaiting the outcome of the day.

'As soon as that fool of a MacKintosh thinks Kerry's fallen in love with him, the MacPherson Fiddle will be mine by right.'

They drank merrily in celebration, and the Chinese fairies

told Morag that as well as being most beautiful she was extremely intelligent, as suitors also will.

The MacLeod sisters sniffed the air as they walked along 17th. Even here, with traffic fumes all around, it was clear to them all that there was a strange breeze blowing from the west. Mairi's second sight was clearing as she grew used to the city, but she could still not tell what it foretold.

She led them with a purpose none the less. She had a clear impression that at the end of this street they would find something interesting.

The four jaggéd-haired warriors arrived at Union Square.

'Well, Mairi,' said Ailsa, 'we've been here before and it looks no more interesting than last time.'

She grimaced at the terrible roar from the far side of the square where a group of men seemed to be attacking the ground, pounding it with strange machines.

An enormous furniture delivery truck crawled its way down Broadway and inched its way painfully round the road-works. Sitting on its roof were a group of twenty black fairies.

'Now that is interesting.'

'Yes,' agreed Kerry, sitting beside Dinnie in the cab home. 'Hair dye can make a terrible mess. I once dyed my bath bright orange by accident and nothing would clean it off. Eventually I tried pissing on it at least once a day and after about a month it began to fade. Strong stuff, uric acid; you can break out of prison with it.'

Kerry was a little drunk. It had been an enjoyable day. She had confidently led a dubious Dinnie into various expensive art galleries for a good look round, bought a yellow plastic necklace from a man selling junk from a suitcase just down from St Mark's Place, had a not very successful attempt at eating a vegetarian meal in a Chinese restaurant, and been highly pleased at the massed guitar noise at the gig.

Dinnie had got quite into the spirit of things, and had danced to the music without making a fool of himself. It was, he thought, the best day he had ever had.

The cab driver, a silent, morose man who did not abuse other drivers but stared fearfully out at them through his windscreen, dropped them on East 4th and grunted unhappily at Dinnie's large tip.

'Well, Dinnie, that was a good day. I am going to go to bed now because I'm very drunk and sleepy. Come round tomorrow.'

Kerry took hold of Dinnie's head, drew it down a little, and kissed him quite passionately, for quite a long time. She wandered off leaving Dinnie dazed on the sidewalk.

Up the road, perched on the sign above the bar, Heather and the Italians cheered.

'That's it,' declared Heather, and swooped down to Dinnie's shoulder. 'A passionate kiss, and she wants to see you tomorrow. The fiddle is mine.'

'Take it,' said Dinnie, his eyes still glazed from the kiss. Heather and her friends flew and scrambled up the fire escape.

Further up the road the kiss had also been observed by Morag and the Chinese.

'It worked,' cried Morag, and the Chinese whooped with joy. Morag swept from her vantage point to clump down on Dinnie's shoulder.

She informed him that she had kept her promise and the fiddle now belonged to her.

'Fine,' mumbled Dinnie, and Morag and her friends advanced up the steps of the theatre.

Johnny Thunders sat on top of the theatre building, musing on existence. Ostensibly, everything should be fine. After all, he had no more drug problems, he had Heaven to go back to . . .

But his friends the Chinese fairies had told him that his Gibson Tiger Top was in the possession of a particularly demented bag lady and this spoiled everything. He felt the same dissatisfaction as he had once felt over the terrible mixes he seemed to be prone to on his records. Both New York Dolls albums and also the Heartbreakers album had been notorious for their poor sound quality. None of them was the magnificent work it should have been, given the great songs and his superb guitar technique.

Across the street lived Kerry, he knew. Should he ever get the chance he would show her a few things, although as he was now a spirit and inhabited a different domain, this would be difficult.

Okailey glanced up at the street sign.

'4th street. We'll be in the territory of the Italians soon. Thank the Goddess. I will never ride down Broadway on a furniture truck again.'

'Okailey,' said one of her companions as they waited at the traffic lights.

'Yes?'

'There would seem to be fairies brawling in the street, just along the block.'

Okailey and her companions looked on in astonishment.

'It's mine!' screamed Morag, and tugged at the fiddle.

'You stupid bitch of a MacPherson, it's mine,' screamed Heather back at her. She was clutching the other end of the fiddle, which, as neither of them had yet had time to shrink it down to fairy size, was much too heavy for either of them to make off with.

'I fulfilled the bargain!'

'What the hell d'you mean you fulfilled the bargain? You didn't have any bargain.'

'Yes I did,' roared Morag. 'I made Kerry fall in love with Dinnie.'

'What?'

Heather, aware for the first time of the arrangement between her human companion and the foul MacPherson, was outraged.

'You disgusting backstabber, you've been interfering in my business again. How dare you sneak in and bargain with Dinnie. And anyway, it does not matter because I made the first bargain and it was me who made Kerry fall in love with him.'

'What?' Morag was even more outraged on learning that Heather had dared to bargain the fiddle against the emotional well-being of her dear friend Kerry.

'How dare you bargain to make that nice Kerry fall in love with that scunner of a MacKintosh. It's monstrous. But it doesn't matter anyway because it was me who did it.'

Morag was tempted here to announce that Kerry was only kidding anyway, but wisely refrained.

'It's mine!'

'It's mine!'

This was not a resolvable argument. Whoever's bargain had been the valid one, each of them was convinced that she had been responsible for its success. As their friends watched, the two thistle fairies shouted and raged at each other. After drinking all day they were both most excitable. Finally Heather, unable to control herself, slapped Morag's face.

Morag immediately let go of the fiddle and began trading punches with her opponent. They grappled with each other and rolled from the sidewalk into the gutter.

The Italians were alarmed. When Morag successfully landed a powerful kick in Heather's midriff, Mario felt he had to do something, and tried to restrain Morag's legs. The Chinese felt that this was hardly fair. Just as Heather managed to get her hands round Morag's throat, they rushed to their friend's aid. It then took no time at all for everyone to start fighting each other furiously.

And thus began the first street brawl of the New York fairies.

Aelis conjured up her mist and the rebels retreated in good order through a magic fairy space into the depths of Tintagel Castle. Once there, a furious argument broke out.

'How did they ambush us?' demanded Aelric's followers. 'You personally went to scout out the ground and you assured us it was safe. What use is it burning Tala's warehouses and stealing his cattle if we all get killed?'

Aelric was hard pushed to find a reasonable explanation. The real reason he had failed to scout properly was that he had in fact been scouring the Cornish landscape for a triple-bloomed Welsh poppy to give Marion. His spy at the court had told him that she needed this to complete her flower alphabet and would be so grateful to receive it that she would inevitably fall into his arms.

His mumbled apologies for the bungled mission were not well received, especially by the fairies who had almost been killed in yet another futile effort to drop propaganda leaflets from the air.

Among any group of fairies there will be some with at least limited telepathic powers, and in the fierce struggle cries for help went out so that in a very short time reinforcements from Chinatown and Little Italy were streaming into 4th Street to join in the mêlée.

'I can't believe it,' said Okailey, striding regally along 4th Street. 'Fairies do not behave in this manner.'

She strode up to Heather, still engaged in close combat with Morag.

'Stop this at once.'

Heather unfortunately assumed that the hand on her shoulder was of hostile origin and struck out wildly. Okailey's companions were stunned. They had never even imagined before that anyone could punch their revered sage in the face.

Dinnie eventually wandered back towards his room. His constant association with Heather had rendered him able to see all fairies, but he crossed the street in such a dream-like state that he did not notice the three tribes battling under his feet and around his head. The Chinese, Italians and Ghanaians were fighting on the ground and in the air, fluttering with swords and clubs from sidewalk to fire escape to lamp-post, screaming war cries and shouting for help.

Ailsa MacLeod watched from above in total incomprehension.

'You have brought us to something interesting, Mairi, but what?'

'Whatever it is, the MacKintosh and the MacPherson are right in the middle,' said Rhona, pointing.

'And they are sore pressed,' said Seonaìd, slipping her dirk from its small sheath on her leg.

This posed a quandary for Ailsa. She did not want to see them killed before returning the pieces of the banner.

'And they are Scots,' said Mairi, reading her mind.

It took only a few seconds' thought. The MacLeod fairies could not stand by and let fellow Scots clanswomen be destroyed by strangers, although among humans, clans had done much worse.

The sisters drew their weapons and swooped into the fray.

Kerry awoke, stretched lazily, and noticed that Morag was curled up beside her in bed. This was as normal, but today Morag was covered in cuts and bruises and her hair was sticky with blood.

Morag woke up, moaned, and burst into tears.

'Tell me all about it,' said Kerry soothingly, as she dangled the fairy over the sink to try to clean her cuts.

Morag, in deepest misery, told Kerry all about it. To Kerry it was a very surprising story. She could hardly believe that her pleasant friend had started a full-scale race war on the streets outside, and had a terrible picture of fairy police arriving with CS gas and riot shields to break things up.

'It was dreadful,' said Morag. 'Fighting everywhere, and me and Heather trying to kill each other, and strange fairies screaming and shouting and— '

She broke off to shudder.

'—and the MacLeods. Right in the middle of it, Ailsa MacLeod brandishing her claymore at me like the savage she is and screaming that once she'd saved me from the foreigners she was personally going to cut me into little pieces.'

The MacLeods' arrival had, however, been fortunate for her and Heather. Well-armed, battle-hardened and disciplined, they had cleared a path through which the Scots had escaped to the side of the street, where they concealed themselves in a garbage can. By now very frightened by the chaos, Heather and Morag had stopped fighting each other and concentrated on hiding.

Morag winced as Kerry cleaned a wound on her scalp.

'What happened then?'

'The fighting went on a long time. Then the noise seemed to fade away. Eventually we looked out and there was no one around. Heather insulted me and I insulted her back but our hearts weren't in it. She went home and I came here.'

'What about the MacLeods?'

Morag shrugged. They had been nowhere in sight. She didn't know why they had just left them. But the worst thing of all was the MacPherson Fiddle. It was now lying smashed in the gutter, run over by a car.

'I have just destroyed my clan's greatest heirloom, one of the great fairy artefacts of Scotland.'

Morag was utterly inconsolable, the most miserable fairy in New York by a long way – apart from Heather across the street, who was not feeling any better.

When Kerry finished cleaning and bandaging Morag she put her to bed and got on with the business of fitting her new colostomy bag for the day. She wondered what she could do to help. And she thought about her day out with Dinnie, which had been surprisingly enjoyable.

Johnny Thunders had been surprised to see fairies fighting on East 4th Street. It reminded him of a riot at a gig one time in Sweden when he was so drunk he fell over on stage and was unable to play.

The street was now quiet. He looked at the flower in his hands, dropped by Ailsa in the heat of battle. A very beautiful bloom, he thought.

THIRTY-TWO

Kerry was lying on cushions, tired and unwell. Today she had pains round her stomach which was always a worrying symptom. None the less she was thinking about Morag's troubles.

'I really think you should hand back the pieces of the flag to the MacLeods. That at least would solve one problem.'

'We can't.' Morag shook her head.

'I know how you feel,' said Kerry. 'But aren't you taking sentiment too far? After all, you will still have the memory.'

Morag looked puzzled and asked what Kerry was talking about. Kerry said she had guessed the reason the fairies would not give up their blankets.

Morag burst out laughing.

'That's not the reason we can't give the pieces back. The reason we can't give them back is because we used them to blow our noses on. It was a miserable cold night and we were both sniffly.'

'You blew your noses on them?'

'That's right. And if the MacLeods ever find out that we used their revered Fairy Banner for handkerchiefs, there will be general warfare and carnage among Scotland's fairy population. The entire MacLeod clan would be over the water from Skye and marching on the MacPhersons and the MacKintoshes before you could blink.'

'Really?'

'Really. I told you before that one thing you could not do to their banner was cut pieces off. Well, that is as nothing compared to blowing your nose on it. A more deadly insult could not be imagined. Jean MacLeod, Queen of the Clan, would have the MacLeods of Glenelg, the MacLeods of Harris, the MacLeods of Dunvegan, and MacLeods of Lewis, the MacLeods of Waternish and the MacLeods of Assynt marching through the glens in a moment.'

'There seem to be a lot of MacLeods.'

'There is a terrible lot of MacLeods. And they'd bring their allies – the Lewises, the MacLewises, the MacCrimmons, the Beatons, the Bethunes, the MacCaigs, the MacCaskills, the MacClures, the MacLures, the MacCorkindales, the MacCorquodales, the MacCuags, the Tolmies, the MacHarolds, the MacRailds, the Malcomsons, and probably a few more. There is a terrible lot of MacLeod allies as well.

'Attacking the MacPhersons and the MacKintoshes would raise the old fairy Clan Chattan confederation, provided they could stop feuding for a moment about who was in charge, and then the Davidsons, MacGillvrays, Farquarsons and Adamsons would come to our aid and there would be a terrible war. And if a war like that happens because Heather and I blew our noses on a flag, our lives won't be worth living.'

Kerry considered this.

'How about washing it so they'll never know?'

'We tried. It can't be done. Nothing will remove the stains. One look at the pieces and Mairi MacLeod with the second sight will know.'

Heather sat sadly at the bottom of the fire escape. She stared hopelessly down at the sidewalk, unable to imagine how things could be worse.

Dinnie, a fellow MacKintosh, had betrayed her, striking a secret bargain with a MacPherson. Ashamed for her clan, she shuddered.

The MacPherson Fiddle was smashed. First the MacLeod Banner, then the MacPherson Fiddle. Thank the Goddess the MacKintosh Sword was still in Scotland or she might have broken that as well. Important clan heirlooms just seemed to crumble in her hands.

Neither she nor Morag would ever be able to go home again, and as they were now bitter enemies, they would both be on their own.

And then there were the MacLeods. Where had they gone? It hardly mattered. There was no longer any possibility of flight. Once Mairi MacLeod had your scent, there was no escape.

Heather felt that she hardly cared. She put her finger through a hole in her kilt, which had re-opened despite her attempt to patch it with Dinnie's cushion cover. For a fairy, Heather was extremely bad at mending.

Behind her, Titania ran through her lines.

'You stupid scunner!' exploded Heather, materialising suddenly. 'That's not how a fairy queen would talk!'

Titania panicked and ran from the theatre.

'Well, Kerry, I have just been up on the rooftops talking with Johnny Thunders and there is some good news and some bad news.'

Kerry looked up from the beads she was stringing.

'The good news is that he has told me every note in the guitar break on "Vietnamese Baby" which I will now be able to teach you, providing the MacLeods let me live long enough. The bad news is that he found the poppy after the battle outside and gave it to the Chinese fairies to trade with Magenta for his guitar. It has slipped through our grasp again.'

Kerry wailed.

Morag scratched her head, slightly itchy from too much hair dye.

'When the Chinese brought him the guitar it wasn't his old Gibson after all. It was a cheap Japanese copy. He's really annoyed.'

So was Kerry. The way that this woman Magenta kept making off with her prize flower was infuriating beyond belief.

Morag found Heather sitting on the steps, still chuckling about the fleeing Titania.

'Give me your piece of the banner.'

'What?'

'Give me your piece of the banner and don't argue about it.'

Heather shrugged, unwrapped her fiddle and handed the green cloth to Morag. Morag flew back across the road to Kerry's. She reappeared moments later and rejoined Heather, but before she could speak, Ailsa, Seonaìd, Mairi and Rhona MacLeod – cut and bruised, but still glowing with health – landed gracefully beside them.

'Let's talk,' said Ailsa, and unslung her claymore.

Heather and Morag slumped in resignation.

The MacLeods had been distracted in the battle by the arrival of the still rampaging Cu Sidth dog which, attracted by the fairies, had raced down 4th Street and attacked Rhona. No sooner had they driven it away and killed it than they found themselves surrounded by unknown tribes. Fortunately the regal Okailey had then managed to halt the fighting.

'The New York tribes have gone their various ways,' said Ailsa. 'But they are hostile and suspicious of each other. Thanks to you pair, I understand. You have a talent for upsetting people.'

'How did the famous MacPherson Fiddle come to be in New York? Mairi recognised its aura before it was broken,' said Rhona.

Heather and Morag admitted they did not know. Nor did anyone know where the pieces had got to.

Seonaìd fingered her dirk.

'Where are the fragments you cut from our banner?'

Four Puerto Ricans appeared on the corner with their tennis ball and tried keeping it in the air with their heads. They took up the whole sidewalk so passers-by had to make their way past on the road. The passers-by included a man taking a weasel for a walk on a leash. This made the MacLeods stare, but not Heather and Morag because they had seen it before.

Heather was at a complete loss. She knew what was going to happen when she handed back her piece of cloth. Mairi would take one look at it and know it had been used as a handkerchief. Death would arrive immediately after, followed by a raising of the clans back home.

'Why,' said Morag brightly, 'we have the pieces safely with us. We are really very sorry we cut them from your banner – it was an accident and we did not know what we were doing. Come with us and we'll give them to you.'

She led the way across the road.

'Are you mad?' hissed Heather. 'You know what's going to happen now.'

'Trust me,' whispered Morag.

'Hello,' said Kerry brightly as they appeared. 'You must be the MacLeods I've been hearing about. You are even more gracious and lovely than Morag and Heather's descriptions of you. Would you like some tea?'

'No.'

'Are you sure? Morag has taught me how to make a good Scottish cup of tea.'

'The banner.'

'Right.'

Kerry opened a drawer and took out two clean bits of cloth, handing them to Ailsa.

'As you can see,' said Kerry. 'Morag and Heather have treated them with great respect.'

Mairi sniffed at them. She pronounced them undamaged.

'And perhaps they may yet be sewed back on to the banner and no harm done.'

'We would have given them back before,' said Morag, 'only you never gave us a chance to explain.'

'I still have a mind to cut you to pieces.'

'Right,' said Morag. 'But before you do, consider this. I see your sporran was cut and ripped during the fight. And, with one of these psychic insights which I am so well known for, I have a strong feeling that your sporran held all your fairy magic, namely your sleep spells, and your means of returning home. Is this not true?'

Ailsa admitted that it was. Her spell for magicking a moonbow back to Scotland was gone, lost on the winds of the Lower East Side.

'But we still have one,' lied Morag. 'Just let bygones be bygones, and we can all go home together.'

'I know a rich merchant who lives in these parts,' Magenta told her men. 'We will trade with him.'

Her force had now passed through the dangerous mountains to the north of Persia and reached the coast. The coast was occupied partly by Greeks, which was an improvement, although even fellow Greeks were not necessarily going to be pleased to see a force of lawless and battle-hardened mercenaries camped outside their walls.

What they needed now was ships to make the last part of the journey home easier. Xenophon would trade some of her booty with the merchant.

In his shop in Canal Street, Hwui-Yin was not displeased to see Magenta. Often in the past they had had interesting talks when the grey-haired lady had brought him something to sell.

'Why do you give her money for such rubbish?' asked his assistant after she left, and Hwui-Yin explained that he was always sympathetic to a bag lady with a sound knowledge of classical Greece.

'If she wants to sell me a broken child's fiddle to buy boot polish, why not? At least I got a good explanation of why the Athenians found it necessary to execute Socrates.'

Kerry, a persistent host, got the MacLeods to accept some tea, oatcakes and honey. After their hardships, they were not averse to a spell of comfort.

'How did you manage it?' whispered Heather.

'Kerry did it,' whispered Morag in reply. 'With modern washing technology. She just shoogled the bits round in her machine for a wee while and they came out fine. Apparently washing is more advanced here than in Cruickshank. They have special powders for washing even the most delicate fabric at a low temperature and making it completely clean. And also something called fabric conditioner which makes it soft, pleasant and as good as new.'

Heather was impressed.

'There are certainly many good things in New York,' she said, immensely relieved.

THIRTY-THREE

Disaster threatened from all quarters. The Italian, Chinese and Ghanaian fairies had retreated to their home territories, but remained alert to the possibility of war. The forces of Tala the King were ready to invade New York, while his special mercenary band had surrounded Aelric in Tintagel Castle.

Dinnie, unaided by Heather's bank robberies, was facing imminent eviction; and Heather, outraged at the treachery of his bargain with Morag, would not lift a finger to help. The MacLeod fairies were for the moment pacified, but still talked of taking Heather and Morag home to Skye to stand trial for theft. Meanwhile they would not let them out of their sight.

'And the MacPherson Fiddle is smashed,' groaned Heather, gloomily sharing a dram with Morag in the bar on the corner. They had themselves settled down into a moody truce. As to whose the fiddle would have been had it still existed, the Goddess only knew. If Kerry really had fallen in love with Dinnie it would have been Heather's; if she had only been pretending it would have been Morag's. Kerry herself was being reticent.

Morag had only wanted Kerry to pretend, but the fairy was not sure any more. She suspected that Kerry had enjoyed herself too much on her last date.

If Kerry had really fallen for Dinnie she was not letting on, but Morag wondered if this might be to avoid upsetting her. After all, if Kerry really did love Dinnie, the fiddle would have been Heather's by right.

By popular vote Aelric was deposed as rebel leader, accused of spending too much time dreaming about the King's stepdaughter.

'A bit less dreaming and a bit more planning and we might not be trapped in Tintagel Castle.'

Their situation was bad. Inside the ruins of the castle the rebels had few supplies and were fast growing hungry. Outside, the forty-two mercenaries, now reunited, patrolled the perimeter and flew overhead, kept out only by Aelis's fast-weakening spell of mystification. If any mercenary tried to set foot in the castle he suddenly and quite unaccountably found himself heading in the wrong direction, ending up confused and dizzy and back where he started. But the mercenaries, being fairies, understood this sort of spell and knew that Aelis could not keep it up for long, particularly if she had no food.

Werferth sent a message to the King telling him that the rebellion would soon be at an end.

Heather and Morag sat on top of the sign over a gun shop, glowering at each other. Heather proclaimed loudly that it was not her fault.

'Yes it is,' retorted Morag. 'You and your hopeless addiction to flirting with any fairy not actually certified dead.'

They had met Magenta outside the bar. She admitted she had had the poppy from Johnny Thunders via the Chinese fairies, but claimed that after taking it out to admire it on Spring Street she had been approached by a winged Roman soldier who asked if he could trade with her for the flower, as he knew it would be the perfect gift for a blonde Caledonian girl he was in love with. He had paid Magenta a good price, and departed.

'In other words,' Morag sneered at Heather, 'some Italian fairy now has the poppy as a means of getting underneath your kilt. Honestly, Heather, the trouble your sex drive has cost us over the years is just ridiculous.'

'Well, what about you and the Chinese fairies?' retorted Heather.

'They are all fairies of great good taste,' sniffed Morag, 'and would not rob a sick young woman of a vital flower merely as a ploy for bedding a well-respected visitor from Scotland.'

Heather sniffed back at her. 'Well, anyway. All I have to do is wait for Cesare or Luigi to arrive and give me the flower. Then Kerry can have it back.'

Brannoc was horrified to learn of the incident on East 4th Street, particularly the part where Heather punched Okailey in the mouth. Apparently Okailey would not have minded so much except she was being carried along the street by the tide of battle and couldn't get in a good blow in return.

'Well, our problems are solved,' announced Maeve, fluttering down to join them.

'You found some Irish fairies?' said Padraig eagerly.

'No,' admitted Maeve, 'I didn't. I don't know why, but there don't seem to be any on this island.'

'I think the Irish communities are probably in Brooklyn or the Bronx,' suggested Ocarco.

'Possibly. I have not had time to hunt in foreign countries. Anyway, it doesn't matter. I have written to my clan asking them to come over the water.'

Brannoc looked perplexed.

'You've done what?'

A young couple seeking peace caused a rare disturbance in the clearing, wandering in with two bottles of beer and an anchovy pizza, and forcing the fairies to withdraw into the bushes.

'I've written to them. I've just posted the letter and they should be here in a few days.'

Brannoc's wings shook with laughter.

'That's the most stupid thing I've ever heard. How is your letter going to get there? You can't send a letter to fairies through the humans' postal system.'

Maeve was indignant.

'You might not be able to in England, but you can in Ireland. The Irish have great respect for their fairies. I addressed it to the O'Brien fairies, just South of Grian Mach, Brugh na Boinne. It will get there fine, you'll see.'

Disgusted with this further piece of stupidity on Maeve's part, Brannoc departed with Ocarco to make love in a tree-top, as a change from under a bush.

He had heard from a squirrel who heard from a sparrow who heard from a seagull who heard from an albatross that the Cornish troops were almost ready to march, and apart from making love while there was still time, he could think of nothing else to do.

'Will the English troops trouble us?' asked Aba, up in Harlem, 'or will they leave us alone if they capture Petal and Tulip?'

'I doubt they will leave us alone,' said Okailey. 'Once these imperialists reach your country, they never go.'

Cesare flew smartly up to the gun-shop sign.

'Heather, I have a present for you.'

He handed over a flagon of whisky and a pouch full of magic mushrooms.

'Where's the poppy?'

'The poppy? I traded it to a Chinese fairy for these. He wanted it for some girl he's met. I thought you'd like them better.'

Heather moaned and covered her eyes with her wings. Morag batted Cesare down off the sign and flew home in disgust.

Dinnie was mightily disgusted. He was being forced to quit his apartment and Heather flatly refused to help, saying that she would not procure money for a traitor to the clan.

With only nine dollars left in the world Dinnie did the only thing possible, and went to buy some beer.

'Things are not so bad, Kerry. I expect a Chinese fairy to bring me the poppy any minute. I understand he is fatally attracted to me and will do anything to please me.'

Kerry was joyful at this news, although not at much else. The judging was only a few days away and she was not feeling well enough to carry on. Her insides hurt and diarrhoea flowed into her colostomy bag.

Morag had been keen to ask about her feelings for Dinnie, but in view of Kerry's poor state of health, she let it pass.

Morag had had one very unsatisfactory discussion about the matter with the MacLeods.

'Whoever the fiddle belongs to, you are not the best fiddler in Scotland,' declared Ailsa. 'Everyone knows that the best young fiddler in Scotland is Wee Maggie MacGowan. She would have won the junior fiddling contest no bother if she hadn't been down with the measles that week.'

'Wee Maggie MacGowan?' Morag was outraged at the suggestion. 'She is nothing but a wee clipe, always telling tales on people and coorying up to her fiddle teacher.'

'None the less, she is the best fiddler.'

This just went to prove how weak-brained the MacLeods were. Wee Maggie MacGowan indeed!

Kerry, despite her poor state of health, selected a new mirror-studded waistcoat and made to leave, saying that she felt like a breath of fresh air.

Morag, well known for her psychic insights, followed silently.

THIRTY-FOUR

Aelis met a thoughtful-looking Aelric at the bottom of a ruined turret. He had been out scouting for some secret means of escape.

'Well?'

Aelric shook his head.

'No sign of a triple-bloomed poppy anywhere.'

Aelis fluttered her wings in frustration.

'You were meant to be looking for a way out. My spell will last for approximately one hour longer.'

'Right,' said Aelric. 'A way out. I forgot about that. Let me think for a while.'

Heather and Morag sat on the railing of a tiny park on 14th Street, discussing how bad things were. This was a popular occupation among fairies these days.

Four young prostitutes were ranged along the sidewalk.

'Only twenty dollars,' they said to men passing by. 'I'll stay a long time. Only twenty dollars.'

Business did not seem to be good and the prostitutes slouched dejectedly against the railings.

From any point of view the affair of Dinnie and Kerry had gone disastrously wrong. Morag, following Kerry across the street, had found Dinnie naked on the floor with the assistant from the health food shop. Kerry was not pleased and now lay unhappily on cushions playing her guitar.

Dinnie protested to the disgusted Heather that it was all a mistake and he still really loved Kerry, but the fairy, after a few cutting insults concerning his probable sexual performance and what an unimpressive sight he made in the shower, had simply packed her things and left.

'I did not spend all that time making you attractive to Kerry for you to fuck the first person to show any interest.'

A Chinese fairy called Shau-Ju had later appeared with a present for Morag.

'At last,' breathed Morag, nudging Kerry. 'The poppy.'

Shau-Ju produced a flagon of whisky from his bag and some magic mushrooms. When questioned by a less than pleased Morag, he protested hotly that it was not his fault he no longer had the poppy. Four Italian fairies led by Cesare had robbed him of it on the way here. Back home, Shau-Ju's kin were already strapping on their swords.

'We started another race war,' moaned Morag.

'One more probably won't hurt,' said Heather.

'Fine,' said Kerry, crossly. 'You all just have fun with the damn thing. Don't mind me.'

Heather and Morag thought that really it was not their fault if they were so irresistible that other fairies committed crimes to bring them presents, but did not say so to Kerry.

Later that evening Mairi, who as far as they were concerned had far too many second sights for her own good, had prophesied that any time now a vast army of evil Cornish fairies would descend on New York.

'Looking for Petal and Tulip, I suppose,' said Heather, eyeing the prostitutes.

'I wonder what happened to them? We haven't seen any sign of them since you got us all separated.'

Petal and Tulip rode down 14th Street on a 1938 Buick.

'We found you!' they exclaimed, fluttering over to the railings.

Johnny Thunders was on the verge of giving up. He had hunted all of New York and nowhere was there any trace of a 1958 Gibson Tiger Top. And yet . . . he was continually drawn back to East 4th Street. There was something about this place, something vaguely familiar. If he concentrated he could almost feel the presence of the guitar.

'Is that really suitable music for the court of Theseus, King of Athens?' queried an actor in the theatre.

Cal looked down at his guitar.

'Course it is,' he replied. 'Why not?'

He waved away the objection. With only three days till the staging of *A Midsummer Night's Dream* and his Titania still in a state of shock, he was in no mood to listen to complaints about his stage music.

Tulip still had a little difficulty adjusting to Morag's appearance. He had not seen anything quite like it since the last Glastonbury festival in England, and even the young and old hippies he saw there were not quite as bright. Heather, after one day at Kerry's, was not far behind, and when she moved now the bells at the bottom of her kilt jingled merrily.

The explanations about what had been going on that flowed between the four were very confusing, but after they had made some sort of sense of it Petal and Tulip explained that with the English army ready to cross the Atlantic, New York's fairies must put aside their arguments and present a united defence.

'Otherwise there is no hope at all. We know all about the fight in your street. Brannoc and Ocarco and Okailey are furious. But even so, we are going to see the Italians and the Chinese and try to mend things.'

'That might be difficult,' said Heather and Morag in unison. 'Try and avoid personal relationships.'

Aelis could no longer maintain her spell of mystification. Tintagel Castle lay open to invasion. Outside, the mercenaries' dogs sensed this and howled. The twenty-five rebels huddled miserably underneath the castle, in the cavern men called Merlin's Cave. They were hungry and in rags.

'So much for the peasants' revolution.'

Aelric lifted his head.

'Of course. I remember. Something I read in the library about Chairman Mao. He one time saved the day with a very long swim.'

'And?'

'We will swim our way out of here,' declared Aelric, a little of his former spirit returning. 'Find a river. Failing that, a well.'

The two Scots fairies took Petal and Tulip to Kerry's apartment. When they explained their mission, Ailsa was sceptical.

'How are you two going to reconcile the warring tribes?'

Petal and Tulip did not exactly know, but claimed to have some skills of diplomacy, as their uncle was a king.

'You could try being cute and appealing,' suggested Heather. 'Always works for me.'

'Could you bring help from Scotland?' asked Tulip, relating the tale of Maeve and the letter. Neither Heather nor Morag thought this would work for them.

'The village postman in Cruickshank is awful grumpy these days. Everyone keeps blaming him for the price of stamps going up. I wouldn't trust him to deliver a letter to the fairies.'

'It's no problem,' declared Ailsa. 'You have the means of magicking a moonbow home, don't you? We'll just go and get help.'

Heather and Morag made a hasty exit, saying that they felt it was their duty to introduce Petal and Tulip to the Chinese and Italians, and also see if they could find Kerry's flower.

'Now you've got us into another mess with your lies and stories,' complained Heather, a complaint which naturally developed into a full-blown argument as to which clan was most likely to bribe the judges at a junior fiddling contest, the MacKintoshes or the MacPhersons, and could easily have led to blows.

'You were meant to be introducing us to the Italians and Chinese.'

A hideous noise emanated from across the street.

'Ha, ha,' chortled Morag. 'Dinnie's got his old fiddle out. There's MacKintosh-playing for you.'

'Nothing to do with me,' replied Heather, hotly. 'I don't believe he really is a MacKintosh at all.'

Upstairs, Dinnie had dredged up the old fiddle he had played at school, and was trying to remember the tunes he'd learned.

I'll show that ignorant bitch of a fairy, he thought to himself. I'll earn my rent busking. No one is going to evict Dinnie MacKintosh without a struggle.

'What an amazing upturn in business,' said one of the young prostitutes to her friend, back on 14th Street. 'I never saw so many eager clients before.'

Both she and her friends were doing a roaring trade, and had been ever since the fairies had perched behind them, because there is nothing like the aura of a group of fairies for spreading sexual desire.

THIRTY-FIVE

It was dusk and in Central Park Padraig and Maeve were just warming up on the pipes and fiddle, running gently through 'The Queen of the Fairies', an air which the famous blind harpist O'Carolan learned from the Irish fairies. They moved through some sedate renditions of hornpipes and slip jigs before breaking into a fierce version of 'McMahon's Reel', and 'Trim the Velvet'.

While Maeve took a brief break to tune her pipes Padraig played his customary version of 'Banish Misfortune'.

'Now what misfortune would you be suffering from, over here on a fine adventure in a new country?' called a voice from far above.

Out of a thin cloud a moonbow in seven shades of green was falling to the ground. On it, marching cheerfully, were around two hundred fairies.

'Well, here are the O'Briens, and some others,' said the female fairy at their head, stepping on to the ground. 'We got your letter. What trouble have you been getting yourself into now, Maeve O'Brien?'

'It is truly wonderful what reasonable creatures we fairies are,' Morag informed Kerry. 'Only the other day three tribes were fighting and battling on the street outside and now, thanks to a few honest words from Petal and Tulip, everything is all right again. Peace reigns everywhere.'

'Apart,' Kerry pointed out, 'from the vast and well-armed Cornish army which is heading our way.'

'Yes, apart from that. Although I'm sure most of them are reasonable too. They are just under the thrall of an evil King.'

'Much like the United States.'

'And now that the streets are safe, I am off to see Cesare. I will be back with your flower in no time.'

Kerry was tired. In the privacy of her toilet she had discovered that some blood had trickled from her anus. This always happened when she overdid things and roused the disease in her intestines into activity. It was a frequent and distressing reminder of her illness which always made her depressed, no matter how often it happened. With the strain of the Community Arts Prize coming up, Kerry had been feeling unwell more and more frequently. She lay down to sleep, leaving the MacLeods to have words with Heather.

'Mairi tells me that you two do not in fact have the ability to make a moonbow between here and Scotland.'

'And how does she know that?' demanded Heather.

'She has the sight.'

Heather sighed. Mairi's powerful second sight was a terrible nuisance. It was practically impossible to deceive her in any way.

'And this lie is a further insult by you to the MacLeods,' continued Ailsa, her black eyes boring into Heather. 'But I shall overlook that for the moment because there are other matters more important. We are of the opinion that all Scottish fairydom is in danger from the Cornish King. If he succeeds in dominating this place there will be no stopping him. Mairi had a vision of his army marching through the borders and right up to the Highlands. This we cannot allow.' Ailsa tilted her spiked hair towards her sister. 'Mairi has sent a message to Scotland for help.'

'How?'

'She has sent a vision of our plight over the water. The Scots will march over a moonbow of their own, and you will guide them down in the correct place by playing "Tullochgorum" at the appropriate moment.'

Morag crawled wearily up the fire escape, worn out by recent events. She was pleased to find Kerry sleeping, although it only delayed telling her the bad news about Cesare being so hospitable to Petal and Tulip that he was moved to give them the poppy as a present, and Petal and Tulip subsequently feeling sorry for a miserable woman they met on the sidewalk that they in turn were moved to give it to her.

'It is such a powerful and beautiful flower,' explained Petal.

'We knew it would cheer her up. And we are good fairies,' explained Tulip.

'You are morons,' growled Morag.

THIRTY-SIX

Aelric and his followers swam for their lives down a secret well in Merlin's Cave and into a cold underground stream, emerging on Bodmin Moor only half alive, but safe.

'Good plan, Aelric.' Aelis weakly tried to shake water from her sodden wings.

A damp breeze blew over the moor.

'What's that?'

Nearby was a circle of standing stones. Rising from the stones was a series of moonbows, and behind them was gathered the full host of Tala's army.

Dinnie did not know what to do about Kerry. He could understand that she would not have been pleased to find him having sex with a casual acquaintance but, never having been in this position before, he was at a loss as to how to rectify things.

'So who gives a shit anyway?' he demanded out loud to his empty room. 'I never liked her anyway. She is a bimbo. Almost as stupid as that dumb asshole of a fairy.'

He was finished with fairies. He did not ever want to see one again. He did not need them to run his love life. Nor did he need them to pay his rent. He would busk. Armed with his old fiddle and his new repertoire of tunes, he was confident of success.

Outside it was hot and clammy, which made Dinnie desire an immediate beer. He headed for the deli. By the theatre steps a tramp's dead body was being loaded into an ambulance. Dinnie was so used to this by now he hardly glanced at it.

'Don't you shithead fairies have anything better to do than hang around on doorsteps all day?' he said loudly, and strode past.

'Aren't you going to visit Kerry?' asked Morag.

Dinnie snorted derisively.

'Who needs her? Plenty of women got their eye on me these days, I can tell you.'

'Well, he seems to be returning to normal,' said Morag, and Heather agreed.

'Bit of a relief really. A polite Dinnie was hard to take.'

'Is Kerry sad about it?'

'I don't know.'

Dinnie made his way to Washington Square and made ready

to play. After two beers and a packet of cookies he was full of confidence. When a stray dog ran up to him he had no hesitation in dealing it a sound kick in the ribs, sending it away hurt and confused. He tucked his fiddle under his now finely contoured chin and started to play. On this hot day the park was full, an ideal opportunity to earn his rent.

Just then a girl who very much looked like Kerry walked past and he found himself severely distracted. His arm shook a little. A slight pain gnawed at his heart.

He lowered his fiddle and hurried away for more beer.

'Where is this moonbow taking us?'

Sheilagh MacPherson, Chief of the Clan, shrugged her shoulders. It was crossing the Atlantic but what was on the other side of the Atlantic, she was unsure. Unlike some of her clan she never spent time in public libraries looking at human books.

'Wherever it is taking us, we will know when we get there, because the MacLeod sisters will guide us in with a version of "Tullochgorum".

'And wherever we end up, I am sure Morag MacPherson will be on the end of it. I will be pleased to have her back safe, providing she refrains from starting any more trouble with the MacLeods. It is a wonder we are all marching here together at all, and only a sign of how serious things are.'

Behind the MacPherson clan came the MacKintoshes and behind them came the MacLeods and their confederates. The message from Mairi, Scotland's most powerful seer and sender, had come not only to them in Skye but had travelled on past the Western Isles into the heartland of Scotland. Now the whole of the Clan Chattan confederation had joined the MacLeods on the march to New York.

It was no surprise to any of the clan chiefs that trouble was brewing with King Tala. According to the wise among them, it had only ever been a matter of time before this happened.

'As his industrial society expands, he will have to seek new markets abroad,' said Glenn MacPherson, a studious young fairy who did spend a fair amount of his time in libraries. 'What's more, to gather in the raw materials he needs at suitably low prices, he will have to conquer these markets by force. A policy of imperialist expansion is inevitable.'

'And what does that mean?' asked Sheilagh MacPherson.

'It means he'll attack us.'

Sheilagh snorted.

'We need not worry about that. Once we have the MacPherson Fiddle in our hands, no one can attack us.'

Agnes MacKintosh, Clan Chief, carried the famous MacKintosh Sword, a renowned weapon made by the fairies for Viscount Dundee. With the prospect of the recovery of the MacPherson Fiddle and the repair of the MacLeod Banner, there was good reason for optimism, for any army carrying these three powerful icons could not be defeated.

Underneath, the Atlantic was vast and grey but over the moonbow progress was swift.

Three beers later, Dinnie felt he was ready to play. The strange feeling inside had subsided. This was just as well. It was ruinous to his finances.

Deciding that to make some quick money an impressive tune was called for, Dinnie once more levelled his violin. To his great dissatisfaction he noticed that none of the crowd in Washington Square was actually looking his way, being busy either sleeping in the sun or shouting encouragement to the numerous junior baseballers who were pitching, hitting and striking out in various parts of the park. A complete waste of time, as far as Dinnie could see.

A young woman who looked remarkably like Kerry walked her dog right in front of him and his bow made a painful scraping noise as it slid down the neck of his violin.

'Go walk your dog somewhere else,' he bawled. 'I'm trying to play some music here.'

'Is that what it was?' answered the girl brightly, and strolled off. From behind she still looked like Kerry.

Dinnie found his arm was shaking again. He hurried off for more beer.

Heather, Morag and the MacLeods sat on top of the theatre.

'Right,' called Mairi. 'I can sense the Scots are approaching. Guide them in.'

'No problem,' answered Heather, scooping her fiddle out of its bag and under her chin. 'One expert version of "Tullochgorum" coming up.'

Morag gaped.

'What? You are going to play it? Your playing of "Tullochgorum" will probably send them into the Hudson River. I'll do it.' Morag whipped out her own fiddle.

Heather was outraged.

'You stupid besom, you can't play "Tullochgorum" to save your life. I'll play it.'

'No, I'll play it.'

Ailsa had a strong desire to strangle them both.

'Will one of you just hurry up and play the damned thing before the Scots army overshoots.'

'Well,' said Heather, rounding on her. 'If you MacLeods spent a bit less time practising with claymores and a bit more learning the fiddle, maybe you could play it. But you can't, so there. I'm going to do it.'

'You are not. I'll do it.'

Morag started up playing, Heather grabbed her fiddle and they started to fight.

Rhona, Seonaìd and Mairi tried to separate the screaming pair. Ailsa just hung her head and wished she was back on the Isle of Skye, where the fairies were neither psychedelically dressed nor feeble brained.

Kerry, finding her apartment unusually empty of fairies, took the opportunity to lay out her flower alphabet, staring lovingly at her latest addition, a bright-yellow bloom of *Rhododendron campylocarpum*. This completed the alphabet, apart from the Welsh poppy.

On display, the thirty-two blooms, preserved as if fresh with loving care, were a soothing and beautiful sight.

Kerry was pleased to have got so far, although the lack of the poppy meant it was incomplete and she could not win the prize. She could not enter her alphabet incomplete. It would offend her artistic sensibilities too much. Botticelli would not have painted half a fresco in the Sistine Chapel. Neither would Johnny Thunders have put down half a guitar solo on record.

It seemed unfair though. A man who had deserted her after promising to teach her how to play guitar did not deserve to win public acclaim.

Cal deserves a punch in the mouth, thought Kerry. And if I ever get strong I will give him one.

She sighed, and made ready for a trip to the drugstore. Every few weeks she had to pick up a large prescription of colostomy bags and the assorted bits and pieces that held them on, cleaned the hole in her side, and so forth, along with a supply of steroids to suppress the disease.

She no longer believed that she would ever get a reversal operation, and the thought of having the bag for ever was more depressing than she could bear.

She was tired. It seemed like a long time since she had been really healthy.

As the rebels watched, the English army marched from the standing stones up the moonbows. Mercenary dogs howled in the distance.

'They're on to us!'

The rebels' wings drooped in despair. After days of hunger

and an exhausting underground swim they could not outdistance their pursuers on Bodmin Moor.

'The moonbows!' cried Aelric. 'We will sneak up into the sky once the army is out of sight.'

The others stared at him, amazed by his audacity. Surely their former leader was returning to his previous brilliant ways.

Aelric had in fact noticed Marion going up the moonbow with a sword strapped to her side, and wherever she was going, he was keen to follow.

While on Heather's health regimen Dinnie had only been allowed one beer a day. Now, after nine cans of Schlitz, his emotional turmoil had quietened but his violin technique was abominable. He struggled to get his fingers round the notes but it was no use. Hearing his atrocious efforts, people's attention was drawn away from the baseball and the sleepers woke, but only to abuse him and demand that he cease immediately.

'How dare you insult me,' bawled Dinnie defiantly. 'You ought to be grateful to hear a fine rendition of "Tullochgorum".'

'Well, is that what it was?' said Sheilagh MacPherson, Chief of the Clan, landing gently beside him. 'We weren't sure. We thought perhaps a Scottish fiddler was under attack and using her fiddle to beat off the enemy. Still, thanks for guiding us down. Where are Heather and Morag?'

Dinnie looked up and groaned. Stretching way up into the sky, and apparently visible only to him, a vast array of kilted fairies were marching groundwards.

'Why me?' he mumbled. 'I'm just a normal guy. I don't deserve this.'

THIRTY-SEVEN

The moon shone on Central Park. A series of moonbows slid out of the sky and down the moonbows came the English fairy host, row upon row.

The fairies below stared in horror at the enormity of Tala's force. Regiment after regiment marched swiftly to the ground, heavily armed fairies and all manner of evil-looking kindred spirits and Cu Sidth dogs by their side.

'We're done for,' whispered Tulip, and beside her Okailey, Shau-Ju and Cesare nodded agreement. It seemed like New York's fairies had made up their differences only in time to be slaughtered by a savage invasion force.

'Where are the Scots?' they enquired urgently of Rhona and Seonaìd MacLeod, who had been sent up as representatives from East 4th Street. The MacLeods did not know. Though they should have crossed the water by now, the clans had not arrived.

'Never mind,' said Maeve, and slapped the backs of a few of her Irish comrades. 'We'll see them off.'

The Irish muttered in agreement, but none of them except Maeve was convinced.

After her further argument with Morag, Heather sat on Johnny Thunders' knee on the corner of East 4th and Bowery. They had just met, although Heather knew from Morag about the dissatisfied guitarist's hunt for his Tiger Top.

Johnny nodded down the Bowery, to where CBGB's was, and told Heather about some good times he had had playing there.

'I guess I should be getting back to Heaven soon,' he said. 'The Festival of Hungry Ghosts must be drawing to a close, and I wouldn't want to be left out.'

Magenta strolled up to them, looking strong and fit. After her recent meetings with fairies and her large intake of Fitzroy cocktail, she had no difficulty in seeing creatures invisible to the rest of the world.

Seemingly free from Persian pursuit and jealous attacks from other Greeks, she sat down for a talk, and the many and various experiences the three of them had had recently made for a very interesting conversation indeed.

In doorways a little way down the street, down-and-outs were doing likewise, just sitting and talking, with nothing much else to do.

'Thanks, Magenta,' said Johnny, accepting a drink. 'A little strong on boot polish maybe, but not bad. He fingered the broken old guitar that he had mistakenly traded with the bag lady. The master artificer Hwui-Yin had fixed it up, but it was still a terrible instrument.

'Anyway, who does have the flower that my fan Kerry needs?'

The small band of English rebels hurried across the moonbow, frightened that they would be pursued by the mercenaries and trapped between the two Cornish forces. They had no idea of where they were going or what they would find, and no notion of where their next meal might come from.

Aelis was still carrying her bag of leaflets. A complete waste of time, and very cumbersome, but after inventing printing among fairies she did not intend to just dump them in the ocean.

In the theatre Cal was directing his final late-night rehearsal. Despite a last-minute scare when Titania had walked out again, things were now running smoothly. She had returned from a long sulk on the street outside bearing a beautiful flower, a present from the fairies she claimed, a story which pleased Cal as it showed she was getting into her part. Tomorrow was their first performance, and the day of the judging.

Theseus, Duke of Athens, and Hippolyta, his betrothed, swept on-stage.

'Now, fair Hippolyta, our nuptial hour— ' began Theseus.

'What the hell is this meant to be?' demanded Magenta, sweeping in through the open stage door. 'Ancient Athenians didn't dress like that,' she declared. 'Looks nothing like an Athenian, and I should know. Who's this?'

'Hippolyta,' said Cal, weakly.

'Hippolyta?' Magenta shrieked, placing her muscular self straight in front of the unfortunate actress. 'Well, what's she doing here? Ancient Amazonian queens didn't get betrothed to Athenian nobles. Last thing they wanted to do. Completely ridiculous. Why don't you get back to your own tribe and get on with massacring the local males?'

Hippolyta wavered on the point of fleeing. The irate Magenta was a frightening sight.

The rest of the actors crowded out from backstage to see what was going on. Cal, desperate for his sensitive cast not to be upset on the eve of the opening, tried shooing Magenta away. She immediately gave him a muscular clout, batting him out of the way. His guitar thudded to the ground.

'Oh God, we're under attack,' wailed Titania. 'I knew I should never have got involved in this production. It's cursed.'

'Don't leave,' screamed Cal. 'I need you.'

'Well, I don't think you need her,' said Heather, materialising brightly on Magenta's shoulder. 'As a fairy queen she stinks.'

'And what's this?' demanded Magenta, grabbing Titania by one imitation wing. 'As I suspected. The triple-bloomed Welsh poppy.' She wrenched it free.

Titania panicked and fled from the theatre, along with a few minor characters.

Magenta grinned triumphantly.

'You soft Athenian dogs. No wonder Xenophon always preferred the Spartans. And what's this?'

She picked up Cal's guitar and read the name on the neck.

'Gibson,' she growled. 'Stolen no doubt from my good friend Johnny Thunders, you swine.'

The English army formed up into ranks. A small group detached itself and advanced towards the opposition. The Chinese, Italians, Ghanaians and Irish numbered around six hundred altogether. The Cornish were in countless thousands.

'Surrender immediately,' demanded the messengers, 'and hand over Petal and Tulip. Otherwise we will cut you all to pieces.'

'How dare you make war on us?' demanded Okailey, regally. 'Have you forgotten how fairies are meant to behave?'

The appeal had no effect. Tala's army was rigidly disciplined and ruled by fear. No one dared disobey an order, no matter how much they may have wanted to.

Ailsa and Mairi stood on Kerry's fire escape and scanned the skies for a sign of the Scottish army, but the sky was empty.

'The Goddess knows where they've got to,' grumbled Ailsa, and turned an accusing stare on Morag. 'All you had to do was play one damn tune. You couldn't even do that without arguing.'

Morag shrugged. It was too late now. After assaulting Heather with her fiddle she now had three broken strings. So had Heather, and they were both sporting bruises from vicious fiddle blows. After the fight Heather had disappeared somewhere to sulk.

'You have destroyed everything of value around you and caused general warfare on the streets. No doubt tomorrow you will find some spectacular new outrage to commit. On the Isle of Skye, you would have been drowned at birth.'

'I have helped Kerry with her flower alphabet,' replied Morag.

'With no success,' countered Mairi. 'If the MacLeods had been involved the Welsh poppy would never have been lost.'

Electronic wailing sounded from the next block.

'Why do sirens go off in this city all the time?'

'Good day's work, Heather.'

Magenta trundled powerfully down 4th Street.

'Caused chaos in Cal's play, regained the poppy for Kerry and found Johnny Thunders' lost guitar.'

But when they met Johnny it turned out not to be his guitar at all.

'Nice Gibson,' he said, running his fingers up and down the fretboard. 'But it's a recent model, not like mine. Look, Heather.'

He showed the interested fairy exactly the way he played 'Born to Lose' so she could show Kerry, which might help her make up with Morag. After a few more tunes, thin-sounding on the unamplified electric guitar, he played an oddly familiar air.

'How did you do that?' asked Heather as he finished a competent version of 'Tullochgorum'.

'I heard you play it enough times, sitting on top of the old theatre.'

A moonbow cut through the night to land at their feet.

'At last,' said Agnes MacKintosh, Chief of the Clan, striding into view. 'I thought we'd never find a familiar face. Well, Heather, what's happening?'

Kerry was out making one last determined effort to find a triple-bloomed Welsh poppy. Morag, in a huff with the MacLeods, wandered out to the fire escape. She was surprised to find there Sheilagh MacPherson, Agnes MacKintosh and Jean MacLeod, mighty Clan Chiefs, climbing towards her, with Heather trailing sheepishly behind.

'We gave back the bits of the banner,' said Morag immediately.

'And it was all an accident,' added Heather.

'We have not come about the banner. We have come about the invasion.'

'Although I would not mind a few words about the banner later,' added Jean MacLeod.

Ailsa and Mairi gave their chief an enthusiastic welcome. Heather and Morag were not quite so enthusiastic about this turn of events. They still suspected that they were about to be dragged back to the Isle of Skye and thrown into a dungeon in Dunvegan Castle.

'The Scottish army was tricked into landing in the wrong place by a grim-tempered enemy of fairies who played an evil version of "Tullochgorum".'

'That would be Dinnie.'

'Well,' said Sheilagh MacPherson. 'We're here now, and no doubt Tala's army is as well. So let's not waste any time. The MacLeods have their banner and the MacKintoshes have their sword. Bring out the MacPherson Fiddle and we will go and scare them back across the ocean.'

'Right,' said Morag. 'The MacPherson Fiddle.'

'The fiddle.'

'The fiddle.'

'Where is it?'

'The fiddle?'

'Yes, the fiddle!' exploded the MacPherson chief.

As it was last seen in several pieces in the gutter of East 4th Street, this was a difficult question to answer.

Dinnie fell asleep in the park, not waking till it had got dark. He trudged home disgusted with life. Instead of making money busking he had wasted what little he had on beer, after which he had been in no condition to play properly. Furthermore, he had been harassed by an army of Scottish fairies and as Dinnie firmly believed that two Scots fairies had been two too many, a whole army made him feel that moving to New York had been a mistake.

'Well, they're not staying with me. I'll hang garlic and crucifixes in the windows. That'll keep them out.'

Of course, Dinnie would not have a room to stay in before long. He could not pay the rent and was due to be evicted.

His misery intensified. He still craved Kerry. It had been a bad mistake to have sex with the woman from the health food shop, or at least a bad mistake to get caught.

On the theatre steps he found Cal sitting with his head propped on his hands. Cal told him gloomily that his production of *A Midsummer Night's Dream* was ruined. Half his cast had fled, either scared by Magenta or panicked by Heather, and he did not even have a guitar to play the music. When the judges came the next day he would be laughed out of the competition.

'Kerry will win.'

Dinnie thought this was probably a good thing but was too drunk and confused to think much about it and slouched upstairs to watch a little television before going to bed.

'Hi, I'm Linda. For the hottest two-girl phone sex in town, phone 970 F–U–C–K. We're waiting for your call.'

THIRTY-EIGHT

After a brief lesson in the geography of New York from the MacLeods the Scottish army marched over moonbows towards Central Park. There were many of them there, fairies from the MacKintoshes and their associates – the MacAndrews, the MacHardys, the MacPhails, the MacTavishes, and others; the MacPhersons had brought the MacCurries, the MacGowans, the MacMurdochs, the MacClearys and more; the largest force of all was the huge grouping of the MacLeods and their numerous allies.

Right at the end marched Heather and Morag, in blackest disgrace. After the fate of the MacPherson Fiddle had been admitted, Sheilagh MacPherson had briskly informed the pair that if they thought they were in trouble before, it was nothing compared to the trouble they were in now. Once they got back to Scotland, incarceration in Dunvegan Castle would seem like a pleasant holiday compared to what she had in mind.

'Not that we will ever get back to Scotland, more than likely. Without the power of our three talismans we will be massacred here by Tala. Well done, Heather and Morag. Between you you have managed to end several thousand years of Scottish fairy history.'

Morag and Heather trudged unhappily over the roofs of the skyscrapers, muttering to each other that it was just not fair the way they were blamed for everything. They weren't to know that any of this would happen.

'What's more,' whispered Morag, 'I don't even want to be

involved in any of this. I'm not interested in clan warfare and feuds and stuff. I want to get on with our radical Celtic fairy punk band.'

'Me, too,' agreed Heather. 'Wait till I play you the Nuclear Assault album I stole for Dinnie.'

Morag nudged her friend in the ribs.

'Look,' she hissed. 'There's that wee scunner Maggie MacGowan, showing off on the fiddle as usual.'

They glowered at Maggie. She was entertaining the marchers with a slow and beautiful air, 'The Flower o'the Quern'.

'Boring bastard,' muttered Morag. 'If she tried that at the 13th Street Squat she'd be bottled off stage.

'And her version of "Tullochgorum" is rubbish, I don't care what anyone says. And look! She's wearing shoes!'

The pair were aghast. Shoes were almost unheard of among fairies.

'The precious little tumshie.'

The kilted hordes descended into Central Park, bagpipes skirling defiance. Ahead of them they could see the dark mass of Tala's army and nearby the small group of friendly defenders.

Everywhere claymores were unsheathed as the fairies made ready for their last hopeless battle. All around were grim-faced and serious. Morag and Heather decided to play a practical joke on the hated Wee Maggie MacGowan.

Johnny Thunders strummed a few tunes on Cal's Gibson, Magenta strode purposefully up Broadway, and Dinnie could not sleep. He headed out to buy an egg in a roll.

Kerry was sitting in the deli, sipping coffee.

She told him that her day had been a failure. There was not another triple-bloomed poppy to be found anywhere.

'Never mind. Enter your alphabet in the competition anyway. I happen to know that Cal's production of Shakespeare is heading for disaster, so you could still win.'

Kerry explained that she could not possibly enter her alphabet unless it was complete.

'I'm pleased that Cal's play is a disaster, but he will win.'

She sighed, and excused herself, saying that she was not feeling very well at all.

Dinnie munched his egg in a roll, and ordered another. Kerry had not looked happy, but at least she hadn't mentioned the incident of the health food shop assistant.

THIRTY-NINE

'I'm not actually blaming you, Mairi MacLeod,' said Jean, her Clan Chief, 'but couldn't your second sight have warned us we were going to be outnumbered ten to one?'

Mairi shrugged hopelessly. Everyone else looked depressed. While some of the fairies were warlike most of them were not; and none of them, not even the fierce ones like Ailsa, had any idea of grand battle strategy.

'I am reminded of Bannockburn,' said Sheilagh MacPherson, referring to a famous battle where a small Scottish force defeated a much larger English one.

'Indeed,' agreed Agnes MacKintosh. 'A grand victory. Do you have any idea how it was achieved?'

'None at all. Of course, they had Robert the Bruce to lead them, which was a help. Personally I have never studied tactical warfare.'

Neither had any of them. When it came right down to it, what the good Scottish fairies liked doing best was sitting with pleasant company in pleasant surroundings, playing music and drinking heather ale and whisky.

And this was fine, as until now that had seemed to be the main preoccupation of the English fairies as well. It would have been unthinkable for them to assemble such a huge host and go to war, before Tala took power.

'What is the matter with that King? He just does not act like a normal fairy.'

'I blame the hole in the ozone layer,' said Agnes. 'I knew the humans would do for us eventually.'

'Terrific,' grumbled Maeve to Padraig. 'These Scots arrive with grand tales of three mighty weapons to repel the English, and what happens? They mislay one of them. Ha!'

The park that evening had an evil atmosphere quite unlike the aura of peace the fairies had been spreading around previously, and while Tala's army was there, many crimes were committed in the area.

The Cornish army began to advance. The defenders braced themselves.

'Help is at hand,' called a robust human voice. It was Magenta, marching in with a small fiddle in her hand.

'Freshly repaired by my good friend Hwui-Yin. You should have mentioned before that it was important to you.'

It seemed like a miracle. The MacPherson Fiddle had arrived at the very last moment.

Sheilagh MacPherson touched the violin lovingly. In her mind she had a picture of its long history, and she knew now how it had come to be in America; MacPherson the Robber's heart-broken mermaid lover had borne it over the seas after he was hanged.

Jean MacLeod unfurled the banner. Agnes MacKintosh brandished the sword. Sheilagh MacPherson kissed the fiddle and handed it to Wee Maggie MacGowan.

'Right, Maggie. You are the finest fiddler in Scotland. Play "Tullochgorum" and watch the enemy flee.'

Maggie took the fiddle and stepped forward proudly in her red and black MacGowan kilt. Unfortunately Heather and

Morag had tied her shoelaces together. She fell flat on her face and the fiddle smashed into pieces.

'If we can make it to Grand Central,' whispered Heather, 'we might get a train to Canada.'

The ambulance took a long time to come through busy traffic and when Kerry was loaded into it she was very ill. She was retching continually and though her stomach had emptied of food she was still bringing up some greenish liquid which dribbled down her chin on to her chest. Sweat dripped from her forehead and her face was deathly pale.

Eventually she reached St Vincent's Hospital. When the doctor examined her he pronounced that the disease had spread from her large intestine to her small intestine and there was nothing to do but perform an ileostomy, which meant cutting it out. Kerry then began to cry because she had been told in the past that if this happened it would be irreversible and she would always have to have a colostomy bag.

The doctor marked a cross on her right side with a thick blue felt-tipped pen where the surgeons were to cut, and the nurses made Kerry ready for the operation, giving her the first of her injections and strapping a little name-tag to her wrist. Kerry moaned and retched painfully as the poison from her ruptured intestines spread throughout her body. She brought up more greenish fluid which splashed horribly into the plastic bowl at her side.

Dinnie sat beside her in the ward. He had found Kerry in the street, too sick to open her front door. He called an ambulance and travelled with her to hospital. Although the doctors had no time or inclination to give him information, he had learned about the disease from a more sympathetic nurse. Seeing Kerry looking like death he felt very sorry indeed.

FORTY

There was no need to ask who had tied Maggie MacGowan's shoelaces together. Before Agnes MacKintosh could actually run the culprits through with her sword, Magenta intervened.

'Excuse me, fellow warrior chiefs,' she said, 'but are you all just going to stand here in a bundle waiting to be attacked?'

'What else is there to do?'

'Form squares, of course. Have you no idea of tactics? I have just led an army through hostile territory against vastly superior forces. Of course, my troops are experienced Hoplites and Pelasts and you are small fairies, but perhaps we can save the day anyway.'

This was obviously a woman who knew what she was talking about. The defenders were quickly organised into two hollow squares. Given time, Magenta would have issued precise instructions for the central squares to withdraw in good order when attacked, thereby drawing the enemy in and trapping them in a pincer movement with her flanking forces (much as Hannibal had done at Cannae), but she knew the fairies would not be able to do this sort of thing at short notice.

When the Cornish army attacked with an ear-shattering roar, the plan seemed to work. Despite the large disparity of forces, the squares held. The Italians, Chinese, Ghanaians, Scots and Irish all stood firm, jabbing with their swords, and the undisciplined attacking horde was unable to break through.

High up in the sky Aelric and his rebels looked down at the scene.

'The Goddess damn that Tala,' exploded Aelric. 'Now he's trying to massacre these poor fairies as well.'

Aelis did not reply. She had noticed that for the first time the Cornish had no scouts flying high in defence.

Up at dawn, Cal checked his scenery, some of which had been damaged during Magenta's last assault on the theatre. What was left of his cast would arrive during the morning, as the performance had to be judged at noon.

Cal dreaded to think what it would be like. His carefully rehearsed play was now full of emergency understudies, some of whom had never even read the script. He himself was playing the part of Lysander after the actor had said he would not work in a building where fairies jabbed at him with little claymores.

Outside on the steps sat Joshua, drowsy but unable to sleep properly. Without his cocktail his body did not feel right. He swore that he would kill Magenta if he did not die first.

FORTY-ONE

Dinnie sat in the hospital restaurant. It was not a pleasant experience. He hated being surrounded by sick people, particularly old hopeless sick people with dressing gowns and bored-looking relatives.

Every so often he would take the lift to Kerry's ward and enquire after her, but the operation was a long one and the nurses had no information. After this Dinnie would go back to the restaurant, each time feeling that he should have done something more, like demanding loudly that the nurses stop keeping the truth from him and tell him everything they knew. Unfortunately the nurses seemed rather intimidating close up. Presumably they developed their muscles hauling patients in and out of bed. Dinnie remained polite, but fretful.

Time never goes so slowly as when waiting in a hospital and after a few hours Dinnie felt as blank as the hopeless cases in dressing gowns.

'We have held them off once, but I do not think we can do so again.'

Jean MacLeod, as dark-haired, beautiful and dangerous as the MacLeod sisters only even taller and fiercer, held the newly repaired green banner high in defiance and prepared to try.

'To hell with this,' muttered Morag, somewhere in the middle of a defensive square. 'Could we not sneak away somewhere?'

Heather was in full agreement but surrounded on all sides as they were, it was impossible.

'We'll just have to stay here and be massacred.'

'I don't want to be massacred. I want to have fun in the city. I like this city. I like all the pizzas and delis and shops open all the time and gigs and nightclubs and bright clothes and bright people and huge buildings. In fact, apart from the poor people dying on the streets, I like everything about it. I am even getting used to the funny sweet whisky.'

'Me, too,' agreed Heather. 'Although it is not a patch on the braw malt the MacKintoshes brew. We could have fun here if all these fools would just behave peacefully for a change. Did Kerry finish making me my Red Indian headband?'

'Yes, and it will look very very fine indeed, if you ever get a chance to wear it. What's that?'

Tala's army was readying itself for its second attack when, from far above on the still visible moonbow, more fairy figures appeared.

'Do you really think this will work?' asked Aelric, emptying out handfuls of propaganda leaflets.

'It might,' replied Aelis, flying beside him. 'I have a talent for propaganda, though I say it myself.'

'WORKERS FREE YOURSELVES', read the leaflets, spinning down from the sky in their thousands.

Kerry was being wheeled back into a quiet ward after her operation. The nurses informed Dinnie that it had not been necessary to remove her small intestine after all. Once she had been opened up the damage had turned out not to be as serious as was thought. This was something that could happen with Crohn's disease, attacks appearing worse than they actually were. So Kerry still had some hope of the reversal operation.

'But what a terrible trauma,' said Dinnie. 'I feel awful.'

'It's worse for her,' said the nurse.

'Will she be better now?'

Apparently not. She might have another serious attack tomorrow, or in ten minutes' time.

FORTY-TWO

Dinnie caught a cab back to 4th Street to pick up some belongings for Kerry. Being concerned about her, he did not resent the fare. Love can change anything. He let himself in with her key, packed a bag, and called over to the theatre just as Cal's play was getting under way. Without pausing to watch, he hurried on upstairs.

Cal's play was exactly the disaster he had expected it to be. The unrehearsed replacements forgot their lines, the emergency tape of background music kept blaring out in mid-scene and the remaining original actors crept nervously around the stage, expecting at any moment to be attacked by bag ladies or fairies.

The small audience giggled and the three judges, all local artists, writhed in embarrassment.

'I knew the standard would be low,' they whispered to each other, 'but this is a disgrace.'

Upstairs Dinnie washed and changed quickly. He yawned. He had to return to the hospital but a wave of tiredness threatened to overcome him. Spying his fiddle on the bed, he had an urge to revive himself with a quick tune.

He picked it up and let go with a strong version of 'Tullochgorum'.

Immediately a moonbow sprang into the theatre downstairs and screaming fairies poured in from all directions.

These were the last skirmishes of the battle in Central Park, a battle which had turned out to be not so fierce after all. The propaganda leaflets, prepared by Aelis with all the skills of a born marketing genius, had roused deep, hidden feelings in the ranks of the English army. Denied access to outside information for so long, the strong and simple arguments in the leaflets went straight to their hearts.

'Why *do* we work twelve hours a day for little wages? We used to be free to do anything we wanted.'

'Why *do* we have to worship this horrible new god? I liked our old Goddess.'

'Why *do* we let Tala and a few thugs rule over us?'

'And what are we doing here, fighting other fairies?'

The ranks of the army began to break up as the fairies, roused from a nightmare, realised the stupidity of their situation. Foot soldiers everywhere refused to advance as ordered. The barons, themselves dubious of Tala's power, felt their authority over their serfs start to crumble.

The situation, however, was far from resolved. Tala's large group of mercenaries showed no inclination to change sides. Nor did the Royal Guard, led by Marion his stepdaughter. Things could still have been disastrous had not Aelric, floating down on the breeze, suddenly spied the triple-bloomed Welsh poppy in Magenta's shopping bag and snatched it up.

'Change sides, lovely Marion,' he said. 'Join the peasants' revolt and this rare triple-bloomed Welsh poppy, in red, orange and yellow, will be yours. Your alphabet will be complete.'

Marion looked at the poppy, quickly scanned a propaganda leaflet, and changed sides, taking the Royal Guard with her. The battle was over and New York was safe.

The only ones not to give in were the mercenaries. Seeing that all was lost but unwilling to surrender, they magicked a moonbow to escape.

'You have to admire them,' said Magenta, as they sped away. 'They are good mercenaries.'

Dinnie, hurrying downstairs, was surprised to hear such a commotion from the theatre. Presuming that the audience were throwing things at the stage, he could not resist a quick look.

Inside there was chaos. Although Dinnie could not know it, his rendering of 'Tullochgorum' had attracted the moonbow, and the mercenaries had barged into the performance followed by a fierce assortment of pursuers.

Confused by the battle in this strange city, and never having seen *A Midsummer Night's Dream* before, the mercenaries were horrified to find themselves surrounded by gigantic fairies. Assuming that these on-stage extras wandering round in cardboard wings were in fact part of the enemy, the mercenaries materialised to fight them, which forced their pursuers to do the same.

Actors fled in panic as fairies of all colours fought and flew round the stage. Cal screamed for everyone to leave him alone. The judges gaped in wonder in the back row.

Dinnie noticed the three judges, and thought briefly that one of them looked rather familiar, but his attention was diverted by Heather pounding down on to his shoulder.

'Hello, Dinnie,' she screamed in his ear. 'Just mopping-up operations. Nothing to worry about.'

She gave him a brief explanation of what had happened, but Dinnie paid little attention.

'You dumb fairies,' he shouted. 'Kerry is sick in hospital. I'm going there now.'

He left, not caring either way about their stupid fighting. He was pleased, though, that Cal's play had been such a spectacular disaster.

FORTY-THREE

With the battle over the fairies partied on the East Village rooftops. Heather and Morag were absent. As soon as they could they had rushed off to visit Kerry in hospital.

They told her the events of the momentous day, and arranged flowers in her hair.

Kerry propped herself up on her elbows.

'Touch my fingers,' she said. 'I need some strength.'

The MacLeod sisters had got good and drunk along with everyone else during the afternoon, but as friends of Kerry they had some interest in the competition and floated down to eavesdrop on the judges.

They were surprised to learn that they knew one of the judges. It was Joshua, recruited from the streets as part of the 'Art in the Community Programme'.

'They will be saying what a grim disaster Cal's play was,' said Ailsa, with certainty. 'It's an awfie shame that Kerry could not enter her alphabet.'

A cab drew up outside the theatre. A skeletal-looking Kerry emerged in a blue dressing gown and yellow fringed waistcoat. Dinnie helped her up the steps.

Much too ill to have left her hospital bed, Kerry had come for her flower.

'Where is this Aelric?' she demanded. Seonaìd MacLeod flew up to the roof and reappeared with Aelric, who held Marion's hand. Marion had the flower wrapped around her beaded black hair.

'Give,' said Kerry, holding out her hand. Marion unwrapped the flower and handed it over.

Kerry's face was radiant with pleasure. She handed the bloom to Dinnie.

'Enter my alphabet in the competition,' she instructed. The fairies clapped and cheered at this act of heroism by someone so gravely ill.

Kerry collapsed on to the ground. She was taken back to hospital and Dinnie notified the judges that the Ancient Celtic Flower Alphabet was now ready for inspection.

Magenta marched triumphantly into East 4th Street. Her mighty generalship had won another stupendous victory and she had come to join in the celebrations.

Everywhere in the street fairies were drinking, partying and fucking; and it was in the aftermath of this gathering that the first mixed-race fairies were born.

The MacLeods, confidently expecting triumph for Kerry's

flower alphabet, were dismayed by an unexpected turn of events. They learned that *A Midsummer Night's Dream* had not gone down so badly after all.

'The most amazing on-stage effects we have ever seen,' said the judges.

'Quite staggering the way the piece evoked the world of fairies. I could have sworn they were really there. Of course, some of it was rather ragged but I have to admit I was very impressed.'

'The flower alphabet is a beautiful and unique piece of Celtic folklore . . . but does it compare to such a vibrant rendition of Shakespeare?'

'Oh no,' groaned Rhona. 'Kerry must not lose after half killing herself to come from the hospital. And feeding us all these oatcakes.'

Heather and Morag appeared back from the hospital. They all had an emergency meeting in the deli, but no solution presented itself.

'We could bribe the judges.'

'What with?'

'We'll rob a bank.'

This idea was quickly vetoed.

Sheilagh MacPherson sought Magenta out to thank her for returning the fiddle and helping them in the battle, proclaiming her a friend of the MacPhersons for life. The intoxicated Chief of the Clan clapped Magenta heartily on the back and told her about the latest progress in the judging.

'What a determined young woman that Kerry is,' said Magenta admiringly. 'I will have her in my army any time.'

'Well she won't be winning this competition if she is a friend of yours,' pronounced Joshua, appearing beside her. 'Because I am a judge. And after I have awarded the prize to Cal I am going to come and beat you to death.'

FORTY-FOUR

'The young woman is undecided, but the young man liked Cal's play best,' announced Morag, back from spying on the judges.

'And Joshua will pick Cal,' wailed Heather. 'He'll win.'

They sat in the theatre on top of a fake pillar, part of the Athenian court. Dinnie slouched nearby. Sheilagh MacPherson and Agnes MacKintosh fluttered up unsteadily.

'We know of your problem,' they said. 'And we are sympathetic because we understand that Kerry has been a good friend to stray fairies here and this man Cal has treated her badly. We do not like boyfriends who act badly. We will help with part of the problem.'

'How?'

'Are you familiar with *A Midsummer Night's Dream*?'

They were, a little.

'Then you will know,' said Agnes, 'that it involves a magic herb which, once spread on the eyes, makes the person fall in love with the first person he sees. Dinnie, fellow MacKintosh, bring me the herb.'

Dinnie, momentarily hopeful, shook his head sadly. The Chief of the Clan was even more stupid that the rest of them. She apparently did not know the difference between a stage prop and real life.

'It's only a weed from the sidewalk,' he said.

'To you, maybe. To mighty chiefs of Scottish fairy clans, not necessarily. Bring it here.'

Dinnie found and brought the weed. Agnes and Sheilagh flew shakily across to Joshua and touched it to his eyes. They propelled him with a few gentle sword jabs towards Magenta.

He screwed up his eyes and opened them.

'Magenta. I have always loved you.'

'Then vote for Kerry in the competition.'

'Of course.'

'Have some Fitzroy cocktail,' said Magenta, slipping her hand into his. 'I will share the recipe with you.'

There was now one vote each. The young woman, a local sculptor, was still pondering.

'I can tell she liked the play best,' sighed the psychic Mairi.

'You stupid fairies,' muttered Dinnie as they passed him in the hospital waiting room. 'All the excitement you caused made Kerry ill.'

'Nonsense,' replied Heather. 'Crohn's disease strikes down many people who have never even seen a fairy. However, as you are now being nice to Kerry, I may yet rob a bank to pay your rent. We're going to visit her now.'

'It isn't visiting time yet.'

'An important difference between fairies and humans is that we are small and invisible and you are not. We don't have to wait for visiting time.'

Dinnie glowered at them. Beside him in the waiting room were two other young men to see Kerry and he was jealous.

Inside, Kerry was weak but pleased to see the fairies. Morag hopped on to the bed.

'You won the prize.'

Kerry let out a small whoop of delight.

'Dinnie did it in the end,' announced Heather, proud of her fellow MacKintosh. 'At the vital moment he walked up to the last judge, introduced himself politely and asked her if, as well as being a local sculptor, she could possibly be the well-known Linda, star of the hottest two-girl phone sex in town. She was thrilled to be recognised, particularly when Dinnie said what a great fan of hers he was and asked for her autograph. After that she was putty in his hands and voted for you.

'The Community Arts Prize is now yours, and well deserved. Cal will regret not teaching you the guitar break from "Bad Girl" for the rest of his life.'

Morag muscled her way back into the conversation.

'There are hordes of men outside waiting for dates with you,' she said. 'I would recommend playing the field for a while. In the meantime, let me introduce my friends.'

She gestured to a group of fairies behind her, each of whom greeted Kerry politely.

'This is Sheilagh MacPherson and this is Agnes MacKintosh and this is Jean MacLeod. They are our Clan Chiefs and as such have great powers of healing. With them is Flora MacGillvray, a healer renowned throughout Scotland.

'This is Donal, a friend of Maeve's. He is the healer of the O'Brien tribe and famous in Ireland for his skill. This is Cheng Tin-hung, healer of the Chinese, Lucretia, healer from the Italians, and Aba, healer from the Ghanaians. All of them possess great skill and great reputations.

'It is the finest collection of fairy physicians ever assembled. Do not mind the powerful aroma of whisky. Even extreme intoxication does not lessen the powers of a fairy healer.

'We would like to point out that things are not as bad as you think, because you are talented, popular, pleasant and beautiful, and that being the case, so what if you have a colostomy bag, you are still streets ahead of most humans. But we will spare you the lecture and let the healers get on with their work.'

'And if eight powerful fairies can't fix your insides,' said Heather, 'we will be most surprised. Morag and I will now withdraw and organise your coming-home party, and say goodbye to the English. They are hurrying home to tear down the workhouses and resume pleasurable lives getting drunk under bushes. Magenta has wandered off happily with Joshua, pleased because she thinks he voted for her as head of the Greek army. Callum MacHardie is fixing the MacPherson

Fiddle. Our Clan Chiefs have forgiven us our few misdemeanours because everything has turned out well in the end.'

'That is news to us,' said their Clan Chiefs.

'Well, haven't you?'

The Chiefs said they would think about it, and Morag and Heather exited while they were ahead.

'What's happening?' demanded Dinnie, outside.

'Powerful fairy magic,' replied Heather. 'And you may come to Kerry's welcome-home party providing you bring a suitably expensive present. I believe she has her eye on a set of silver bangles from an Indian shop. You may yet end up going out with her if you take a sound line on which flowers are best in her hair, pretend to like Botticelli, and bring good presents.

'Meanwhile we are off for a few drams and a bit of serious fiddling. If the Irish and everyone else think they've heard Scottish music at its best just because Wee Maggie MacGowan managed to struggle through a few simple tunes without making any mistakes, they have a lot to learn.

'Callum MacHardie has promised to make us some amplifiers. When our radical Celtic band gets going, the hills and glens will never be the same.'

Johnny Thunders left Cal's Gibson in the theatre. It was a good guitar but he could not bring himself to keep it. He knew how bad it felt to have your guitar stolen.

It was time for him to be off, though his mission had been a failure. Thinking that before he left he might as well take one last look around, he headed for Kerry's. He had a desire to see the flower alphabet that had caused so much excitement.

Inside, he was impressed. The flowers, dried by Kerry and spoken to kindly by Morag, emanated great beauty and power. The thirty-three blooms were laid out on the floor and behind them as background Kerry had arranged all her favourite things, including her New York Dolls bootlegs and her remixed copy of the Heartbreakers album.

Another of her favourite things was her guitar.

'My 1958 Gibson Tiger Top.'

Johnny picked it up.

'She had it all the time. No wonder she is obsessed with the New York Dolls.'

Whichever lover had given Kerry the guitar must have been the person who stole it all those years ago.

He made to leave with it but stopped, staring again at the beautiful flowers. He thought about Kerry, lying sick in hospital.

'Oh, to hell with it. I'll take the old beat-up thing I got from that bag lady. I always could play better than anyone else on any old guitar.'

He left Kerry's guitar where it lay, and was not dissatisfied.

Ruby & The Stone Age Diet

Living in Battersea I one day arrived home in the early morning and found a corpse, it was the body of a girl who has been around for a short while, I didn't really know her. She spent her time with the heroin users up the road.

Outside my squat there is a little garden with scrubby grass. She is dead in the scrubby grass.

Never having seen a corpse I wonder if they are really stiff. I poke her skin and it is indeed stiff, and very cold.

She has some mess around her lips like vomit. She is very young.

Finding the corpse perplexes me. It is not a normal experience and I am unsure what to think.

'A dead body,' I say.

'Yes,' agrees Ruby.

Ruby is my friend. We squat together in an Army Careers Office. She never wears any shoes.

We stare at the corpse and at that moment it starts to rain.

'Look,' says Ruby. Two small raindrops have fallen right under the dead girl's eyes.

'Raindrops like tears', says Ruby. 'It is hugely symbolic.'

I feel some relief. Everything is all right once Ruby names it.

Minds at rest, we go inside and wait for someone else to find her so they can call the police.

'What it needs now,' says Ruby, 'Is for the radio to play *You're sixteen, you're beautiful, and you're mine*.'

'Yes,' I agree. 'If that was to happen it would be immensely poignant.'

But when I switch on the radio the only station we can

find is broadcasting a report from the Tokyo stock market instead, and no matter how we try we cannot work this up into any really effective kind of imagery.

I try humming it, but it's not the same.

Some years later, Cis wants some flowers. I'm pleased. Now I can go and get something for her.

She wouldn't mind if I didn't. She doesn't even expect me to get them. She just mentions that it would be nice to have some flowers around the house.

I leave the flat and walk round the corner, searching. I find a flower stall. It has appeared by magic.

I have never bought flowers before. I try and imply this, looking vacantly at the paper-wrapped bundles.

The young woman doesn't mind me being vague, and I buy some daffodils.

'Here, Cis, I brought you some flowers.'

She smiles. She wasn't expecting them. I said I was going out for cigarettes. I bought cigarettes as well.

Cis is very happy with the daffodils. She smiles more and finds an old glass vase and puts them in water and puts the vase on the table and kisses me for bringing them.

I am deliriously happy. Nothing could make me any happier. I love Cis. I could not love anyone any more than I love Cis. I will go to any lengths to bring her flowers.

Later I tell Ruby all about it.

'Cis said they were lovely flowers,' I say, and Ruby tells me it was a good thing to do. She says there is nothing wrong with a bit of romance, even in a world where poor people have to sleep in cardboard boxes and young girls sick themselves to death on heroin.

One time I am walking home a long way after a party in North London. I have no money for the bus and possibly there is no bus, so I walk and walk. Half way home I start to feel feverish and it comes on so rapidly that just a street or two after I first notice it I am sweating and tiring and my throat is starting to swell.

The pavement is strewn with crushed glass. It sparkles under the streetlamps. The notion enters my head that it is a design put there for me to enjoy and I say thank you for making such a pleasing design to entertain me when I am walking feverish along the pavement.

In the centre of town where the night buses start I beg money for a long time. I am too tired to walk all the way home. I'm hot inside, hot, feverish, drunk and drugged. Finally I raise the bus fare.

At home I wake up with some virulent flu germ and I lie in my one room for a long time in a flood of sweat and self-pity and dream about the rain. My muscles hurt and my joints ache, particularly my knees, which won't support me to the sink so I have to be sick on the bedclothes.

I am sick for a week and no one visits and if I died then no one would find me till maybe the landlord thought it was time to rent out the room again.

The fever rages. After a week. I feel better and go out to buy a book to get me through. In the bookshop the assistant is wearing two long silver earrings with opals in them. The opals catch the light and it reminds me of the sparkling pavement.

Back in my room I make a cup of tea and read one page of the book when the fever starts to rage worse than before and I can't read or even finish my tea. I lie on my own for more days and wonder where you find a doctor if you don't have one, but I'm too sick to find out.

The fever makes me shake and shake and I hallucinate

slightly. I wonder why no one visits and I feel lonely and one day I am so lonely I start to cry.

After a while I recover. It was a bad illness but when I tell people about it later I can't impress on them how sick and lonely I felt, though as it turns out that lying sick and lonely in a room somewhere with no one visiting is not such an uncommon experience, perhaps they know anyway.

I wake up in the morning with Cis wrapped around me, still asleep.

I look at her closed eyes and think about what we did last night, which was mainly nothing, watching television, making food.

Cis is a bad cook. So am I. We don't worry about it. We ate our bad food and looked at the flowers, then went to bed and made love.

This morning I am perfectly happy.

Cis gets up. I watch her getting dressed and rummaging her hair into position. Her hair is bleached white and cut in to a flat top, but Cis is so beautiful it doesn't really matter what she does with her hair, or anything else. Cis is the sort of girl you see for five seconds in the street then think about once a week for the rest of your life.

Hair finished, she has to go and visit her mother. I go back to sleep, thinking how good it is to wake up with someone you love wrapped around you. I am still perfectly happy. I am happier than I have ever been before.

Ruby and I are living in a council flat. We have shared many different places to live and we get on very well. When I get home the whole place is a shambles and she tells me she had some friends round for a few drinks the night before.

'How is Cis?' she asks, always willing to make pleasant conversation. 'And can you help me with my hair?'

I help her with her hair.

'Cis is wonderful,' I say happily, and she sneers a little, but pleasantly.

She tells me what good acid she had last night with the few friends and drinks and I say it sounds nice but really I am not keen on acid because I tend to get strong and unpleasant hallucinations.

'Have you found a drummer for your band yet?'

'We're auditioning some tonight,' I tell her.

'Look. I cut my foot.'

'You should wear shoes.'

'I hate shoes.'

Ruby is always barefoot which is practically unique in the city. The only things she ever wears are a lilac cotton dress that comes down to just below her knees and a pair of sunglasses. She wears nothing under the dress and nothing over it, except a donkey jacket if it is cold.

With her dress, bare feet and sunglasses, she looks wonderful.

A broken bottle has proved too much even for her toughened soles. I bring a basin of water and wash her feet, then stick a plaster over the cut.

'Thank you,' says Ruby.

Cis comes round. I bound around the flat trying to do things for her. She gives me a pot plant and tells me she doesn't want to see me any more. I think I might die on the spot.

Ruby wanders in and offers us some tea.

'Yes, thank you.'

'Why don't you want to see me any more?'

There doesn't seem to be any particular reason for it.

Ruby brings the tea and Cis goes away. I look at my pot plant. It is a little cactus.

'Will you go and cash my Giro for me?' asks Ruby, and signs the back.

I go to the Post Office. It is robbed. I am surprised at this. Normally it is a quiet place. Robbers come in with machine-guns and hold me and all the other customers at gunpoint and demand a small jet to fly them to Libya. All the hostages shake with fear.

The siege lasts for hours and hours till finally specially-trained police burst in and shoot all the robbers dead. There is blood everywhere, blood and television cameras.

I cash our Giros and go home.

'Ruby, I'm sorry I was so long cashing our Giros but when I was in the Post Office robbers with machine-guns came in and held me hostage.'

Ruby says don't be silly and I say it is true and she says it is just the acid making me think funny things and I say what acid and she says the acid she put in my tea to make me feel better about Cis leaving me and after that I can't think of anything good to say.

'I wrote a werewolf story while you were out,' says Ruby. 'Do you want to hear it?'

'Yes.'

'Then sit down comfortably.'

Cynthia Werewolf – her early life

Cynthia, a good but hungry werewolf, always tries her best not to eat people. Sometimes, however, it is an uphill struggle. They taste nice.

An outcast from society, she lives alone with her mother. They do not get on very well. Cynthia is always lonely.

At school she has no friends. The other children do not know that she is a werewolf, but they can sense she is different.

Every full moon Cynthia has an unbearable urge to eat someone. This, however, is absolutely forbidden by her mother.

'Under no circumstances are you to eat a human being,' her mother instructs her sternly.

'Not even a little baby that no one would miss?' pleads Cynthia.

'Particularly not a little baby. Babies are absolutely not on the menu as far as we are concerned. And nor is anybody else.'

Cynthia, never very happy, annoys her mother, who tells her continually that she has a lot to be thankful for.

'Outside it is a beautiful world.'

Hungry and lonely, Cynthia can't see it herself.

I get a job for three days on a building site in Wandsworth. It is meant to be for longer than three days but the foreman tells me not to come back because I am not much use.

I am a little hurt because I have been trying my best but I know that it is true. I can manage clearing rubble in wheelbarrows, although I am not very strong, but when it comes to levelling out wet concrete with a sort of vibrating machine I am hopeless.

I often do this sort of temporary work when I am broke. It is the only work I can get.

On my last day a man in my shift tells a joke.

Everyone laughs. I am still waiting for the joke to end. I seem to have missed a bit. I will have to ask Ruby to explain it to me.

But Ruby is not home so I go to my room and feel bad about being sacked after only three days. If I had been able to practise a bit more I'm sure I could have worked the concrete-levelling machine.

Outside my window a nice looking boy walks past. He is just the sort of boy that Cis would like. He might even be her new boyfriend. He might be going to see her right now. The thought of Cis with a new boyfriend is too terrible to contemplate.

I would like to phone Cis but I know she doesn't want to hear from me.

Where I am standing everything becomes unbearable. I walk to the other side of the room to see if it is any better there.

No success. This side of the room is just as bad.

I figure maybe I should do something to take my mind off Cis. I will tidy the flat.

My room has cobwebs in the corners but when I think about how to clean them away it seems to be an awful difficult thing to do and maybe not worth the trouble as they are sure to come back in a while.

Ruby must be across in the next block with her boyfriend Domino. I wish she was here to talk to.

I don't like Domino. Ruby is very smart. He is dumb.

Ruby is writing a book. Domino can hardly read.

Outside the window is a pathetic little window-box with a dead weed and five cigarette ends. I think about planting some flowers in it then taking them to Cis. Looking out the window I see her go past. I walk back to the other side of the room but nothing has changed there.

The next day I am captured by a spaceship. It swoops down on me when I am walking through Trafalgar Square and takes me away for some tests. The aliens look quite normal but I am worried they might be wearing masks and underneath they are really horrible and scaly. Still, I am not one of these people who is totally paranoid about space aliens. After all, there is no real reason for them to be unfriendly.

So I try and co-operate the best I can with their tests and after a while, when I have taught them some English, we get on quite well and they show me round. Their spaceship is full of luxuriant flowers, all lilac and yellow and bursting with life. They try bringing me some tea as they read in my thoughts that I am very fond of tea but the machine that makes it gets it a little wrong. Still, I appreciate the thought.

Ruby arrives back. I go for a talk with her but she is busy writing a letter.

'Who are you writing to?'

'I'm writing to my genitals.'

I borrow her book of myths and fables and sit beside her, reading.

'Where do you want to go now?' asks the Captain of the space aliens.

'Just back to Trafalgar Square,' I say, and they drop me off.

I wander round for a while thinking about the aliens and wondering if I should tell anyone about it but just down the road at Charing Cross I lose concentration when I suffer a dreadful hallucination that there are rows and rows of people living in cardboard boxes, so I hurry on past and catch the bus back to Brixton. It is raining and this makes my knee hurt and I wish I had remembered to ask the space aliens if they could cure it, because my knee is often sore.

Back on Earth I start missing Cis again. I cannot think of any reason that she would have left me. Disappointingly, Ruby is unable to explain the joke the man told on the building site.

I show her the pot plant that Cis gave me as a leaving present. Two tears dribble from my eyes.

'Never mind,' says Ruby. 'At least it is a nice cactus.'

Afreet, says Ruby's book, *is the evil God of Broken Relationships. If you offend him your lover will leave you.*

'I met Izzy today,' says Ruby. 'She is having terrible problems with her boyfriend and she has bought two weights to build up her body.'

'What sort of weights?

'Little ones. She wanted something bigger but the woman in the shop told her that she had to start off small. Apparently it is the repetition that counts. Her boyfriend is secretly fucking someone else.'

I would like to phone Cis but I know she doesn't want to hear from me.

Cynthia eats the first of many victims, or the first one that is discovered

Cynthia and her mother live on a small croft in the Scottish Highlands. They live alone. A few years ago her father left the family. He ran off with a younger werewolf.

Cynthia's mother insists that her daughter should go to university. In the modern world werewolves always try to integrate themselves with society. Cynthia is not keen. She wants to go and sing in a rock band and play her guitar loud.

One day she is out for a walk through the heather. She comes across a pregnant woman.

Aha, thinks Cynthia. A nourishing sandwich. And there's no one around. She eats the pregnant woman. Unfortunately her mother, sharp-eyed, is not as far away as she thinks, and sees the crime.

Her mother is furious. So is the Werewolf King. Cynthia is forced to flee to London with only her guitar for company.

I can never find a reliable drummer for my band. This is on my mind while I am patching my jeans and feeling hungry. My jeans are a shambles and we can't afford any food.

I think we should become Buddhists,' says Ruby.

'I am busy patching my jeans.'

'See? You are too concerned with the material world. Once we are Buddhists you won't worry about patching your jeans or stuff like that.'

'Are you religious about your drumming?' I once asked a drummer, in a shabby all-night café in Soho.

'Not really. There is no god of drumming. But I do follow the way of the Tao.'

'What will Domino say if you became a Buddhist? Will you still be able to fuck him?'

'Domino can fuck himself,' says Ruby.

They have been arguing again. I think about Ruby's suggestion.

'If I become a Buddhist will I stop being sad about Cis?'

'Right away.'

Next day, in heavy rain and very hungry, we go up into town to join a Buddhist temple.

They give us a vegetarian meal which tastes very good and we sit around banging tambourines for a while. I pretend I am banging a tambourine in tribute to the God of Drumming so he will send my band a good drummer.

'I am enjoying this,' I say to Ruby, and she seems quite enthusiastic as well.

Everyone has shaven heads and we wonder if we will have to have this done. Ruby says she doesn't mind, even though she has lots of meticulously cared-for hair, because spiritual people don't bother about this sort of thing. Also we will get nice orange robes.

After we've banged our tambourines and chanted and had some more vegetarian food a man comes and sits with us.

'I am your instructor,' he says.

'How long have you been a Buddhist?' asks Ruby.

'We're not Buddhists,' says the man. 'We're Hare Krishna.'

We pick up our shoes on the way out.

'What a disappointment,' says Ruby.

'How come we picked the wrong temple?'

'At least it was nice food.'

'The act of eating disgusts me,' says Ruby.. 'Do you think I am putting on weight?'

'No.'

Ruby worries about her weight. It is stupid. She is not overweight.

A string of shaven-haired devotees marches past, chanting and banging drums.

'Don't ask them to join your band,' advises Ruby. 'You'll be wasting your time.'

'Is that –'

'No it isn't. Cis isn't here. And it doesn't look anything like her.'

'Why did you write a letter to your genitals?'

'I was just telling them how much I dislike them. It is a procedure recommended in my new book. Next I have to write them another letter telling them how much I like them.'

On the way home we meet Izzy who is eating a pizza in the street and carrying a small weight.

'I have to screw this onto my dumbells,' she tells us. 'It's time to make them slightly heavier.'

She is wearing a leather waistcoat. She flexes her bicep.

'Do you notice any difference?'

Ruby and I say yes although actually we don't.

'How are you getting on with Dean?' asks Ruby. Dean is Izzy's boyfriend.

Izzy shrugs. There is a definite kind of shrug that means you are not getting on too well with your boyfriend.

Back home I go through to look at my cactus.

Ruby follows me into my room.

'Let me have a look at that cactus.'

She studies it for a while.

'This is sensational.'

'What?'

'This cactus. According to my book of myths and fables it is the sacred Aphrodite Cactus. Once it flowers your love is sealed forever with the person that gave it to you.'

'When will it flower?'

'Any time.'

It is February. Any time cannot be far away. I am pleased to have Aphrodite on my side.

Cynthia is very poor, but meets a pleasant companion

In London Cynthia squats with a few people she meets around. She is very poor. The Social Security will not give her any money and she is forced to scavenge the streets to survive. She tries mainly just to eat dogs and cats, because she does realise that it is not such a nice thing to eat humans, but sometimes she devours one. Humans are very tasty.

And, when she thinks about it, humans have never been all that pleasant to wolves, and they do eat animals themselves.

Still, after eating a human Cynthia always feels a little guilty. But when she meets a nice boy called Daniel and starts going out with him she soon forgets all about it, because Daniel is a friendly lover and they both like to fuck for hours on end. Afterwards they watch television or listen to records, and Cynthia plays Daniel a few simple songs on her guitar.

Ruby comes back from Domino's, slamming the door, holding a cactus and forcing a smile.

'Domino bought me a sacred Aphrodite Cactus. I made him do it. He wanted to spend the money on beer instead.

Look after it till it flowers.' She storms off, apparently unhappy despite the cactus.

I put it next to mine and feed them both some plant food. Outside it is thundering and lightning and lashing down rain.

One time around midnight I met a girl called Anastasia at a bus stop in the rain at Clapham Common. This sticks in my mind because Anastasia is an unusual name. No buses came so we started walking together. At this time I was still in the Army Careers Office.

'It would be nice to control the weather,' said Anastasia, pulling her collar tight against the rain. 'Like a rain god. I'd walk around in sunshine all day long. Maybe I might have a little bit of rain so I could make some rainbows.'

I go through to Ruby's room and ask her what is wrong and she says that Domino is a complete moron who wants to drink beer all the time and he reminds her of her father.

I try being sympathetic but I am not a very convincing liar and Ruby sees through me. We disappear into our separate rooms and I get back to staring at my pot plant. I had considered writing a poem but now I don't feel much like it because with Ruby in such a bad mood I will have no one to show it to. But this is probably just as well, because I am a terrible poet.

It rained till the gutters overflowed onto the pavements. At the corner of Battersea High Street Anastasia quoted me three lines of a poem by Byron and told me she would like to come home with me. This was a surprise, but fine.

Possibly I am massively attractive that night. Possibly she is dreadfully lonely. Probably she is just fed up with getting rained on.

At my front door I find I have lost the keys.

'I have lost the keys.'

We look at the front door. It is barricaded like a good squat should be, with a rough sketch of Tilka, Guardian Goddess of Squatters, protecting the entrance. Hammering on it produces no results. No one is home.

'Never mind,' I say. 'I'll get in the back.'

I walk round the corner and beat on Paul's door to let me in and then I climb his back wall and walk through the gardens of some rented houses and avoid a barking dog to clamber into our backyard. I force the window at the back of my room. Once inside I can't get out because I now remember I have padlocked my room on the outside as a security measure against everyone else who squats there.

So I have to hop out the back and break the window of the next room. Unfortunately once inside the room I find that the person who lives there has followed my example and this door too is padlocked outside.

I curse him for being so suspicious of his fellow human beings and wonder what to do. By this time I am growling with frustration and Anastasia is somewhere outside in the rain wondering where I am, so I just take hold of the door and beat it till the locks break. The door is in shreds.

I run to the front door and haul it open.

'Hi Anastasia, come in.'

We enter my room via my neighbour's room, the backyard and my window.

Up above spaceships fly through the night sky, puny human craft and mighty alien movable worlds. Somewhere on a mighty alien movable world two beings are clambering through a window and into bed. Being mighty aliens they will have conquered all sexual diseases and will be able to fuck with complete abandon.

'This is an interesting way to get into bed,' says Anastasia, clambering over the window-ledge. After undressing she takes a diaphragm from her bag, smears it with spermicide, and pushes it into her vagina.

After fucking I have the longest journey ever up to the kitchen to make some tea and carry the teapot back through the obstacle course of the shattered door. Two windows and a backyard is no easy matter. Later I have to make the same journey again to rummage round for some dog-ends to roll a few cigarettes, but all in all it is a pleasant experience, though as I never see Anastasia again, possibly she does not enjoy it as much as me.

The following day Danny in the next room is furious that someone has torn his door off its hinges but I just deny all knowledge of it, and when he gets round to taking some glue and some heroin he soon forgets all about it.

Cynthia gives way to her appetite

'Let's go out for a walk in the beautiful full moon,' suggests Daniel.

'No,' says Cynthia. 'It's not safe outside at night.'

'Don't be silly,' says Daniel. 'Of course it's safe.'

Round the first quiet corner Cynthia changes into wolf-form, kills Daniel and eats him. The full moon always gives her a powerful appetite.

'I told you it wasn't safe,' she says.

Daniel did have the slightly unfortunate habit of often not listening to Cynthia's opinions carefully enough.

Ruby comes out of her room and starts being friendly. I immediately co-operate because if Ruby is friendly to me I will always be friendly right back, even if she has been unpleasant to me only minutes before.

'Here is some tea,' she says. 'Help me with my hair.'

She is tying some small lilac ribbons into her plaited locks.

'They are lovely,' I tell her. 'They look beautiful with your dress.'

'I'd like to show them off. Let's go out.'

We walk down into the centre of Brixton and call on Izzy. Izzy lives with Marilyn. They are both Ruby's friends rather than mine. Marilyn is not in and Izzy is busy lifting her weights. They seem like very small weights but she must have been lifting them for a while because her body is glistening with sweat.

'See the improvement?' she says flexing her biceps.

'Yes,' we say, although neither Ruby nor I can see any difference.

Izzy is wearing a dull yellow tracksuit with the sleeves ripped off and holes in the knees. For some reason I feel sorry for her, standing there in rags, pretending her muscles are growing.

Before we go Ruby asks her how she is getting on with Dean. Izzy tells us she is mad at him because he is busy rebuilding an old motorbike and never has any time for her. And then when he does call round he expects her to drop everything and pay him lots of attention. What's worse, she always does. And she still thinks he is fucking someone else.

We leave Izzy to her weights. Outside Ruby says she feel a little sorry for her, though she isn't sure why.

We set off again to visit some more of Ruby's friends. When we arrive they are busy putting some padlocks on their front door.

'Can't be too careful,' says Phil, who is a small-time cocaine dealer, and attracted to Ruby.

When they hear about how Domino has been unpleasant to Ruby and I have been left by Cis they do their best to cheer us up.

'How could Domino be so unpleasant to you?' says Phil. 'Compared to him you are a goddess.'

Later on I go home and Ruby stays. Close to our flat I am so full of things to cheer me up that I find myself lying face down in a puddle with a vivid memory of someone telling me that you can drown in only two inches of water.

I struggle to my knees. Only an inch and a half, I estimate. A lucky escape. Four young men pass by, singing and shouting and causing a disturbance. I hate them. They ask me if I am all right and they go to a lot of trouble to help me home. I still hate them.

Next morning I wake up in bed with the Great Goddess Astarte.

I am surprised, of course, that the Great Goddess Astarte has chosen to visit a council flat in Brixton, let alone sleep in my bed, but I go along with it because I do not want to offend her in any way. I have nothing but respect for the Great Goddess.

At this time I am working for a man in Dulwich who does painting and decorating. I have to strip off wallpaper with a steaming machine. It is unpleasant and difficult.

Some people do easy jobs and earn huge amounts of money. I do dreadful jobs and am always poorly paid. I am not quite sure why this is. Maybe I didn't pay enough attention at school.

When I am doing these menial things I think about whatever band I'm playing in at the time. I imagine us being successful. I imagine that one day I will not have to visit any more building sites or factories because I will be making records and making money and having fun. Even though I am realistic enough to know that this is unlikely, I still think about it.

However, I abandon the decorating because I cannot leave the Great Goddess to go and strip wallpaper. It would be a terrible insult.

For some days I go around making food and keeping the flat tidy and generally being organised because I am sure that the Great Goddess will be totally fucked off if she keeps tripping over old clothes on the floor or finds there isn't any soap in the bathroom.

She seems to adjust to the modern world very well, working the TV doesn't cause her any problems at all and she consistently plays all the best records in Ruby's and my collection. Ruby seems to be away somewhere, which is a shame as I know she would have liked to meet Astarte.

'Can you make Cis come back to me?' I ask, respectfully bringing her a cup of tea.

'Of course,' she replies. 'I can do anything. But I'm not going to. She has a life of her own to lead.'

'Oh.'

I think about asking her to find me a good drummer but I do not want to burden such an important being with my petty problems. She has told me that she is presently engaged in trying to stop the world being destroyed by heartless humans. Apparently it is a very close thing. She does however take the time to say a few words to my cactus and afterwards it is always spectacularly healthy. It starts to grow, but there is no sign of a flower.

Cynthia finds happiness with another lover

After eating Daniel Cynthia is very very lonely. She deeply regrets it. So she takes her guitar and goes busking in tube stations to try and earn some money and take her mind off things.

She is quite successful at busking. Cynthia has a good voice. Also, something about her eyes makes the police hesitant about moving her on.

Later, still lonely, she has a drink in a pub.

A girl comes over and talks to her. Her name is Albinia. They go home together.

Cynthia moves in with her and they are happy for a while. Albinia is a dress designer and works every day in a studio surrounded by other young artists who she finds very pushy. She appreciates Cynthia's relatively simple manners, and she likes her singing.

Cynthia, of course, does not let on that she is really a werewolf. She knows that Albinia will find this hard to understand.

I meet a man who can't relate to the world because he is too shy to talk to anyone. He is too shy to talk to me and we don't have any fun. I meet a woman who hates herself because she is fat and she apologises for not saying she was fat in the contact advert. I tell her not to worry about it because I don't mind but she says she knows I am lying and that really I hate her for being fat and she wishes she'd never met me. I meet a man of fifty who runs a company making yachts and he says he is looking for a nice young houseboy who he can fuck on his own personal yacht but I am not good-looking enough so it isn't going to be me. I meet a man who lives in a cardboard box under the National Theatre and he promises that he is only living there whilst pursuing a sociological study of the homeless and if I will take him home and let him fuck me we will be very happy together. I get rained on and wet waiting for a woman who wants a young lover to take her to art galleries and she never shows. I meet a young man with a withered arm who says he used to be a drummer until he got burnt in a fire. I like him but he says he never wants to have sex because he is ashamed of his withered arm and he is sorry he wasted my time. I brush my hair downstairs in McDonalds whilst waiting for a young soldier who promises he has books, magazines and videos, but he never shows and I don't wait long because four noisy young men at the next table are making me nervous. I meet a man who wants to teach me to fly helicopters but when we get undressed he is nervous that I will steal his suit so he cannot concentrate. I meet a woman who says she is embarrassed about placing an advert but since her husband died she has not been able to stop crying and the doctor told her to get out of the house more. I meet a young woman from Iceland who is so bright, intelligent and attractive that it seems like a bad miracle that she cannot meet anyone she likes and has to sit every night alone in a bedsit with one ring of her gas cooker lit because her electric heater is too expensive. On reflection she decides that she does not want to sit there with me. I do not want to sit there with her. I do not want to do anything with anyone. I want to wake up in bed with Cis.

I wake up in bed with Ruby.

'Good morning, Ruby. Where have you been? Why are you in my bed? Where is the Great Goddess Astarte?'

Ruby tells me to stop rambling and says she will make us some tea. I rush out of bed to make the tea myself.

While the kettle is boiling I have to go and be sick in the

toilet and while I am sicking up a little blood I try and think what has been happening the last few days. However, with the vomiting and the kettle boiling over and Ruby screaming will I bring her a bit of toast as well I can't get much thinking done so I abandon the attempt.

I wonder what day it is.

'What day is it?' says Ruby.

Neither of us have any idea.

In the mirror I look like a corpse. I am sorry the Great Goddess has gone but pleased Ruby has come back. After a while, when I don't feel like vomiting any more, I walk round to the shops for some cigarettes and a bar of chocolate for Ruby. When I'm there I look at a newspaper to find out the date and I find it is Saturday, which is in some ways a pity as we both should have signed on at the Unemployment Office on Wednesday and forgetting to sign on is practically the worst thing you can do when you are on the dole.

On the way back I think that I see Cis coming towards me with a dog, but when the person gets up close she is nothing at all like Cis, she is an old woman of eighty with a carrier bag containing her weeks shopping and I can see from the way she carries her shopping that she is the loneliest person in the world. Probably all she has to talk to is a cactus.

'Here's your chocolate, Ruby.'

Ruby looks distressed and says she does not want any chocolate as chocolate disgusts her.

'But you asked me to buy it.'

'How are the pot plants coming along?'

'Very well. I think mine's grown with all the food I've given it. If Cis was to come back right now she'd be really pleased how well I've looked after it. No flowers though. Are you sure you don't want this chocolate?'

'Yes. What do you know about diaphragms?'

'I know what they are.'

Ruby is surprised. She does not really expect me to know anything.

'I am having trouble with mine.'

I make her some tea and Ruby tells me how lonely she feels when Domino is not around, and how good she feels when he brings her little gifts like bars of chocolate.

Ruby is the most intelligent person I know and also very strong. Why she is bothered by a fool like Domino not being around to bring her chocolate I can't imagine.

Cynthia suffers a series of misfortunes, and thinks of home

'Isn't it nice,' says Albinia, 'the way that our periods have started to coincide since we started living together.'

'Yes,' says Cynthia, the scent of blood in her nostrils.

The full moon shines through the window.

Cynthia eats Albinia.

The neighbours hear screaming and break down the door. Cynthia is forced to flee.

She finds a rubbish tip and lies down to cry.

I am cursed in love, she thinks. Why did I do it?

Later that night she suffers further misfortune when the rubbish tip internally combusts and her leg is burned in the fire. She limps off to nurse her wound. Thunder crashes in the sky above and it starts to rain.

Soaked, lonely and injured, Cynthia thinks about her comfortable home far away in Scotland, and her mother.

'I do not think it is a very beautiful world, no matter what you say,' she mutters, and tries to find somewhere dry.

Ruby and I are sitting quietly. Sometimes we sit quietly for hours. Domino is incapable of this. He talks continually because he has to hear his own voice all the time. I hate him.

'Look.'

Ruby has made a spaceship out of the chocolate wrapper. We fly it round the room for a while till it is time for me to rehearse with my band. Wrapping my guitar in a black plastic bag I walk down to the studio, but when I arrive only Nigel is there and he says the new drummer we recruited has decided not to play with us after all but to go away for a long holiday in Denmark instead.

'Is it nice in Denmark?'

Nigel doesn't know. I offer him some chocolate but he refuses because not having a drummer makes him too depressed to eat. Also the chocolate is not too appetising after resting wrapperless in my guitar case. He departs in silence and I try and visit some people but no one is in so I have to go home.

The next launch is particularly successful. Crowds cheer ecstatically and in no time at all we are plunging into deep space. I like our spaceship except this time I notice all the daffodils and lilacs are plastic, and I am not at all fond of plastic. Before take-off I strongly request some real daffodils but apparently they are bad for the oxygen supply.

The President radios his congratulations on the successful launch. I complain to him about the plastic daffodils.

'And where is my guitar?' I ask, but he pretends not to hear.

All the crew are busy with scientific experiments. I am busy trying to tidy my little cabin, brushing away a few cobwebs and programming our computer on how to make me a guitar, when suddenly we are bombarded by a ferocious meteor storm.

'Why didn't the computer warn us?' cries the Captain.

'Its memory banks are all full of instructions on how to make a guitar and long love poems about some woman called Cis,' reports the First Mate.

We are battered mercilessly by the meteors. The door to the airlock is ripped to shreds and only heroic action by some crew members prevents total disaster.

Eventually we struggle through. Afterwards no one will speak to me because they are all annoyed at me endangering their lives by jamming up the computers. Fortunately by this time the computer has made me a guitar so I sit on my own in my cabin and work out a few songs and when the person in the next cabin bangs on the wall complaining about the noise I just ignore it. They disturb me by exercising, always banging weights around and doing push-ups.

I become quite friendly with our robot.

Later in the day Ruby appears with Domino and they act like they are the happiest couple in the world. I wait for Cis to appear so we can also act like the happiest couple in the world.

After a few hours it seems like she is not going to call round today. Maybe she is busy. Possibly she will call first thing in the morning. Suddenly it strikes me that if today is Saturday then it is time for me to get round to the art class where I work one day a week as a model.

I get washed. I never like to think that I smell bad when people are painting me.

'Hello,' says the teacher, a woman of about thirty-five with a cultured voice.

'Hello,' say all the students of all ages also with cultured voices. There is a little screen for me to get undressed behind which always strikes me as strange.

I have no real idea why the art class needs someone to get undressed to be their model but if they are willing to pay it is fine with me, also they are always very nice to me and sometimes buy me a drink afterwards. In fact, sometimes afterwards they all fall over themselves to talk to me and be pleasant. Possibly they are keen to let me know they do not regard me as being in any way inferior because I have been sitting there for two hours being painted with no clothes on.

Today the teacher puts lots of boxes beside me. I am disappointed. I was hoping for some daffodils. She piles up the boxes a bit like a robot and tells all the students to make their paintings like boxes. Or robots. Or something like that, I am not too clear about it.

Sitting being painted I am very lonely. I talk to Cis in my head.

Only another twenty minutes, I say to her. *Then I'll be finished. What would you like to do tonight*? I get the feeling that it is unbearable where I am and I want to walk to the other side of the room to see if it is any better there, but as the one thing the art class requires of me is that I stay still this is not possible. A pity, because the other side of the room looks like it might be better.

I wonder if I should tell the art class my problems. Probably they would not like being interrupted in their painting. Everyone always concentrates hard at the class. Also I realise that being left unhappy by your lover is such a common experience that everyone would just be bored by it.

Cynthia's uncontrollable appetite brings her to the attention of the Werewolf King

The Werewolf King is called Lupus. He is immensely rich, and lives regally in Kensington. He has business connections all over and rakes in money from sex magazines and private mailing companies.

When he hears reports about Cynthia eating people he is furious. He hates for his werewolves to eat anyone. Lupus is very keen for werewolves to integrate fully with society. Eating people is disastrous for their image.

Lupus is never happy. His wife ran off with a mathematics student from Africa. Since then he has always looked for people or werewolves on whom to take out his anger.

He summons his werewolf detectives.

'Bring Cynthia to me,' he instructs them. 'Preferably alive, although I won't stretch the point.'

They set off on the hunt. It will not take them long to find Cynthia because werewolves are supernaturally good at tracking.

After his agents depart Lupus relaxes with a bottle of wine and a copy of Voltaire's complete works.

The goddess responsible for people whose lovers have left them is called Jasmine and she is always very busy. Sometimes she gets out her flaming sword and battles with Afreet the God of Broken Relationships when she sees that he is about to strike. She is hugely compassionate but she has a high failure rate. Her difficult job sometimes makes her turn to drink, and then there are broken hearts everywhere.

At the end of the art class I get dressed and the teacher brings out some wine. This is not normal but it seems to be a little celebration for something or other and they all drink wine out of paper cups. When the teacher pours some for me she makes a little wine joke and everybody smiles, but as I have no idea whatsoever what the wine joke is about I just look vacant. Later I have the vague notion that I am pretty dumb compared to these artists who can go around making paintings and wine jokes.

Afterwards I have to go to Stepney to meet a violent sadist who advertised for me in a contact magazine. He is terrible to me and after he beats and fucks me I am half dead and have blood all down my back. I do not approve of violent sex.

'I don't fit in with the art class.'

'You don't have to fit in,' says Ruby. 'You are only the model.'

'Still, I am pretty dumb compared to them. I used to like it better there but since Cis left me I feel stupid. Also I think my soul has gone missing.'

'Yes,' says Ruby. 'That is possible. You could well have lost it.'

'Where could it be?'

But Ruby is too busy reading her giant reference book of myths and fables. This book is an endless source of wonderment.

I shuffle round the flat trying to find a space where I do not feel bad about Cis. I have bought a little yellow cloth to brush the dust off my cactus. After cleaning it I study it closely for any sign of a flower. I wonder if Cis will reappear as soon as it buds or will she wait till the whole flower appears?

It is now March and there is no sign of a flower.

Cynthia has many unpleasant experiences

Cynthia is evicted from her squat.
She tries eating the bailiffs but some policemen arrive and there are too many of them to fight.

Not for the first time she is left homeless, with only her guitar for company.

Where oh where is a young werewolf to find happiness, she asks herself, and can't think of an answer.

Out busking she is run over by a bus. Fortunately werewolves are very tough and she is not seriously injured, but it is still a bad experience.

Later two men try to mug her and take her day's earnings.

Cynthia turns into wolf-form and eats them angrily. She gets back to busking. A policeman moves her on. It starts to rain. Her guitar breaks a string.

Two werewolf detectives appear.

'We've come to arrest you,' they say.

This is a fucking lousy day, thinks the young werewolf. Everyone is against me. I haven't a friend in the world and I've nowhere to live and I've no one to fuck. The only things I feel are hunger and loneliness. This is far from being a beautiful world. It isn't even pleasant.

Hardened by living rough, she kills and eats the detectives without much trouble, but in the process she loses her earnings down a manhole and finds herself penniless even after a hard day's busking.

The old woman is still waiting on her balcony. I wish she had someone to talk to. She reminds me of a woman called

Sylvia I used to see in Battersea. Sylvia was around sixty and her Spanish accent was too thick for anyone to ever understand what she said. She lived with a man called Victor who had a cleft palate and no one could understand him either. They could understand each other.

No one ever wanted to see them because they were so filthy and shabby and difficult to understand. Sometimes, for companionship, they would hang around with the local Socialist Workers Party and sell papers for them.

No one cared anything about them and no one ever visited although they lived in a squat in a street full of squats. Just them, sick and old, and a horrible sick dog and not a visitor for months and months. I used to wish that someone would go and visit them.

'Did you ever?' asks Ruby.

'No. I could never understand what they were saying.'

It rains outside and the little balcony floods and we have to bail it out with a bucket and a pot and this is quite fun because we can pretend we are pirates. Ruby would be a good pirate captain, I think, because she would never have to leave the ship and she could just order the crew about all the time.

Ruby goes to lie down after her exertions and I go downstairs where I meet the postman, the woman from the ground floor and Ascanazl, an ancient and powerful Inca spirit who looks after lonely people. He is drying his feathers after the rain. His feathers are magnificent.

I tell him about Cis leaving me. Almost immediately he makes a polite excuse and flies off.

'You are in a sorry state,' says the woman downstairs. 'Even the powerful Inca spirit dedicated to looking after lonely people is bored with your company.'

I ask the postman if he has any letters for us. We hardly ever get letters.

Ruby emerges from her room flushed and annoyed.

'Help me with my diaphragm,' she says.

'What sort of help do you need?'

'I can't fit it. I am going to see Domino tonight and I have this diaphragm from a doctor because I don't want to take the pill any more but I can't get it fitted right.'

Ruby brings out a tube of spermicide and squeezes some onto her finger, then rubs it all over the round piece of plastic.

'I'll have one last try.'

She lifts up her dress and squats on the floor and squeezes the diaphragm in half way and tries to fit it but somehow she can't. It keeps slipping out.

'Stupid fucking thing,' she rages.

I try and help. Ruby lies on the floor and opens her legs wide and I insert it.

'Make sure it is stationed securely behind the pubic bone.'

Her vagina is slippery from spermicide but when I fit it, it stays inside.

'There,' I say, always pleased to do Ruby a favour.

'It's not right.'

'How not?'

'It's not covering my cervix,' says Ruby, glowering, feeling inside her with her fingers. 'Do you have any cigarettes?'

I light some cigarettes although this takes several tries as the matchbox also becomes slippery with spermicide.

'Are you sure?'

'Of course I'm sure. Don't you think I know when my cervix is covered?'

She takes my hand and puts my fingers up her vagina.

'See?'

'Not really.'

'Why not?'

'Well, I'm not really sure what a cervix is.'

'You must know what a cervix is.'

'Well I do, in general terms. Just not exactly.'

Ruby frowns some more and removes the diaphragm, then she shows me exactly which bit is the cervix.

'This little bit in here that sticks out.'

Ruby tells me it moves around. I am fascinated.

'Does it move around fast? I mean, do you have to wait till it stays still for a minute, then try and get the diaphragm over it quickly?'

Apparently it doesn't. I try again and this time I am successful.

'Thank you,' says Ruby, standing up and adjusting her dress.

The room is covered in spermicide. Any sperm that comes in will have no chance of survival whatsoever.

I tell Ruby that I like her new sunglasses and remind her that my band is looking for a new drummer, just in case she comes across one on her travels. She leaves to visit Domino.

Cynthia, pursued by detectives, meets her true love

After a few days sleeping rough Cynthia meets some punks who live with some hippies in a huge old vicarage near King's Cross. She makes friends and moves in with them.

One night the hippies annoy her by banging drums when she is trying to sleep. Cynthia stares out of the window. A full moon stares back at her. She goes and eats the hippies.

My my, she thinks. That was a good meal. Something between brown rice and a lentil casserole.

Werewolf detectives surround the house. They are armed with machine-guns loaded with deadly silver bullets.

Cynthia is forced to flee. Tumbling down the stairs she

meets Paris, a young newcomer to the commune. She falls in love with him on sight.

But she only has time to brush her lips against his before the detectives pound down the stairs after her, and she flies off into the night.

Sometimes I work for an industrial agency which gets me casual work in factories.

Ruby phones them up for me because I am not very coherent on the phone. When she does this she tells them she is my wife.

I get a job cleaning in a huge industrial garage in Gunnersbury. The floor is black with oil and I have to clean it till it is white. It takes me around a day to clean a space the size of a car, grinding away at years of grease and filth with a scrubbing brush and a mop and a bucket. Also I have to clean the toilets.

The first day I make the mistake of cleaning the toilets too early and at the end of the shift all the workers come in and make everything dirty again. So after that I leave cleaning the toilets till last.

The company tells the agency that I am a good worker and the man in the agency is pleased and says that it is very rare for one of their clients to pay a compliment to one of their workers.

At lunchtime I sit on my own in the canteen and listen to everyone talking about what they saw on television the night before.

One day a white worker calls out, 'Hey, Mandela!' to a black worker and there is a big argument because the black worker says he is not called Mandela, he has a name of his own.

I do not mind this cleaning work as everybody just leaves

me alone to get on with it because I am obviously a good cleaner, but after about a month I don't go in one day because I wake up with the sure knowledge that Cis will call round and visit me.

'Not working today?' asks Ruby.

'No. Cis is going to visit.'

I spend the day thinking what I will say to Cis when she calls and rushing to the window at the slightest sound outside. I make up all sorts of speeches in my head, but eventually I decide that I will just tell her how pleased I am to see her again.

Ruby appears at around two in the morning with wet feet and sunglasses.

'She didn't call?'

I shake my head.

'Don't worry,' says Ruby. 'She might call tomorrow.'

I don't feel like cleaning any more floors or toilets so I don't go back to the garage and afterwards I have trouble even remembering where Gunnersbury is, although I miss the meals in the canteen because they had good pies and I used to enjoy sitting there eating them.

Marilyn and Izzy live in a housing co-op flat with three tiny rooms and red curtains. I wonder about visiting them. This is always a slight problem because I am friends with Izzy but I don't know Marilyn so well and if I visit and only Marilyn is in then I feel awkward. I decide to go anyway.

They are on the first floor with no bell so I have to throw stones at the window and I am careful not to throw anything too big because Marilyn gets really fucked off if she's watching TV and a big rock crashes into the window.

She gives me a friendly smile at the door. Upstairs Izzy

smiles at me as well, and this is not so bad, two smiles in one day.

There is an advert for pensions lying on the floor. It shows a happy couple on a yacht, drinking wine.

I have no idea why people pay for pensions when you don't get the money back for more years than you can think about. I have no idea how people get enough money to buy yachts. I have no idea why yachts cost so much money. I have no idea why I spend even a second thinking about yachts.

'What are you thinking about?' says Marilyn.

'Pensions and yachts.'

'So you are still feeling bad about Cis leaving you?'

'Yes.'

Izzy has put up a poster in the hallway of a female bodybuilder. She is wearing a purple leotard which shows off most of her body. Her back is V-shaped, muscular and strong.

Marilyn and Izzy both play in a band and so do I so we talk about how difficult it is to get gigs and how appalling all other bands are and how much we detest all the other bands in the area.

'How is the weightlifting going?'

'Very well,' says Izzy. 'I am twice as strong as I was two months ago. I'm on a special healthy diet and I'm thinking of joining a club. Except I can't find a good club. There was a women-only bodybuilding class at the local institute but they closed it down. And I don't want to go somewhere where men will laugh at me.'

'They wouldn't laugh if you were serious about it.'

'Yes they would. Dean thinks it's hilarious.'

'How is Dean?'

'I haven't seen him for a week. Do you think I'm looking stronger?'

'Yes,' I lie.

'Say hello to Ruby for us,' they say, as I head off home.

Cynthia thinks about her love, and suffers at the hands of the weather

I love the boy whose lips I brushed, thinks Cynthia, lying alone on her rubbish tip. I have only seen him for three seconds, but my love is more powerful than any love that has ever been.

She writes him a love poem on the outside of her sleeve.

One time Cynthia ate a boyfriend because he brought her a love poem and it was really bad.

Feeling sentimental, she now regrets this.

I will never eat another human, she vows. Or rather, I'll never eat another nice human being. I may chew on a few nasty ones, but only if they really deserve it.

She wonders how she can get to see Paris. The werewolf detectives are bound to be watching the old vicarage.

Rain starts falling in large slow drops and the wind carries some of the moisture under the railway arch that overhangs the rubbish tip. Cynthia shivers and seeks refuge under some sheets of cardboard. She dislikes the rain, especially when she is living rough.

A few yards along from her more bodies shiver in their temporary cardboard shelters, tramps and derelicts who live with her on the rubbish tip under the arches.

In friendship they sometimes offer her some of their methylated spirits to warm her up, but Cynthia is not a big drinker.

Back at my flat I ask Ruby if she thinks I should invest in a pension plan but she doesn't think it is a good idea at my stage of life, even though I specifically remember the advert said it was never too early to start. And I'm worried about forgetting to sign on because now we will have been thrown off the Social Security register. It will take weeks to get our claim sorted out and we will have no money for anything and we'll have to sit around for hours in the DHSS.

'Don't worry,' she says, 'I have a good idea for making money.'

'How come you got back with Domino?'

She shrugs.

Ruby tells me to read good books, although why she wants me to do this I am never quite clear.

She is always reading good books and she is a writer. She never shows me any of her writing except for the ongoing werewolf story, but I know she will be good.

Now she is busy plucking her eyebrows, so I give her artistic advice and make us some tea.

'How was the rehearsal?'

'It was good except we don't have a drummer any more and I can't play my guitar so well now my soul is missing.'

'Maybe you left it in your guitar case.'

I hurry through to my room and look.

'No. It isn't there.'

'Well, don't worry, it is bound to turn up somewhere, probably when you least expect it.'

'I could ask the Goddess of Electric Guitar Players if she's seen it.'

Ruby frowns.

'There is no such thing as the Goddess of Electric Guitar Players.'

Later on Domino arrives and criticises Ruby's eyebrows even though they are looking terrific. After a while they start fucking in the living room so I can't go in and watch television, but the picture isn't very good anyway since Ruby battered it with a brick when she couldn't find a good programme.

I sit in my bedroom and play my guitar some more, trying to remember the new things I worked out with Nigel.

The Goddess of Electric Guitar Players is called Helena. She looks after you when you are trying to learn a new song and if anyone throws a bottle at you when you are going on stage she reaches out a graceful hand and diverts it onto an amplifier. Also, if you have been assiduous in paying tribute to her, she will prevent your guitar strings from breaking and give you a gentle nudge if your solo is starting to bore everyone. She brings comfort to everyone whose fingers are sore from trying to learn a new chord and, if the occasion merits it, she will personally get inside your fuzzbox and make it scream and shriek.

A lovely goddess, Helena.

After a few minutes the people upstairs bang on the ceiling because I am disturbing them.

I sit and feel lonely. Sitting and feeling lonely is something I am a spectacular success at. I can do it for hours. Everyone is good at something.

There is a knock on the door. It is Izzy. I make her some tea and show her my cactus.

'Ruby says it is a sacred Aphrodite Cactus. Once it flowers Cis will fall in love with me. It is a wonderful coincidence that she picked it as a present for me.'

Izzy says that love is not necessarily all that good a thing and asks if I can lend her two hundred pounds because she needs an abortion.

Through in the living room there is a furious argument with screaming and shouting and banging. The front door slams.

Ruby storms into my bedroom. Her face is streaked with anger and tears and she screams about what a bastard

Domino is and how she had better not see him again or she will kill him, then she sits on the edge of my bed and complains that I don't have any comfy seats in my room. I wonder where Cis is. Cis had a comfy seat in her bedroom. But probably she is not in the comfy seat, probably she is in bed with someone nice, wrapped around him. Probably she is in bed with someone who is secure with a lucrative pension plan.

Izzy looks depressed and Ruby looks furious and I think about Cis and how difficult everything is but, lacking anything sensible to say, I keep quiet and let Ruby rage.

There is a tiny spot on the side of my cactus. It looks like it might be the start of a flower. There is nothing on Ruby's and I feel sorry for her, although really if Domino were to fall permanently in love with her it would be a very bad thing.

Cynthia hungrily thinks of home, but manages to find a meal in the end

Next morning Cynthia is dreadfully hungry. Remembering her promise not to eat reasonable humans, and not having any money at all, she wonders what to do about breakfast. She still has a few friends from her days at the vicarage, but she does not want to go begging food off them, though she would like to see Paris again.

She looks around for a stray a cat or two, but nothing moves save for the homeless inhabitants of the railway arches folding up their cardboard beds and storing them carefully for the following night.

Back home on the croft her mother fed her regular meals.

Today is Thursday. Every Thursday her mother made lamb stew and baked a cake. Cynthia craves for some lamb stew and a piece of home-made cake.

Three young men walk past and one of them wolf-whistles at her. Cynthia can see immediately that they are not very pleasant. She decides that it will be all right to eat them, and probably every bit as good as her mother's lamb stew.

So she does. Afterwards she vomits for three days till the lining of her stomach is dribbling through her nose.

My next contact is with a man who describes himself as fortyish and looking for a younger lover. He doesn't show. Probably this is just as well as I do not feel like a younger lover. I feel like a washed-out old person.

I feel bad when I wake up, so on the way to the toilet I kick the door and I almost break my foot and this is such a ludicrous thing to do that it cheers me up.

I limp through to Ruby's room with some tea. Ruby is in bed with a robot made out of metal boxes. Unprepared for this, I wonder if I should stay. I hover around for a few minutes, resolving finally to go out for a while and come back later with another cup of tea.

How did the robot get in? Usually I would hear anyone knocking on the door in the middle of the night. Of course, if it is a flying robot it could have come in the window.

I pour another cup of tea and look round at the mess in the kitchen. Neither me nor Ruby is very good at tidying up.

Back in Ruby's room the robot has gone and Ruby is talking to Izzy. Ruby holds the sheet over her, although I have seen her naked body many times. For some reason this must not be permissible when Izzy is in the room.

Izzy wants some breakfast, but Ruby refuses because she

says she cannot bear to eat in the morning, or any other time really.

'How is your knee?' she says.

'What do you mean? There's nothing wrong with my knee.'

'I thought it was sore,' says Ruby, and drinks her tea.

I walk down to Brixton. My knee starts to hurt.

Marilyn is out buying apples and she asks me if I've seen Izzy but I say no.

I go to buy some apples.

Cis is serving behind the counter.

I am stunned by her beauty and memories of good times.

'Hello, Cis. Four apples please.'

I point to the kind of apples I want.

Cis puts four of them in a scale and weighs them, then puts them in a brown paper bag.

'How long have you been working here, Cis?' I ask, heart pounding.

'What are you talking about?' says the assistant who, on close observation, looks nothing at all like Cis.

'Nothing,' I mutter.

The assistant classifies me as a harmless crazy person and gives me a fairly sympathetic smile. I hurry away.

This cactus is sacred to Aphrodite because on one occasion she was pursued through the southern desert by Ares, God of War and unwanted suitor.

Unsuited to such a rigorous chase and unable to fight him off (Aphrodite is no coward, but Zeus refused to give her proper fighting skills, leading to her being pursued from the field of combat at Troy) Aphrodite falls to the ground.

A brave shepherdess, seeing her plight, rushes up, rips a

nearby cactus out of the ground and rams it between Ares's legs. He is forced to retire from the scene, badly hurt.

'Thank you,' says Aphrodite. 'Why are you crying?'

'My lover left me by this cactus,' wails the shepherdess. 'It reminded me of him. I used to sit and watch it grow. Now it is dead.'

Aphrodite, graciously sympathetic, replants the cactus and it comes back to life.

'When it flowers your lover will return,' she says. 'And now and forever, in memory of my rescue, this cactus will be sacred to me, and will bring good fortune to all lovers who are gentle and kind.'

'We will make money from writing,' announces Ruby.

'What writing? Is your book ready?'

'No. Magazine writing.'

I wait for her to explain. Ruby is very smart and I know that her idea will be good.

'I have been down to the library and stolen all their magazines. And I have stolen some more from the newsagents. I got sex magazines, karate magazines, football magazines and romance magazines. And photo-love stories.'

'So? Are we going to sell them? It won't get us much money. Couldn't you steal something more valuable?'

'No. What I mean is, we will write stories for them and they'll pay us.'

I am dubious. But Ruby insists it will be easy, in fact what she has in mind is copying stories practically word for word and just changing a few names here and there and then sending them off.

'The stories are all crap,' she tells me, 'so there is no reason for them to reject ours.'

Cynthia falls ill, seeks help, and learns she is still pursued

Cynthia werewolf has only one friend in the world of werewolves, her kindly Uncle Bartholomew.

An eccentric professor, Uncle Bartholomew lives alone with his experiments. He never got over his wife leaving him for a movie star.

'Let me in, Uncle Bartholomew, I'm sick.'

'Cynthia, what are you doing here? It's not safe. Only the other day the detectives were here looking for you. Lupus the Werewolf King wants you dead.'

'I'll be dead soon enough, Uncle. I can't eat.'

Uncle Bartholomew makes her some tea and wraps her up in a warm blanket. He can see she is not well. This makes him sad. He always liked Cynthia and her rebellious ways.

'Tell me your problems.'

'I can't eat. I vowed only to eat bad people but they make me vomit. For some reason the only people that taste nice are my friends. Now I don't have any friends left. I'm so lonely I could die. And I'm in love, but I can't go and see him because I know I'll eat him. Help me before I eat all the nice people in London, and die of loneliness.'

Uncle Bartholomew offers her some vegetables but Cynthia has never been keen on vegetables. Anything green makes her want to scream.

My foot still hurts from kicking the door, in fact it hurts worse than before. My knee seems to be better. Ruby's idea about writing stories seems quite good to me.

It is March. My cactus shows no sign of flowering. The

spot on the side has disappeared. Ruby's is barren as well. Perhaps they only flower in the summer. Although if they come from a desert in the southern hemisphere this might be their summer. I don't know if this matters. Do the months change round for a cactus when it is transported to another hemisphere?

Months later we are still flying through space.

The Captain comes to see me.

'Why are you not doing any scientific experiments?' he demands.

'I am busy writing a new song.'

'You are meant to be doing experiments.'

'I'm bored with them. Anyway, when we reach a new planet it will probably be full of primitives. They will not care at all that we have discovered a new scientific data. But if I play them a few songs it is bound to get us off to a good start.

The Captain leaves in disgust. I can tell he hates me.

When my fingers are sore from playing the guitar I ask the computer to give me something to read. It puts a file on the screen called ancient myths.

Ascanazl, I read. *The ancient Inca Spirit Friend of Lonely People. He would appear to anyone who was lonely and talk to them.*

That would be nice.

Another crew member comes into my cabin and I play her my new song. She says she likes it because the guitar notes remind her of rain on Earth, and she misses the rain. She forgives me for almost getting us all killed in the meteor storm.

She even asks me if I would like to come through to her

cabin and lift some weights together, but I decline the offer. I have no enthusiasm for exercise.

And I am very sad, because I left my girlfriend back on Earth and I know I will never see her again.

I call up the book of myths and legends on the computer screen again. *Ascanazl's mother*, it says, *was well known for her friendly manners. She lived quietly at the end of the rainbow, but every so often she would go round villages bringing food and medicine to poor peasants.*

On one occasion she was bathing naked in the woods when a mortal hunter came across her by chance.

'It is forbidden for mortals to see the unclothed form of a goddess,' she said. 'But never mind. Just go on your way and we'll forget all about it.'

Ruby sends me out to steal some more magazines. On the way to the shop I pass the flower stall and I stare at the daffodils for awhile.

A large jet flies overhead and I stare at it as well, but I am surprised and perturbed to see five small fighters fly over and start attacking it with rockets and lines of tracer fire.

The airliner does its best to fight off the unexpected attack but as its only armament is a small machine-gun that the navigator pokes out the door it has little chance. Soon a rocket blows its tail off and it hurtles to the ground. More pieces break off before it hits, scattering the area with burning debris that starts fires in all the houses.

Luckily the paper shop is unaffected and I quickly pocket a few magazines while the assistant is still stunned by the explosion following the crash.

At Ruby's suggestion I am wearing my army trousers with big pockets specially for the occasion.

Loaded down with dubious magazines, I hurry home.

Cynthia feels sad about Morgan and learns about her psychic appetite

Cynthia watches television in her Uncle's house. The day-time soap operas are full of difficult romances. This reminds her of Paris, and makes her immensely sad.

She wonders if he is in sleeping with anyone. The thought of Paris fucking someone else makes Cynthia want to plunge a knife into her stomach and twist it round and round. And maybe jump off a cliff as well and take poison and jump under a tube train and slash her wrists with broken glass.

Uncle Bartholomew shambles through in his carpet slippers.

'I've analysed your blood sample,' he says. 'And I know what is wrong with you. You've eaten too many hippies. Your system is infused with LSD. LSD has a very bad effect on us werewolves. You've developed a psychic appetite.'

'What is that?'

'It means you can sense who is a good person and who is not. And only the good ones will taste nice to you. In fact, the nicer someone is, the better they'll taste.'

Cynthia is about to enquire further when the werewolf detectives arrive. She is forced to flee, silver machine-gun bullets bouncing and ricocheting around her.

'There may be other symptoms,' calls out her Uncle after her.

After the young girl's body was found outside my Battersea squat the police asked me some questions. Not very many questions, really. A few days later I saw four men in a car in the street who looked like policemen. That was all.

I got a temporary job helping in a chemical factory

somewhere near Chiswick, and carried drums of chemicals around and mixed them in huge metal vats. The person who worked with me was a fifty-year-old Kenyan who read Latin at tea break and classical Greek at lunch. He had studied for a law degree but switched half way through to mathematics. Then he had some personal problems and was unable to finish his degree. Now he just read Latin and Greek in his breaks at the chemical factory.

The third member of the shift was heavily tattooed with blood-dripping roses crawling down his arms and he told me he never went out with his wife any more because she had put on too much weight.

Every morning, because of the times of the trains I could catch to work, I was three minutes late arriving and for this I would be docked fifteen minutes' pay. But as the alternative was arriving twenty-seven minutes early this seemed like the best thing to do.

The foreman thought I was a good worker and encouraged me to take the job permanently, but after a few weeks some chemicals splashed out of a drum and burned my eyes.

My burning eyes were the most painful thing I have ever experienced, by a long way.

There was no doctor in the factory and nothing in the medical supply box but bandages, so I went to the toilet and washed and washed them with water, hoping that I would not lose my sight. Then I went home on the bus with my eyes burning under a bandage, lifted at one corner to let me see, and lay around crying and burning for a while.

I gave up the job. The Social Security suspended my benefit for leaving work without good grounds.

My eyes got better. My next job was the one laying cement, which was horrible as well. I didn't get my eyes burned but it ruined my boots. After every shift I would shake with exertion and if it rained on the way home my feet would ooze with mud and cement.

All the buildings in the street were burning after the fight in the sky, but I make it home safely through the police and fire engines and ambulances screaming this way and that.

Back home Ruby is in her bedroom, listening to music.

'There were some aeroplanes fighting in the sky,' I tell her. 'But I managed to get some magazines.'

Ruby goes and puts the kettle on. She says that she is hungry and wishes we had some food.

She gets her typewriter out and we start copying some stories.

I read out some stories and Ruby types them out, changing them a little. It takes longer than we think it will and after making up a karate story and a doctor-nurse romance I am bored with the whole thing because as far as I can see the stories we are copying already say everything there is to say about karate tournaments and doctor-nurse romances. But Ruby wants to do some more because she is convinced we can earn money and Ruby and me both need money. Sometimes I have jobs but Ruby never works. I think she is becoming more and more disinclined to leave the house. Everything we need, I bring in.

Ruby hunts out another magazine from our bundle. It is called *Blow* and is comprised entirely of photographs of men spanking women or hitting them with canes.

'One of Danny's,' she says. 'We are bound to get published in it.'

Danny, the person whose door I ripped off in frustration some years ago in Battersea is now a sex magazine editor. We still know him.

'But it is total nonsense,' I protest. 'And objectionable in every way.'

'No one will ever know. And these specialist sex magazines are sure to pay well.'

I read out the story and Ruby puts it down, changing it round a little.

There is a knock on the door. When I answer it I find Cis outside, delivering our new telephone directory.

'Cis has just bought us a new telephone directory, Ruby.'

'Stop being foolish and get on with the story,' demands Ruby.

I have no idea why she says this. It is true, I have the telephone directory as proof.

When we have a break for a cup of tea we go and look at the cactuses.

No flowers, and it is the beginning of April. Ruby, however, is getting on well with Domino and does not seem too worried. She sympathises with me.

'It will flower soon. Probably Cis knew that it was a sacred Aphrodite Cactus and gave it to you deliberately.'

Ruby tells me that we have to move next week.

'Why?'

'Pauline is coming back.'

It is Pauline's flat. We are only living there temporarily. I forgot all about it. We can never find anywhere proper to live.

'What will we do?'

'I'll find us somewhere,' says Ruby, matter-of-factly.

In the Battersea Squatters' Association we planned to defend a house against Wandsworth Council after they gave the tenant notice of eviction. The Squatters' Association was determined to resist this eviction because everywhere there were homeless people and everywhere there were empty houses.

We formed a defence committee and appointed one person in charge of the physical defence and one person in charge of publicity, and made ready to resist the eviction.

'I met Izzy today,' continues Ruby. 'She was buying some new weights. Well, actually she was standing on a corner about to burst into tears because she's pregnant and Dean doesn't want to see her any more because he has a new girlfriend. But after that she was going to buy some new weights.'

'Was she looking any more muscly?'

'No. Izzy is one of the least muscly people I've ever seen. But it keeps her happy.'

We have a break from writing.

'Relationships are terrible,' I say, and Ruby agrees. I ask her if she thinks it would be a good idea for me to go and visit Cis but she says probably it wouldn't be.

'How about if I phoned?'

'That might be better.'

'Will you phone for me?'

'What good will that do?'

'I don't know. But I'm terrible on the phone.'

'I bought some new earrings when I was out,' says Ruby. 'Look, little rainbows. One for you and one for me.'

Cynthia eats a motorbike messenger

Cynthia is in worse trouble than ever. She can only eat people she likes.

The rest of the werewolves scattered throughout Britain hardly ever eat people at all. They live as normal humans. Unfortunately Cynthia has never been able to adapt.

A motorbike messenger stops to ask her directions. New on the job, he has lost his way between Marble Arch and Brixton. He has a nice smile and a friendly manner.

Cynthia eats him while his radio crackles in the background.

A pleasing snack, she thinks, riding off on his motorbike. That's strange, I never knew how to ride a motorbike before.

Suddenly she realises that she never meant to eat him in the first place.

She would rather have made friends and seen more of his friendly smile. Her appetite has become completely uncontrollable.

Outside it is raining with maybe a few hailstones and I wish the sun would shine so I could see a rainbow because I like rainbows and if I don't see Cis soon I will go totally mad.

'I wish I could see Domino,' says Ruby. 'And I'm fed up with all this rain. This must be the wettest year in history. I'm going to go and paint some sunshine.'

I make her some tea and she strides through to her room to paint. I am envious of Ruby's ability to paint. I am envious of all artists. I have a good plan for seeing Cis.

Lamia the Eastern Huntress Goddess used to exercise daily to keep her body perfect. She fell in love with a mortal painter and asked him to paint her. Unfortunately, none of the paintings could capture her perfect beauty. Eventually, dispirited by his failure, he took his own life by drowning himself under a waterfall. Afterwards Lamia cried for her lover for forty days and forty nights and her tears fell like rain, washing away crops and houses in a flood of grief.

Izzy told me she heard that Cis was going to art school. I hope she does well. I would hate it if Cis became discouraged and drowned herself under a waterfall.

'Ruby, I have a good plan for seeing Cis and also it will probably help you to see Domino, and my zip is stuck can you help me with it please?'

Ruby kneels down in front of me and tries to loosen my zip. Her room smells of paint and I notice she is losing weight.

The person in charge of the physical defence of the squat in Battersea went slightly overboard and barricaded the bay windows with railway sleepers, filling up the gaps with cement and barbed wire. To fit the railway sleepers in he organised the removal of half the floorboards and part of the ceiling. With the windows barred and barricaded and the doors nailed shut the house was practically invulnerable. The only way in was by ladder into the upstairs window.

We made a yellow banner with 'Battersea Squatters' Association' written on it. On the day of the eviction we would hang it out of the window.

Three people were nominated to stay inside the house when the bailiffs arrived. The rest of the squatters were to stand outside protesting. Nominated as one of the three, I was less than enthusiastic. I knew that when the bailiffs couldn't get in they would call the police and we would be arrested. But I had not done much for the Squatters' Association and it was my turn to be useful.

Ruby has to struggle with my zip for a long time but I trust her implicitly to fix it without doing me any damage. And if by chance she did do me some harm then she would call an ambulance right away. She is the sort of person who would have no problem in calling an ambulance and demanding they came right away, no excuses accepted.

Ruby is a wonderful friend and I worry about her losing weight. Ruby is the best friend I've ever had. Ruby is the best friend in the history of the world. It enrages me that she will lose weight and maybe harm herself all because of Domino. I hate Domino.

'There, your zip is free. If Domino saw me in such close proximity to anyone else's penis he would go crazy. Do you like my sunshine painting?'

'Yes, it's wonderful. The lilac sun matches your dress. How is your writing coming along?'

'Fine. I'll show you a story soon. When's your gig?'

'We had to postpone it again. We still can't find a drummer. Do you want to hear my plan for seeing Cis?'

'OK. What's your plan for seeing Cis?'

'Well, first you ring up and check if she's home. If she answers the phone you put it down immediately like it is a wrong number, but if she's out then there's a good chance we could accidentally run into her. It is Thursday and Cis will cash her Giro today and probably go for a drink. There are four pubs in Brixton she might go to and we can call in to each one casually as if we were just there for a drink ourselves and if she is there I'll naturally just have to say hello. She won't realise I've planned it. If she isn't at any of the pubs she might be at some friend's house so we can call round her friends on some pretext and if that fails we could wait at the end of her street and see if she happens by.'

'What pretext are we going to use for calling round on her friends?'

'I don't know,' I admit. 'I hoped you could think of one.'

'And what will you do if you meet her?'

'I'll say hello.'

'What then?'

'I don't know. I haven't planned that far ahead. But there is a good chance we'll run into Domino along the way.'

'Fine,' says Ruby. 'It seems like a good plan to me. Let's do it.'

Cynthia does not accomplish very much

Cynthia werewolf rides around on her motorbike. She loves to take corners dangerously and threaten pedestrians. Unfortunately she cannot stop thinking about Paris. She is tormented by the thought of him sleeping with other women. When she –

There is a sudden silence as Ruby comes to a halt.

'What's the matter?'

'I have writer's block. I don't know what happens after Cynthia rides away on her motorbike.'

'Make her eat a few more people,' I suggest. 'I like it when she eats people.'

Ruby frowns, and plays with the material of her dress, and she tells me she is feeling bad. She is troubled because Domino has not been around for a few days. He might be sleeping with someone else. Just like Cynthia.

'Do you think about Cis fucking someone else?'

'About twenty or thirty times a day.'

'What do you do to stop thinking about it?'

'I don't do anything. Nothing works. I can remember every inch of Cis's body perfectly. I can picture her fucking someone else like it was happening right next to me. Usually after a while I get to wondering if it hurts very much when you slit your wrists.'

'It would here,' says Ruby. 'We don't have any sharp knives. We'd better get drunk instead.'

We hunt out our money. I like whisky but Ruby likes brandy, so I buy a bottle of brandy at the off licence. The off licence is full of Irish women buying Irish whiskey. They have all come over to have abortions in Britain because it is illegal in Ireland. In London they are lonely, separated from their friends and families, forced to travel abroad like fugitives. They buy the Irish whiskey to cheer them up.

I wish them good luck and take home a bottle of brandy. Then Ruby and I drink it as fast as we can till it makes us fall asleep. It is quite a good idea of Ruby's, because you can't really think of anything when you are collapsed drunk on the floor, and next morning you have a terrible hangover and this is good for taking your mind off other things as well.

Come the day of the eviction the publicity person had done his job fairly well and other squatters from south London were there to help us picket. Some pressmen from small local papers arrived with cameras.

All the squatters were cheerful but I was nervous. The week before one of the women in our group had been arrested for causing a fight at the dole office and she described to me how the police put her in a cell all night and the cell seemed as big as a matchbox. I did not want to be locked up all night in a tiny cell.

Upstairs in the barricaded house we three occupants had a pile of things to throw at the bailiffs. Plastic bags full of paint and piles of rotted fruit and, strangely, cold porridge.

I became more and more nervous and wondered if I could escape over the rooftops when the police arrived. I wondered if it would be normal police or the Special Patrol Group, because the Special Patrol Group was very active in south London at this time.

Sitting in the window I looked up at the sky and wondered if some beings in a spaceship might fly down and rescue me.

'I like your new earrings,' says Marilyn, who has called round for a visit and a cup of tea.

'Thank you,' I say.

'Thank you,' says Ruby.

'Your flat is cold.'

'We're having problems with our bills. How is Izzy?'

'Stuffing herself with steak to help her muscles grow. And depressed about Dean, and her pregnancy.'

Ruby and Marilyn disappear and Cis is there in their place. She is wearing a lilac T-shirt I gave her with a cloud on the back and a rainbow on the front.

'I have wandered in here by mistake,' she says, 'I was on my way to spend my Giro at the pub.'

'Right,' I say. 'Perhaps I'll run into you there.'

'Nothing would induce me to eat a steak,' says Ruby. 'I hate steaks.'

Three bailiffs in suits arrived and shouted at us to come out.

'We have nowhere to live!'

They did not seem inclined to discuss it. But before we could throw anything at them they went away. Inside the house we were shivering with cold.

Some hours later still nothing had happened and the pickets from other areas began to drift away. By mid-afternoon it seemed certain that the bailiffs must have abandoned their efforts for the day and would not be coming back till the next day. We were tired, having been awake all night, so all three of us left to get some sleep while another member of the group climbed the ladder to keep look-out, just in case.

I was very relieved not to have been arrested by the Special Patrol Group, although I knew that after a break of a few hours I would have to go back.

But I didn't have to go back. Half an hour after we left to go round the corner to our squats, the bailiffs returned with some police and the look-out immediately fled out over the roof and down into the back alley. The bailiffs repossessed the house without any difficulty.

As an act of resistance it was a pathetic failure. And it ended the Squatters' Association because while previously we had been negotiating with the council for possible rehousing, the council was now extremely irate at all the damage we had caused to the house in fortifying it.

'What about our re-housing negotiations?'

'Pay us twenty thousand pounds for the damage you did to the house and we'll think about it.'

We were all evicted soon after and no one made much fuss. The local news programme showed pictures of the inside of the house, all cemented and barbed wired and no longer habitable. This is what these vandals do when they squat, they said.

This all sticks in my mind very clearly. I'm not sure why.

I moved to Brixton with Ruby and we still could never manage to find a secure place to live.

Cis had a nice council flat in her own name. I liked sleeping there. But she argued too much with her sister and moved back in with her mother. I don't know what the arguments were about. I suppose there was lots of Cis's life I didn't know anything about.

Maybe it sticks in my mind because it was all so futile. But it wasn't a ridiculous effort. There shouldn't be empty houses when people have nowhere to live.

Possibly removing the floor and the ceiling was a tactical error.

Cynthia looks for a leather jacket and eats another lover

'I suffer from terrible claustrophobia,' says Marion, a very agreeable young woman who sells clothes in Kensington Market.

Cynthia has gone there looking for a cheap leather jacket.

The jackets are all too expensive but she is pleased to meet Marion.

They eat carrot cake and arrange a date.

Out at a disco they have a happy time together. Cynthia thinks that if she can't be with Paris, being with someone else she likes is bound to make her feel better. And she is determined not to eat Marion, no matter what happens.

'Would you like a snack?' says Marion, back at her flat.

'Yes please,' says Cynthia, and eats her without thinking.

She goes back to her rubbish tip to cry. Her psychic appetite seems to have left her with no control whatsoever. It only needs someone she likes to offer her food and she will eat them.

Why oh why was I born with such terrible problems, she thinks. And where oh where is Paris, the great love of my life?

Some council workers arrive to clear away the rubbish. Cynthia is forced to move on. A homeless refugee and the unhappiest of werewolves, she skulks around in alleyways, rummaging for food in dustbins.

Afterwards she notices that she has started to suffer from claustrophobia.

I wonder about Izzy's pregnancy.

'If we sell enough stories we can lend Izzy the money for an abortion,' says Ruby, telepathically.

'Maybe she will build huge muscles and win a bodybuilding competition.'

'I doubt it,' says Ruby. 'Not in the next month, anyway.'

I am helping her with her hair. She has a mass of matted dreadlocks and ties thin colourful ribbons into it. I like helping with it.

'I will post the stories,' says Ruby, 'because I don't trust you not to lose them.'

She takes the bundle in a large brown envelope and I wander out to see what I can find.

Down in Brixton market I meet Rosaline from the Dead City Dykes and she tells me to come to their gig next week and I say I will although every day someone tells me to come to their gig, the place is full of people putting on small gigs for their bands and telling me to come to them.

'I just wrote a new song,' she tells me. 'It's called 'My Spaceship Is Full of Plastic Daffodils.''

Next I meet an actress called Kath I know slightly. She tells me she is going to be in a play and I should come and see it because it will be a good play. It is about gypsies having problems living their life and always being moved on because no one wants them living next door.

I used to be an acting student, that's how I met Cis, we were acting students together. Our class was being taught by a famous director from Poland and Cis and I were playing the parts of lovers.

After having a drink in the pub with Kath I find myself being tattooed. I am shocked at this because I never really wanted a tattoo. It hurts. The needle looks like a dentist's drill and where it pierces the ink into my flesh the skin bleeds. Blood and ink run down my arm over the muscle and onto the hand of the tattooist, a fat man covered in tattoos who grips my arm tightly so the skin doesn't move.

Behind him is his assistant, a young skinhead only half covered in tattoos but catching up fast. His jeans are ripped to show off a tattoo over his knee. Today my knee has been hurting a lot.

'What your studio needs is a nice bunch of flowers,' I say, trying to make conversation. They are not great talkers.

Outside it is raining hard and two gypsies offer to sell me some sprigs of heather.

Back home I am very annoyed.

'Ruby, this has got to stop. I keep having these terrible hallucinations. I just imagined I was being tattooed, it was dreadful.'

'What are you talking about?'

She pulls up my sleeve.

'Nice tattoo.'

I look at it. It is a nice tattoo, under the matted blood. The blood is dark red going brown, just like the base of my cactus, which is dark underneath the green on top.

I apologise to Ruby.

'Did you post the stories?'

'No. I left them on the bus.'

'What?'

She left them on the bus. Somewhere in London bus drivers are sitting at their tea break pouring over sex and karate stories with our address at the bottom.

'Unless of course someone else picks them up on the bus.'

We look out the window to see if there is an angry group of feminists preparing to storm the flat, outraged at our not-very-liberating sex stories.

The coast seems to be clear. We decide to go out for a while, just in case.

'I brought you a sprig of heather.'

'Thank you,' says Ruby. 'It is a nice sprig of heather. It matches my dress. I met a drummer yesterday who is looking for a band. I gave him our phone number.'

I show everyone my new tattoo and they all seem to like it.

The director from Poland told us we had to start living our

parts more fully and made Cis and me become lovers right then so we made love on stage in rehearsal with the other students watching and learning their lines. When we were acting in a bodybuilding play we lifted weights all day together.

Cynthia goes home to visit her mother, who gives her a useful present

Cynthia's problems increase. Not only can she only eat nice people, but she is starting to take on their attributes as well. After devouring Marion she is claustrophobic for a month.

Still, she is pleased to know how to ride a motorbike.

Where oh where is Paris, she thinks, staring up at the moon. I will die if I don't see him. On the other hand, if I do, he might well die. My appetite seems to be beyond my control. What is to be done?

Risking an attack of claustrophobia, she jumps on a train and goes to see her mother on the croft in Scotland.

'Mother, you have to help me. How can I have a love affair without it turning into a tragedy?'

Her mother is not pleased to see her.

'What sort of shade of purple is that for a werewolf to dye her hair?' she demands. 'And how often have I told you, you have to wear shoes? You're not in the forest now, you know.'

'Right,' says Cynthia. 'I can see you don't want me here. I'll leave.'

Moved by some remnants of parental affection, Cynthia's mother fetches a necklace from her jewellery box.

'Take this. It is the family's hereditary werewolf soul jewel. Give it to the one you love and you will never want to

eat them. Now, get out of here before I phone Lupus. You disgust me.'

Cynthia leaves.

'No real daughter of mine would put seven earrings through each ear,' her mother shouts after her.

When I wake up the cactus is in full bloom. Its flowers, yellow, lilac and mostly beautiful, exceed everything I have dreamed of.

Cis shouts my name through the letterbox and I run down the hallway to open the door.

There is no one there. I have imagined it all.

'Why are you wandering naked in the hall?' asks Ruby, her lilac dress crumpled from sleeping in it.

'No reason.'

'Make me some tea.'

I put on a pot of water. We have an electric kettle but we are having trouble paying our last electricity bill.

The God of Foolish People Who Walk Around Naked in the Hallway Thinking Their Lover Is Shouting Through the Letterbox is called Alexander and really there is nothing good to say about him at all. He is more of a demon than a god.

His brother is called Philip the Terrible and he is responsible for delaying people's Giro cheques in the post and sending out electricity bills that no one can afford.

Yesterday Ruby and I spent four hours wandering Brixton trying to accidentally bump into our lovers but my plan was a failure. We met neither Cis nor Domino, despite calling into every place we could think of where they might be.

'Sometimes it's difficult to manufacture coincidences,' says Ruby, sharing a drink with me before closing time. 'A pity. I would have liked to fuck Domino right this minute.'

'We could try again tomorrow.'

'It won't do any good,' says Ruby, morosely. 'Nothing does any good. You fall in love with someone and they leave you and you feel like dying. You meet their friends in the street and you tell them how unhappy you are and you hope this news will get back to your ex-lover and they'll take pity on you. Or else you meet their friends in the street and you tell them you're having a great time and you hope this news will get back to your ex-lover and make them jealous. You think about things you could have done and what you would do differently if you had the chance, you wait for the phone or the doorbell to ring, you hang around the fringe of conversations hoping to hear some snippet of information about how they are.

'You can write poems and send them or not send them, you can turn up drunk at their house and plead with them to come back or turn up drunk and pretend you don't give a damn, you can send flowers or love notes or a few intellectual books, you can discuss it endlessly with your friends till they're sick of the sight of you, you can think about it all day and all night, imagining that somehow your mental power will win them back, you can sit on your own and cry or go out and make yourself frantically busy. You can think about killing yourself and warmly imagine how sorry they'll be after you do it, you can think about going on a trip round the world and probably when you got back you'd still hope to run into them on the street. You can do anything at all and none of it is any good. It is completely pointless. Lovers never come back. You can't influence them to do it and you would realise this if only you weren't so dementedly unhappy all the time.'

The pub is noisy with little room to move, and we have to guard our drink against a marauding barman who keeps trying to snatch it off the table even though there is a good half-inch left at the bottom.

'So we won't try again tomorrow?'

'We might as well. What else is there to do?'

'Write poems?'

'What was it like in bed with Cis?'

'I can't remember.'

'That's a pity. If you could remember it it might cheer you up.'

The rain beats on my bedroom window and seeps through the warps in the frame to make small puddles on the window-sill. With my finger I draw the puddles into little shapes like spaceships and pretend they are flying free through the sky.

The drummer that Ruby gave my phone number to has joined the band and we are already planning to play our much-delayed gig. I am writing a new song. It is about Cis. It will be wonderful. We will make a record out of it and it will be a success. Cis will hear it, realise she really does love me and come back. I think this sort of thing all the time.

It will be a rush to get the song written and rehearsed in time for the gig, but it will be worth it.

I shout to Ruby to come and listen and I play her the chords. She says she likes it.

'Do you think it might touch Cis's heart and make her want to see me again?'

'It might.'

'If I don't see her again I'm going to commit suicide.'

'How?'

'I'm not sure. I thought I might carve my goodbye note on my chest with a kitchen knife, then go and die on her doorstep.'

'Well at least she'd remember you. But don't do it yet, I'll miss you.'

'OK, I'll leave it a while.'

Nigel appears with a bundle of posters, drawn by us and photocopied at the cheap place in Coldharbour Lane. Tonight we will go and stick them up all over Brixton. I do not enjoy flyposting but I like seeing our name on walls. Also, if we don't do it no one will know about the gig.

Ruby says she will cook a meal so I can eat when I get back, but when I arrive home she claims that just looking at food made her feel sick so she had to throw it all down the toilet.

'I spent the evening writing a story instead. It's about you and Cis fucking. You want to hear it?'

'Of course.'

'Right. Sit down comfortably.'

The lonely old lady on her balcony never looks as if she is sitting down comfortably. Maybe when you are old you can't get comfortable if you are lonely, no matter how many well-made chairs you have saved up for your retirement.

'It's my period,' said Cis, one day. 'I love having sex when it's my period. Let's fuck till we're swimming in blood.'

So we do. Cis is wearing a tampon. I take it out for her and it is red with menstrual blood. Cis likes her menstrual blood. So do I. In the air it quickly dries and goes brown.

I lick the blood from around the lips of her vagina. Cis likes this but the pressure of my tongue is often not quite enough to make her come so when she is excited I press harder on her clitoris with my finger and I slide another finger up her anus and then she comes quite quickly in a noisy flurry of blood and urine and some other liquid that I can't put a name to.

Next she sucks my penis. I like her doing this and when I come she keeps the sperm in her mouth and stretches up to kiss me quickly so she can spit some of it back into my mouth while it is still warm.

After a little while we start fucking. First Cis lies on top of me, then I lie on top of her. She puts her legs around my neck and while she is doing this she rubs her clitoris with her fingers till she reaches orgasm. She turns over so I can fuck her from behind. Her vagina is very wet and when I glance down I see that my penis and the inside of her thighs are covered in her blood. After I come she sits up and sperm and blood and vaginal fluid dribble from between her legs and we stick our fingers in the liquid and paint it on each others bodies. I paint it round her nipples and she paints it round mine so when we next embrace both of our chests are smeared with a sort of brownish glue.

We fall asleep for a while and when we wake Cis wants to lie on top of me while I suck her breasts and reach my hands between her legs. She trembles slightly when I do this and digs her nails into my skin. I can smell the stink of our sweat-covered bodies and it is the thickest smell of sex I have ever experienced. As Cis comes I again slide my finger up her anus. 'Fuck me there,' she says. Needing lubrication, I smear more of her menstrual blood onto me and mix it with saliva and she rubs some cream on my penis so that it slides easily into her. I fuck her like this from behind and then she turns over, telling me that we can fuck anally from in front as well, which we do, while she stretches her arm around me and inserts her finger in my anus and pushes it in and out fairly violently, and slightly painfully.

After I come Cis wants me to lick her cunt again. Good. It takes around an hour for her to orgasm and she makes enough noise to wake the whole street. We fall asleep for a long time.

Next morning our bodies are smeared with every human excretion. On our thighs and genitals, and on the sheets, is a hardening mixture of blood, sweat, semen, saliva, vaginal fluid, penis lubricant, shit, urine and the bright red lipstick Cis bought in the market last week.

We wash our bodies but the sheet seems beyond help, so after a few days we throw it out.

Fucking with Cis is wonderful fun.

'Did you like it?' asks Ruby.

'I certainly did. It sounded terrific. No wonder I miss her.'

Our toilet is blocked because of all the food Ruby has emptied down it.

We discover that neither of us has ever cleaned a toilet. We are not keen to start now. Ruby suggests pouring bottles of bleach into the bowl and so it happens that we have lots of spare bleach because I had to buy six bottles to get a free booklet on looking after house plants.

After a day or so the toilet is clear again and Ruby promises to throw our food only in the bin in future.

Lovers never return. Stories about people who go out and win back their lovers are all lies.

Cynthia successfully makes love, and feels less lonely

Back in London Cynthia wastes no time in trying out the necklace. She disguises herself as a postman in case the werewolf detectives are still watching the old vicarage, and sneaks in to see Paris.

He is delighted to see her.

Cynthia gives him the necklace. They fuck happily all night.

He is not a very good lover but Cynthia shows him how to be a better one. All werewolves are wonderful lovers.

When he falls asleep, late on into the morning, Cynthia lies contentedly beside him. Lonely no more, she thinks, and it is a very happy thought.

Ruby and I move house.

We grind through the process of sorting out our benefit claims, visiting the Unemployment Office and the Social Security Office. Sitting waiting to be called I worry that some clerk has already shouted out my name and I've missed my appointment, even though I know that I haven't.

Looking round vacantly at all the noisy and quiet people sitting there, I wonder what it is that they all do. I am eager to get home in case my pot plant has flowered.

Our spaceship crashes on a sparsely-populated world killing all the crew except me and the robot.

Outside the world is made up of bleak and empty plains split up by a few canyons where small groups of humanoids cluster amongst black vegetation, eking out their existence under a feeble blue sun.

The spaceship is beyond repair. I take the robot and go to the nearest community, looking for help.

At the edge of the canyon I am stopped by a force field. Scientifically primitive, the inhabitants have developed powerful mental abilities.

'Go away,' says an elder.

'Where?' I say.

'Anywhere but here.'

I trudge on across the plain. The robot is able to synthesise a little food from the rubble but, insufficiently powered by the blue sun, the food it provides is thin and unsatisfying.

On the edge of the next canyon the same thing happens. The inhabitants will not let me in.

I walk on alone.

'Make a radio,' I instruct the robot. 'So I can talk to Earth.'

The robot shakes its head. It cannot make a radio. It can't talk either.

It is not much of a robot.

The house that we move to is a flat on the Loughborough Estate and it is the only squat that I ever actually open myself. I borrow a jemmy and jemmy the door, ripping off the security cage the council has fixed over the door. With the jemmy it is easy and gives me a feeling of power. Ruby has obtained some fuses from a friend and she fits them into the fusebox.

'A brief prayer,' she says, lowering her head.

'Great and kind Tilka, Guardian Goddess of Squatters everywhere, please make our electricity work.'

Right away we have electricity. The whole thing has gone very smoothly, although being on the fourth floor and the the lifts not working I have a lot of hard carrying to do.

Days later me and the robot reach the next community. There the elders also refuse me entry. They are dressed in yellow robes, with long silver earrings studded with opals.

'Please let me in. I have been walking for days and I'm coming down with fever.'

They refuse. Sweating with an alien disease, I sit down on the edge of the canyon and watch them going about their business, although under the poor light of the blue star I can't really make out what their business is.

When I rest against some of the black vegetation it crumbles into ash and settles quickly on the windless plain.

'OK robot,' I say, resigning myself to a friendless existence. 'It looks like I'll have to teach you to play chess.'

But it never really gets the hang of it and after a day or so I abandon the attempt and we just sit and watch the humanoids scuttling about, doing whatever it is they do.

The robot synthesises some medicine to cure my fever. It is not completely useless.

Around this time Ruby is involved in a fight with Domino and he hits her on the side of the ear and bruises her. When she arrives back in the flat she is trembling with fury and she has a cut on her foot from storming across the concrete outside. I am outraged but Ruby doesn't want to do anything about it, just not see him again. When any of her friends say that Domino deserves some violence himself, she brushes it off as an irrelevance.

She spends days writing in her room, and paints a little. Ruby is a good artist but generally doesn't bother doing anything when things are going well with Domino.

Because it seems like we might starve to death, I think maybe I should find a job. Ruby, busy writing, agrees to phone up the agency for me.

'How does thirteen-hour nightshifts in a private mailing warehouse sound to you?' she calls, covering the mouthpiece of the phone.

'No, I don't want it.'

'Fine,' says Ruby down the phone. 'What's the address?'

Cynthia is happy living with Paris

Cynthia and Paris have a wonderful time. She lives in his room and he does all the shopping. This way the werewolf detectives will not find her.

Except when Paris is out shopping, they fuck all the time. Werewolves can have wonderful orgasms, and so can their lovers. And she never has any desire to eat him, apart from a few small bites here and there.

Later in the day Ruby helps me make some sandwiches. I am too gloomy about the prospect of a thirteen-hour night-shift to put much energy into sandwich-making.

'Don't worry, it's well paid and you only have to do it for a few weeks.'

'But thirteen hours? At night?'

'It's only four shifts a week. Anyway, it will take your mind off Cis.'

'I will not have enough time left to look after our cactuses.'

'Two cactuses are called cacti. And you'll have plenty of time left. I think your one is starting to grow a flower bud.'

Waiting for the bus to take me to my new job I am harassed by werewolves. They are not sure whether to eat me or not because they have already had few good meals today but they think they might anyway.

Izzy appears in the distance.

'That's my friend Izzy,' I say to the werewolves. 'She is a champion weightlifter. She has immense muscles. If you give me any trouble she will beat you to death.'

The werewolves run away.

'Hi, where are you going?' says Izzy.

'I'm going to a new job doing nightshifts.'

'I'm going to the gym,' says Izzy. 'Look at my forearm development. Pretty good eh?'

'Yes.'

She is deluding herself. Her forearms just look the same to me. It is lucky the werewolves didn't look very closely.

Working at the mailing firm is like a punishment from God. The workplace is a draughty warehouse near Waterloo, and outside there is nothing but other warehouses with no one around so it seems that I am working alone in a desolate city, although only a few streets away there are busy shops and restaurants.

At the start of my shift I have to stand in a big wooden frame with pigeon holes everywhere. I collect a pallet of mail from round the corner, then sort it out into all the countries it has to go to.

It is all business mail. The businesses save money sending it through the mailing firm instead of the Post Office and the mailing firm makes a profit large enough for the owner to arrive in a Rolls Royce, though I never understand exactly where this profit comes from.

Each job of sorting can take hours and the foreman is keen for the work to be done quickly because if it is not then he will suffer for it.

There is an hour for a meal and two fifteen-minute tea breaks, which makes eleven and a half hours work.

At my meal break I think about Izzy. She doesn't want to have her baby. When I asked her if this was because she was getting on so badly with Dean she seemed slightly annoyed and said no, that had nothing to do with it, she just doesn't want a baby.

After many hours sorting it is time to load the truck. When the truck pulls up to the goods entrance and opens its back door it seems as big as a football stadium.

The mailbags are so heavy I can only just lift one to shoulder height, but loading the truck means carrying hundreds of them up a shaky ramp and then piling them up as far as I can reach above my head.

I am on 'E' shift. The other four workers are stronger than me. They sweat but they can cope. Towards the end of loading the truck I can hardly lift a mailbag above my knees.

Back home Ruby is writing a letter to her genitals and arranging the flowers I brought in to brighten up our new flat. Cis has forgotten all about me and is having fun with a string of devoted boyfriends.

It is four in the morning, my muscles are shaking and the forklift is bringing up another huge metal cage of sacks to be loaded.

'Mind your feet.'

The cage bangs down.

Here's a gentle ballad for all you lovers out there, croons the DJ from the radio on the wall. I pick up another sack and struggle into the truck, embarrassed that I am weaker than everyone else.

I feel ill. I want to phone up Cis and ask her to pick me up in her mother's car. If Cis did that all the other workers would be impressed by her beauty and would not mind so much that I am weaker than them.

She would take me home in her car. Then she would talk and talk like she liked to do and we could cook some terrible food.

I can see her in front of me. Here, Cis, have some business mail.

Cynthia learns that life is still full of problems

Cynthia prowls happily around in the backyard. Paris is away buying tea bags and a new plectrum for her guitar.

She has not eaten a human for weeks. Contented with her life, she is prepared to make do with vegetables.

Everyone in the house is a vegetarian.

Paris is away for a very long time. When he arrives home Cynthia throws herself into his arms and kisses him passionately, but Paris holds back slightly. She senses this immediately. A werewolf can always sense when someone is holding back, especially while kissing.

'What's wrong?'

Paris says he has met someone else.

'Do you love her more than me?'

Paris isn't sure.

There is a splintering crash. Cynthia thinks for a second that it is her heart breaking, but it is in fact eighteen werewolf detectives flooding in through the windows.

Ruby has many friends but she usually only sees them when her and Domino are not speaking. When they are together she mainly just sees him. I find this hard to understand because all of her friends are nicer than Domino. Everyone else in the world is nicer than Domino.

I practise my new song but I can't get it right so I go and make some tea for Ruby and she tells me about the contact article.

'But why a contact article?'

She looks at me patiently.

'I explained it all already. What's wrong with your memory these days?'

I shrug. I don't know. It seems to have disappeared.

'You remember that guy who used to live next to you in the Army Careers Office? The one whose door you ripped to shreds the night you arrived home with Anastasia?'

'The one who used to overdose all the time and lie around shivering? Of course I remember him, I could never get a bowl of cornflakes in the morning without stumbling all over him. Isn't he dead by now?'

'No, he is the editor of *Triple X Adult Fantasy Magazine*. And he told me he would pay us good for articles about meeting lots of bizarre contact people and fucking them. Or not fucking them, depending on what they want.'

'What else would they want?'

'I'm not sure. Maybe they might want to piss on us and stuff like that.'

I look at Ruby.

'Do we really have to let strangers piss on us to earn some money?'

'Well, maybe not. I figure maybe we could make some of it up. But anyway, we'll answer some ads and post a few ourselves and see what kind of replies we get.'

'Can I put an advert in for Cis?'

'No.'

I think maybe I will anyway. She might be lonely. She might be desperate to start going out with me again but too shy to ask, frightened that I will not want anything to do with her.

'Go and steal some more magazines after you've helped me practise with my diaphragm. And see if you can find some nice flowers, these ones are dead.'

Walking round to the shops I can't find the flower stall but I do meet Helena, benevolent Goddess of Electric Guitarists. She is resplendent and beautiful in a ruby-coloured dress.

I pay her proper respect, then I ask her if she could maybe help me with the chord changes in my new song.

'I'll try,' she says. 'But I am finding it difficult to concentrate. My girlfriend has left me.'

'You too?'

'I'm afraid so. This morning she kicked down my door and told me she never wanted to see me again. Take these daffodils for your flatmate. I don't need them any more.'

I buy a romantic fiction magazine and steal a sex magazine and take them back to Ruby. I feel sorry about Helena losing her girlfriend. Obviously it is a universal problem.

Ruby is pleased with the daffodils. I put most of them in the living room but I save two for my room where I put them next to the cacti. 'Look at these nice flowers. Why don't you grow some nice flowers too?'

It is now May. Although it is pouring rain outside we are well into spring and I am sure it must be the flowering season for cacti.

'Look at that tree,' says Ruby, pointing out the window. 'It is covered with lilac buds. Just like my dress. What do you think it is like being a tree?'

'I don't know. Peaceful, I suppose. But you would get wet all the time.'

Next day Ruby says she will take me for a day out. I ask her if I have to bring a bucket and spade but she says no, we're going to the British Museum.

At first I am not enthusiastic, but when we arrive I start to enjoy myself. Ruby holds my hand and we walk round roomfuls of exhibits: ancient Egyptian mummies, Greek armour, Persian carpets, all sorts of things. Groups of schoolchildren hurry about them from this glass case to that and serious tourists look at their guidebooks.

Some of the children point at Ruby's bare feet and she smiles at them before their teachers drag them off to look at more exhibits. The teachers are looking after large groups of children, but they do not seem to be harassed by it. I suppose they are specially trained.

After a while Ruby hunts out the information desk.

'Can we get a cup of tea anywhere?' she asks. 'And where is the armour that Hector stripped from the body of Patroclus at the siege of Troy?'

'The restaurant is at the far end of the ground floor,' the assistant tells us, pointing the way. 'And Patroclus's armour is in the room immediately above.'

'Thank you,' says Ruby.

We have to queue a long time for our tea but it comes in a good silver pot. Ruby tells me the story of Hector and Patroclus at the Siege of Troy and right after we go to look at the armour. It is still stained with ancient blood.

Next we look at huge carved lions that used to guard the gates of Babylon and in the ancient Syrian jewellery section we spend a long time staring at the earrings and deciding which ones we like best and which ones we'd like to wear if we could take them away.

When the museum shuts we buy a drink in the pub along the road. Ruby is happy, though I expect she wishes Domino was here.

'Who is the guardian spirit of museums?'

Ruby doesn't know. 'But whoever it is is doing a good job.'

It was a good visit. If Cis was still talking to me I'd ask if she wanted to come here and if she did she would like it a lot. She'd like to be at the seaside too, with a bucket and spade.

'If I'm stuck for some conversation with these contact people I can tell them all about the museum,' I say to Ruby, being practical.

Cynthia fights ferociously to save her life and finds herself in the sewers with rats

Cynthia is involved in a terrible battle with the werewolf detectives. Despite being fairly small, she is in fact one of the strongest, most ferocious werewolves ever to walk the midnight streets.

While Paris and the rest of the inhabitants flee, Cynthia plunges into her assailants' midst where it is difficult for them to bring their silver-bullet-filled machine-guns to bear on her.

Jaws crunching with rage, Cynthia sends several of her attackers to the werewolf afterworld before finally her legs are riddled with bullets and she has only strength left to plunge out through a window. She escapes on a motorbike.

Round the first corner she realises she no longer knows how to ride a motorbike. The effects of eating the motorbike messenger have worn off. The motorbike skids under a bus and Cynthia's ribs cave in under the impact.

Fortunately she is very resilient. It takes more than bullet-riddled legs and broken ribs to stop a ferocious young werewolf, particularly one that grew up strong on a lonely croft with porridge for breakfast every morning.

While the detectives pour out of the warehouse, Cynthia stumbles down a manhole into the sewers and paddles her way to freedom.

Rats flood out of every opening in the sewers, attracted by the blood that pours from her wounds, but Cynthia savagely fights them off and carries on swimming, blinded by blood, crazed with passion, and fearfully claustrophobic in the underground maze.

Ruby has disappeared. I have not seen her for three days. She is not at Domino's. None of her friends have seen her. I am frantic with worry. I trudge from place to place and after the first place it starts to rain. My clothes are soaked through and no one knows where she is. Dead images of Ruby in a torn lilac dress dance in front of me.

I meet Cis carrying some parts of a drum-kit but she won't talk to me. I meet a man with a terrible birthmark down one side of his face and bad acne on the other side and he trembles and tells me that nothing I suffer is as bad as the staring and avoidance of staring that he endures everyday. I meet a former flatmate of mine with a suitcase who is walking down to the Maudsley psychiatric hospital for a brief stay as an in-patient. I meet Gerry who plays bass guitar and doesn't like me because he thinks I tried to steal his girlfriend years ago. I denied it to everyone although it was true. I meet Mary who has had a baby and produces so much breast milk that she is on her way to the children's home with a spare bottle for the motherless babies alone in their cots. I meet all of the Dead City Dykes who claim to be the only lesbian speed metal band in the country and they tell me they will shake the nation when they find a new guitarist, but they haven't seen Cis and they haven't seen Ruby. I meet Izzy who is on her way to see a doctor to start abortion proceedings after calling into the sports shop for some heavier weights, and she hasn't seen Ruby either. I meet Alice who works in a travel agency and Maggie who is being evicted and Jane who is selling communist newspapers and Barry who has nowhere to stay, but none of them know where Ruby is and I become wetter and wetter and colder and colder and I end up in the centre of London looking in alleyways and other than this I don't know what to do.

A few years ago I walked round the centre of London with nowhere to stay the night, not knowing what to do. It was raining heavily and my clothes were soaked through. I wanted to be somewhere warm. Just being somewhere warm would make me very happy.

I meet a person at the edge of Soho who is friendly and we get talking and share a cigarette. His name is Phil and he is a drummer. He shows me a comic he is carrying and he says I can read it if I want. It is a tale about some spacemen lost after a meteor storm. I read it in a café he takes me to where we can sit all night.

The café is full of hopeless degenerates and I feel quite at home. One of them is called Spider because of the spider's-web tattoo across his neck. His long hair is filthy and even sitting in his seat he manages to give the impression of someone shambling about in an alleyway. As the night passes he starts to shake slightly and tap his foot to an imaginary rhythm.

I feel all right in the café, at least I have somewhere to sit for the night. On each table there is a vase with one yellowed plastic flower drooping over the edge and I find these quite pleasant.

Another person walks past and offers Spider a cup of tea and nods to me and I get bought a cup of tea as well. Pretty soon the tea buyer sits next to us.

He is about forty with a small tough face and thin hair tied in a little pony tail.

'Call me Jocko' he says, 'although it's not my real name. No one in London knows my real name.'

He seems pleased that no one in London knows his real name, and regales us with stories of his time as a security guard at the local amusement arcades.

'I used to carry a chopper. I found that better than a knife. I've had people come up and point shooters at my head.'

About three o'clock he invites me and Spider home.

Spider tells me that normally Jocko would not give him house-room so it seems that I am the attraction.

Jocko's door is bright green and battered. The original lock has been torn off and a new one has been fitted underneath with some metal panelling to strengthen it. Jocko has lots of pornography. A magazine called *Bits of Boys* sticks in my mind. When I was eight I wouldn't have known how to give a blow job.

Jocko is pleased that he has a nice room to stay in close to Soho, and very cheap, and pleased that he is at home with violence.

I sleep with Spider, although Jocko says I am welcome to stay in his bed if I will be more comfortable there.

Probably I will be more comfortable with Spider. He is very dirty but I am not very clean myself.

'Will I toss you off before you go to sleep?' says Spider, trying to be friendly, but I decline his offer.

Next day Jocko tries to make me stay in the flat but I say I have to leave. Seeing his small axe lying next to the knives and forks on the sink, I am very polite about it and promise I'll come back.

I desperately want Ruby to come back.

The nightmare in the mailing firm continues. After two weeks of thirteen-hour nightshifts I have turned into a zombie. During the day I seem to have no time to sleep because I am busy trying to organise our gig, and rehearse my new song about Cis, and look for Ruby. I struggle up the ramp, loading the truck. The DJ is playing records.

'Get a fucking move on,' says Mark, the shift foreman, as I start to wilt.

Mark knows all about being a shift foreman. He told me he learned it quickly because he doesn't just want to be a shift foreman all his life. And when he worked cleaning cars he learnt everything about cleaning cars in one day as well.

I pound down the last sack and collapse onto the floor. It is three o'clock, time for a fifteen-minute break. By the third shift of the week all five of us are so exhausted that we curl up on empty sacks and sleep during these fifteen minutes, although sleeping for fifteen minutes only makes you feel worse when you have to get up for the next lorry.

I think about Cis. I have never felt so lonely and hopeless as when lying on these mailsacks.

I want to go and tell Ruby about it. Ruby has disappeared.

'She's visiting her mother,' says Ascanazl, Spirit Friend of Lonely People, making a brief appearance. I know he is lying.

Here's a record for you, says the DJ. *It's from Cis, and the message is, come back, I love you.*

When I arrive back at the flat Ruby is home. I hug her and tell her how worried I was. She says she was visiting her mother and didn't I see the note she left in my room?

'No.'

'Or the one in the kitchen?'

'No.'

'Next time I'll spray-paint a message on the wall.'

She tells me it was a pieasant visit except her mother moaned about her not wearing any shoes.

She has brought back some fishfingers as a present from her mother so we cook them into sandwiches.

The sacred Aphrodite Cactus was first brought to Britain by

Brutus. Britain is in fact named after Brutus. He was a refugee from Troy.

Aphrodite, sympathetic to the defeated Trojans but unable to help militarily, gave the refugees food and supplies for their journey, and a few cactuses to help them with their love affairs.

Geoffrey of Monmouth won his true love, the daughter of a local noble, in this way. As soon as the cactus he presented her with flowered, she fell powerfully in love with him.

Mine will not flower. Neither will Ruby's. It is almost June. June must be a good flowering time for cacti.

I ask Aphrodite if there is any problem but she is too busy to talk to me because there are broken hearts everywhere. She refers me to Jasmine, Divine Protectress of Broken Hearts. Jasmine says she will see what she can do but she is also very busy. The number of broken hearts there are is increasing all the time.

'I know,' says Ruby. 'And there is not much to do about a broken heart. But don't worry. I heard that Cis is missing you.'

I finish the fishfinger sandwiches and bring them through on our metal tray, green with a tobacco advert.

'I think it is a little banal,' says Ruby.

'You told me you were keen on fishfinger sandwiches,' I protest.

'Not the fishfinger sandwiches. I love fishfinger sandwiches, as long as there is plenty of mayonnaise. I think your story is banal.'

'What story?'

She looks a little impatient.

'The one you told me last week. About your spaceship crashing and you walking around on the planet with a robot.'

I have no idea what she is talking about. I never told her any story like that. I have never been in a spaceship that crashed onto another planet. But I go along with it while we're eating our sandwiches.

'Why is it banal?'

'Because you stare at people doing things in canyons and don't know what they're doing and really that is a very obvious image and not original at all.'

I am hurt, despite having no idea what she is talking about. The amount of times I have helped Ruby with her hair, not to mention her sandwiches and putting in her diaphragm, she could be more polite than to call me banal.

She starts writing a letter.

'Is it to your genitals again?'

'No. This one is to my orgasmic response. I am really fucked off at my orgasmic response. Sometimes it is pathetic. I am gong to give it a good telling off.'

'I want to write something too.'

'How's your orgasmic response?'

'All right I think. I haven't had much use for it recently. I don't think I could write it a very interesting letter.'

'How about writing a hippopotamus story instead?' says Ruby. 'That would be nice.'

Cynthia descends into hell, develops a liking for country music and eats some more friends

Cynthia drags her broken body out of the sewers and back to her rubbish tip. She lies on a cardboard box and bleeds.

This is the end, she thinks. Life is unbearable. I am pursued everywhere and my body is mangled beyond repair. But this is as nothing compared to the fact that Paris doesn't love me any more. All I want is a friendly lover and a roof over my head. Is that too much to ask?

'Why are you bleeding all over my cardboard box?' demands a tramp. 'I have to sleep on that tonight.'

Cynthia loses consciousness. The tramp, a kindly soul, takes her to hospital where she almost dies. The doctors wonder how a young girl came to be riddled with silver bullets and have her ribs smashed to a pulp, but they battle to save her life.

Unconscious in hospital, Cynthia sinks into a terrible nightmare where she descends into the werewolf underworld. All around are the faces of the people she has killed and eaten.

'Die now,' they say. 'You deserve it.'

On the verge of being trapped there forever, the power of her love for Paris drags her back. She refuses to give up life while he is still in the world, and recovers.

She discharges herself from hospital and buys a bundle of sad country music tapes. All night long she lies on a rubbish tip howling at the moon and listening to Patsy Kline and Tammy Wynnette, a terrible state for any creature to be in.

Hopelessly and helplessly alone, Cynthia visits the South London Women's Centre for some company. There she meets a few friendly women who invite her to join their plumbing company. Cynthia considers the offer but as she is on the point of agreeing the full moon shines through the window. By this time a fairly crazed werewolf, Cynthia is unable to resist, and eats them all up.

She goes back to her rubbish tip in despair. She is tired after being hounded through the streets by irate friends of the mangled plumbers.

She changes back into human form and listens to some country music. Later that night she sneaks around the streets near to Paris's house, hoping she might accidentally run into him. Unfortunately, she is not successful, even though she checks all of his favourite pubs.

The young werewolf is in misery over Paris. Her only true

love and he fell for someone else. Cynthia loves him to distraction. She gave him part of her soul.

We have no food and I am hungry.

'Why don't you go round the shops for some chocolate?' asks Ruby.

'I am scared of the werewolves. Yesterday they almost trapped me at the bus stop.'

'Right. You better just wait till daylight.'

Ruby is surrounded by bits of paper and magazines and seems pleased with herself.

'Maybe I could risk the shops anyway. Do you have any money?'

'No. But we'll be rich after our contact article rocks the nation. I've sorted out the ads to reply to. Here's your bundle.'

There are about fifteen, mostly from sex magazines, a few from other things with contact columns. I read them.

BEAUTIFUL THIRTY-FIVE-YEAR-OLD RED-HAIRED WOMAN SEEKS YOUNGER MAN, PREFERABLY ARTISTIC AND ATHLETIC. MUST BE SEXUALLY SUBSERVIENT.

SINCERE GUY, FORTYISH, SEEKS YOUNG FRIEND FOR MUTUALLY SATISFYING FRIENDSHIP. INTERESTED IN DISCIPLINE.

OLDER GUY, GOT BOOKS, MAGS, VIDEOS, SEEKS SLIM YOUNG GUY FOR TRAINING. ACCOMMODATION NO PROBLEM.

MOTHERLY FEMALE, FORTY-THREE, INTERESTED IN FLOWERS, MYTHOLOGY AND DISCIPLINE, LOOKING FOR YOUNG MALE FRIEND IN NEED OF LOVE, AFFECTION AND CORRECTIVE TRAINING.

MUSCULAR GUY, INTO BODYBUILDING AND WALKS IN THE COUNTRY, SEEKS SINCERE YOUNG FRIEND TO EXPLORE THE WORLD OF SUBMISSION – PHYSICAL, MENTAL AND PSYCHOLOGICAL. ALL LETTERS ANSWERED.

'Do you notice anything about your ads?' asks Ruby.

'No.'

'Right. I'll help you write some replies. Go and get those photos you had taken last year when you weren't looking such a shambles as you are now.'

Still hungry, I go out to rehearse with Nigel. He tells me our drummer has left the band to go to acting school instead. We will have to postpone our gig again.

'I wanted to play my new song to Cis.'

Nigel has brought his drum-machine so we can rehearse on our own. It is a small drum-machine, an out-of-date model that cost him thirty pounds from the second-hand shop. All it does really is keep a beat. Compared to some drummers however, this is not too bad.

We are rehearsing in a makeshift room downstairs in a squat that we rent for four hours at a time. The microphones will not stay on the stands so we have to tape them in place and sometimes the amplifiers stop working, but it is convenient and very cheap.

I get on well with Nigel. If we could find a drummer we would be a good band. No one would care if we were a good band and, playing the sort of gigs we would get, no one would ever hear us. But we would still be a good band.

Rehearsing is fun sometimes. Putting your guitar up full and thrashing it takes your mind off everything else and there is always the thought that today's rehearsals might be tomorrow's big success. And sitting round on rickety old chairs in a shabby rehearsal room smoking cigarettes between playing is fun as well.

Carrying my guitar home through Brixton is a little worrying. If someone stole it off me I could not afford another one. I like my guitar. It is a Burns, an unusual old British make. Actually it looks better than it sounds, but it has a nice aura.

Walking home I carry on a conversation with Cis in my head.

'It's cold tonight. Can you feel the drizzle? We can cut through this road here. It's quicker. Yes it is, really.'

I imagine her smiling, willing to go along with my short-cut although she doesn't really believe in it.

These imaginary conversations go on all the time.

I have the sudden inspiration of calling on Cis and telling her I'm locked out. She will be sympathetic about this and let me sleep on her couch, or rather her mother's couch, as that is where she is living just now. Her mother answers the door and refuses to let me in and tells me not to come back. I head on home and cut through the little park, past some trees.

Ruby is standing beside a tree. Her feet must be cold in the damp grass, unless they have become immune to all feeling.

'What are you doing, Ruby?'

'I'm seeing what it is like to be a tree.'

I stand beside her for a while. Nothing much happens.

'I think this is a little boring.'

'Yes.' agrees Ruby. 'I had hoped for better.'

'Should we go home? I'm hungry.'

'There isn't any food. But we can have some tea.'

We walk home, holding hands.

At the bottom of our tower block I think I see Cis but she is holding hands with Fanfaron, God of Electric Guitar

Thieves, so we run up the stairs as fast as we can. The police would never be able to protect us from the God of Electric Guitar Thieves, and anyway there is never a policeman around when you need one.

Next day Cis phones me up and screams down the phone for a while and then she sends me a letter telling me how much she hates me. I am pleased to hear from her. I wonder if she would like me to send her some flowers.

Ruby is quite sympathetic when I tell her all about it. Domino is with her and they seem to be back together again and outside the next block the old woman is having a friendly conversation with Ascanazl, ancient Spirit Friend of Lonely People. She has made him a cup of tea and is telling him how hard it is to manage on her pension.

He tells her that she should have joined a private pension plan while there was still time.

I phone up the people we hire our PA off to tell them our gig is cancelled again and they are quite annoyed about it and say I have to send them some money anyway or they will sue me.

I wonder if they are serious. I do not want to be sued. I go to ask Ruby what to do but she is busy fucking Domino and I sense that she will not want to hear about my PA problems right now. Another important question springs into my mind however, so I go into her room where Domino is lying on top of her.

'Ruby, about this contact article, I have replied to all these gay adverts and I am not gay. Is this not a bad thing to do?'

'Well, you never fuck anybody these days so it doesn't really make much difference, does it?'

There is some logic in this.

'But they are bound to sense something is amiss.'

'Amiss? That's a funny word.' Ruby pushes Domino away and sits up, quite interested.

'I've never heard you say amiss before.'

'I must have picked it up somewhere. Perhaps Cis said it. Do you think Cis -'

'Will you get the fuck out of here!' screams Domino, who is probably wanting to get back to fucking, although as he doesn't live here and I do he has no right to shout at me. But I leave anyway and spend some time looking after Cis's cactus. I have a book called *How to Take Care of Your House Plants* that came free with six bottles of bleach and I am following its advice assiduously. If Cis was to walk in the door right this minute she would be proud of the way I have looked after her plant, although there is no sign of a flower.

Then I give some care and attention to Ruby's cactus, although she is at this moment fucking Domino there doesn't seem much need to help their relationship along.

I wonder if I killed her plant would Domino go away? I would like that. But I would not like to hurt Ruby.

I decide to make a sign.

I get some paper and write on it 'Cis's pot plant', but I don't know where the apostrophe should go in Cis's because it is always a little confusing when the word ends with an s.

Back in Ruby's bedroom Domino has his head between Ruby's legs and she is looking like she is quite enjoying herself, but when I ask her where the apostrophe should go in the word Cis's she edges away from him a little to give the matter some consideration.

'C-I-S apostrophe S,' she spells out for me, hand on Domino's head. 'Anything else?'

'Do you know where the Sellotape is?'

'I think it's in the kitchen drawer.'

'Thank you. While I'm in the kitchen, do you want me to make you some tea?'

'Not this minute. In a little while.'

Domino has a terrible scowl on his face and seems to be

shaking. I get back to making my sign. I do not really like Domino. I letter the sign with infinite care and Sellotape it onto the pot and I am very pleased with the result. When I give it some water and three carefully-measured drops of plant food I am sure I can hear it saying thank you.

'Grow me a little flower,' I say to it. 'I am fed up with not being able to eat and thinking that every person I see is Cis and being sad all the time. And it's all your fault.'

And then I have nothing to do. I rummage through some papers in my cupboard. I find a home-made ticket for one of our gigs, and a love poem. Ha Ha.

Cynthia, still sad, exhibits a social conscience and kills everyone in a wine bar

Cynthia calls in to visit her Uncle Bartholomew. He is having some trouble with his plumbing. Cynthia, fresh from eating some plumbers, knows all about pipes and drains, and fixes it.

'I've come to say goodbye,' she says, wiping her tools. 'My true love doesn't want me any more. I'm either going to kill myself or become a pirate. I haven't made up my mind which.'

'Goodbye,' says her Uncle, unable to help her decide.

Down the road Cynthia develops a powerful hunger. She changes into wolf-form and sniffs around.

There on the pavement is a shabby tramp. He only has one foot.

I know I shouldn't eat humans, thinks Cynthia. But no one will miss him.

'Stop Ruby,' I say. 'Don't make Cynthia eat the tramp with one foot. I get depressed just thinking about him.

Ruby looks up from her story.

'Yes,' she reflects. 'So do I.'

We saw him last week in New Cross. He was lying on the pavement with an empty can of Special Brew cradled in his arms. His crutch was leaned up against a shop-front and his ankle stump stuck naked out of his filthy trousers.

'Another one slipped through the welfare safety net,' said Ruby, hunting in her bag for a little change.

'OK,' she says, looking back at her story. 'How about this? "Cynthia, moved by sympathy for the one-footed tramp, immediately bursts into an elegant wine bar just round the corner. She savages the rich customers to death and steals their wallets. Stopping only to eat a spare plate of soup, she gives all the money to the tramp, and also a few bottles of wine." How's that?'

'Fine. I like it.'

'Right. But don't expect any more social conscience. Cynthia is crazed in love, and is not responsible for her actions.'

'Sit down comfortably,' says Ruby, opening her book of myths and fables, 'and I'll tell you a story.'

'Does it have a happy ending?'

'Yes.'

I sit down comfortably.

With all the standing around sorting mail and loading up trucks in the warehouse my knee starts to hurt continually and I begin to hate business magazines.

There is nothing interesting to read in the magazines, nothing interesting to look at in the warehouse, nothing to do but look forward to the next tea break or the end of the shift.

Where the truck comes in there is a metal door that opens by hydraulics, but at some time in the past a truck has run into it and ripped one side of it open so the warehouse is always cold.

One night a fox ran past the entrance and I found something funny in a magazine. Even businessmen need cartoons.

I show it round but it turns out that three of the other four people on 'E' shift can't read. This is embarrassing and the embarrassment seems to be my fault. When there is a radio quiz on and I say some of the answers out loud I am generally mocked for being an intellectual. I am also mocked for my Scottish accent. In factories and building sites I am always mocked for my Scottish accent although it is usually friendly, people calling me Haggis and Hamish and saying 'Och aye the noo.'

'Abeline,' begins Ruby, 'a minor music deity who once use to play the harp to amuse Zeus on Mount Olympus, came to Earth looking for some adventure. He was bored after centuries of bliss on Mount Olympus and also annoyed because Zeus kept on doing terrible things to women he was attracted to, like pretending he was a swan and forcing them to have sex. Also he had a big argument with Apollo after telling him his harp playing was out of date.

'Abeline strolled around for thousands of years, playing music and having adventures until, some time in the late nineteen-seventies, he realised that there were no adventures to be had any more and also music had become rather boring.

'Still unwilling to return to Olympus, he decided to create an adventure of his own, so he gathered up four musicians and started up a band to make radical music. Abeline played mighty guitar chords that deeply impressed all who listened to them.

'Apollo came to visit Earth.

' "Abeline," he said. "I need you. An upstart young Tree Goddess from Vietnam has been telling everyone that her music is the most divinely beautiful in the Universe. She claims that it drove the Americans from her country. I disapprove of such presumption. We are going to have a contest and I want you to judge it."

' "I'm too busy with my band," protests Abeline. "And I'm not very interested in your sort of music any more." '

Apollo tells Abeline that he'd better judge the contest if he knows what's good for him. Abeline, not wishing to bring divine punishment down on his head, is forced to agree.

'The contest is attended by all the world's major deities, except the Buddha, who is beyond competition, and Jasmine, who is too busy trying to comfort all the people with broken hearts.

'Apollo plays his divine music and the audience applaud rapturously. But when Daita, the Vietnamese Tree Goddess, sings there is no comparison. Her singing is the most beautiful sound ever heard in the Cosmos.

' "Well?" says Apollo, ominously.

' "Daita from Vietnam was the best," says Abeline, honestly.

'Apollo storms off in a fury but not before taking his revenge. He alters the sales figures so Abeline's band never make it into the charts and he maliciously influences the critics so they never receive any good reviews.

'What's more, Apollo curses Abeline so that no one will

ever listen to his ideas about music ever again, so after a brief career as a music journalist Abeline fades into obscurity. And the enraged Apollo also inflicts all of Daita's descendants with a toxic fever so that, despite their best efforts, the trees will never grow in her country again.

'Daita, with no trees in her homeland, is unable to sing any more, but wanders the planet giving help to the poor and oppressed, particularly labourers who have to work all day for low wages.'

Sitting round the table in the rest-room with the other labourers on my shift, I listen to them talking about football and women and I try and join in, but I am not good at it and my contributions never ring true. When I make some comment about football there is usually a brief awkward silence, and if someone shows me a pin-up in the paper I can never manage to say the right thing. One time Mark looks at a pin-up and says, 'Imagine fucking that, be like throwing peas down the Blackwall Tunnel,' and everyone laughs but I am completely at a loss as to how to react and it must show because Dave says, 'What's the matter, you queer or something?'

I do not know why I can never join in the conversations between groups of men.

I tell my shift that my band has at last recruited a drummer but they are not really the sort of people who are interested in music.

It is the Sunday shift, our last. We finish all our work about two hours before the shift ends. I slump down exhausted on a pile of orange plastic sacks that scratch me through my clothes. A gang of robbers looks in briefly, but they leave almost immediately because we have nothing worth stealing.

The rest of the shift play with the mini forklift and shoot elastic bands at each other. Next week I don't go back because I can't stand it any more so now I have the problem of signing on again. My knee hurts for weeks and I can't find a PA for the gig.

'Where is the happy ending?' I ask Ruby.

'I lied about it,' she says.

Cynthia becomes a highway robber, but suffers unfortunate consequences

Cynthia, lacking a ship, decides against becoming a pirate but does embark on a life of crime.

Hunted through the streets by the ever-vigilant werewolf detectives, she tries to forget her love for Paris by holding up cars and robbing the occupants.

She is wearing a purple shirt and green trousers. Ever since eating a man who designed book jackets, the young werewolf has been exhibiting terrible taste.

Reports of her crimes reach the ears of Lupus. The Werewolf King loses patience. He wants Cynthia brought to Justice. He instructs his detectives to bring her to him, or else.

Now these detectives are very wary of Cynthia. They have already lost several of their number to her ferocious fangs. They would rather just leave her alone. Lupus, however, is not to be defied, particularly when he is angry, so they formulate a plan.

Cynthia lies down on a lonely road. A car approaches, drawing to a halt at the sight of her apparently injured body.

'Stand and deliver,' she cries, leaping to her feet. 'Your money or your life.'

Cynthia can be quite theatrical when she wants.

Werewolf detectives pile out of the car. It is a trap. She is surrounded and captured, bound immediately in magical silver chains and thrown in the cellars of the Werewolf King to await trial.

Ruby's benefit claim is sorted out but mine is not. Ruby shares her money with me which gives us fourteen pounds a week each to live on, plus the six pounds I make as an artist's model. I scour the music papers for cheap PAs but all the cheap ones are booked up in advance and the only ones available cost eighty pounds. Eighty pounds is more than me and Nigel can afford. Perhaps John our new drummer can borrow it.

Nigel phones and says that John is leaving the band.

'He can't leave the band. He's only just joined. We have a gig in two weeks.'

'He's been offered a job drumming for someone else. He's going on tour.'

I tell Nigel about not having a PA either. Things look bleak for our gig.

Helena, Goddess of Electric Guitarists, is sympathetic and shows me how to play a difficult new chord but tells me again that she has no influence over drummers. And she is still sad because her girlfriend has left her. She has run off with Ezekial, God of Acoustic Guitarists, and I find this shocking because acoustic guitars are very boring.

'Who was that on the phone?' asks Ruby, who has a big yellow towel round her hair to dry it.

'Nigel.'

'Oh. I thought it might have been one of our contacts.'

'You sent off the postcards?'

'Yes.'

'Oh.'

When Ruby's hair is dry I help her tie the thin ribbons into it.

'What day is it?'

'I don't know.'

We look at the television to see what day it is but it won't tell us so I go round to the shops to buy a paper. The flower stall doesn't seem to be there any more, perhaps without me to buy flowers for Cis it is no longer viable.

Cis is buying some sausages in the butcher's and I am wondering if I should have a word with her and maybe borrow a few sausages when I am suddenly kidnapped by four gangsters in a huge American car. I think it might be a Chevrolet but I do not really know much about cars.

'Is this a Chevrolet?' I ask, gun at my throat, but the gangsters are desperate men and don't reply, except one of them asks me briefly what part of Scotland I'm from as his parents came from Falkirk.

'Give us the rights to the new oil well or you'll never see your friends again,' says the leader, a small man of Italian extraction with an Uzzi sub-machine-gun and a suit of violet that is brilliantly coloured although not as attractive as Ruby's dress.

'I don't have any rights to oil wells,' I protest. 'All I have is fourteen pounds a week and six pounds from the art class. Also, I don't have any friends.'

'You're lying. We'll cut your ear off and send it to your mother.'

The car is thundering down through Brixton. Too wide for the narrow streets we crash into the Ritzy Cinema, where this week they are showing a series of Marlon Brando films.

I am catapulted out just before the car explodes. Uzzi machine-gun bullets hail in every direction as the survivors battle it out with riot police. Bystanders everywhere are mown down in puddles of blood.

I scramble for safety into the Ritzy.

'The film has already started,' says the woman in the kiosk.

'Damn. And I really wanted to see "The Wild One".'

I decide to catch it later and shamble down into the market to see if anyone will buy me a pizza.

Izzy is there at the pizza stall. Although she has no money to buy me one, she tears me off a good chunk and I sit beside her and chew away at it. She tells me about a party tonight.

'I am feeling a little sad about Cis leaving me,' I tell her. 'How about you?'

'Dean is mad at me because I'm having an abortion.'

'I thought he had left you anyway?'

'He had. But he's decided it's his business if I have an abortion or not. Well he can go fuck himself.'

She pulls up her jacket a little way.

'Can you see an improvement in my trunk rotators?' she asks.

'Yes,' I say, although I do not know what a trunk rotator is. 'They are looking much better.'

'Marilyn borrowed me two hundred pounds off her parents to get me an abortion. Have you got everything ready for your gig?'

Immediately I am gloomy and can't finish my pizza fragments. Izzy reclaims them, saying she has to eat to develop muscles, although really it should be steaks and not pizzas. But she supposes every little helps.

Next to the pizza stall a few people hang around the door of a reggae shack and slightly shake to the music.

The robot and I trudge on across the blackened plain. I am fed up trudging. We have stopped communicating and the robot is entirely concerned with completing its life's work, a huge encyclopaedia of mythological mechanical deities.

Suddenly there is a total eclipse of the sun and the robot falls to its knees.

'Come on, make some light so we can keep trudging.'

There is a small whirring noise and a print-out appears from its side.

Silence, it says. *It is time for me to pray to the deity.*

It brings out a picture of Marlon Brando on a motorbike.

'You like Marlon Brando too?'

Who is Marlon Brando? it prints. *I am praying to the Harley Davidson.*

The party Izzy told me about is in a squat in Kennington. The street, full of licensed squats, is buzzing with three parties, two black and one white.

At the kerb there are a few old cars and three majestic looking motorbikes. Underneath the motorbikes a few shards of glass glisten in a small pool of oil.

Downstairs in the white party it is too full to move. There is a smoke-machine and beer on sale for a pound a can and one light shining horizontally across the ceiling. I stand around and talk for a while and I meet my friend James and his girlfriend Maz, who have a plastic bag full of drink which they share with me.

'Every time I meet Izzy she is always going on about her

muscles,' says James. 'But they don't look any different to me.'

I have a good conversation with Maz about caring for cacti.

It is bitterly cold on this planet. While the robot prays I shake and shiver and wonder how you go about building a new spacecraft. Suddenly I come across a small cactus, the only green thing I have seen on this world. It is small and beautiful and I stare at it for a long time.

Next morning I wake up in bed with Maz. This is a surprise. These days my life is full of surprises.

I hunt for my clothes, Maz gives me a nice smile.

'Don't worry about last night,' she says. 'It happens to everyone sometimes.'

'What,' I say. 'Having sex with your friends' girlfriends?'

'No. Getting drunk, being unable to have sex with your friends' girlfriends because the drink has made you impotent, being sick over the bedclothes and screaming out that the cat is a demon out to drag you to hell.'

I have a terrible headache.

Walking home I see Cis right outside Brixton Town Hall doing an exotic dance with a bowl of fruit in front of a TV camera but I don't stop to watch because it is starting to rain and water is running into my eyes and making it hard to see.

Despite the rain the woman is still sitting lonely on her balcony so I wave to her and she waves back.

'What day is it?' says Ruby.

'I don't know. Should I go and get a paper?'

'No,' she says. 'Don't bother.'

Cynthia howls

Cynthia lies in the cellar, bound with unbreakable chains of iron and silver. In the morning she will stand trial. As Cynthia is too much of an embarrassment to werewolves in general to be let loose again, Lupus will most probably have her quietly killed.

Cynthia, however, is not concerned about this. She is not even thinking about it. She is thinking about Paris. She is picturing him in bed with someone else.

She lets out a mighty howl and rolls around in misery. Her heart feels like it has been pierced with a stake. Her soul is leaking out in a small silver stream.

The guards outside the door tell her to be quiet, but Cynthia ignores them and keeps on howling.

My first contact is called Steve. He is forty and interested in films. We meet in a wine bar in Camden and he takes me back to his flat where he tells me his theories about discipline. On Ruby's instructions I try and remember all the details and everything he says. He ties me onto his bed and whips me with a leather thong a friend brought him back as a present from Surinam, and then he puts a gag in my mouth and fucks me.

'Would you like to go and see a film next time?' he asks as I leave.

'Yes,' I reply. 'Is "The Wild One" showing anywhere locally?'

Ruby is fascinated by my tale of the night's events and goes so far as to leave the house to bring back some antiseptic cream from the chemist's. When she rubs it into my wounds she says she is surprised that such a violent person would advertise in a left-wing magazine like *City Limits*, but it just goes to show, you never can tell.

'Nigel phoned. He has found a good drummer and wants you to go and meet him tonight. Tomorrow I am going to see my first contact. Some man who wants to be dominated.'

I tell her about waking up in bed with Maz and also about how I had apparently drunk too much to be able to have sex.

'That happened to Domino last night,' says Ruby.

'Maybe we could form a club.'

Eventually me and the robot become bored hanging round the valley and we strike out boldly for the next continent.

On the whole planet there are no animals.

The robot converts into a boat and we sail across a dead sea.

The next continent is much the same, dead plains, small groups of shambling humanoids.

Unexpectedly, one village gives us a warm welcome.

'The great Rain-Singing God,' they say, and bring us some food.

I eat the food and sit around for a few days. Everyone treats me well. I seem to be some sort of star. They are friendly to the robot as well and I can tell it is happy.

After a few days, however, I notice they seem to be expecting something.

The headman approaches me respectfully with a bowl of fruit.

'Thank you.'

'When can we expect the rain?' he asks.

'What rain?'

'The rain to end our terrible drought. The rain that follows the Rain-Singing God.'

I admit frankly that I have no idea.

'But you are the Rain-Singing God?'

'No, I am a lost spaceman.'

He grabs the bowl of fruit off me and I am ejected from the village.

'You can't sing for rain,' I protest. 'Rain is the scientific result of certain meteorological conditions.'

Cis appears in a tattered spacesuit, singing happily. It starts to rain. Immediately she is bombarded with presents of fruit.

In her tattered spacesuit she looks immensely stylish.

I trudge away with the robot.

'Oh, fuck it,' it says, the only time I ever hear it speak.

The robot is becoming less and less inclined to synthesise food for me and I am becoming increasingly hungry.

Ruby has promised to cook me a meal because I have done all the cooking for the past month.

'What is that awful smell?'

'I have burned all the food you bought at Sainsbury's,' she says. 'and thrown it in the bin because it is all so unhealthy. From now on we are going to go on a Stone Age diet.'

'What does that mean?'

'It means we only eat the sort of healthy things our Stone Age ancestors would have eaten. Raw grains and fruit and stuff like that. That's what our bodies are made for.'

'OK, what healthy grains and fruits are we eating tonight?'

'None.'

'Why not?'

'We don't have any.'

'But I'm hungry.'

'Fasting is good for you.'

Right.

It is time to tend to our cacti. Now that it is July I am sure there should be some sign of a flower but there is not. Looking at my cactus, I start to feel some dislike for it. I suspect it is deliberately refusing to flower. It is unwilling to mend my rift with Cis.

'I am beginning to think this is all your fault,' I say, quite harshly. Ruby is watching television.

'I'm hungry,' she says.

I look in the fridge. I have never seen an emptier fridge. I think Ruby is only happy when all she has in the world is her dress and her sunglasses.

'You know, when I was being whipped with that leather thong I forgot all about Cis.'

'That's good. Something positive came out of the occasion. Also, I will be able to work it into a terrific magazine article. If Domino calls, tell him to go away. We had an argument and I never want to see him again.'

'What happened?'

'I took him some flowers and he spat on them. He threw my book of myths and fables down the stairs.'

She strokes her book protectively.

'He is upset because he drunk too much to fuck. Did you know the Spirit of Evil Zoroastrism is called Ahriman?'

'No. But I'm pleased you told me.'

It seems that it is Clio, the Muse of History, who looks after museums. I tell her how much I enjoyed visiting the British Museum and I compliment her on her earrings, which are silver and gold with rubies and opals dancing at the ends. She tells me they are made by her brother Andryion who, as well as making jewellery, builds houses and always tries to help people who have no proper place to live. But often he is busy with his boyfriend Marsatz who is a painter. They are very happy together, always bringing each other little presents, but it sometimes means that housing does not get as much attention as it should.

Ruby hustles me out the house. It is time for the art class.

Today all the students have to do a series of fast drawings so that every few minutes the teacher shifts me into a different position. This is better than the normal two hours of motionless cramp. As some sort of prop the teacher puts a cactus next to me and she makes another little joke about hoping the cactus will not sting my naked skin.

Clio also looks after painters so she is interested in the art class. I tell her that all the exhibits in the British Museum were fine and also they serve good tea although it is quite expensive, and I confide that I am a little worried because I have heard that there is no money to keep museums open and they might have to introduce an admission charge.

'My friend Jane who sells communist newspapers tells me that the government hates giving money for things like art.'

Clio frowns.

'A strange accusation,' she says. 'I would have thought they were doing their best.'

'Well, she's not really my friend. I just run into her now and then.'

My feet are dirty. I hope no one at the class notices. I do not want them to talk about me afterwards and say to each other that I had dirty feet.

Back home with my six pounds I am very bored.

Ruby wanders through.

'I'm bored,' she says. 'Let's buy a new can opener.'

'A new can opener?' I say, a little surprised.

'Yes, I saw a brilliant new kind of can-opener on television, the advert had hundreds of them all dancing round doing the can-can. We have to get one, it will be wonderful.'

We spend a while getting properly dressed and wondering whether it will rain, then we hunt the shops for the radical new can-opener. I am dubious of course that it is really going to improve my life but I trust Ruby's judgement.

We find the new can-opener in Tesco. I am interested to be in Tesco. I have not been here since Cis and I were thrown out for shoplifting.

Seconds after slipping some bright yellow electric plugs and a packet of coleslaw into our pockets we were surrounded by security guards. We were surprised how quickly they came. We were also surprised to be merely thrown out and not arrested.

But I was not surprised to be caught. Tesco is full of bad demons and evil spirits.

It was no fun at the time but now it seems like quite a good memory. Except it reminds me of Cis.

Depressed by the memory of Cis I am unable to move.

'Come on,' says Ruby. 'I don't like it out here, I want to get home.'

'This new can-opener, please,' she says at the check-out. She does not want to steal it. I am relieved. Barefoot with sunglasses, Ruby is not inconspicuous.

'And twenty tins of beans and a loaf of bread.'

'Why did you get a loaf? Does the new can-opener slice bread as well? It must be a wonderful machine.'

Ruby says no, it doesn't slice bread, but as we are going to be opening lots of beans we can make toast and eat them. Sometimes I am lost in admiration for Ruby. I cannot think ahead like she can.

Walking home there is a man taking photographs in the street so we have to sneak past him because we do not want our souls to be stolen. Ruby has told me that when a stranger takes your picture the camera sucks up your soul and gives it to bad spirits like the ones in Tesco. I am anxious that this should not happen.

'Look at that boy's hair,' says Ruby. 'Isn't it nice?'

Tied up with plaits and white dreadlocks it is indeed very impressive.

'Get him to be your drummer.'

'But he might not play the drums.'

'Of course he does,' says Ruby, 'I can feel it in my feet.'

He says he will be pleased to audition.

Cynthia faces trial, and loses her guitar

Ruby tells me she is stuck. She is not sure how to rescue Cynthia from prison.

I think about it while I'm helping her with her hair.

'Can't you just have her eat all the guards in a savage fury and burst out through a window?'

'I was hoping for something more subtle.'

She ponders it for a while.

In the morning Cynthia is dragged upstairs to face the werewolf court. Armed guards are everywhere.

Lupus is sitting on his jewelled throne.

'To my certain knowledge,' he says commandingly, 'you have eaten two hundred people. Despite my express desire that we should not harm anyone in these civilised days, you have become the bloodiest werewolf in the history of our race. Have you anything to say for yourself?'

Cynthia is hard put to find a good answer. She has undeniably eaten a lot of people.

'I had a hard and loveless childhood in a lonely croft. As soon as I left I became tangled up in a series of tragic love affairs. I am not responsible for my actions.'

'Pathetic,' sneers Lupus. 'Is that the best you can do?

Look at you. No shoes, purple hair, and fourteen cheap earrings. You are a disgrace.'

Cynthia is not pleased at this personal criticism. Her natural good taste has returned, and she has been taking a lot of trouble with her image.

Lupus picks up her guitar and brandishes it in her face. Whilst raging against her many crimes, he smashes it. Cynthia is appalled. She loves her guitar. Roused by an incredibly savage fury she attacks the guards. The room dissolves into a volcano of blood before Cynthia makes her escape by chewing through the bars and plunging out of a window.

'You were right,' says Ruby. 'A savage fury and an escape through the window was the best thing to do. Do we have any brandy left?'

'No. But I could get some. Is Cynthia still suffering the psychic appetite?'

Ruby shakes her head.

'No, I'm bored with that now. She can eat who she likes and it doesn't affect her.'

Half-way across another desolate plain we come across a ruined building. The robot forces in the door but there is nothing inside.

'Back on Earth I once had to force a door so I could get into bed with a young woman I met at a bus stop.'

I wait for some sign that the robot would like to hear the rest of the story but it does not give me one.

The robot does not think that I am a good storyteller. When I tried to interest it in a tale of some hippopotamuses it just looked at me with contempt.

Also it is busy compiling the encyclopaedia of machine myths and occasionally worshipping the Motorcycle God.

Everywhere on the planet it is raining. As a Rain God, Cis has been a spectacular success. I have given up hope of ever finding a home here and am resigned to trudging round for ever with a mad machine.

My only comforts are some ruby earrings that the robot synthesised for me to keep me quiet. Unfettered by any stylistic conventions I am wearing seven earrings in each ear. If there is room to pierce any more holes, I might put in some more.

I know that I will never have any fun again, and I wish that I was back on Earth.

Sure enough the new design can-opener is immense fun. It takes the whole tops off cans, and Ruby and I take it in turns to take the tops off and stare admiringly at the results because neither of us has ever had a good can-opener before, only the very cheapest one that you buy from a stall in a market and you have to wrestle with it for twenty minutes to open your beans and even then you still get your fingers ripped to shreds on the tin.

After all the tins are opened we pour all the beans into the sink and start on the other ends of the cans. By this time we are becoming hysterical and when there aren't any cans left we try it on the loaf and cover the room with crumbs and then we ask the people next door if they'd like any cans opened and when they say no, not right now, we ask them to be sure to bear us in mind when they do.

I have a few minutes sadness when I think how much fun I could have had if Cis was here to see the new can-opener, but when Ruby gathers up all the tops from the cans and stars frisbeeing them down the hall I cheer up again and join in and all in all the new can-opener is probably the most fun I have had all year.

Afterwards, when the entire house is a slithering swamp of beans, breadcrumbs and mangled aluminium cans, I think that possibly life is not so appalling after all. Ruby gets me to massage her shoulders and she says I am easily among the best shoulder-massagers she has ever come across. I am pleased at this compliment.

I am not pleased to learn that she is back with Domino and he is coming round this evening to borrow a little money.

Out my window I can see the old woman on her balcony. She is looking lonely so I try and communicate with her telepathically, but she does not seem to be very adept at it and her replies are too weak for me to make out properly. I do get the strong impression, however, that her son is in prison for repeated chequebook fraud and that she disapproves of the Pope for being inconsiderate to the needs of women.

Cynthia finds that loneliness is good for your guitar technique

Without her guitar, Cynthia is unable to busk. Hopeful of remaining inconspicuous, she does not want to return to her life of crime. With Lupus still hot on her trail, really it would be best for her to leave town, but she cannot bear to be so far away from Paris.

There is only one thing to do. She finds a temporary job in a factory, making components for robots. Unfortunately, on her second day at the factory she is forced to chew the foreman's head off after he bores her for twenty minutes with a funny story about how he was thrown out of a nightclub at the weekend for starting a fight.

This brings Cynthia's industrial career to an end. She decides that she had better not work in any more factories because in her day-and-a-half making robots she came close to eating almost everyone she met.

So she moves into a disused warehouse and lives on stray cats and dogs. She eats down the door of a music shop one night and steals another guitar, which she practises and practises on till she becomes a master of the instrument, and when the moon shines through the cracked windows above her head she exercises her voice by howling out sad country songs.

She thinks that maybe she will just stay in the warehouse for the rest of her life. Paris has no doubt forgotten all about her and she will never see him again.

My next job is as Assistant Head Storeman in a large hotel in Knightsbridge. There are two porters there who know the job already, but the hotel does not want to make either of them Assistant Head because they are both Indian.

I am embarrassed to be put in charge of them. I never once tell them to do anything.

'I think that story is worse than the last one,' says Ruby, who is dyeing a leather wristband.

'What story?'

'The one about Cis being a Rain God.'

'I don't have any story about her being a Rain God.'

'Yes you do.'

I don't have any story about Cis being a Rain God. Ruby is

getting crazier and crazier, it is probably Domino's fault, he is an awful boyfriend. I have known thousand of nice girls with terrible boyfriends.

Domino knocks on the door and when Ruby eagerly shows him her newly-dyed wristband he says it is a mess.

'But wear it if you like.'

Ruby tries to hide her disappointment and quietly throws it away. It sinks down into the plastic bag full of yesterday's beans.

'We have a brilliant new can-opener,' I say, trying to cover the slight embarrassment caused by Domino's disregard for Ruby's endeavours.

Domino is not interested in any can-openers so I decide to go out and walk around. It starts to rain, which reminds me of Ruby's strange accusation that I have been telling Rain God stories.

At the next corner I meet Shamash the Sun God.

'I see Cis has been busy today making all this rain,' he says. 'I am lonely up there in the sky by myself. I could do with a friend. I am on my way to buy a book of mythical history which will tell me who the sun is meant to be friends with.'

'How will you get in touch?'

'I might place an advert. I think I would like to go out with a moon worshipper. Maybe even a werewolf. It's a long time since I had any excitement.'

'Hello.'

'Hello Izzy, what you doing?'

'I've just come back from having my abortion and now I'm going to eat a pizza in the market then I'm going home to exercise the muscles round my knees and thighs, what are you doing?'

I explain I have just been talking to Shamash the Sun God and Izzy says really, was it nice, and I shrug my shoulders because I don't want to make too much of it.

'Do you think if Cis was to walk along here with her little sister and her little sister was suddenly to run out into the road and then a massive truck was about to run her down because its brakes had failed and I rushed out and saved her then Cis would start going out with me again?'

'No.' replies Izzy. 'And anyway, Cis's little sister is seventeen and could dodge the truck herself.'

'Suppose she was drunk?'

'Is this likely to happen?'

'Well, yes, her little sister cannot hold her drink.'

'I mean, is the whole scenario likely to happen?'

'It was just a thought. I miss Cis terribly.'

Izzy says that she has noticed. When we reach the market she offers me some pizza but I don't enjoy it very much.

I do not last long as Assistant Head Storeman. The Head Chef, a very pompous man, is annoyed when he walks into the underground food store and catches me juggling oranges. I am reported to the Head Storeman. He gives me a terrible row and I resign in disgust. My benefit is suspended because the DHSS does not think that resigning in disgust is a reasonable thing to do.

'Ruby, why am I condemned to doing terrible jobs all the time?'

'Because the country is in the grip of evil demons.'

'Jane who sells communist newspapers blames the economy.'

'What would she know about anything?'

During my few weeks at the hotel I am, however, very well fed. Smoked salmon hang in the fridge and I eat strips off them and drink from gallon cartons of cream and devour boxes of expensive chocolates and every day I take a big peach home for Ruby.

When I get home after the pizza, I find that Ruby has moved house. This is a terrible shock. She has left without telling me.

But when I rack my brains I eventually remember that today was the day that we were due to move because our eviction notice arrived last week. In fact now I think about it I was meant to be out buying bin-liners to pack our clothes in.

The council have been and boarded up the door with a huge iron anti-squatting device.

Cynthia meets two international terrorists, and has to leave the warehouse

Cynthia's stay in the warehouse is interrupted by the return of Millie Molly Mandy and Betty Lou Marvel, international terrorists, drug smugglers and good-time girls. The warehouse is their secret hideout and they do not want to share it with a werewolf, even one they like.

I am doomed in everything, thinks Cynthia. Not only did my true love desert me but I will never even find a peaceful place to be sad.

'We're sorry about your tragic love affair but you can't live here,' says Millie Molly Mandy, dressed as always in a flowery frock. 'We need it as base for a new smuggling operation.'

'But I've nowhere else to go,' protests Cynthia.

She is considering eating them but they both have machine-guns and it is bound to be very messy.

'Here is some money,' says Betty Lou Marvel. 'Enough to live on for a while. We are going to assassinate someone now. Please be gone when we get back.'

There are many interesting stories about Betty Lou Marvel and Millie Molly Mandy and the trail of destruction they have left behind them, and all the fun they have had living it up on the proceeds, but they will have to be told another time.

They load up their sniper rifles and depart. Cynthia gathers together her guitar and spare sunglasses and leaves shortly after.

Outside she spends some time meditating in a Hare Krishna temple. They offer her some vegetables, but she refuses politely. Later she wanders round the British Museum, wondering what to do.

Ruby has gone and our flat is boarded up. I am alone in the world. I am engulfed in a huge flood of self-pity.

One of the many things I have in common with Ruby is that we are both expert self-pityists. We regard it as a good positive emotion. If I can't find her again I know I will never meet anyone as good for sitting round being miserable with.

Homeless, I stare at it, a little perplexed. I shake it but it won't let me in. Where has Ruby gone?

She is my only real friend. If she has gone away and left me I don't know what I will do.

I wonder if she took my belongings. I wonder if she took good care of my pot plant. I wonder if I was meant to help us move. It seems almost certain I would have been. Ruby will be furious. I have to spend five days sleeping on the floor of a slight acquaintance's flat and wearing the same clothes, and after I get rained on I am wet and shivering all the time.

Ascanazl appears, resplendent in his lilac-and-yellow feathered cloak. I ask him for help because now, without even Ruby to talk to, I am as lonely as I can possibly be.

'I'm afraid I am too busy to help,' he says. 'And my girlfriend has left me.'

My next contact refuses to fuck me because I am too dirty. Ruby will be furious.

'Please,' I say.

'No. You are too filthy for me to abuse. I have a horror of cold shivering bodies.'

Eventually I bump into Ruby in the street when she is out buying some margarine and she says where the hell have you been and why did you disappear when it was time for us to move? She seems quite annoyed about the whole thing and really I am stuck for a good explanation.

Eventually I have to claim that I was kidnapped by a spaceship and Ruby seems to accept this as a reasonable story.

She takes me to our new home, a squatted flat on the Aylesbury Estate. Having arrived five days before me Ruby has taken the best room, but I would have let her have it anyway. I notice she is looking a little fatigued. No doubt it was hard work moving all our things. Also she will have had to make all her own cups of tea and go round to the shops herself. Her dress is badly stained because she can never remember to buy soap powder.

I am a little sorry about all this so for the next week I try and make up for it by making continual cups of tea and helping her in every way possible. Soon she is feeling better and her dress is clean again. I buy her three new pairs of sunglasses and everything is fine.

We postpone our gig again. I rehearse with Nigel but we still don't have a drummer. The boy with attractive white dreadlocks turns up for the audition and he is quite good but he says he doesn't like our music and the weather turns colder and it rains everywhere and Cis's mother is living next door.

'Cis's mother is living next door,' I say to Ruby.

'No she isn't,' says Ruby, pulling down the top of her dress. 'Feel this lump, I think I have breast cancer.'

'Yes she is, I saw her.' I feel Ruby's breast but it doesn't seem like cancer to me, although I am not an expert.

'No you didn't,' says Ruby. 'You're imagining it. Do you think it is a malignant tumour?'

'No, I don't think so, but maybe if you're worried you should see a doctor. You're breasts are very white, you have skin the same colour as Cis's and I'm sure her mother is living next door.'

Ruby prods at the lump for a little while more and I can see she is worried, although she does take the time to tell me that the flats on either side of us are occupied by black families and as she seems to remember that Cis is white then it is not likely that any of the people there are her mother.

Reassured I go and look for a clinic of some sort and when I find one I ask for a booklet on how to check for breast cancer and the receptionist is very nice about it and loads me up with leaflets and pamphlets about all sorts of things. I am impressed by her efficiency.

'Would you like to be the drummer in my band?'

'No,' she replies. 'I am already a drummer in someone else's band and I wouldn't like to take on any more work because I am really involved in our music.'

'Oh well, thanks for the leaflets.'

'Be sure and have the young lady come in if she's still worried.'

'Right,' says Ruby. 'If I'm not going to die of breast cancer then we can get on with the insurance fraud.'

'What's that?'

'Come with me,' says Ruby. 'Mind the door when you leave, it's still weak after I jemmied it in.'

Ruby takes me round to the house of some friend of hers

who I have never met and we immediately start loading up rucksacks with stereo equipment and videos.

The house is full of pot plants and flowers in vases.

'Will I take the flowers?' I ask, but Ruby says you cannot claim insurance for stolen flowers.

Cynthia meets Paris, is heartbroken, gets betrayed, but has a good meal at the end of it

Well, thinks Cynthia. I may as well go and visit Uncle Bartholomew. It is a long time since I have seen a friendly face.

On the way she bumps unexpectedly into Paris.

Cynthia throws her arms round him. They go for a drink together.

'Did you miss me?'

He says he missed her last week. This week, not so much.

Cynthia is more heartbroken than before and starts to cry in the pub. She is embarrassed at this, though Paris is reasonably kind about it.

Cynthia leaves and visits her Uncle.

He pretends to be pleased to see her but really he slinks off and telephones Lupus, because Lupus has threatened him that he'd better co-operate, or else.

So Cynthia is betrayed by her only friend.

When the detectives come, Cynthia, fired up after meeting Paris, eats them all without any trouble.

Fuck this, she thinks, finishing off her bad Uncle. I have enough problems without werewolf detectives chasing me all over the damn place. I am going to sort out King Lupus once and for all.

The pretended robbery continues until everything is packed into bags.

'Now we just wait for the van to take all the stuff down to Izzy's. Then we get a big cut of the fake insurance claim.'

The van doesn't arrive. After waiting for two hours Ruby says we had better just set off on foot. At one in the morning I have to walk the streets of Brixton with a rucksack full of stereo equipment and a video recorder in a black plastic bag, trying to protect them from the thick cold rain.

There seems to be a policeman on one corner and a gang on the next. At any moment I will be arrested or robbed.

Ruby strides confidently on, however, and we deliver the goods safely to Izzy's house.

'I'll help you carry them upstairs,' says Izzy. 'These days I'm pretty strong.'

'Now we have money,' says Ruby. 'And the rain has stopped. The pub round the corner is still open because there are bands playing, let's get a drink.'

We over-indulge in drink relieved that we have not been arrested or robbed in the street.

The toilet in the pub has no glass in the window but still smells bad.

'Stop killing Irish children with plastic bullets' says some graffiti on the wall.

Two men in the pub make a comment about Ruby's bare feet and she tells them to go and fuck themselves. The band plays and they are quite good, which is a surprise.

'Do you know anyone with a chequebook and cheque card?' asks Ruby. 'I know where we can sell them for a good profit.'

'How is my cactus? It is August. It should have flowered.'

'Yes, it should. And so should mine. But they haven't. Perhaps something is holding them up. Did you notice Izzy had been crying?'

'No. What's wrong with her?'

'Dean hates her for having an abortion and so do her parents. She told me the whole world is against her. Would you like to hear a story I just wrote?'

'Yes.'

'Sit down comfortably, then.'

Cynthia flies a helicopter

Why oh why did Paris desert me, thinks Cynthia, landing her helicopter on top of Lupus's palace.

'Where did she get a helicopter?'

'She stole it,' says Ruby.'

'How did she learn to fly it?'

She shrugs.

'Are you going to write any more about Millie Molly Mandy and Betty Lou Marvel?'

'No. They belong to another story. Now stop interrupting or I won't finish before dinner.'

'We don't have any food. You burned it all.'

'Good. Food disgusts me. Now listen.'

I wake up with Cis wrapped round me. A tiny bug walks over the quilt. I brush it off, taking care not to kill it.

When I sit up it wakes Cis.

'I have an idea for a new song.'

I get out of bed and drag my guitar out of its case, a good case, second-hand from the music shop in Coldharbour Lane, and start strumming. Cis joins me on the floor and works the tape recorder because it is fun to record a few chords and listen to them later.

Crawling around we are soon all wrapped up in guitar leads and tape recorders and when Ruby comes into the room to see if she can borrow some money she laughs at us naked on the floor with musical instruments draped around us. Then we laugh too because it seems funny, although before we had just been having a good time and had not considered the fact that we hadn't got dressed.

My guitar lead stretches round Cis's thigh and between her legs, black against her very white skin. Beside her I look a grubby sort of light brown colour. Cis says that today she would like to buy some new earrings, small silver pendants with fake ruby stones she has seen in the market.

We play my new song, sit next to each other's bodies and think about making tea and buying earrings.

At four in the morning I walk past Cis's window. I stop and stare for a while, wondering what she is doing. Standing looking at her window is a ludicrous thing to do.

A policeman cycles up. I have never seen a policeman on a bicycle before. Bicycles are bad for the knees. After working in the private mailing warehouse my knee hurt for months.

'Ruby, do you know what I can do about my –'

'My knee is sore,' said Ruby. 'Can you go out and get me an elastic bandage?'

She had stolen my injury.

I walked round to the chemist but it was shut so I had to walk on further. At the next chemist I met Izzy.

'I'm just buying a bandage,' she told me. 'I hurt my knee doing exercises.'

It was an epidemic.

'What are you standing here for in the rain?' asks the policeman on the bicycle.

'Staring at my ex-girlfriend's window.'

He takes my name and date of birth and radios it in to the police station to see if I am a wanted criminal. I am not.

'You look bad,' he says. 'Try and get more exercise. Sleep with the window open. And good luck with your staring. I often stare at my ex-girlfriend's window myself. She left me for a guitar player.'

'Acoustic or electric?'

He doesn't know. He cycles off. It is still raining.

The stairs up to our flat make my knee hurt. My leg shakes inside as the muscles try to pull away from the cartilage.

Some time ago I bought Ruby an elastic bandage but I can't find it. I make straight for her bedroom, a room which, as is quite normal for Ruby's various bedrooms, has one wall painted black and the other three whatever colour they originally were, because Ruby's feeling that a black bedroom would be nice never extends beyond her first tin of paint.

I wake her up.

'Ruby, my knee is sore, remember you said I should see an osteopath, how do I find an osteopath?'

'Why do you want to know at five in the morning?'

'Because I'm feeling bad about Cis leaving me. I've just been staring at her window.'

'Never stare at someone's window in the middle of the night. It is a creepy thing to do. Also, you'll get arrested.'

'I almost was.'

Ruby struggles into her dress and brings a towel to dry my hair. Then I make us some tea and we talk about things and switch on the television.

An American comedy actress is being interviewed in front of an audience of fans.

'What is your inspiration for working?'

'The Big Guy in the sky.'

She says what a wonder and a privilege it is to be a mother, particularly in America. The audience applauds and Ruby says she is starting to feel sick.

I am a little hungry and offer to try and make breakfast, something I can do because yesterday we imposed some iron discipline on ourselves and went shopping.

Ruby declines the offer.

'The act of eating has started to repel me.'

'Has it? OK, I'll just get something myself.'

Ruby tells me I can't because she has burned all the food.

In the bin there is an unbelievable mess.

I was wondering what the bad smell was. It reminds me of the bad smell in the biology class where me and Cis first met, dissecting frogs.

She defied the teacher and refused to dissect a frog. She said that dissecting frogs was a wicked thing to do. Naturally I went along with this and both of us refusing to dissect frogs in the face of strong opposition brought us together.

The local paper wrote a story about us, underneath a small article on flower arranging.

Ruby says that she would like some more sleep now, so I go and strum my guitar and walk around the room looking at the damp patches on the walls. The damp patches will be bad for my sore knee. I wish Ruby hadn't chosen last night to carry on her crusade against food. I feel better for talking to her.

Suddenly I have a good idea. I will look at Ruby's book.

If your sacred Aphrodite Cactus will not flower it may be being held back by the Archangel Gamrien. As a prime mover of patriarchal Judaic religion, he has little sympathy for Aphrodite, and none at all for sex.

Depressed, I put down Ruby's book of myths and fables. It is hopeless. I always wondered why everything went wrong all the time but now I realise it is because of all the powerful spirits ranged against me.

Before I go to bed I make sure the window is open.

Cynthia fights an epic battle

Cynthia silently eliminates all of Lupus's guards and creeps down to his bedroom.

There she finds him mournfully contemplating a photograph of his wife who left him.

She pads up to his shoulder and lets out a low growl. Lupus spins round. A moment's concern shows in his eyes but he composes himself regally.

'What are you doing here?'

'I've come for a little talk. Don't bother ringing for your guards. There aren't any left. You were right. I am the bloodiest werewolf in the history of our race.'

Lupus transforms into wolf-form, something he rarely does these days. As a wolf he is huge and malevolent. They fight.

They fight for three hours till the whole building is a tangle of blood- and fur-stained wreckage. They fight through every room and hallway till nothing is left whole and they fall to the ground, battered and exhausted.

Lupus is unable to move. Cynthia drags her body across to his. Slowly and painfully, she puts her jaws to his throat.

'Swear now to leave me alone in future,' she hisses. 'Or I'll kill you.'

Lupus knows when he is defeated. He doesn't want to die.

So he whispers out a Royal Pardon. The Werewolf King will never break his word.

Cynthia grins, and starts to crawl away in triumph.

'Your mother died last week,' calls Lupus after her. 'She didn't leave you any farewell message.'

Cynthia leaves, her triumph spoiled by the death of her mother.

My next job is as a temporary clerk for Securicor in an office with a coffee machine on the wall and a sign in the bathroom: IF YOU ARE LONELY THEN GOD WILL HELP YOU.

Will he? Good. Please send me Cis.

I wait all day but she doesn't appear.

There are pages and pages of numbers in fractions. I have to convert them to decimals in the morning and file my results in the afternoon.

Every minute I am expecting bank robbers to arrive but they never do. I only stay there two days and later the agency tells me that I was not well enough dressed to work in the Securicor office.

Watching television with Ruby a man comes on and makes a joke about not being able to tell if the light in the fridge really goes out when you shut the door.

Ruby is outraged.

'What a boring tedious thing to say. I must have heard a hundred people say that.'

I am busy putting a patch on some jeans and do not pay much attention till some time later Ruby shouts at me from the kitchen.

'Come here a minute.'

She is staring at the fridge.

'I'll shut the door and you see if you can see a light through the crack.'

But when she shuts the door there doesn't seem to be any crack to see through. We spend about twenty minutes trying to work a knife through the plastic seal around the door to see if there is any light inside.

'Maybe you could sit inside while I close it,' suggests Ruby, but the fridge is too small to sit inside. It looks like we will never know.

I notice something strange about the fridge. It is completely empty.

'What happened to our food?'

'I felt disgusted by the act of eating,' Ruby tells me. 'So I threw it all away.'

'You seriously expect divine help in a reconciliation with your old girlfriend when you are so wasteful as to throw away food?' says the Archangel Gamiel, hovering outside the window.

I try to explain that it wasn't me, but he doesn't seem interested.

There is a knock on the door. It is a neighbour asking us if we would like to open some cans of cat food for her. She acts like we should be pleased.

We lend them our can-opener but we are still a little puzzled as to why they should come to us.

'Maybe their can-opener broke.'

Broke again, I ask Ruby to phone up the industrial agency for me and she finds me a job as a temporary labourer in Kennington.

Before leaving for work I make Ruby promise to take good care of our cacti. Ruby says she will but she also says she no longer thinks that her relationship with Domino will turn out well, no matter what the cactus does. But I still have faith. When I am in the flat I check every half-hour for the start of a flower.

As soon as I walk onto the site in Kennington they give me a pneumatic drill and tell me to help level out the rocky earth.

I have never used a drill before and it keeps jumping around and threatening to cut off my toes. I do the best I can and no one seems to mind that my progress is very slow. In the earth I am levelling there are a few small yellow flowers. I hate killing them. If all plants are friends then my cactus will be annoyed at me.

It starts to rain and I keep on drilling. After a few minutes I notice that everyone else has taken shelter under the roof of the labourers' hut.

At lunchtime I try and make conversation by asking if anyone knows any good drummers looking for a band, but no one does. I am so obviously ignorant of what to do on a building site that no one takes much notice of me.

When we have levelled out the site we have to clear everything away in wheelbarrows. The rubbish tip is across a deep ditch and to get there I have to struggle my wheelbarrow uphill across a sloping and shaky plank of wood. Each time I do this I almost fall in the ditch and if I fall in the ditch the wheelbarrow full of rubble will come down on top of me.

I'm scared of this, Cis, I say in my head.

No one else has any problems doing this and, struggling over, I feel increasingly stupid and incompetent. At the end of the day the foreman tells me that tomorrow there is not so much work on so I need not come back.

'I am a poor labourer,' I tell Ruby.

'At least you got one day's wages,' she says, comfortingly, and afterwards she runs me a bath and washes the building-site filth out of my hair and massages my shoulders. When I go down to the agency's offices to pick up my money they give me two day's wages by mistake.

Ruby tells me that Daita the Vietnamese Tree Goddess is also the Friend of Poor Labourers everywhere and probably she is responsible for my extra day's wage so I buy some incense and light a stick for her. I also buy Ruby some more new sunglasses and some nail-varnish. She is very pleased at this and brings home a boy to fuck who is not Domino. This is unusual but not unheard of.

I wonder if she is managing with her diaphragm.

Lying in bed I can hear them fucking.

Bandits enter through my open window. Bad advice from the police. They kidnap me and try to carry me off but I escape and hide on a council estate till they have gone. I hide in a stairwell along with a lonely cat and a ripped plastic bag full of flowers and beer cans.

When I am safe from the bandits I wander over to Cis's sister's flat. It is on the third floor. I stare through the window.

'Help me with my diaphragm,' says Ruby. 'It keeps coming out.'

'Are you sure it's the right size?'

'The doctor measured me.'

I put it in for her. On her vagina I can smell the breath of her lover.

Cis is visiting her sister. With her is her new boyfriend. I notice that he is not all that good-looking. But he is good company and they are having fun discussing an old wreck of a motorbike that they're going to try fixing up together.

Moans come from Ruby's room. Sometimes she makes a lot of noise when she is fucking. I am glad she is not with Domino. I hate Domino.

Next morning I make them some tea.

'Last night I dreamed I was kidnapped by bandits,' says Ruby. 'But I escaped and hid on a council estate.'

'How is your orgasmic response?'

'Much better. I am going to write it an appreciative letter.'

Her new lover plays drums and I ask him to play in my band.

Cynthia sick, howls at the moon again

Cynthia, weak from loss of blood after her battle with Lupus, limps along in the freezing rain through a miserable south London street where all the shops are boarded up and all the boards are covered with cheap posters advertising last month's meetings and last week's gigs. Fevered, she hallucinates that Paris is selling fruit from a market stall. He is with another girl, holding her hand and smiling into her eyes.

Behind the next block is her rubbish tip. She lies down on it and contemplates her life: no friends, no family and her mother dead; betrayed by Uncle Bartholomew; worst of all, her soul still trapped by a man who doesn't love her. And she's lost her guitar again.

Unable to think of anything better to do, she starts to howl at the moon.

'What is that terrible noise?' asks a young woman, picking her way over the rubbish tip.

'It is me, Cynthia Werewolf, howling at the moon. Go away or I'll eat you.'

'You're too weak to eat anyone.'

'Who are you?'

'I'm Ruby Werewolf – pirate, slayer, thief, reaver, painter, poet, writer, artist and uncontrollable adventurer.'

'Pleased to meet you,' says Cynthia, impressed.

A necklace glints at the throat of the stranger. It is Cynthia's werewolf soul necklace.

'Where did you get that?' she demands.

'A man gave it to me,' replies Ruby. 'He said he loved me but most days he doesn't seem too sure about it. I've been at home all week but he hasn't called round.'

'You don't really sound like much of an adventurer,' comments Cynthia.

'I'm having a short holiday.'

Cynthia passes out and Ruby helps her home and bathes her wounds.

All Autumn I carried on being mainly unemployed with a few days' work here and there, looking forward to finally getting my gig organised, and thinking about Cis. I wondered what she was doing. I had no doubt that whatever Cis was doing she was particularly happy doing it, although it was raining all the time, and I remembered that Cis did not like the rain.

Trudging around on the blackened plain, the robot gives me a print-out saying it has an important piece of news for me. However, I am at that moment late for work and I can't wait around to hear it.

I am working in a carpet warehouse in Hackney, loading rolls of carpet onto trucks. This job lasts for three days and during it one of the other people employed there seriously hurts his back lifting a heavy carpet and has to go home in a taxi.

Izzy, expert on weights, has told me to be careful with my back when lifting things. I manage not to hurt myself, but it is no fun loading all the trucks.

The other workers are slightly jealous of the men who drive these trucks. We imagine that driving a truck must be easier and more lucrative than loading them. I expect it has its problems as well.

When the warehouse is emptied the job comes to an end.

'OK robot,' I ask, 'what was this important piece of news?'

But the robot has disappeared. It is nowhere in sight. I hunt over the blackened plains of three continents but I never find it again. I miss the robot. It was not much of a companion but there is no one else for me to talk to.

Ruby is in a slightly bad mood because Domino has been being particularly unfriendly, claiming that he is too busy to see her this week.

She tells me that she has utterly given up on him. She is lying of course, and when we go to a party and she meets someone who she thinks might possibly be having some sort of relationship with him she is very displeased.

Depressed, she lies around doing not very much. The contact article seems to have been forgotten about. Occasionally she gets drunk and plans out more werewolf stories, although she is actually in a bad mood with her werewolf story as well, because Domino asked her if there was something Freudian in all this talk of werewolves eating their lovers. Ruby was outraged at this, telling me crossly that Freud was a notorious moron with ridiculous theories about female sexuality, quite apart from the fact that Domino couldn't tell Freud from a carrot cake if his life depended on it, in fact Domino couldn't do anything whatsoever if his life depended on it, except drink beer and talk loudly all the time and make sure his hair was looking good.

'I'm depressed in here,' says Ruby. 'Let's go visit Izzy and Marilyn.'

I'm surprised at Ruby wanting to leave the house.

'It's raining.'

'Well, we'll take an umbrella,' she says.

Ruby sees that I am not enthusiastic.

'Come on,' she says. 'We might meet Cis in the street. You know she used to like being out in the rain.'

Izzy and Marilyn are not home so we sit in a café instead and drink cups of tea and have a good bout of self-pity, with Ruby telling me what a terrible life it is when you are constantly messed around by your lover and me telling her much the same thing. Ruby is frustrated because she knows someone who will buy chequebooks and cheque cards from us at ten pounds a cheque which would be a hundred and fifty pounds if the chequebook was full, but we do not know anyone with a chequebook and cheque card. Even petty fraud can be difficult to make a good start in. I am distracted during this conversation because Cis walks past the window of the café at least fifteen times while we are sitting there, but no matter how hard I try to catch her eye, she never looks in.

Cynthia regains her health and leads a quiet life for a while

Ruby makes Cynthia nourishing soup and nurses her back to health. They become friends immediately, neither of them ever having met a werewolf before who they really liked – apart from Uncle Bartholomew, and even he turned out badly in the end.

A strange coincidence, muses Cynthia, that we should both be sad over the same man.

'I've brought you some new clothes,' says Ruby. 'And a few newspapers in case you get bored while I'm pirating and adventuring.'

'Thank you. But I don't need the shoes. I never wear any shoes.'

'Neither do I. What are you going to do when you are better?'

Cynthia shrugs.

'I have no idea. My life is empty and meaningless.'

As Ruby Werewolf, despite her claims, is not really doing much adventuring right now, they spend the evenings together decorating Ruby's room with black walls and bright pictures.

After a while, Cynthia decides she should move on. She doesn't have to, now that she is safe from the detectives, but being in any one place for too long depresses her.

Before she leaves Ruby gives her back the necklace, because Ruby has utterly given up on Paris.

On the day my cactus flowers I am offered a job in Brixton dole office. If there is a connection here I can't see it. The cactus grows a wonderful flower, radiant yellow, a little desert oasis in my damp bedroom.

In the dole office I have to take fresh claims, people signing on for the first time or people signing on after finishing work.

I do not want to work here but as one of the criteria for signing on is that I am available for employment, I cannot refuse the offer. At least it is only temporary. Another of the clerks in my section knows Cis and sometimes he tells me news about her.

Izzy and Marilyn have to move house when their short-life tenancy comes to an end. They move into a new squat with three other people because they cannot find anywhere decent otherwise.

Ruby visits them and later she tells me that it is a nice place and Izzy is still lifting her weights, without any visible results.

'But it keeps her happy. I told her they should ask Tilka the Goddess of Squatters to look after them, but they didn't seem to think it was necessary.'

John, Ruby's new lover, is a good drummer and easy to get on with. He joins the band and we organise our gig.

'My cactus has bloomed. When will Cis knock at the door?'

'Any day,' says Ruby. 'Of course she might just wait till your gig. Probably she will want to see you on stage. Make us some tea.'

'Do you want to eat? I bought a bag full of healthy Stone Age things.'

Ruby shakes her head.

'Eating disgusts me.'

She must feel bad about Domino. She is still sleeping with John the drummer.

We are evicted and move to a squat in Bengeworth Road. There is no electricity and we find out after we've moved that it is disconnected in a way that means we cannot put it back on. By coincidence Bengeworth Road is the site of the main electricity offices in Brixton.

'Strange,' says Ruby, in the gloom. 'They have plenty of electricity up there but they won't give us any. I'd better find us somewhere else to live.'

I meet Jane who is selling socialist newspapers outside the tube station.

'We can't find anywhere to live.'

'Of course not. The government won't provide houses for poor people. They don't give local councils any money to build council houses. They are only interested in rich people buying property.'

A strange accusation, it seems to me. Everyone knows that if you can't find somewhere to live it is because you have offended Ixanbarg, the Bad Housing Demon. I'm sure the government is doing its best.

Some people in the government introduce a bill to restrict abortion rights. Ruby, outraged, decides to join the local campaign against this bill and I join along with her. Every Tuesday we go to a meeting in the Town Hall and every Saturday we hand out leaflets in the street and get people to sign our petition.

I am good in this campaign because I am a reliable person for handing out leaflets and I never try to make any decisions or decide policy.

Ruby is slightly more vocal but I am happier just being told where I have to go and what leaflets I have to hand out.

At the same time the government introduces more legislation which is anti-homosexual and there is a large campaign against this and sometimes our whole pro-abortion group goes on demonstrations for gay rights. I help carry our banner.

My cactus is in full flower and the gig is next week. John finds a PA. I can play all our songs. Ruby stops sleeping with

John and finds us a place to live, a council flat which we can stay in for three months till the tenant comes back from her holiday in Vietnam.

'Will we say a prayer to Tilka?' I ask, when all our belongings are moved in.

'Tilka only looks after squatters,' Ruby tells me.

'Who is the god of council tenants?'

'There is no god for council tenants.'

It is December and I hand out leaflets in the snow. Ruby strides through the snow barefoot and still wears her sunglasses and we live on chocolate biscuits and bananas, which is a satisfying diet. I worry about her feet but they seem to be tough enough for any weather conditions. She does put a donkey jacket over her dress, though, and sometimes she has to stop and wipe the snow off her sunglasses.

In the dole office I take hundreds of fresh claims every day and sometimes people ask me when they will get their first Giro because they are desperate for money. I tell them that it will probably be soon even though I know that it won't be. If I don't say this they will shout and argue at me and I am just the lowest clerk and I can't do anything about it. I don't even want to be here.

When anyone needs to find the papers relating to a client they are always missing. The dole office has clerks whose only job is to try and link up missing papers. Sometimes among the long depressing queues there is shouting and scuffling and angry people pleading for money, and when a middle-aged man bursts into tears in front of me because he has forgotten to bring his P45 I start to think that maybe it is all my fault after all.

Cynthia makes a commendable vow, and fails to keep it

Cynthia, free from the worry of pursuit by Lupus, has no idea what to do with herself.

Where oh where is my Paris, she thinks sadly. And will I ever see him again?

Penniless, she eats the new door off the second-hand music shop in Brixton and makes off with another guitar and a portable cassette player. Being a powerful werewolf has its compensations. She gets back to busking and listening to country music. Ruby is very keen on country music.

Cynthia decides to go through the rest of her life never harming anyone.

Cheered by this thought, she strums her guitar as she walks along the street.

Hungry, she is going to use her day's taking from busking to buy a vegetarian pizza.

The full moon shines weakly through the dusk. Cynthia momentarily mistakes a young girl for a pizza and snaps at her throat.

Oh fuck it, she thinks. Another one gone. I will never learn any self-control.

She drags the young girl's body into a small patch of scrubby grass in front of a desolate looking Army Careers Office. She stares morosely at the dead face for a few minutes, then leaves.

In the snow I hand an abortion leaflet to Cis.

'Thank you,' she says. 'I have never seen you do anything useful before.'

Ruby and I have been petitioning for two hours and we are frozen.

Izzy sees us in the street and she signs our petition and then brings us some pizza from the market and cups of coffee in polystyrene beakers.

'I do not feel the cold so much any more,' she says, 'because I am more muscular than I used to be. Do you want to see my biceps?'

'Not right now,' says Ruby, a little harshly.

'We were all arrested yesterday,' Izzy tells us. 'The police broke down the door of our new squat and took us to the police station. They kept us in overnight. We've been charged with stealing electricity and they've boarded up the house.'

We sympathise with Izzy. She is having a hard time.

Back home Ruby puts her feet in my lap to warm them. I massage her toes and rub her calfs till the blood starts to flow again.

We have chocolate biscuits and bananas and with my wages from the dole office we are well off for a while.

Every day Cis and her new boyfriend drive past the window on their new motorbike, but I am not worried any more now that my cactus has flowered.

The cold weather makes my knee hurt. My knee is damaged and badly scarred from an inglorious motorbike accident. I fell off when I was learning to ride it. The scar looks like it has been sewed up with a fish-hook.

'I think your stories are getting worse,' says Ruby.

'What stories?'

'The ones where you are trapped on a foreign planet. The ones where you say you are resigned to walking round with a stupid robot and never having fun any more.'

'Ruby, I never told you any story like that.'

'Yes you did and it is a very obvious image. You'll have to start either living in the real world or writing better stories.'

Ruby is slightly upset. I know why. Last week I could not get into work because I was waylaid by a pack of snow-wolves in Coldharbour Lane. When I went home Ruby had been crying because she had seen Domino walking along with another woman. Now she won't eat.

If any of Ruby's friends stopped eating and acted sad because of a fool like Domino, Ruby would give them a severe talking to.

I apologise to my supervisor about not coming in to work and tell her that I could not get past the pack of snow-wolves.

'Werewolves? In Brixton?'

'Not werewolves. Snow-wolves.'

While I am working in the dole office the old woman who sits on the balcony throws a little party. She invites Ascanazl, Spirit Friend of Lonely People, Shamash the Sun God, Tilka the Goddess of Squatters, Jasmine the Divine Protectress of Broken Hearts, Daita, Vietnamese Tree Goddess and Friend of Poor Labourers everywhere, and a few others.

They have a good time together. Helena, Goddess of Electric Guitarists, turns up. She is still upset about her girlfriend leaving her and Jasmine does her best to cheer her up. Helena tells everyone that she is keeping herself busy so as to not think about her personal problems. She has started lifting weights to improve her body and she has helped my band organise our gig at last.

'Good,' says Daita. 'He needs some help, he is having a hard time. Last month I got him two days' wages for only one day's work.'

'Good party,' says Ascanazl. 'Any more wine?'

The day after I make the excuse about snow-wolves making me late for work my supervisor tells me that I will not be taken on as a permanent clerk at the dole office. This is such good news I feel like partying.

One time I went to a sauna party where everyone took off

their clothes and had saunas, then draped themselves in towels and drank wine. But on the wasted planet there are no good parties. There is not even anyone to talk to, now the robot has disappeared.

People hammer on the door of the dole office but the door won't open. We are on strike because one of the union representatives has been victimised.

I hand out leaflets telling people what the strike is about. Many policemen come down to watch over our picket and they make most of us stand on the patch of grass on the other side of the road. One superintendent is particularly unfriendly and he tells us that anyone who even says the word scab will be arrested and charged with threatening behaviour.

This strike covers my last few days at the dole office and I had already booked these last few days as holiday, so I get paid while everyone else doesn't. I offer to give all my pay to the strike fund but the union representative says I should not because now I am unemployed again and will need the money myself. I keep my wages but I always feel guilty about it.

The abortion bill is defeated so our campaign is a success and Ruby says that Domino is going to meet her at the gig tomorrow and this makes her happy. I am also happy. My cactus is in full flower. Cis is going to come and see me play my new song about her.

'Things are looking good,' I say to Ruby.

It is bitterly cold outside and we have wrapped ourselves in one quilt in front of the fire to keep warm.

'Yes,' she says. 'They always get better in time.'

Ruby says that being wrapped up in a quilt like this reminds her of being a child. I see what she means, although I have no memories of being a child. Ruby claims that she can remember sitting in her pram but, no matter how I try, I cannot recall anything at all before I was sixteen.

Cynthia does not find happiness

Cynthia buys some flowers and takes them to the nearest graveyard. She distributes them randomly on the graves. This is her penance for killing so many innocent people.

Sat down by the walls of the graveyard are five men, very shabby, very thirsty for some wine from the communal bottle. Their fingers are yellowed with nicotine and their trousers are filthy brown with excrement.

The sight of their poverty depresses the young werewolf. Outside there are more derelicts hanging round aimlessly, waiting for the day to pass, begging money for drink and something to eat. Everywhere she looks there seems to be some poor person unable to cope with living. And even the prosperous passers-by don't seem to be very happy.

An ambulance wails its way past, trying to hurry but caught up in heavy traffic. Cynthia imagines that inside there is some person trying to fight off death, and losing.

This is terrible, she thinks. Everything appears to be totally hopeless. I wonder where Paris is? I wonder why he let me down. All this successfully not eating anyone and not being pursued by any assailants has plunged Cynthia depressingly into the real world. She has no friends, her heart aches over Paris, and she is poor all the time.

Sometimes whole days pass without her exchanging a word with another living being, so that even a shop assistant saying a cheery hello to her seems like a happy event.

She buys a newspaper every day. Occasionally she reads

the lonely hearts column, but has too much sense to think you could ever fall in love through a contact advert.

Every day she goes for a long walk. Always she hopes to run into Paris, but she never does. The old vicarage he was living in is long since boarded-up, and she has no idea where he might be.

'What a life,' she mutters, trying to work her fingers round a difficult new chord. There is no happiness anywhere. It is a lousy world, in every respect. I will never see Paris again. I will never have any friends. I will always be poor and hungry. It would have been better if I had never been born, and if I had to be born, I wish I had never fallen in love, because being in love is a worse curse than being born a werewolf.

She fingers her werewolf soul jewel, which she will never ever give to anyone else, and stares at the moon and howls for a while. But soon she gets tired even of howling, and tired of playing guitar, and tired of everything in the whole world, so she just sits and looks blankly in front of her, and wonders how long the average lifespan of a werewolf is, and if she might get lucky and die young.

'Well?' says Ruby. 'What d'you think?'

'I like it. What happens next?'

'Nothing happens next. That's the end.'

I am shocked.

'It can't be. Where is the happy ending?'

Ruby says she doesn't believe in happy endings. I feel a huge depression creeping towards me.

'Make a happy ending,' I say, slightly desperate. 'I'll be depressed if Cynthia just sits there being sad for the rest of her life.'

Ruby, however, will not relent, and there is no happy ending for Cynthia Werewolf.

I dream about the old woman who I used to see on the balcony. I dream she is a goddess. She stands before me in the most resplendent jewelled robe that has ever been woven and tells me to stop being stupid and moaning and whining all the time about my girlfriend leaving me.

Then she advises me not to do any more thirteen-hour nightshifts because it will be terrible for my health and I'm not getting any younger. She wishes me good luck for my gig.

On the day of the gig it rains. This week has been continually wet and none of our posters are still on display. Those ones that haven't slid off the walls or been ripped off the bus shelters have been covered by other posters advertising the meetings of the ever-active local revolutionary parties.

Our friend Matthew arrives with the van and we load up, slightly anxious as always about carrying our instruments off the council estate, anxious as well that nothing should get wet.

Ruby comes with us in the van and we arrive at the pub at six o'clock to wait for the PA to arrive.

'Ruby, why do all these goddesses you tell me about wear flowing robes? Why don't they wear trousers or dungarees?'

'I haven't been telling you about any goddesses.'

'Haven't you?'

'No.'

I'm sure someone has.

'Is Izzy coming tonight?'

'I'm not sure. She told me yesterday she was depressed about being evicted and arrested and her parents nagging her and Dean moaning at her.'

The PA is three minutes late which is three minutes of terrible anxiety. When it arrives I have to pay forty pounds.

The God of Sound Engineers is called Manis. He is a very clever god, always fixing things, but he is also avaricious.

'Hey,' says Izzy, striding through the door. 'You want a hand in with your equipment?'

She takes off her leather jacket and flings it in a corner. The sound man stops connecting leads and stares at her. She is wearing a small vest and underneath her arms ripple with strength. She is burning with health and energy. Her shoulders are sculpted like an artist's illustration of the perfect anatomy. Ruby and I are awestruck. Beside her we are as weak and sickly as broken twigs.

'How are Dean and the parents?' I ask, outside at the van.

'Who cares?' says Izzy, hoisting the mixing desk over her shoulder. 'Who needs them?'

We help carry all the equipment in, large speakers, a mixing desk, monitors, reels of wire, microphones, more stuff than we really need.

It takes an hour to set up and meanwhile the support band arrives to do their sound-check.

Ruby is on her own in the bar next door.

'Where's Domino?'

She shrugs. 'He hasn't turned up.'

We share a drink and I look outside for any sign of an audience, but all there is is rain.

'Don't worry,' says Ruby, passing me our drink. 'It's early yet.'

We lock one door and set up a table to collect money at the other and Ruby brings in an ashtray to keep it in. She has a rubber stamp to stamp people's hands once they've paid.

'Dear Helena, Goddess of Electric Guitarists. Please protect me from guitar thieves. Please do not let me forget any of our songs. Please prevent me from breaking a string, particularly in the first number. Please don't let the lead come out of my guitar when I dance on stage. Please don't let my fuzzbox become disconnected from my amplifier. Don't let my amplifier stop working again. Don't let Nigel cover up everything I'm playing because he has a better amplifier than me. Please distract everyone's attention when I play some wrong notes. Good luck with your girlfriend.'

Nigel puts the lights down and gives a tape to the sound man to try and create some atmosphere in the empty room.

Me and Nigel and John sit in a corner, making ourselves ready. Ruby sits at the door on her own, trying not to be sad that Domino has not turned up.

I am nervous. Cis might be here. I told her sister about the gig.

Some spacemen appear for a second but they disappear without talking to me. I haven't talked to any spacemen since my cactus flowered.

I look around, and I realise for the first time what a drab room this is. Drab and lifeless and totally dull. Too dull for anyone to enjoy themselves in.

When the support band plays there is an audience of five. We wait as long as we can before going on in case more people turn up, but when we start playing there are eight people watching us.

In the other bar there are many people but they are not interested in coming in to watch us play.

During our set five more people come in and two leave. That makes an audience of eleven. All eleven clap.

After a while I forget about my nerves. We finish our set and the eleven people drift away.

We help the PA people out with their equipment. I have to give them another forty pounds, so on the night we have lost fifty-four pounds, and another ten for the posters plus five pounds to Matthew for driving us.

Izzy wishes us a cheery goodbye and strides away confidently into the night, a very powerful presence. Every eye follows her as she leaves.

As a gig it is a total failure and I am completely depressed. So are Nigel and John. We are all silent as Matthew drops us home.

Enough human suffering

Enough human suffering, I think, wandering aimlessly round my room. I hunt out some paper and a pencil.

Cynthia Werewolf places an advert for musicians in a music paper. She is surprisingly successful with this advert because werewolves sometimes do get lucky breaks. A guitarist she likes answers right away and he knows a good bass guitarist. They have no trouble at all in finding a drummer, in fact they have several to choose from.

They practise downstairs in the basement of a squat and soon Cynthia's demented love-crazed genius begins to produce powerful results. They develop into the most violently beautiful country punk band ever to see the light of day, sounding somewhere between Extreme Noise Terror and Loretta Lynn.

Soon they are playing local gigs and making a name for themselves. Cynthia, verging on success, has friends and admirers everywhere. Almost happy, she no longer feels the urge to rip people apart and eat them, even on the brightest of full moons. Standing on stage, singing and playing, with feedback whining all around and her stetson perched on top of her head, she is as contented as she has ever been. When the band play the song she has written about Paris the audience riot in appreciation.

Only her lingering heartache over Paris prevents her from being completely satisfied. But while in the real world lovers never return, and stories about people who go out and win back their lovers are all lies, Cynthia, being a mythical being, is not strictly bound by these rules.

One night, after a gig in which representatives from several record companies are seen enjoying themselves in the audience, Paris walks into the dressing room.

'I heard your song about me,' he tells her. 'It was wonderful. I realise now that I have always loved you. Please take me back.'

Cynthia is overjoyed. Really she should hate Paris for all the misery he has caused her, and certainly she should at least give him a hard time about the whole thing, but she is in fact too happy to bother. She embraces him passionately, and takes him home.

Back in her flat she slips the soul necklace round his neck again and they go to bed. They fuck for hours on end. Paris is still not all that good a lover, but Cynthia knows she can improve things, given time.

And ever afterwards, Cynthia and Paris are famous for being a happy couple, immune to the stupidity and misery of the world around them. The band goes from strength to strength, and Cynthia is never ever lonely again.

'What do you think?' I ask Ruby. She says she doesn't really think much of it, but she doesn't mind if it makes me happy. It seems like a big improvement to me.

'We have lost sixty-nine pounds,' I say, back in the flat.

'Never mind,' says Ruby. 'I'll think of some way to get money.'

We have a long silence.

'Cis never came.'

'There wasn't any chance she would.'

'I know. But I would have liked her to hear my song.'

Ruby makes me some tea.

'My life has seemed strange recently.'

Ruby says she has noticed.

'You remember you said you always feel better in time?'

'Yes.'

'I feel worse.'

'That can happen as well.'

Right.

Ruby shrugs. I am empty-headed. My whole body is hollow and without feeling. No, I am lying. There are little bits here that don't feel too good. I imagine that Ruby is feeling immense pain inside about Domino messing her around all the time. I'm not entirely sure if she is. I do not know if it is really possible to know what anyone else is feeling. Maybe she is just hollow as well.

'Ruby, could you tell me something optimistic and cheerful before I go to bed?'

'My knee is feeling better.'

'So is mine.'

I am a little cheered.

'And we are good friends,' says Ruby, smiling.

'Yes. You are the best friend I ever had.'

'Do you remember the can-opener? And all those beans?'

We start to laugh. We laugh and laugh till Ruby starts to roll on the floor and complain about her sides hurting, we laugh about nothing till we are completely worn out.

Then we kiss and go to bed. Ruby has the best bedroom, because she got here first, but I would have let her have it anyway. A friend like Ruby is hard to find.

My cactus thrives although Ruby's never flowers. Despite this she later moves out to live with Domino. After a while they have a terminal argument and she goes back to live with her parents. We lose touch.

I find a job as a library assistant in a college and I am quite well suited to this, sitting quietly behind a counter stamping books, watching the students. Without Ruby's support I stop squatting and start paying rent. I miss Ruby terribly.

And I miss the spaceman and Tilka and Ascanazl and the flowers and the old woman who is never on the balcony any more and the mad schemes for making money and the robots and the art class and everything else. Most of all I miss Cis. I see her sometimes walking in the street and sometimes on her bicycle, but I never talk to her.

Lux the Poet

Lying with a Friend under a Burnt-out Truck

Lying under the burnt-out truck, head still bleeding and cocaine still rampaging around his body, Lux the Poet begins to ramble.

'I have definitely had a hard life you know. When I was nine I fell under a lawnmower. It was an experimental model my dad was testing for the company. It could've been a disaster. It could've cut my head off. Worse, it could've left me so horribly scarred I'd've been ashamed to walk the streets. All it did though was give me this nice little scar over my eye which as you can see makes me even more attractive. This is why I'm permanently optimistic. Even a terrible lawnmower accident turned out well.'

His companion listens in silence.

'In fact,' continues Lux, megalomaniac vanity coming to the surface, 'I am universally acknowledged to be the prettiest man on the planet. Also I'm the greatest poet. Despite this I am unappreciated. I always suspected my dad deliberately shoved me under the lawnmower. He hated me because I was a test tube baby. It is not widely known but I am the first test tube baby to become a nationally recognised poet.'

'You're not nationally recognised.'

'It's only a matter of time. I wrote my first great poem when I was seven. An epic.'

'What was it about?'

'Oral sex with a shark. It created a sensation. I got expelled from my primary school. They said I'd disgraced them in the road safety contest. Apparently it was the only sex-with-a-shark poem in the under-nine category. But it worked out well enough. Everyone at my next primary school wanted to hear my poetry. And ever since then I've been thrilling the nation. Do you want to hear a poem?'

'Not right now Lux.'

'Why not?'

'Because we're lying under a burnt-out truck in a riot.'

Lux can't follow this, it seems to him like the ideal time. Never mind.

'Is my hair still perfect?'

'Shut up Lux.'

CHAPTER ONE

At seventeen, Lux the Poet is a natural optimist, undeterred by life's misfortunes.

Being hopelessly in love with a girl called Pearl who doesn't care for him all that much could count as a misfortune, but Lux always imagines that people he likes enough are bound to like him back sooner or later and in view of the wonderful new poem he has written for her it will probably be sooner.

He thinks about her all the time, and supposes that she thinks of him.

Pearl is at this moment trying to shepherd her friend Nicky through a riot. Nicky is practically comatose with worry, the shops in the main street of Brixton are starting to burn, it is becoming hard to hear over the sound of shouts and sirens and breaking glass, hard to move in the crowds that are alternately advancing in triumph or retreating in disarray, and generally no fun at all for someone intent only on finding some safety.

So right now Pearl is not spending much time thinking about Lux.

'I killed my computer. Don't let them artificially inseminate me,' moans Nicky obscurely, and Pearl drags her on.

The misfortunes that Lux is not too worried about include having nowhere to live and no Giros coming from the social security but he figures it will work out all right in the end.

He strides through the riot, not too worried about it, on his way to Pearl's house. 'Hello,' he says, passing by someone he knows who is busy throwing rocks at the police across the street.

He gets a nod in return.

Lux is friendly to most people, and polite.

Passing by the corner of a small street he ducks his head down, not wanting to be spotted by the woman who lives on the top floor, an ex-lover who on learning that as well as sleeping with her and eating her food he was also going to bed with her sister, her brother and two of her friends tried to throw him out of the window. A total over-reaction as far as Lux could see, but not an experience he wants to repeat. He is just not strong enough to fight off irate lovers.

Due to his devastating good looks, the area is full of men and women who want to fuck him although they wouldn't necessarily want him to stay around and talk about it afterwards because Lux has a terrible habit of trying to make people listen to his poetry.

'I don't want to go down to Brixton just now,' protests Mark, listening to the news on the radio. 'There is a riot going on.'

'So what?' Gerry is entirely dismissive of the objection. 'If there is a riot on then that is where we should be. The people need our support. Besides, we have to get the manuscript back.'

When Lux arrives at Pearl's house he finds it burned to the ground.

Tears well up in his eyes. As a young artist he can cope with almost any aspect of a tragic love affair but not his girlfriend being burned to death.

'Little poppies, like Hell flames,' mutters Lux, a fan of Sylvia Plath.

'Pearl is all right,' a neighbour tells him, bringing out a cup of tea for a sweating fireman. 'She went off with a friend.'

Well that's a relief, thinks Lux. I couldn't have coped with an incinerated Pearl. And now she needs me more than ever. He sets off in pursuit.

A shame it had to happen before he arrived. Possibly he might have been able to fight his way into the burning building and rescue her and been a hero.

Lux has no idea what the riot is about. It just sort of started while he was walking along the street. When he first saw a gang of youths running towards him he thought perhaps it was some fans come to hear some poetry and was disappointed when they ran on past without paying him any attention.

This feeling persists, however, and the whole night Lux has a subconscious suspicion that possibly the riot is in his honour.

The riot, grumbling away from the early afternoon, heats up as the evening comes.

Pearl had the misfortune to have her house burned down very early on, before things were even really under way. A stray petrol bomb bounced off a policeman's riot shield, shattered her window and set alight the curtains. Modern technology has made riot shields very efficient, which is good for the policemen but bad for anyone else around when petrol bombs get thrown.

Old and threadbare, the curtains blazed up in seconds and that was that. Pearl barely had time to grab a few possessions, including her valuable film, and flee, dragging along her friend Nicky, currently hiding from Happy Science PLC and going through a massive trauma over what she did to her computer.

So now she is trying to work her way through Brixton to Kennington where she can find refuge with a friend for her and Nicky and her film, but with the police blocking off roads everywhere to isolate the riot it is very hard going.

* * *

Lux was evicted from his squat five days ago. This took him by surprise because he hadn't bothered to look at any of the official letters of eviction he had been sent so all he had time to gather up was a few clothes and some prized possessions like his Star Wars toothbrush and picture of Lana Turner, whom he resembles. He didn't have all that much stuff anyway, but it did mean leaving behind his collection of brightly coloured carrier bags and some poetry books he'd stolen here and there, and also his dungarees. As he is commonly acknowledged to look sensational in dungarees, this is a sad loss.

So now he has no proper place to live and has been staying with Mike and Patrick, who don't mind him moving in for a while so long as he doesn't try to read them any of his poems.

This is difficult for Lux to do, as he likes reading his poems to people, in fact he loves it, but he controls the urge as best he can because as well as giving him a roof over his head they have been feeding him and this is not something to be laughed at, especially when the DHSS is saying that he has to make his benefit claim all over again because he didn't tell them about his change of address, and a new benefit claim takes long enough for a person to starve.

However, his habit of borrowing or stealing anything not too heavy for him to carry and then shamelessly lying about it afterwards has been causing some tension in the household.

Nicky is unfortunately being no help to Pearl because she is virtually in a coma having suffered severe shock when she destroyed her computer at work. Her computer was her only friend apart from Pearl and now she regards herself as a murderer. Furthermore she is convinced that Happy Science are after her and it is all too much for her mind to take so it has started to switch off intermittently and she is liable at any time to wander off into a looting mob or a police Transit van without realising what she is doing. So Pearl has to coax her along and the going is becoming increasingly difficult as more and more people flood out onto the streets with wild smiles and petrol bombs and more buildings start to burn.

The riot begins in the young black community and spreads to the whites and they join forces to fight the police.

Cars trying to pass through Brixton are stopped and the occupants robbed and their vehicles set on fire so the police try to prevent any more vehicles coming in by setting up roadblocks but with frightened drivers going all ways and everything and everyone a mass of excitement, terror and confusion the streets are soon impassably blocked with burning and abandoned heaps of scrap metal, some overturned like horrible giant beetles, some sitting quietly with their tyres smouldering and all with their doors and windows open to the world – in-car-radioless, stereo-speakerless, tyreless, never-to-be-traded-in, valueless hulks.

The sky rains with stones and any other missile that comes to hand and the police, reinforcements arriving in their special green buses, start forming up with their shields and batons to make advances towards the rioters and Pearl, caught in the middle with a sick friend and a film to look after, becomes more and more worried.

Like Lux, she can cope with another riot, but this time she has things to protect.

Kalia, exile from Heaven, goes through reincarnation after reincarnation doing kindness after kindness. She has to.

Exiled from Heaven after being framed in a celestial coup that went wrong, Kalia is dragged in front of the Heavenly Court where she is sentenced to perform five hundred thousand acts of kindness before being re-admitted into Heaven. She will have to eternally reincarnate until she has worked off the badness of being involved in a coup against the Gods.

'But I never did anything,' she protests. 'I was framed.'

'Silence,' roars her judge. ' You spend your time writing subversive poetry. You were obviously involved. For talking back you are now sentenced to do a million good deeds. Now go.'

The next thing she knows she is waking up as a newly born child in a poverty-stricken peasant community on the southern tip of India.

After the splendours of Heaven it is a terrible comedown. A million acts of kindness. How long is that going to take?

'If we go down to Brixton we might get attacked.' says Mark, worried.

'Attacked?' Gerry looks at him with disgust. 'Why would we get attacked? The riot is against police and oppressison. I am not the police or an oppressor, am I? Why would I be attacked?'

Mark gazes at Gerry admiringly. He is so smart. He writes for *Uptown*, a left-wing arts magazine. There is nothing he doesn't know.

'As soon as I finish this writing we'll catch the tube,' he says.

CHAPTER TWO

Lux is not too worried about the riot because it is the third one he has lived through and he never came to harm in either of the others.

He is slightly perturbed however to find Pearl's house burned down. Neither of the previous riots have had any effect on him but this could have been a tragedy.

He tramps the streets looking for her, knowing that he can be of assistance, knowing that he will be a star one day, muttering snatches of other people's poetry, making up his own.

A white van pulls up beside him and Lux is interested to see a camera crew emerge. He would like to be on television.

'Hello,' he says politely as they set up their cameras. 'I am Lux, an important local poet. Would you like to hear one of my poems?'

'No,' says the reporter. He is busy looking round for a hot story and local poets are rarely hot stories. Lux is a little disappointed, although he is used to people not wanting to hear his poems. He appreciates that there is little taste for the truly artistic in the world any more.

The camera starts filming the riot. Lux, however, guardian of artistic sensibilities, is not so easy to get rid of and starts working his way in front of it.

'Are you sure you wouldn't like to hear a poem?'

'Absolutely'

'Why not?'

'I'm busy.'

'Doing what?'

'Will you get the hell out of here! We're trying to film a riot.'

Lux starts declaiming a poem anyway, figuring it is more interesting than a riot, but the soundman, used to outsiders trying to muscle in on the act, works the controls so that no one can hear him and Lux declaims his poem into the void.

The people that Lux is living with, Patrick and Mike, live far up Brixton Hill and are so far unaffected by the riot. They are watching it on the news.

'Another riot,' says Patrick. 'Oh God, there's Lux trying to get in front of a camera again.'

Mike laughs but Patrick sniffs with disapproval. He does not really want Lux in the house and only puts up with it because Mike likes him, and as he thinks that the reason Mike likes Lux is that he wants to fuck him he does not really approve at all. It makes him jealous.

They watch as the camera swings back and forward trying to focus on rioters while Lux determinedly pursues the lens to keep himself in the picture, all the while mouthing off something that nobody can hear.

* * *

Happy Science is in turmoil. Their well publicised research project to breed a new generation of geniuses is in big trouble.

The project involves a vastly complicated genetic programme and gathering of semen from old geniuses and implanting it into suitable women.

They plan to breed a very clever new generation.

The prime minister is thrilled with the idea. It has caught the public imagination, partly because they are also running a beauty contest to decide on some suitable mothers.

It was originally planned to find some genius mothers as well, but the Happy Science publicity department vetoed the idea, feeling that they would get more attention from the press with some beauty queens.

Unfortunately the genetic programme has gone missing and without the genetic programme all they have is a few test tubes full of frozen sperm.

Doctor Carlson, head of the project, buries his face in his hands. Disaster is looming on every front. His Nobel Prize hangs in the balance. He should never have tried to blackmail Nicky into entering the beauty contest.

Lux is easily recognisable on the TV screen, looking something like a cross between a scarecrow and Lana Turner, if Lana Turner had red and yellow hair standing in a jagged bush two feet off her head and the scarecrow topped its ragged old coat with a face of extreme girlish beauty, bearing a little piratical scar over its left eye.

Lux is regarded by some people, particularly himself, as the prettiest man in London, if not the whole world.

Patrick thinks he is a little brat.

'Little brat,' says Patrick.

'Leave him alone,' replies Mike. 'I like him.'

'And we all know why.'

'Whadya mean we all know why?'

'You know what I mean we all know why.'

'No I don't know what you mean...'

This goes on for a while.

'You're in a bad mood because Liberation Computers is losing money again.'

'That's not true!'

Mike is very sensitive about Liberation Computers, a business he has set up with his friend Marcus using the social security set-up-your-own-business scheme for reducing the unemployment figures. They start to argue about the washing up.

Recently their relationship has not been running very smoothly and were it not for the fact that their sex life is very good they might well have broken up some time ago.

OK, thinks Lux, walking away from the TV crew. So you don't want to hear my poems. Fine. Fuck you. You wouldn't know a good poet if he bit you in the leg.

But it is a little dispiriting, the way no one ever wants to listen to him. Everyone just automatically assumes that what he has to say is nonsense.

'It is prejudice,' he mutters. 'They won't listen to my poems because I have perfect legs like Betty Grable. If Shakespeare had had legs like Betty Grable he wouldn't have stood a chance either.'

He catches sight of himself in a flame-illuminated shop window and this cheers him up, as always. It is a good thing, he thinks, that I am so attractive. I would have found it hard to cope with life if I wasn't. I wonder how everyone else manages?

Having given up the attempt to read the camera crew some poems, Lux has resumed his search.

Pearl cannot be all that far away, he reasons, particularly if she is with Nicky. Nicky is no doubt being difficult. She is practically in a coma these days.

Lux is not all that fond of Nicky. He suspects that she is sleeping with Pearl and that this is why Pearl has so far refused to fall in love with him. They have fucked several times but Lux knows that Pearl's heart was not in it. Lux can fuck all day long if he wants. He has many admirers. But he is desperate for Pearl to fall in love with him.

Momentarily a feeling that life is very hard descends upon him. Here he is, monumentally good looking and the most talented writer the world has ever seen and still Pearl doesn't seem to be particularly attracted to him. He can't understand it.

When he sends his work off to magazines they never say nice things about it. Yes, he muses, it is a solitary life, guarding the artistic heritage of the nation. He bumps into some people he knows, hurrying home away from the riot.

'Have you seen Pearl?' he asks.

'Pearl who?'

'Just Pearl.' he says, realising that he doesn't know her surname. He wonders if she has one. Presumably.

Seeing no alternative, the Gods being too powerful to fight against, Kalia sets about her million acts of kindness. Almost as soon as she can walk she is carrying water for the women of the village and helping chop firewood for the family and volunteering for extra skinning duties on the odd occasions that the hunters bring in a deer or a gazelle.

'That child is a saint,' says her mother to a friend.

'Only another nine hundred and ninety nine thousand, nine hundred and eighty two to go, sighs the young Kalia, sadly, already finding it difficult.

Johnny is an important man these days in Personal Computer Services, otherwise known as the computer police. He is now engaged on a mission to track down Nicky who has committed the terrible crime of destroying a computer at Happy Science. You can't do this sort of thing to a big company and get away with it.

Lux stops everyone he knows and some people he doesn't and asks them if they have seen Pearl but nobody has. He asks people if they will help him look but everybody is too busy rioting.

At the offices of *Uptown* magazine Gerry is rushing through his work so he can get down to Brixton and report on the riot. He is editing the letters page.

You dumb bastard, he writes in response to a complaint from some fool who has gone to see a film he recommended and found it dull. *I said it was a good film and I meant it. No doubt you were too busy eyeing up the woman in the next row to pay attention properly. Don't whine to us about wasting a valuable portion of your Giro and then not liking the film, we can't help it if you have the taste of a warthog.*

As well as not being appreciated as a literary genius, Lux has to sleep on a couch at Mike and Patrick's and it is not a very nice couch. It is the sort of couch that is dragged by its owner from squat to squat before ending up in the front room of a hard-to-let council flat covered by an old blanket in a futile attempt to hide the beer and cigarette stains and it is really not all that pleasant to sleep on.

Lux, however, veteran of a score of temporary unfurnished squats and never much good at getting hold of any furniture, has rarely had anything very pleasant to sleep on unless someone with a proper home takes him in for the night so he wouldn't mind the discomfort too much except that downstairs live all the members of the Jane Austen Mercenaries, a local thrash metal band who he hates because he keeps having to listen to their demo tape through the floor. Thrash metal offends his artistic sensitivities at the best of times and listening to a four-song demo tape a hundred times a night really makes him feel that the band should be tied up in a sack and drowned, although he has never actually said this to them as sometimes they give him free cocaine.

Bricks and bottles fly overhead but Lux takes no notice, too intent on scanning the streets for a sign of Pearl.

'Was Milton ever evicted from his squat?' he mutters. 'Did Thomas Hardy have to listen constantly to a thrash metal demo tape? No chance. These people had it easy.'

And now he is having to walk through a riot when really he feels like a bit of peace and quiet to compose a poem and maybe have a chat with Pearl.

But his optimism immediately reasserts itself. Lux is very, very optimistic. Lux is in fact the most optimistic person that ever lived.

'And love's the burning boy,' he mumbles.

CHAPTER THREE

'Let's stop arguing and go to bed,' suggests Patrick and Mike agrees.

'Where is the KY jelly?'

They hunt the flat.

There is no KY jelly to be found.

'That's funny,' says Mike, 'I bought a giant-size tube just the other day. Where's it gone?'

'Lux!' explodes Patrick. 'I saw him with it. He must have been setting his hair with it again!' Sure enough, there in the living room they find the evidence. Lux has squeezed the whole tube of lubricating jelly into a breakfast cereal bowl, mixed in some sugar and gelled his hair with it.

The bowl is stuffed under a chair along with a comb filled with the sticky mixture.

Patrick is livid.

'How could he use the whole tube?' he rages. 'Now we can't even fuck because that little monster has set his hair with our jelly. This is your fault. You invited him into the house.'

'Calm down,' says Mike. 'We can use something else.' He hunts for some moisturising cream.

When they find out that Lux, always keen to keep his skin looking nice, has used up their new bottle bought only last week from Tesco, Patrick is utterly livid and they lurch back into a dreadful argument, full of personal details and scurrilous suggestions.

Lux, hair set in a spectacular red and yellow forest fire around his head, skin looking very young and smooth, finds that he has reached an impassable roadblock. On his side of the road are masses of rioters. Separated by some burning cars are hordes of police. The rioters throw stones and petrol bombs. The police throw them him back and beat on their riot shields with their truncheons, trying to unnerve the rioters prior to making an advance.

Lux looks on, wondering what it is all about.

'What's it all about?' he asks the nearest person. The nearest person looks at him like he is crazy.

Lux tries to peer over the crowd, looking for Pearl. Small, he has difficulty gaining a clear view over all the heads and riot shields. She could be only yards away and he wouldn't see her.

His heart starts to ache.

What I need here is a little help. A group of people he recognises shuffle closer, bricks in hand.

'Help me look for Pearl.'

'Drop dead Lux.'

It is a section of the local anarchist collective. They do not like Lux because he laughed so much about them putting up a silly candidate in the last general election. Lux thought he was meant to laugh, he never realised it was serious.

'She might have been kidnapped by police or fascists,' he says, trying to interest them. It is useless. They are too busy jostling for position to throw their bricks.

'Well I'm glad I never voted for you,' shouts Lux at the departing figures. 'Don't count on my help in any future struggle.'

They don't hear him.

Meeting the anarchists diverts Lux into a slight fantasy.

'What has happened to Pearl Kropotkin?' he mutters. 'Kidnapped by secret police and fascists as part of the class struggle? Tortured by spies for information? Only Lux can sort things out...'

He goes on hunting.

The smell of smoke is everywhere, slightly troubling Lux, who has an exceptionally acute sense of smell.

'Either he goes or I go,' says Patrick, with finality. 'He just doesn't fit in with our household.'

Mike is glum. He doesn't want to see Lux thrown out onto the street. But as good sex is all that holds him and Patrick together and Lux now seems to be an obstacle in the way of good sex, he is forced to agree.

Kalia is reincarnated in one poor peasant village after another till she starts to feel that she is being persecuted. As far as she understands it these reincarnations should be random and she should at some time be reincarnated as a rich princess or something, enabling her to do a lot of kindness by just giving away money. But no, she is always a peasant. It seems to her that someone in Heaven is trying to make it even more difficult for her and this feeling is magnified when many of her good deeds start to go wrong.

When she piles up firewood outside the home of an elderly priest, the priest trips over it and breaks his neck.

Helping to dig a new well, she turns her back for a moment and a child falls in and drowns. Oh dear, she thinks, fleeing the village pursued by the irate family. Do these still count as acts of kindness? She hopes they do. With another eight hundred thousand still to go she is already fed up with having to act as the country's greatest saint.

But she can't give up. She must get back into Heaven. After living in Heaven, Earth is unbearably tedious. She hates it.

* * *

As the police draw near a vicious mêlée breaks out and the sky fills with rocks and stones and flying glass and Lux is wondering which way to go when a half brick hits him behind the ear and he falls down.

The police are dragging away everyone they can lay their hands on so he has to leap to his feet and run despite feeling dizzy and shaken from the blow. Several corners later he has to stop to rest and crouches under a hedge, feeling sick.

CHAPTER FOUR

As Kalia's lives wore on she found that she would occasionally meet the same people again, themselves now reincarnated. She used to enjoy these meetings as they gave her some sort of relief from the dreadful loneliness brought about by everyone she knew always dying while she had to go on living, even though none of the souls remembered her in their new reincarnations. Only Kalia is born again and again with memories intact.

She learned how to recognise them by the colour of their aura and the shape of their spirit, things she picked up here and there. One person she met quite a few times, in various incarnations, was Lux, and he was always quite entertaining.

She encountered him in Athens in 420 BC where she was a slave at the theatre and he was always hanging around trying to get sponsors to put on his plays or publish his lyric poems. He never managed it.

'It is a terrible injustice,' he complained to her. 'The rich patrons are falling over themselves to sponsor Aristophanes and everyone knows I can write Aristophanes under the table any day of the week. Any time I am invited home to discuss business by a rich patron he ends up trying to seduce me on a couch. These people have no morals.'

Kalia tries to do him a good turn by bringing him to the attention of her rich master but it turns out badly when Lux is suspected of being a Spartan spy because of his long hair and has to flee quickly, never to be heard of in classical Athens again.

Kalia felt envious of people like Lux who could just have a good time because she never could. Of course she was on her way back to the splendours of Heaven and Lux was doomed to be eternally reincarnated because his spirit would never be in a fit state to be admitted into Heaven, in fact after several of his more degenerate lives he is lucky not to be sent back to Earth as a bug, but as he never knew anything about it this never bothered him. Only Kalia is going through eternity with all her past-life memories intact.

Her loneliness increases. On Earth she comes to hate the people she has to help as they are largely stupid and brutal and any time she meets someone she likes they die after only one short life and then she is lonely again.

To make matters worse, her acts of kindness continue to backfire, as when Lux is denounced as a spy. Someone always seems to be on hand to spoil them. She begins to suspect that her enemies in Heaven have sent down an agent to frustrate her efforts.

A week or so before the riot, Nicky, old friend of Pearl's, turns up at her house looking for sanctuary.

She is so upset that Pearl has difficulty piecing together her story. 'I have decided not to let them artificially inseminate me,' she says eventually, utterly distressed. 'I need a place to hide for a while.'

'Who is trying to inseminate you?'

'My employers. Happy Science.'

'Are employers allowed to do this sort of thing these days?' asks Pearl, knowing that the government had brought in a lot of new anti-worker legislation.

'I signed a contract with them. I was blackmailed into it by Dr Carlson.'

So Pearl gives Nicky sanctuary although she feels that really she has enough to do already, what with trying to finish her film while desperately warding off Lux, the social security and the man at the bank who looks after the overdraft she was allowed to build up as a student.

When Lux comes back to his senses after being hit by the brick the riot seems to have raged on to another spot and the street is relatively quiet. There is blood all down his neck and shoulder from the wound on his head and he decides that he had better go home and clean it up before carrying on his search in case an ambulance decides to whip him away for treatment and he ends up confined to a hospital bed.

Possibly Mike and Patrick will come out with him to help him look. He knows that they are a friendly couple. Making his way up Brixton Hill he finds it still relatively trouble free and reaches his temporary home.

When he lets himself in he almost trips over a small bag in the hallway. Why, that is nice of them, thinks Lux. They've tidied up all my stuff into a little bag for me. How thoughtful.

'Hello Patrick. I've just been out in the riot. Pearl's house burned down and I had to rush in and save her, I got hit by the roof falling on me but I managed to save her and I didn't get hurt very much except a girder cut me on the head. Anything interesting happening here?'

'Yes. You're leaving.'

'What?'

'You're moving out.'

Lux is astonished.

'Why?'

'Because I'm sick of you, you little brat. You use everything in the flat. Since you've been here you've been nothing but a parasite and now you've stolen all our lubricating jelly and moisturising cream.'

Lux is upset. He realises, in a flash, that Patrick doesn't like him. This is a shock because he never usually realises that anybody doesn't like him.

'I never used the jelly,' he lies. 'I gave it to some needy child outside to put on his bicycle chain.'

'Don't lie, it's all over your hair.'

Damn, thinks Lux. Normally a talented liar, the shock of being hit by a brick has made him come out with an unconvincing story.

'I might have used a little bit,' he admits. 'Would you like me to scrape some off for you?'

'No.'

'I'm sure I could manage to give you some back.'

'No thank you. I don't intend to fuck through a layer of your hair dye.'

'It wouldn't do you any harm. I'll scrape off a clean bit.'

It is no use. Patrick, sexually frustrated, is not to be reasoned with. Also Lux's hair, attractive from a distance, is, close up, an incredible mass of various gels and home-made setting agents and Patrick figures it would probably give him a disease that would be impossible to explain at the clinic.

'Get out,' he says. 'Take your toy robot and Star Wars toothbrush and never come back.'

Lux leaves, sadly, clutching the carrier bag. It is at least a well-designed carrier bag in pleasant colours, not like the monstrosities some shops give you. Lux, despite losing his collection, is still a carrier bag fan.

Sebastian Flak is Deputy Chief Accountant at Happy Science PLC and he is not a happy man. He is frustrated because he has not been headhunted by a major American company to be a chief executive somewhere.

Ever since one of his fellow acountants, a man below him in the company hierarchy, was sought out by General Motors to run their European division, Sebastian has been feeling miserable, unappreciated and overlooked.

'Why haven't they headhunted me,' he thinks, sadly flicking the pages in his *Soldier of Fortune* mercenary magazine which he has concealed behind a copy of the *Financial Times*. I am a brilliant accountant. Also I am a man of action. Someone must have been spreading bad stories about me.

He has an idea that this someone might be Dr Carlson, head of the genetic research programme and an important man in the company.

Downstairs Lux knocks on the door of the Jane Austen Mercenaries.

Eugene, the singer, lets him in.

The Jane Austen Mercenaries are friendly to Lux because he has told them, quite untruthfully, that he has started doing gig reviews for a music paper and is just waiting for the right opportunity to write them a good review and make them stars. Lux tells Eugene about saving Pearl from the burning house along with the four children that were trapped on the roof and asks if he can wash the blood off his head and Eugene says yes, but when Lux asks if the singer will come out and help him search for Pearl Eugene says he can't although he is just going down into Brixton for a while to look at the riot. But if Lux will stay a while and look after their guitars he is welcome to wash his wound.

Eugene takes off the comforatble jersey he wears in the house, puts on his leather jacket and leaves.

Every day Sebastian waits expectantly by the phone, hoping that Ace Headhunters or We Get Your Man Executive Personnel Ltd will phone him up to arrange a secret meeting in a park somewhere where he will be told that General Motors or IBM is after him and how much salary would he like, but so far it hasn't happened, despite Sebastian spreading it around discreetly at business luncheons that he could be tempted away by the right offer.

He has some accounting to do but he is bored with it so he gets back to his mercenary magazine and notes with pleasure that at last there is a really effective portable one-man-operated anti-aircraft missile on the market.

He sees a picture of himself, sent by a major company to sort out a spot of bother with a subsidiary in Central Africa, a sheet of creative accounting notepaper in one hand and a portable missile in the other, bringing down a communist jet fighter whilst simultaneously putting the company back into high profit margins. If that happened then he might get a special profile done on him by *Business Week*. He would like that.

Lux washes off the blood and feels better.

Time to get back out and look for Pearl.

He feels a little fatigued.

What's this bundle of white powder lying on the table?

Tasting it he finds it is cocaine.

Lux figures they will not notice a little bit missing and anyway they owe him a favour as he is going to review them for a music paper and it will give him some energy for searching, so he rolls up a piece of paper and starts to separate a small line with a kitchen knife, but just at that moment there is the sound of a violent struggle and a policeman bursts through the door wrapped in combat with a rioter.

Oh dear, thinks Lux, and starts sniffing frantically, knowing that more policemen will be in hot pursuit. The constable and the civilian crash round in the hall and more heavy footsteps sound outside. Lux snorts away furiously, desperate not to be arrested for cocaine when he has to get out looking for Pearl. When his nose is totally congested he lowers his head to the table and eats what is left, licking his tongue over the mirror till no trace of the drug remains.

'Sorry to disturb you like this,' says the policeman, now handcuffing the man as some others appear. 'We've chased this coon all the way down the street and I wasn't going to let the bastard go.'

'Right,' says Lux, eyes starting to glaze.

'Take care of yourself,' says the policeman, remembering his Community Training Programme.

Lux, of course, young artist, does not like policemen bursting in being insulting about coons but he is not going to argue with them as he discovered long ago that the best you get for arguing with a policeman is a trip to the police station.

The constables leave. Huge lumps of cocaine start pouring down Lux's nasal passages. A breeze blows in the shattered door. Temporarily forgetting what he is meant to be doing, Lux strums on a guitar, picking out the notes with his perfect nails.

'I wonder if I'll get another house,' says Pearl. It took her two years' membership of a housing co-op to get the one that has just been burned down. Nicky makes no reply and Pearl leads her on, one arm round her friend and the other round her bag of salvaged possesions.

Pearl's prize possession, virtually the only thing that she saved, is a roll of film, a film that she has spent almost a year making with some friends from art school.

Making an independent film is almost impossibly difficult. The print in her hand is the only one in existence. Badly harassed and somewhat frightened by the increasing violence around her, Pearl will nonetheless kill anyone who tries to lay their hands on it.

Lux suddenly feels that he is on top of the world. He often feels like this so it does not really strike him that it is the massive dose of cocaine working its way round his body.

At five feet three inches Lux does not have a lot of body for it to work round. He is small everywhere. Although he thinks his legs are perfect like Betty Grable's they are really a little bit thinner. Still, they are good legs. Often he wears short trousers to show them off and then he is whistled at by men on scaffolding and when they realise he is male they shout abuse at him. And, he muses, I am getting pretty good on the guitar. I wonder if I could steal one somewhere.

Being seventeen, hopelessly in love and maniacally vain, it would be natural if Lux was a terrible poet. But in fact he is quite a good poet which makes it hard for him that no one ever wants to listen to his poems, except occasionally Pearl, who has a kind heart, sometimes.

He makes up strange cut up verses in his head, shuffling around the lines like beads on an abacus till they fall in place to his satisfaction. Inside Lux's head is a literary computer, unwanted by the rest of the world.

No publication has ever published anything he has sent them, or even talked kindly of it. Nobody has ever really said to him that he has any talent. But Lux is not downhearted by this because he is too optimistic to be downhearted even when the *Times Literary Supplement* went out of their way to send him a special letter saying please don't send us any more poems and *Uptown* tried to pretend to him that they had changed their address.

Lux is at least loved by animals. Dogs and cats follow him around in packs, which he likes. Sometimes he speaks to them. He feels that they appreciate his work.

Hunting round in the flat for a while he finds some make-up and touches up his face, a little pale from loss of blood, thinking that he can't disappoint his public by appearing out on the streets looking bad, also there might be more TV cameras about.

He knows it is only a matter of time until he is a star of some sort and he wouldn't like some cheap tabloid to publish a bad photo of him taken at an unfortunate moment.

Then he comes across the Jane Austen Mercenaries demo tape, a tape that has caused him some distress due to the band playing it over and over again at massive volume when he is trying to sleep upstairs.

Aha, he thinks.

At work, Nicky never got on very well with anyone else in Happy Science but she made very good friends with her computer.

She doesn't get on very well with anyone because she is the sort of person who just can't see the joke when a strange man in a pub tells her that she has nice tits. So with all the fun-loving young executives and computer operatives in Happy Science happy to say this sort of thing all the time while she is trying to get on with her work she never reacts well and is never really popular.

Still she is very good at her work and Dr Carlson promotes her in the department and lets her help with the genius project, even proudly showing her the frozen sperm collected from all the nations' geniuses, although Nicky does not manage to sound as enthusiastic about this as he might like. But generally most people leave her alone except for Sebastian Flak, who is particularly keen on her.

She starts to form a deep bond with her computer.

Lux does not like the Jane Austen Mercenaries. He thinks they are crass and unpleasant sounding. Also he thinks they are sexist. Lux's sexual politics are now very good, because if he ever came out with anything bad Pearl would clap him round the head and he learns quickly when he is being clapped round the head.

As well as this they have refused his persistent offers to write lyrics for them.

At the last count fourteen Brixton bands have refused Lux's persistent offers to write lyrics for them.

He puts the demo tape in his carrier bag along with three more copies lying on the floor.

Now so wrecked as to be totally irresponsible he takes a lipstick and writes on the wall.

> DEAR JANE AUSTEN MERCENARIES, THANK YOU FOR LETTING ME GET WASHED IN YOUR FLAT. A POLICEMAN BROKE DOWN THE DOOR. DO NOT WORRY ABOUT YOUR DRUGS I MANAGED TO FINISH THEM ALL BEFORE THEY WERE DISCOVERED. YOU CAN REPAY ME THE FAVOUR SOME OTHER TIME. I AM TAKING YOUR DEMO TAPE BECAUSE IT IS AN INSULT TO THE NATION'S EARS. IF YOU WOULD LIKE ME TO WRITE YOU SOME GOOD LYRICS, GET IN TOUCH.
>
> LUX

Making sure that his notebook is handy in case he feels a poem coming on, Lux sets off again, heart starting to ache because Pearl is struggling along somewhere without him.

CHAPTER FIVE

A week before the riot Mary Luxembourg the novelist phones up Gerry at his desk at the offices of *Uptown.*

Mary Luxembourg is soaring up the alternative bestseller charts with her first novel, largely due to the wonderful full-page review that Gerry gave her.

Mary Luxembourg is Gerry's hero.

A wonderful feminist classic, he called it, *full of startling imagery and memorable characters involved in a long dream of freedom.*

The book is now being picked up on by the straight press, whose book editors would not like to be thought of as old fogeys.

'Gerry,' says Mary, after Gerry has finally answered the phone, 'My publisher is clamouring for the next one. It is all thanks to your review. Next week I am being interviewed by the *Sunday News.*'

'The workers are on strike at the *Sunday News*,' replies Gerry, 'It is being put out by the management and scab labour. Should a left-wing feminist author be talking to them?'

'I need the publicity,' says Mary. 'And anyway it will spread the message among people who would otherwise not hear it. And also I will put a good word in for you with their book editor so that he will read your novel when it comes out. How is it coming along?'

'Pretty well,' replies Gerry, 'I have some startling imagery in it. And some notable characters. It is sort of a long dream of freedom.'

'Sounds terrific. Incidentally, can I have the manuscript of my new novel back?'

'I haven't finished it yet.'

'I need it. I've lost the only other copy. It was stolen out of my Audi.'

Gerry's heart sinks. He knows that he has lost the manuscript. He manages to keeps calm.

'I'll drop it right round,' he says blithely. 'Bye.'

Gerry considers the situation. It seems bad. He has lost the only copy of Mary Luxembourg's new novel and this could be a terrible blow to his credibility because he is always going on at his friends about what a wonderful novelist she is and bragging about how friendly they are. What is more, he is utterly depending on a good quote from Mary Luxembourg for the back of his first novel. It will make all the difference to his sales. Since Mary Luxembourg is becoming a big novelist thanks to his reviews, this seems like a convenient arrangement.

He can't quite remember where he lost the manuscript.

Lux is back in the riot. He has no idea why it is going on.

'Why is there a riot going on?' he asks a stranger, an elderly man who is standing beside him watching some people across the street throwing stones.

'We are suffering more than usual,' says the man.

'Oh. Who is?'

'Us. Black people. No jobs, no money, policemen stopping the youth in the street all day.'

Lux is concerned to hear this.

'Can I do anything to help?' he asks. But the man doesn't think so, and Lux goes on his way.

Lux, not much in touch with the real world, doesn't really know anything about these things, although in this he is not alone, even among the people who live locally. Like many of the whites in Brixton he co-exists with the blacks without actually knowing much about what is going on among them, and if a sixteen-year-old black is stopped and questioned by the police five times in one day, it doesn't make the TV news.

Still, he doesn't quite understand why anyone would riot if they couldn't get a job. Lux would be more inclined to riot if he had to get one. He looks around to ask the man, but he has disappeared.

'Have you seen Pearl?' he asks some more complete strangers, expecting that they will have.

'Pearl who?'

'Just Pearl,' says Lux.

'What does she look like?'

'She has finely textured cropped red hair like blood-soaked grass,' he tells them, quoting loosely from one of his poems. No one recognises the description.

Unnoticed by Lux the police on the far corner are about to advance. One last fierce shower of missiles and the crowds in the road retreat, carrying him with them, so that he does not catch a glimpse of Pearl, who was only yards away in the crowd but is now carried off in the opposite direction.

Pearl and Nicky are deposited in a doorway where a moment's peace breaks out.

Nicky breaks out as well in one of the frantic bursts of speech which occasionally pierce her psychotic silence.

'The whole place was a nightmare.'

'Where?'

'Happy Science. It was full of madmen. I never understood what they were all up to.

'There was an accountant called Sebastian who was going mad because he was a failure and read mercenary magazines and chatted me up all day long and my head of department was Dr Carlson who was going mad as well because his serious scientific project had been taken over by someone called Mr Socrates in the publicity department who wanted to run a beauty contest to attract public sympathy and stop environmental groups going on about them ruining the countryside all the time. It was a nightmare.'

Pearl motions Nicky on and they hurry down the street which is for the time being clear of obstruction though littered with minor riot debris and fast-food cartons.

'Perhaps people riot because they're full of fast-food poison,' says Pearl, a little sick of tales of Happy Science which she has already heard many times, but Nicky ignores the interruption.

'Mr Socrates had huge influence in the company because he had the idea of adding fifty per cent water to all their beauty products and then saying on the labels that they were now fifty per cent purer. They thought he was a genius. I would have resigned because they are so stupid but I'm in so much debt I need the money. Where are we going?'

'Somewhere safe.'

Kalia's acts of kindness start to go more and more wrong. She can hardly sweep a floor without someone tripping over her and breaking their collarbone. When she saves food to give to holy men it turns out to be rotten and poisons them. For a while there are no healthy priests left in the province.

When she is reincarnated as an Eskimo almost the first thing she does after learning to walk is to sharpen up her father's harpoons but when he comes to use them they have been mysteriously weakened and he is eaten by a walrus.

Someone is definitely dogging her footsteps. Her enemies in Heaven have sent someone down to Earth to make sure she never gets back.

Pearl is slightly lame in one foot. She always wears strong boots. Lux now likes women in boots.

They run into another fierce patch of rioting and Nicky becomes blank again. Struggling through the riot, Pearl's foot hurts so they take temporary refuge behind a huge crowd of people, onlookers. All round there are people rioting and people onlooking and sometimes the rioters cross over into the other crowd for a rest and sometimes an onlooker gets worked up and joins the rioters and sometimes people are somewhere in between onlooking and rioting, but everywhere the police are forming up into impenetrable phalanxes prior to clearing the streets because by now they are well used to this sort of thing and specially trained to deal with it.

Another camera crew hoves into sight, shrouded in smoke from the burning buildings.

Aha, thinks Lux.

'Hello, I'm Lux, an important local poet. Would you like to hear some of my poems?'

'Get the fuck out of here.'

'What way is that to speak? I never heard you tell the prime minister to get the fuck out of here. Do you wanna hear a poem or not?'

'No. We're covering the riot.'

'It was one of my poems that started it. Would you like to hear it?'

The cameraman would rather kill Lux than hear his poem. Restraining himself from violence he swings round the camera on his shoulder to film some policemen scattering in the face of a petrol bomb attack. The petrol blazes up out of the shattering milk bottles and lights up the fading day with blue and yellow flames.

'Such yellow sullen smokes make their own element,' says Lux, pursuing the camera. 'That's Sylvia Plath. Now I'll read you one of mine.'

Personal Computer Services exists to make sure that businesses using computers don't get any aggravation from anyone. When they hear about the terrible aggravation that Nicky has caused Happy Science they are immediately hot on the trail, hunting her down with the intention of bringing her to justice and also recovering the vital genetic programme without which the nation will crumble, not having a new generation of geniuses to lead it.

Happy Science has predicted that the nation will be particularly short of geniuses very soon because educational standards are falling all the time and nobody has to sit an Eleven Plus exam any more but spends all their time in primary school playing with sandpits and guinea pigs instead of learning the twelve-times table. The education system is practically in ruins.

No wonder we are falling behind in the export market, they tell government committees. No one knows enough any more to export anything. You don't catch them playing in sandpits in Japanese primary schools. In a Japanese primary school everyone is learning the twelve-times table before they can walk. They never get near a guinea pig. Without our genius project we might as well just throw in the towel.

The government committees give them full support and the project races along, until it is ruined by Nicky.

'I need to rest,' says Nicky, somewhere between Brixton and Stockwell.

'Me too. What's in that bag?'

'A genetic programme,' says Nicky. 'And the manuscript for a new novel.'

Oh god, thinks Pearl, she really is cracking up.

Pearl is of course not feeling very good with her house being burned down and all her possessions lost. She is not insured. Her guitar is gone and the tapes of music she was trying to knock into shape to get her band going have gone and so have her paintings.

All her artistic endeavours burned by a stray petrol bomb.

Some ashes float into her short red hair. They stain her face. In front of her there seems to be no way through.

Some rioters speak enthusiastically to them about a big attack they are going to make, but Pearl just wants to get down to Kennington where she knows the riot will probably not reach and her friend will give them shelter for a while.

'How come you never have any good programmes on TV?' demands Lux, working his way in front of the camera. 'Why didn't you even reply when I sent you a tape recording of me reading poetry?'

'Get the fuck out of here,' bawls the cameraman, manoeuvring desperately into position round Lux as a ferocious battle breaks out only yards away, with ten rioters trying to haul back the furiously kicking body of a colleague that the police are dragging away.

'Could I get my own TV programme?' says Lux, hopefully, himself desperately manoeuvring round into the viewfinder.

'Go away,' scream the crew. 'You're ruining all our pictures.'

'What're you filming?' asks Lux, too wrecked by now and too involved in the prospect of his own TV programme to remember much about the outside world.

'Lux!' screams a voice from across the road. 'Give us back our demo tape. I'm going to fucking kill you.'

'Damn,' curses Lux, lurching back to reality. 'Interrupted at the vital moment. Another minute and I'd've had my own programme.'

He scurries off up the street.

Patrick sees him scurry up the street on television as the camera picks out his distinctive figure, hair flying, long coat flapping.

CHAPTER SIX

Johnny is leading his squadron of trained operatives from Personal Computer Services into the riot zone. He is a popular leader.

Johnny has tattoos over his shoulders and arms, most of then done while he was in the army. He has thick black hair cut short and a small moustache. He is popular with his friends because he has a fund of good stories and tells them well in the pub. There is the one about wanking in an armoured car in Belfast, the one about going to a disco and picking up a girl in a wheelchair, wheeling her home and taking her off the wheelchair in the park to fuck her, the one about how he ran his car at a nigger in the road and made him fall in a puddle, the one about how when he was a police-cadet he pushed his truncheon up the vagina of a prostitute they had in for questioning.

He is a great storyteller.

Lux, nimble despite his head wound, shins over a wall to escape from Eugene. Along with Eugene is Grub, one of the Jane Austen Mercenaries' four guitarists.

'I'll kill the little bastard,' says Grub, flexing his muscles in his filthy leather jacket. 'He's took every copy of the demo tape.'

They keep searching. Their tape going missing is a disaster. Just that evening they had a phone call from a record company where an executive has been listening to the riot on the radio. The executive knows that Brixton will be big news for a while, and he has a vague memory of receiving some tape from a band in Brixton. Sure enough, when he hunts around in the drawers where he stuffs all the tapes that get sent to him he finds the demo from the Jane Austen Mercenaries.

At least he finds the cover, but when he plays it he finds that he has taped some of his Beatles favourites over it. Never mind, he knows they will have another copy. I must sign them up for a quick single, he thinks. If I get it out immediately it will sell.

Eugene, receiving the call, is ecstatic about this attention from a record company but a little distressed to find that all their tapes have gone, along with their cocaine.

The band set out to look for Lux. When they find him they will recover the tapes and probably give him a good kicking as well, which will not be bad for their image.

* * *

Kalia's guess that someone has been commissioned by her enemies in Heaven to frustrate her return is correct. Yasmin, assassin, has been sent to dog her every move with instructions to ruin her efforts, wreck her acts of kindness, make her position so hopeless that she will eventually give up.

He arrives on Earth around 800 B.C. and immediately starts giving her a hard time. The minor prince in the heavenly palace who framed her is frightened that if she returns, now a creditable being who cannot be ignored having performed the million good acts, she may be able to prove that it was him who was the real villain of the heavenly coup.

Seeing Kalia getting on so well with the kindness he sends Yasmin down to stop her. Yasmin, a nasty piece of work who only got into Heaven because the prince forged his Karmic record in return for services rendered, began to plague Kalia's every lifetime. The rate of good deeds completed slumped dramatically and Kalia, seeing endless lifetimes of hopelessness stretching out in front of her, began to feel depressed and defeated.

Now, however, wandering around in the riot doing acts of kindness to everyone who needs one, she is cheered up to see a figure she recognises. It is Lux.

For some days after Mary Luxembourg's call Gerry casts around desperately trying to find what he has done with the manuscript. Finally it strikes him that he left it at the house of a girl called Nicky he was trying to pick up after a Nicaragua benefit gig in Brixton Town Hall. It might be a little embarrassing seeing her again as she threw him out the house, not wanting to fuck him, but at least now he can get it back.

During this time he is in a terrible mood and every review he does is killing. Any film or book unfortunate enough to come under his scrutiny is destroyed outright and everyone else at *Uptown* goes very gently around him because they know that if they rub him up the wrong way then he will denounce them as oppressors and they all hate to be denounced as oppressors, particularly by someone who is such good friends with Mary Luxembourg, the novelist of the moment.

Once denounced as an oppressor by *Uptown* magazine there is no way back. Everyone knows that if they don't like you there must be something pretty badly wrong with you.

'My father hated me,' mumbles Nicky, sheltering with Pearl behind a wall.

'Right,' says Pearl. 'We should be able to work our way through if we head on towards Stockwell.'

'Everybody made fun of me at university.'

'Right.'

'You're not listening.'

'I'm trying to get us to somewhere safe.'

'I don't care if we're safe. I'd as soon be dead. I might kill myself anyway. I killed my computer. My only friend.'

'Oh thanks,' says Pearl.

'My only friend apart from you. Everyone else hates me.'

'No they don't.'

'Yes they do. Lux wrote a terrible poem about me on the wall.'

'That wasn't Lux. He isn't vindictive. Anyway, I'd recognise his handwriting.'

'He still hates me. He's jealous of us. Personal Computer Services are coming to get me.'

'There is no such thing as Personal Computer Services.'

'Even you don't believe me,' says Nicky, wide-eyed. 'They do exist, they're evil. It was them that assassinated the man who broke into the Queen's bank account. Now they're after me and they're after you as well, because of the film.'

'What?'

Nicky falls silent and won't speak any more.

Wonderful, thinks Pearl, and pokes her head out to see if the coast is clear.

A phalanx of policemen is marching up the road. They take cover again.

Pearl has been going to self-assertiveness classes where they have taught her how to shove her way through aggressive strangers and frighten them off by using her voice powerfully. As far as she can remember there was no class telling you how to deal with forty aggressive policemen. Possibly that was next term.

'What's that smell?' says Nicky.

'My organic moisturising cream,' replies Pearl.

'I recognise that smell,' thinks Lux, who has a very acute sense of smell. It is Pearl's natural organic moisturising cream. She must be somewhere close.

I recognise that aura, muses Kalia.

'Hello Lux.'

'Hello.'

'Nice to meet you again.'

'Right,' says Lux, not having any idea who Kalia is but never willingly impolite.

'I haven't seen you for a few hundred years. Not since the Spanish Inquisition, if I remember correctly. What are you doing?'

'Hunting for Pearl. Do you want to help?'

'Certainly,' says Kalia, and joins in the search.

Johnny, now in hot pursuit of Nicky and Pearl, joined the police after leaving the army. He loved it at the police college, where they taught him how to work his police radio and how to drive a car fast with the siren going neeneneene and how to deal with coons without starting riots all the time.

But due to a terrible injustice he was thrown out of the force almost as soon as he settled in when he had the dreadful misfortune to beat up a black student who was staying in the country with a family of rich whites. The rich whites made a terrible fuss and Johnny was expelled.

Since then his life has been hard. He no longer has big wages and has had to sell his car, which caused him great distress because he firmly believed that a big car was very good for impressing women, in fact he thinks that his recent lack of success with women may be due to his not having such a big car any more.

But now, re-employed by Personal Computer Services because of all his valuable experience, he has a chance to start all over again. He is determined not to foul it up. He will bring back the genetic programme if he has to kill Nicky to get it.

'Well,' says Mark, if we're going to Brixton we might as well leave.'

'I should finish these book reviews first,' says Gerry, 'I have a volume here that has been cited all over as the major novel of the decade.'

'It's getting late.'

'Is it? Oh fuck it then.' He sweeps the novel of the decade into the bin. 'It is probably trash anyway. Let's go.'

When Nicky crouches down she puts her hand out to lean on and makes contact with a still dribbling condom.

Terrific, she thinks, shaking her hand.

One time she went to a party and some students played a game of putting condoms over their heads and blowing them up. The game was called Horses. To Pearl it didn't seem like a lot of fun but it gave the students hours of enjoyment.

Thinking of the party makes her think of Lux because he was there, trying to write a poem on the kitchen wall with a red crayon until the person who lived there found out and threatened to throw him out of the window.

'What d'you mean throw me out the window,' protested Lux. 'I'm doing you a favour. When I'm world champion poet this kitchen wall will be worth a lot of money. People will come from miles to see it. Probably TV crews will come to make programmes about it.'

Lux has some vague and confused notion about being world champion poet, picked up during some drunken reading of a newspaper report about some obscure poetry contest.

'I know plenty of poetry,' he told Pearl. 'As well as writing my own I know bits from Homer and Sappho down to ee cummings and Stevie Smith. I could quote you the whole of Milton's *Paradise Lost.*'

'Go on then, ' said Pearl.

'It's slipped my memory. Still, I am a prime candidate for world champion poet. You'll be sorry you wouldn't sleep with me when I'm being interviewed on breakfast television and photographed for the *Reader's Digest.*'

'I did sleep with you.'

'Only partially,' replied Lux, dragging up an old argument. 'Your heart wasn't in it. I don't reckon it counted.'

The only time that, to Kalia's knowledge, Lux ever had any success in life is when in twelfth-century Japan he turned out to be a spectacular success at the perfume guessing game.

With no warfare going on, the Japanese aristocracy sit around all day being civilised and playing games and one of their favourites is perfume guessing, in which various aromas are offered round blind and they have to guess what they are.

Lux, turning up as usual in a kimono that has seen better days and a hairstyle that would probably get him beheaded by a samurai were it not for him being an artist and therefore allowed some degree of liberty, begs some food from the rich household in return for his poems. Possibly because he is more than usually hungry he does not declaim any of his own works and sticks to the classics, so he is quite well received and, full up with rice and fish, is invited to play the game.

He amazes everyone with his skill. He is sensational at guessing perfumes.

The household invite him to stay a while as they have an important perfume-guessing contest coming up soon with some rivals from the next hamlet.

Gerry and Mark make it to Brixton later in the evening, having had to get off the tube several stations early and walk the rest of the way.

Outside the riot they are stopped by the police but when they say they live in the area and have to get home they are let through.

Brixton Road is now fairly clear and the riot, though still growing in intensity, has moved sideways into the streets and estates. A police helicopter flies deafeningly overhead and more and more buses of police crawl into the area, green single-deck buses full of officers from other areas.

Almost immediately they meet Lux, who is standing adjusting his hair in front of the remains of a shop window while Kalia stands around watching.

The window belongs to a butcher's shop. As a vegetarian he is not sorry to see it wrecked. Eating animals makes him feel upset.

'Hello,' says Gerry. They know each other through having met at Pearl's when Gerry was visiting Nicky.

'Hello,' says Lux, without enthusiasm. He does not like Gerry because *Uptown* refused to publish any of his poems. Although Gerry didn't have anything to do with the decision Lux regards him as working for the enemy.

'We're going round to Pearl and Nicky's.'

'No use,' says Lux, and tells them that the house is burned down and he is just now searching for them.

'Damn. The house burned down. Did they save the manuscript?'

'No,' replies Lux, despite not having any idea what manuscript Gerry is talking about. 'All they had left when I handed them out through the window to the firemen was the clothes they were wearing and a book of my poems. There wasn't time to save anything else.'

'Where are they now?'

'I don't know. They drove off in the fire engine.'

'Did you see the riot start?' asks Gerry.

'No.' Lux shakes his head, fairly violently, body tingling with the cocaine. 'I just walked out of the house and it was going on. I don't even know what it is about.'

Gerry gives him a look of contempt.

'It's anti-police oppression and racism and the repressive state of the nation,' he tells him.

'Right,' agrees Lux. 'I am pleased to know. I got hit by a brick.

I wasn't doing any oppressing at the time.'

'Well you should have got out of the way,' says Gerry. 'Anyway, there will be innocent casualties. Although you are probably not that innocent.'

Lux thinks of Pearl being an innocent casualty and becomes frantic again.

CHAPTER SEVEN

Thrash metal guitarist Grub, man of action, chases round after Lux with Eugene. Grub has a degree in astro-physics from Cambridge University but, unlike his guitar, keeps it quiet.

The other three members of the band are back at the flat, guarding the instruments from the riot in case any one decides to riot through their shattered door.

Lux is nowhere to be found but the two hunt with the sheer determination of any struggling musicians who see the prospect of imminent success. Nothing is going to stop them from getting their demo tape to the record company and putting out a record. They would commit murder to put a record out.

As far as Sebastian could see he was at a dead end in Happy Science. Although an important company it was not the sort of business that rates deputy accountants very highly and he realised that without some high profile exposure he was never going to come to the attention of IBM or Coca Cola and they would never send a headhunting company after him with a big offer.

The only good thing in his life is Maybeline, brought over from the USA to be chief computer programmer. Sebastian has been talking to her and she seems to like him.

Sebastian might like Happy Science better if he was party to the secret plan being formulated to genetically code everyone in the country and make sure that only nice people have babies, or the illegal Happy Science genetic experiments which are going to make them the company of the future, but these plans are being kept quiet in case rival companies steal them. So it seems to Sebastian that Happy Science is a dead end.

Lux talks to Gerry for a time while Kalia hunts in her pockets for ten pence for a passing tramp who is struggling along in urine-drenched confusion but is trying not to let the riot affect his income.

Eugene and Grub appear round the corner.

'Bye,' says Lux, nipping through a garden and over another wall, band in pursuit.

'What do you think that was about?'

Gerry shrugs. 'No doubt he's stolen something off them. I've heard he is light-fingered.'

Kalia finds ten pence for the tramp and leaves.

Gerry wonders what to do about the lost manuscript. It is a disaster any way you look at it. Mary Luxembourg's copy has been stolen and his copy has been burned in a fire. He will never be able to hold his head up at *Uptown* again after Mary Luxembourg denounces him. Unless of course no one particularly cares about her any more.

'Quick. We have to find a phone.'

'We'll never get through this way,' says Pearl, exasperated. 'I wish these people would all fuck off and let me get out of here. Come on, let's try this way.'

'He used to try and make other companies employ him,' mumbles Nicky. 'It was pathetic.'

'What?'

* * *

'A close escape,' mutters Lux, having evaded the Jane Austen Mercenaries. 'Closer than the time Patrick demanded I went shopping with him and helped cook a meal.'

'Well, well, look what the cat dragged in,' says a voice full of husky sensuality.

'Hello John,' says Lux. 'Nice dress. Have you seen Pearl?'

John yawns, deliberately.

'Stop pursuing that female, Lux. You're wasting your time.'

They look at each other. John, in his dress and high heels, has known Lux for a while but their friendship has never really got much beyond swapping tips about make-up because John is one hundred percent concerned with being gay and in some way regards Lux as a traitor, because Lux is so attractive, wears such nice make-up, but isn't homosexual, or not very.

They are standing outside the terrace where John lives, flanked on either side by more people who form a small gay community.

'Hello,' screams Tim, John's lover, and grabs Lux up to kiss him in greeting. Lux kisses him back and the process takes quite a long time.

'We're having a riot party. I've just been collecting the Judy Garland records. Will you stay?'

'I have to look for Pearl.'

John and Tim both yawn, dramatically.

They are very camp, unlike Mike and Patrick. Lux is not keen on campness and thinks he should be on his way.

'Some people were asking after you. Some musicians.'

'Wanting me to write them a new song again?' suggests Lux brightly.

'I don't think so. Sure you won't stay for the party?'

'I got to find Pearl. She is alone in the riot.'

'I knew there would be a riot,' says John, adjusting his hemline. 'The socio-economic factors were exactly right for – ' He stops as Tim digs him in the ribs. 'Sure you wouldn't like to hear some Judy Garland?' he finishes.

'No thank you,' says Lux, and walks on.

He likes Judy Garland but right now he is a man with a mission.

* * *

It was a moment of maniacal genius when Sebastian struck upon the idea of creating some market interest in himself.

'Hello. Is that Ace Headhunters? I am speaking on behalf of Coca Cola.' He puts on an American accent. 'We're looking for a new man to run our South American operation. He has got to be someone exceptional, capable of clearing rainforests in Brazil and building sales figures in Chile. Is there anyone suitable you could get for us. Who's that? Never heard of him.'

Sebastian dismisses all the proffered suggestions.

'These are all third-raters. What we need is something special. The Chilean army is a huge Coca Cola market. How about this man Sebastian Flak? We've been hearing a lot about him over here in the States.' Sebastian makes a little clicking noise to make it sound like it is a trans-Atlantic telephone call.

The Ace Headhunters agent confesses to never having heard of Sebastian Flak.

'Well in that case we had better try another headhunting company. You are obviously not on the ball.'

With that he rings off, satisfied that it is a good start, and takes a turn round the building to see if there are any secretaries or research assistants he can sexually harass for a while as Maybeline is away on a course for the week, learning some advanced management techniques and probably having a good time.

Lux is well treated in the Japanese household. Every day they feed him rice and fish and give him a new kimono and the family lets him read out his own poems which they pretend to like because he is their secret weapon in the perfume guessing game.

They have never beaten the neighbouring hamlet. This counts as a disgrace to their village, but the neighbouring hamlet has a man who is reputed to have a god-given nose and never makes a mistake. In all the time they have been playing the game they have never come across anyone to rival him, except perhaps Lux.

He is put in strict training and spends hours every day sniffing perfumes in unmarked containers while the family coach marks down the results.

'Excellent, excellent,' exclaims the coach. 'You have a superb nose.'

Lux is pleased at the compliment and pleased at the unusual hospitality.

Kalia meanwhile does her duties in the household. The youngest daughter, she is not very important in the family, but after scores of unimportant lives she is used to this and carries on cooking and cleaning with her usual forced enthusiasm, wondering how many hundreds of thousands of kind acts she has left to complete.

Lying with a Friend under a Burnt-out Truck

Under the burnt-out truck Lux continues to ramble.

'Tonight has been a waste of time. I could've been writing poetry instead of running around in a riot. But people do a lot of things that are a waste of time. Mike and Patrick go surfing. Do you know what surfing is? I saw it on television. You go out to sea on a plank of wood and then you float back to the shore. Then you do it again. Imagine. It is almost as pointless as jumping out of a plane on a parachute.

'Once I knew a girl who worked in a hamburger restaurant. I was horrified. Imagine working in a hamburger restaurant. Do you think they get deliveries of whole cows at the back door and then make them into hamburgers? People do terrible things to cows. It shouldn't be allowed.

'The social security wanted me to get a job. They tried to force me to work in a hamburger restaurant and cut up cows instead of writing poetry. They seemed to think it was more worthwhile. If my

signing-on clerk hadn't been crazy about my good looks I'd be up to my elbows in blood at this very moment.'

He pauses.

'I keep getting this funny feeling I'm heading naked into battle.'

His brilliant red and yellow hair splays all over the tarmac, but under the truck they are hidden from the outside world.

Chapter Eight

A few accountants come in for a meeting with Sebastian, which frustrates him a little as he is impatient to get on with whipping up interest in himself. Also, he has a new issue of *Soldier of Fortune* to read.

The mercenary magazines have given Sebastian some confusing images when he masturbates. One involves marching into some village in Africa and raping all the women at gunpoint. Another has him making love to some woman who is carrying a Kalashnikov and wearing an army uniform such as he has seen in pictures of the Nicaraguan army.

Sebastian is confused about his sexuality and this surfaces occasionally.

The first time he meets Lux is when the young poet arrives at the door of Happy Science just as the accountant is leaving and demands to be allowed to add his sperm to the genius collection.

'Why?'

'Because I am a genius of course. Also, I came out of a test tube and have experience of this sort of thing. Would you like to hear a poem?'

'No.'

'Well is there a genius selection committee? I could read them some of my work. They'd let me in, no bother. How exactly do you collect the sperm? Do you suck it out with a big machine or do you have to have an operation or does everybody just masturbate into a test tube? If so could I bring along a friend to help?'

Sebastian starts to feel a little uneasy. Lux, hair resplendent, trousers ripped to show off his legs, sticks out in the business section of the city like a kind heart at a management meeting. People walking past in their suits are starting to stare and Sebastian is embarrassed.

Worse, he is slightly attracted. 'I'm sorry, I can't help you,' he says, and walks off briskly, scared that Maybeline might appear and somehow guess that he is not unattracted by Lux.

'I am the first test tube baby to be a nationally recognised poet,' calls Lux after the accountant, a little forlornly, but it has no effect. Disappointed, Lux hunts for someone else to volunteer his services to. Ever since Nicky told him about the project he has been keen to do his bit for the next generation.

He thought they would be pleased to have him.

Gerry finds a phone and phones *Uptown*.

'Are you reporting on the riot?' they ask.

'No,' he says. 'I want to dictate a retrospective re-appraisal of the works of Mary Luxembourg. Are you ready? Right. *Mary Luxembourg has been much over-rated in the past by critics unable to see the ultimate unworthiness of her work...*

Mike argues and argues with Patrick until he is forced to storm out of the house saying that he is never coming back because he is not willing to share a house with anyone uncharitable enough to turn Lux out into the street in the middle of a riot.

Patrick wishes he had never set eyes on Lux and sits angrily in front of the television, watching game shows interspersed with up-to-the-minute riot reports.

Mike makes his way through the seething streets which is easy in some places, difficult in others. Some side roads are blocked by police, others aren't. Some are pouring with missiles, some aren't. There are not enough rioters or police to entirely fill all of the streets.

He meets a friend who is carrying a leather coat and a pair of jeans liberated from a shop and the friend is very pleased about this because he has not had a new coat for three years. He tells Mike that the main road is presently impassable but if he makes his way along Acre Lane and through the back streets from there he should be able to reach the office of Liberation Computers, his destination.

Well, thinks Gerry, ending his phone call with some satisfaction. That's fixed that. When people read that retrospective on Mary Luxembourg no one will care if she never publishes another novel again.

Of course now he won't be able to get a quote from her for the back cover of his soon-to-be-completed first novel and this is bad, but not so bad as being a pariah among his peers.

They walk into the centre of the riot, turn a corner and come across a group of five young blacks, one of them bleeding from a wound in his head.

'Tell me what's happening,' says Gerry, excited.

'Are you serious?' they say, presuming he is some sort of police spy.

'No,' he chuckles. 'You don't understand. I'm a journalist.'

'A white journalist,' says one of them, wryly. 'Fuck off, white journalist.'

'You don't understand. I work for a left-wing magazine...'

'Fuck off, white journalist, before we cut your throat.'

They leave.

'In any revolutionary movement there will always be reactionary elements,' he explains to Mark, who admires him for his knowledge of this sort of thing.

The five youths hide behind a wall. They have just been chased by some policemen and are planning to get their own back. Two policemen are walking towards them. They go tense in readiness, weapons to hand, ready to pounce.

'Hi everyone,' says Lux cheerfully, appearing over the wall 'Anyone seen Pearl? She's sort of this height with short red hair and probably carrying a friend.'

'What is this?' they demand, staring at Lux, who is looking more than usually strange with blood still seeping out of his wound and KY jelly starting to run over his face, melted from the heat of the burning butcher's shop.

'No one seen her? Oh well. Fancy hearing a poem?'

'Will you get the fuck out of here, you white bumbawally,' hisses one of the youths, seeing that Lux is going to ruin the ambush.

Lux becomes indignant. This continual unthinking rejection of his poetry is a little hard to take, particularly when only he stands between the nation and complete barbarism.

'What do you mean get the fuck out of here?' he says, raising his voice. 'Let me tell you the poem I was going to read you was pretty fucking good. Now I might not bother.'

'Kill him!' screams the leader, totally frustrated at Lux being so stupid. And they might well have done it had not the two pursuing members of the Jane Austen Mercenaries appeared on the scene at that moment, clambering over the wall a lot less nimbly than Lux.

'Where's the tape?' they scream. The police, hearing all the noise, call for help and rush to the scene. Everyone flees.

'You'll all appreciate me one day,' shouts Lux over his shoulder, and disappears.

Dr Carlson and Sebastian Flak do not get on very well.

This is mainly because Sebastian is always telling him to spend less time and money doing research and start making some more profitable products like stay-fresh hamburgers and medically-recommended toothpaste.

'Where is the new toothpaste?' he demands. 'We have a team of dentists all ready to make tests showing it leads to fifty per cent less fillings. The report is already written. Mr Socrates has the

TV commercial well in hand. So where's the toothpaste?'

'The new toothpaste can wait. I am carrying out a serious scientific project.'

This goes on all the time. Another reason for bad feeling however is that Sebastian is always trying to pick up the doctor's research assistants in the canteen, particularly Nicky. Sometimes he even comes down to the laboratories brandishing free tickets for the Hippodrome.

Finally the doctor confronts him with this and tells Sebastian that if he bothers any more of his assistants then he will complain to the Managing Director and after this they are deadly enemies so that when Sebastian finds that he is not getting on too well in the company he naturally assumes that it is because Dr Carlson has been spreading stories about him to the directors.

Sebastian, already bitter about his lack of career progress, becomes more frustrated and blames the directors for believing the stories and completely loses the company loyalty they taught him in business school.

He stops accounting altogether and spends all his time reading magazines and dialling up Maybeline's extension.

'I'm just not getting on in the company,' he confesses to her.

He finds her soft American accent soothing and easy to confess to. Maybeline, a little bored after her course on management techniques, asks him to join her for lunch.

Meanwhile Dr Carlson composes a biting memo to the Chairman complaining about Sebastian always hanging around his laboratories troubling the assistants and trying to get them to come out for drinks.

Lux, in flight, is grabbed by a hand and hauled behind a wall.

'I have a good explanation for everything,' he begins.

'Don't bother,' says Kalia. 'You don't need to explain to me. I already know you are a born thief as well as being hopelessly vain.'

'How do you know I am a born thief as well as being hopelessly vain?'

'I've met you before in other lifetimes.'
'Oh.'
They are in a garden that fronts one of the many large houses in the side streets of Brixton.
Only yards away some people are struggling home with some booty looted from the high street, but Lux is not very aware of his surroundings.
'What is your name?'
'Kalia. I expect you want some explanation about me saying I've met you in former lives?'
Lux's mind is too full up with cocaine and Pearl for him to really understand what Kalia is saying. 'Not right now. I am too worried about Pearl. I don't seem to be any nearer finding her. I can't find anyone who's seen her. I can't get anyone to listen to a poem.'
He becomes slightly maudlin.
'I don't have anywhere to live. I'm being chased by a bunch of dumb thrash metal merchants. Pearl refuses to fall in love with me. Perhaps it was a bad idea to fall in love with her. Plenty of other women like me. Just the other day someone wanted to take me away to a life of luxury but I didn't go because of Pearl. It is hard being in love.'
'Maybe you should have taken the life of luxury.'
Lux shrugs.
'I didn't really like the person that much. I only went home with her because she said she wanted to hear some of my poems. When I got there she tried to grapple me into bed. This happens to me a lot. People seem to get the wrong impression when I offer to come home with them and read them some poems.'
'Yes,' says Kalia. 'It is hard being an object.'
'It would definitely have been more convenient to fall in love with someone who wants to fall in love with me. Much less trouble. Well, I'd better get looking.'
'*Then on to the Pnyx*
With urgent tread
A fearful threat
Hangs over our head,' he mutters. 'Now, who wrote that?'
'Aristophanes.'
Lux frowns. 'I'm not sure why, but I never liked Aristophanes.

Is my hair looking all right?'

'Perfect.'

'Good.'

Pearl's film is about some women with magic powers who live in an old block of flats.

They kidnap the hero, played by Pearl, and put her through a painful cathartic process which will be liberating in the end but causes her a lot of hardship at the time.

Also, it is about witches being burnt in the seventeenth century. It has been a long process making it without any money.

Lux, however, has been very supportive with help and ideas, and when Pearl needed someone to play the part of a demon scarecrow Lux was a natural choice. Everyone agrees he is a sensational scarecrow although Pearl never lets him read any of the scarecrow poems he writes specially for the part.

'Wasn't I good in your film,' says Lux continually.

'Yes,' says Pearl. 'Shame you couldn't have helped with some money.'

Lux has never had any money.

'I heard it rumoured that some headhunting companies were after me with some substantial offers from large American corporations,' Sebastian tells Maybeline over lunch, slightly altering the truth. 'But it hasn't come to anything.'

This last part is true. Despite his best efforts, Sebastian has failed in his bid to generate interest in himself.

'I envy you,' he continues. 'You have just been promoted. You are obviously heading for success. Everything you do goes well.'

'It's all due to chanting,' she tells him.

'Chanting?'

'Yes. Every day I chant Nyam Myoho Rengi Kyo for fifteen minutes. It has brought me success. Before I started I was merely a computer programmer and now I am managing the whole department.'

Sebastian is interested, if dubious. He can't see himself chanting.

'How does it work?'

Maybeline shrugs. 'No one knows. It is a Buddhist technique but you don't have to be a Buddhist to use it. I learned it from my brother back in Dallas. He used to be a down-and-out street artist and now he paints murals for oil companies.

'But chanting? It seems like such a strange thing to do.'

'But it brings sucess'

CHAPTER NINE

Kalia spends several lifetimes without pushing up the balance of kindness at all. Inside she rages against Heaven for making things so unfair for her. Powerless against the evil Yasmin, she has seen her hopes fade. The last person she tried to help, a starving beggar she gave some food to in the central Russian steppes, was torn to death by Mongols after Yasmin led them to believe the food was stolen.

This incident makes her despair. Here she is trying to be kind and what happens? The recipient of her kindness is ripped into four small pieces by wild horses.

Yasmin, helped by his heavenly supporters, always seems to turn up in a more powerful position than her. She is always a peasant or a slave or something, and though her lifetimes of accumulated wisdom sometimes make things easier it is never any help against some brute of a warlord, and there seem to be a lot of brutish warlords about.

Next lifetime, however, she receives an unlooked-for stroke of luck when she is born into a family of wise women in the Hopi

Red Indian tribe.

Lux admires some rioters with scarfs tied round their faces but decides against copying it as his face is too nice to tie a scarf round. Every few moments he stops someone to ask them if they have seen Pearl while Kalia waits patiently for him to catch up.

'Someone must have seen her.'

'Don't worry,' says Kalia. 'We'll find her.'

'I hope so. I'm aching inside.'

'Did you argue with her?'

'Certainly not,' says Lux, working his way round a group of people giving away some sort of news-sheet. 'We never argued. Even when Pearl was being horrible I was pleasant and cheerful.'

This is a lie. They did in fact have an argument, brought on by Lux being insensitive when Pearl was suffering a depression about the film not going well.

'The cameraman does not take me seriously,' she complained. 'Basically he can't work with women. Woman have always had a hard time in the arts.'

Lux nods sympathetically.

'We've no sooner stopped getting burned as witches than cameramen start fouling up our films,' she continues. 'I'm fed up with being disregarded. No one knows any women film-makers, philosophers, poets...'

'I don't know about that,' interrupts Lux. 'There's Sylvia Plath, my favourite. Then there's Maxine Kumin and Rosemary Dobson and Stevie Smith and Fleur Adcock and Ellen Bryant Voigt – '

'Lux'

' – and Elaine Feinstein and Margaret Atwood and Selima Hill and –

'Lux'

' – and Marianne Moore and Charlotte Mew and Ruth Pitter and – owww!'

Lux is brought to a halt by Pearl yanking his hair. Afterwards she won't speak to him because she thinks he is trying to make fun of her, but really it isn't Lux's fault that he happens to know all the world's poets.

'It isn't my fault if I happen to know all the world's poets,' he says. 'No reason to get upset.'

'Pardon?' says Kalia. 'Excuse me, I'm just going to help that young man to his feet.'

In a comprehensive and efficient act of kindness she picks up a fallen victim, wipes his face, helps him adjust his dreadlocks back into his big hat and gathers up a few coins that have rolled out of his pocket before sending him on his way. Unfortunately a watching policeman decides that probably anyone lying on the ground with dreadlocks must have been doing something worth arresting him for, and arrests him.

'Are you in love with anyone?' asks Lux.

Kalia shakes her head. 'I got bored with it a thousand years ago.'

At the offices of Happy Science Dr Carlson is arguing bitterly with Mr Socrates from the publicity department about the perfect-mother contest.

'You don't seem to understand,' he explains, patience running out, 'that what we have here is a serious scientific study involving years of research, not to mention the purchase of the most obscure pornographic magazines in order to collect the sperm from the nation's geniuses. Some of them were very old. We can't just stuff it into any woman who happens to look nice. We need someone who is genetically correct and also intelligent.

Socrates waves away the objections. He has already explained to the Doctor that they can only continue with the project if they generate public interest in it. No high-profile interest for the company and they are liable to cancel the whole thing. It has already cost a phenomenal amount of money and were it not for the fact that the prime minister has personally spoken out in favour of it it would have been cancelled long ago.

'Furthermore, where is the new toothpaste you were meant to be developing?'

Nicky appears, holding a clipboard, preventing the Doctor from coming out with a cutting reply.

'I've got your results,' she says, and hands him the clipboard.

'Don't ogle my staff!' says Doctor Carlson to Mr Socrates as he stares after her departing figure.

During all this time Nicky is having a progressive mental breakdown because she can't relate to the world at all, but no one is very bothered about this because she is never really very friendly to anyone and if you are never all that friendly then who is going to worry about you having a mental breakdown?

She sits at her computer terminal and talks to it.

Good morning, did you sleep well? That sort of thing.

She does not see her friend Pearl very much because Pearl is putting all her time and energy into making her film, and Nicky resents this a little.

Sebastian, still dubious, but impressed both by Maybeline's success and her confident personality, starts his chanting. He does it in secret, slightly worried that people might think he has got religion, or maybe just lost his senses.

For fifteen minutes each day he chants the mantra, without really believing anything will happen.

Of course he has zero interest in Buddhism, but a lot of interest in success in the material world, and Maybeline said it would work.

Lux and Kalia walk on until they are halted by a policeman who tells them to wait while he searches their pockets for anything they may have looted.

'Don't worry,' he says in a strangely friendly tone, 'we aren't bothering about dope tonight, just stolen goods.'

Not finding any stolen goods on either Lux or Kalia, he lets them pass.

'Though why should I whine,' says Lux 'Whine that the crime was other than mine?'

'Very nice,' says Kalia. 'Yours?'

'No, Gwendolyn Brooks.'

They walk on, surrounded by a shallow stream of people, all searched and found to be without stolen goods.

'So,' says Kalia, picking her way over the broken glass of a shattered shop window and raising her voice slightly as a siren starts up somewhere close, 'you don't remember me at all? Well, never mind, I wouldn't expect you to. But I knew you immediately. The aura around your body never changes. Still going around falling in love with unsuitable women and trying to get people to listen to your poetry?'

'Now you mention it, yes.'

Lux's brain clears slightly.

'Who exactly are you?'

'I am Kalia. I have been exiled from Heaven for three thousand years. I am engaged in a quest to regain my rightful place in Paradise. Also, I have an idea that some descendant of Heaven is in danger tonight and I am going to try and help them.'

'That's a relief,' replies Lux. 'For a while I thought you might be connected with the Jane Austen Mercenaries. I heard they were looking for a new drummer.'

'Have you seen anyone who might be a descendant of Heaven?'

'Do they have any distinguishing marks? A halo or anything?'

'No. But they might have an aura of magic around them.'

'Maybe it's Pearl. She would fit the bill. Unless it's me.'

'No, it's not you, although you are fairly magical. I always liked the cheerful way you failed at everything.'

'Have we met?'

'Often. But you wouldn't remember.'

'No, I have a terrible memory. My mind is all full up with cocaine and poetry. And Pearl.'

'Why don't you leave her alone?' says a voice from behind.

'What?' says Lux incredulously, turning round to see what maniac is telling him to leave Pearl alone. He finds a young woman giving him some very unfriendly looks.

'Oh, hello Pat,' says Lux, still polite but edging slightly behind Kalia. 'How is the woman's refuge doing? You haven't seen Pearl anywhere, have you?'

'No, and I wouldn't tell you if I had,' declares Pat. 'Everyone's sick of you running round after her. What's the idea of bothering a lesbian? You ought to leave her alone and maybe if you don't we'll throw you in the Thames. And don't send any more of your dumb poems to the refuge. We're not going to put them up on the noticeboard.'

She leaves.

Kalia looks at Lux. 'Well?'

Lux sighs. 'Pearl has already lectured me about it. I still have some bruises. But we did sleep together. Anyway,' he brightens up, 'I figure this sort of thing doesn't apply to young poets in love. Young poets in love are allowed to do anything. Everyone knows that'.

Kalia doesn't agree but she doesn't reply. After her thousands of years of tedium on Earth she rarely argues about anything.

'How do you regain your place in Heaven?' asks Lux.

'I have to do a million acts of kindness?'

'Maybe I could help you with one or two,' says Lux, 'I'm well known for my acts of kindness.'

Pearl has fought off the social security people trying to make her get a job in order to keep on with the film and she is not going to let a riot spoil it all.

She would have been safely through to Kennington and her friend's house by now were it not for the fact that she is having to chaperone Nicky and Nicky is finding it difficult to walk because she feels so guilty about destroying her computer and this brings back more bad memories about Happy Science. When they come across a destroyed electrical goods shop and Nicky finds the remains of a small computer lying mangled and unwanted on the pavement she is reduced to tears.

'Come on,' says Pearl.

'Maybe I could fix it.'

'It's ruined. Put it down.'

The sad occurrence starts Jane off on more bad memories.

'I hated it at work because every time I wore anything different all the men had to make some comment about it.' She mimics their voices: ' You're looking nice today. Another funny outfit?

That's a bit normal by your standards, isn't it? Smartening up are we?'

Pearl, of course, as Nicky's part-time lover, is normally sympathetic to this sort of thing, but now she is too busy concentrating on avoiding the missiles that are flying fiercely.

Down by Stockwell there is a thick mass of people, young blacks from the council estates and young whites from the local squats, all throwing stones and bottles and petrol bombs and sometimes whole ignited garbage cans at a force of policemen who are retreating, outnumbered.

A girl beside Pearl throws a petrol bomb and it spills over the top of a policeman's riot shield to burn round his helmet and some other policemen beat out the flames and this creates a gap in the ranks and more and more stones and bricks start pounding down onto them.

'Sugar and washing up liquid,' says the girl to Pearl. 'It's no good just putting petrol in, you have to make it flare up and stick to the skin.'

'You know,' says Lux. 'Tonight I have met two TV crews and neither of them wanted to hear any of my poetry. I can't understand it.'

Kalia is temporarily busy, helping a man to his feet and setting him on his way.

'Well Lux, they won't take much notice of you because you are not very important.'

'But I am a great poet.'

'That isn't very important. Not to them anyway.'

Lux finds this depressing. He kicks a stone in his path and it sails down an alleyway.

'Good shot,' says Kalia.

'Yep,' says Lux, pleased. 'I was always a good footballer. I could have played for my school.'

'Why didn't you?'

'All the other boys refused to go into the changing rooms with me.'

'Why?'

Lux shrugs.'I'm not sure. I think they were jealous of my skill. Look, there's another television crew.'

He strides up to them.

'Hello,' he says, politely. 'I am Lux, head of the local council. Would you like to hear some of my poems?'

'You're not head of the local council. I've just been interviewing him up the road.'

Damn, thinks Lux. What a stroke of misfortune.

'Well, the head of the local council is a terrible poet,' he says, trying to work the situation to his advantage, 'whereas I am a genius. Also, I saved some people from a burning building and then I helped the Jane Austen Mercenaries get a recording contract by writing them some good reviews and now I'm on my way to hospital to give blood as I have a unique blood group and am always on call for saving a few lives when neccessary, so how about letting your listeners hear a decent poem?

'No.'

'Why not?'

'I'm here to report on the riot.'

'Who cares about a riot?'

'The whole country.'

'Well I don't. I think it's a bore. Have you seen Pearl anywhere? She has a small thin body like an F1-11 jet fighter.'

'Please go away.'

Lux shuffles away, disappointed, with Kalia, who sympathises.

'Why do I bother being polite to these people?'

A Jane Austen Mercenary appears in the distance and they are forced to hide.

Jesus, thinks Patrick, still moody in front of his television. Lux is everywhere. Every time a news report comes on he is harassing the cameraman.

Brooding, he wonders if Mike might have been fucking Lux in secret. He wouldn't put it past them. He knows that Mike is attracted to Lux, and might have won him over by agreeing to listen to some of his poetry. Lux, well known for having no morals at all, would probably do anything for a person who is willing to listen to his poetry.

Out for a drink after work, Sebastian hears from a reliable source that We Get Your Man Personnel have been making some discreet enquiries about him.

Deliriously happy, he pays for his round and rushes home to do some extra chanting.

Eugene and Grub are joined by the three remaining thrash metallists who have left some friends to guard the flat.

They gather on a corner to discuss the affair.

'We got to get the record out. What will we do if we can't find Lux and get the tape back?'

'We could record it again,' suggests one of them.

'It wouldn't be as good,' protests Eugene, the singer. 'I could never do my vocals as well again.'

'Well that wouldn't really matter,' says Grub. 'No one cares too much about the vocals in our sort of music. As long as I could get the lead guitar down right, we'd be OK.'

Eugene is outraged. 'What the fuck do you mean no one cares about the vocals? My singing makes the band.'

'I wouldn't go that far,' protests the drummer. 'I always thought it was my powerful beat.'

'Fuck your powerful beat. Any drummer can make a powerful beat. My vocals are special.'

'My guitar solo was a classic.'

'Your guitar solo was the same one you always play.'

'It fucking well was not. I spent three days getting that guitar solo right.'

'Well it just sounded the same as all the others...'

The argument rages for a while, as does the riot.

* * *

Johnny sees Kalia pass in the distance. He grins.

'She is never going to get back into Heaven,' he says.

'Pardon, sir?' says his second-in-command.

'Nothing.'

Around 45 AD Kalia is a fully qualified Hopi wise woman and can cure illnesses and find water in a drought. More importantly, by studying the behaviour of the birds in the sky, she can predict the future.

Predicting the future will be, she knows. a very useful weapon against Yasmin, who up till now has always had the upper hand.

In the tribe she is able to do hundreds of good acts, curing illness and war wounds, helping to fix tepees, staying up late to mix up body paints – all sorts of things.

Yasmin appears in the shape of a psychopathic young warrior but, now able to tell what is going to happen, Kalia starts to frustrate his evil plans.

For the third time she meets Lux, now reincarnated as a vagrant singer of traditional songs who makes his living by going round all the tribes singing to them.

He is not a very good singer, in fact he is terrible and the reason he wanders around is really that no one will put up with him for very long. But Kalia makes sure he gets a good meal for his singing and, knowing in advance that Yasmin is going to poison it, switches plates round the campfire so that Yasmin is poisoned instead and Lux goes away well fed.

'He was the worst singer ever to visit the tribe,' says one of her friends the next day. 'I think it was very kind of you to give him some bison stew.'

Kalia's credit rating starts to move up again.

Lux, of course, never remembers these reincarnations. Only Kalia does. But traces of them remain in his succeeding lives. It is, for instance, the reason he knows so much poetry, having spent thousands of years learning it all over the world.

* * *

Lux seems to find himself doing a lot of hiding. Still, with police charges and violence everywhere he is probably as well to keep out of the way, being too small to be very successful at violence, also he is not very keen on it. It doesn't seem right for a poet to go around flinging bricks at people, even if they deserve it.

'Of course I could be wrong about that,' he says. 'After all there have been plenty war poets. Homer maybe even fought in a war.'

'What are you talking about?'

But with the cocaine still rampaging round his body, new lumps still disentangling themselves from his nose and throat to slip into his bloodstream, Lux isn't really sure what he is talking about. What he most feels like doing is going to a party or a nightclub.

'What I most feel like doing,' he says to Kalia. 'is going to a nightclub.'

'Yuck.' says Kalia. 'What's this?'

It is a used condom.

'Pearl has touched that condom,' says Lux. 'I can sense it. I have good intuition about this sort of thing.'

Lux's intuition is correct. He does have a touch of magic about him.

'Condoms can be a terrible problem. Have you ever stepped on one when you get out of bed to go to the toilet or something?'

'No.'

'I have, lots of times. It is a terrible experience. It clings to your feet like a magnet. I think maybe they put glue on them so they don't accidentally come off while you're fucking. Very helpful at the time but no fun afterwards when you're groping around in the dark with sperm dribbling over your toes. Are you sure it's never happened to you?'

'No. I got bored with sex long before prophylactics were invented.'

'Did you? Oh well. We must be hot on Pearl's trail now.'

Lux's arms are getting a little tired from carrying his bag of possessions and his feet are sore from walking becasue he is wearing a threadbare pair of baseball boots that are not made for walking long distances and jumping over walls.

Inside the carrier bag he has a few clothes and a few precious possessions. One of them is a toy robot he found on a bus one time, inside a biscuit barrel. He is very very fond of this robot. Back in the high street, with the night becoming dark and a crowd of looters tearing the heavy metal shuttering off a jeweller's shop, he notices some batteries lying inside the smashed frontage of Woolworth's.

'Wait a minute, Kalia, I need a battery for my robot.'
He stoops down and gathers one up, thinking that if he gets it working he can cheer up Pearl with it as she is bound to be depressed after her house being burned down.

'Aha, a looter,' says a policeman, and drags him off to a police van.

Up above the helicopter has switched on its spotlight and the powerful beam lights up the rooftops where the police are pursuing someone, and inside the police van the noise of the helicopter's blades is amplified so that it rings out on the metal walls and shudders around inside the young poet's head.

The noise reminds him of some time he can't quite remember and again he feels as if he is preparing to go naked into battle.

Even when Nicky used to visit Pearl and they would go to bed Pearl would always end up talking about her film. She was consumed with the creative urge.

'What it needs, is something to offset all the scenes of the witches in the mansion. How about you getting me some shots from Happy Science?

'I hate Happy Science.'

'That's all right, just get a camera and take a few pictures in the laboratory of something that looks like it's evil technology and I'll cut it into my film.'

Nicky agrees, if only to get Pearl off the subject and back to lovemaking.

So later she takes some pictures at random, sneaking into the science laboratories when the scientists and technicians are all over at the pub celebrating a pay rise.

Unfortunately she takes pictures of the top secret genetic programme experiments. If anyone finds out that Pearl's film is going to contain incriminating shots of illegal foetus experiments and pictures of secret computer documents, she is doomed.

'Hello? Is that We Get Your Man Personnel Limited? I am speaking on behalf of IBM. This is very secret but we are looking for a good man to take over our newly restructured European division. We have scoured the company but there is no one here that is up to it. Have you any suggestions? How about this man Flak?'

Sebastian, motivated by his inside information, is re-applying himself to his cunning scheme to have himself headhunted. Meanwhile he is getting in bad with the company directors because his work is suffering as he is too preoccupied with his machinations to do any accounting. This, however, is of little concern to him.

'I have heard that some large corporations are again expressing an interest in me,' he tells Maybeline. 'No doubt it is due to your advice on chanting.'

Maybeline is pleased to have been of help but refuses an invitation to lunch as she already has an appointment.

Sebastian is aghast. She is having lunch with someone else. His heart aches. He resolves to chant even more to bring him success in his relationship with her.

Meanwhile he dumps the bundle of papers he is meant to be working on in a drawer, cancels an appointment with a client and shuffles off through the building to see if he can find a secretary or someone to have lunch with.

Outside the van containing the captive Lux, massed police talk over their radios, waiting for instructions about the next move.

'Personal Computer Services, let us through,' says Johnny, importantly, leading his squad of elite men.

They file through Brixton.

'Do you know what's in there?' asks one of the operatives, passing the big old building that houses the Enterprise Centre.

'What?'

'Liberation Computers.'

'Really?'

Johnny is interested to learn this. So this is where Liberation Computers, deadly enemies of PCS, do their subversion.

He briefly considers going in and wrecking the place but decides against it. He has a job to do.

The blessed damozel leaned out of the gold bar of Heaven, quotes Lux to himself, locked in the police van. *She had three lilies in her hand and the stars in her hair were seven.* I wonder if Pearl is thinking about me just now? She might even be looking for me.

CHAPTER TEN

An ambulance draws up and the crew try to load some of the fallen policemen into it, but it is difficult for them as the missiles keep flying and one of the ambulancemen is floored by a piece of paving stone so that he falls down right over the policeman he was trying to load onto the stretcher.

Pearl and Nicky cannot get through and they cannot go back. The crowd advance on the police and seem on the point of breaking through when round the corner a huge double file of reinforcements arrive with their shields in position and their special long riot batons at the ready. These batons were specially manufactured after the last riot to make sure the police could effectively deal with troublemakers without having to come too close.

They form up and start to advance. Trained for this sort of thing, they force the rioters back. Snatch squads appear from among their ranks, targeting particular people for arrest and dragging them off face down with their arms pinned behind their backs.

They have been well trained. Funds have been diverted from other places to strengthen the police and prepare them for riots. So now the government can deal with riots without having to come too close.

Beside Pearl a young woman is poleaxed by a constable, and the crowd, sensing they are about to be overwhelmed, start to panic and everbody tries to escape.

Pearl tries to grab Nicky but Nicky panics along with the crowd and struggles away. A snatch squad comes between them and they are separated.

Lux is sitting in the police van waiting to be charged with looting a nine-volt battery, but he is not too worried. For one thing he is too stoned to worry much and for another he never lets anything trouble him, save for his painful love affair.

This optimism is soundly rooted.

'My optimism is soundly rooted, ' he exclaims out of the blue to the man sitting next to him in the van. 'When I was six years years old I fell underneath a lawnmower my dad was testing for the company. It could've been a terrible disaster. It could've left me so mangled and disfigured I'd be ashamed to walk the streets. But all that happened was it gave me this little scar over my eye. I kinda like it. Sort of pirate-like, don't you think?'

He gets no reply. But if even falling under a prototype lawnmower turned out well he is sure that nothing really bad can happen to him. And, so far, all his life he has enjoyed the luck and protection of the truly innocent, and every time he is thrown out of a squat he finds a new one quickly enough, or someone attracted by his looks puts him up for a while and when he spends all his Giro an hour after he gets it on drugs, robots and carrier bags then someone looks after him for the next fortnight or he finds twenty pence on the street and twenty pence is enough to live on for a day if you can manage on a bar of chocolate, which Lux can.

Sometimes the people he is looked after by get fed up with him thieving everything and spending hours in front of the mirror doing his hair and make-up and sometimes he gets bored and leaves, because he is never really able to merge his life with anyone else's.

'Mind you,' he continues. 'I never really trusted my father after that. It was rumoured in the family that he pushed me deliberately.'

Even inside the police van the air smells of burning.

'The prolonged candle flames flung their smoke into the laquearia,' he says out loud. 'That's T.S.Eliot.' The line sort of sticks in his mind because he has no idea what a laquearia is. Possibly it is something you spray on hair lacquer with.

'Shut up,' grunts another of the van's occupants, having a cracked rib and not being in the mood to hear any poetry or stories of Lux's childhood.

Lux takes out his crayon and starts to write on the side of the van, making up a poem as he goes along.

The Jane Austen Mercenaries continue their search although they have had a furious argument about who is the most important member of the band and are now barely speaking to each other. This makes it difficult for them to agree on which street to look in next and with the police everywhere shoving people about and some streets impassable with burning debris it is proving to be a difficult task.

'Where now?' rasps Eugene.

'Don't ask me,' says the drummer. 'I am just a worthless accessory. According to you anyone can keep a beat. If you're so smart, you find him.'

Nicky runs off and hides in a council estate behind a rubbish skip and Pearl can't find her.

Alone except for the colonies of insects that make a good living hunting through the rubbish left by the refuse truck, Nicky lies quietly, unable to move.

Her psychosis is getting worse and worse as she becomes more and more guilty about killing the computer. As a master programmer she had her own little computer on her desk. When she thinks about how she set fire to it and threw it through a window she hates herself. After all it wasn't the computer's fault that she had such a bad time at Happy Science.

She imagines it lying in a grave somewhere, cold and unloved, circuits dead and casing all rusted. Worse, she imagines Personal Computer Services coming and taking her away and putting her in a secret prison where no one will ever find her.

To make it even more frightening, no one else but her believes in the computer police; they think she is just being paranoid when she talks about them. Even Pearl does not really believe in them.

'Hello, Personal Computer Services?' Dr Carlson is on the phone. 'Any progress yet? No?'

'Fraid not,' they tell him. We haven't been able to find her yet.'

'Well this is not very satisfactory. This woman has committed one of the major anti-computer crimes of the century, you know, wrecking the machine and making off with the programme. It is time you did something about it.'

They tell him to be patient. They always get results.

The Chairman happens by and asks him how things are progressing.

'Not well. We are stuck without the genetic data in the programme. I could kill that woman. And Socrates wants more and more publicity. The man is practically insane.'

The chairman tries to calm him down. He knows that the Doctor no longer gets on with anyone.

Kalia watches Lux being hauled off into the police van. Unable to do anything about it, she continues on her way, doing what acts of kindness she can.

The riot is making little impression on her. Having lived hundreds of lives, she has seen hundreds of riots.

The twentieth century has made an impression on her. She doesn't like it. Particularly she doesn't like where she has to live, a bedsit in Camberwell. The bedsit is terrible. She has been more comfortable sleeping in a swamp with a wolfskin for a blanket. Thousands of years after being exiled from Heaven she still finds her surroundings hard to take and has never forgotten the luxury of her heavenly life.

Earlier that day a starling had flown past her window.

That is interesting, she thinks. There is going to be a riot.

Furthermore, the birds tell her that somewhere in the riot a direct descendant of the Queen of Heaven will be endangered.

She thinks that she must now be close to her tally of one million kind acts. Completely worn out by it all, she hopes she is, but she lost track somewhere around the sixteenth century, when she was an Inca and the Spaniards invaded South America. If I rescue this descendant of the Queen of Heaven from danger it might be the very thing that gets me re-instated, she muses.

So far in this lifetime she has not encountered the evil Yasmin.

Gerry and his friend Mark wander the streets, looking at the riot without participating. Gerry takes mental notes for the article he is going to write for *Uptown*.

In a crowd they run into Sheila, a friend from the days when Gerry was big in his student union.

Discussing the riot, they are both enthusiastic.

'I met someone you know, a little while ago.'

'Who?'

'Nicky. Do you know she has a manuscript of Mary Luxembourg's new novel?'

Gerry frowns.

'She had. It was burned.'

'No, I met her and another girl a while ago and she still had it. I held it while we hunted in the bag for some cigarettes.'

'Quick,' yells Gerry to Mark,'I must find a phone.'

They struggle out of the crowd to look for a phone but it is not easy, hardly any phones work in Brixton at the best of times and now most of them are either freshly wrecked or unreachable.

I can't let that retrospective go out if the book still exists, thinks Gerry, worried.

Back in twelfth century Japan the perfume-guessing contest is under way with Lux and two brothers from the family on one side and three important locals from the next hamlet on the other, including the man with the god-given nose.

Kalia's heart sinks when they arrive. Another of the important locals is Yasmin. With her growing ability to read the future she has been expecting this, but in the rigidly hierarchical society of ancient Japan it is difficult for her to avoid him. As usual Yasmin has been reincarnated in the more important position. While Kalia is youngest daughter and someone to be married off as quickly as possible, Yasmin is lord of his hamlet.

He lets loose a malevolent grin. By now both Yasmin and Kalia can easily recognise each other's spirits whatever bodies they are inhabiting at the time. As Kalia brings out some tea for everyone, Yasmin cunningly trips her up, just to keep his eye in, and the tea spills everywhere, ruining Lux's new kimono.

Lux is practically in tears as he has spent hours in front of a mirror arranging his clothes till they are perfect and it takes all of Kalia's skill to calm him down. He makes such a fuss about his kimono that if it were not for the fact that it would set her back in her task such a long way she would have strangled him with it.

Chapter Eleven

Get a grip, Nicky tells herself. Stop being so appalled at everything. The world may not be so bad.

While she hides under the skip seven men with knives drag a young woman into the entance of the flats to rape her, removing her clothes and taking turns to make her do what they want.

While one has his turn the others look on and make comments and pass round a can of beer.

Nicky is too scared to help the victim and there is nowhere to run for help.

The woman trembles with sick terror and does what the men want so as not to be killed.

Above her eyes the rapist's face looms huge and wet with folds of skin hanging down, filling with excited blood.

'How d'you like that, bitch.'

'Keep her legs open.'

'You do it good or I'll cut your face into bits.'

'Yes,' says Gerry, further up the road, as missiles still fly and fighting rages. 'It is very true that a riot is the voice of the unheard.'

'Hi,' he says, meeting Eugene on the fringes of a large crowd which is shuffling unwillingly up the street, directed and occasionally prodded by a line of policemen.

Knowing each other slightly they talk and Gerry hears about Lux stealing the tape.

'Can't you record it again?' he suggests, but all this suggestion gets is some angry silence from the other members of the band.

'How about I take some pictures of you in the riot?' asks Mark, brandishing his camera. 'Be great publicity material for the single. If you get it out.'

'We're busy looking for Lux,' says Eugene.

'It'll be good publicity. Let's do the pictures,' says Grub, keen to disagree with the singer.

'I wanna be in the front of the photo this time,' says the drummer. 'I'm fed up with being obscured by everyone else.'

'It's my turn to be in the front,' complains the bass guitarist.

'What the fuck are you doing?' demands the large body next to Lux.

'Writing a poem,' he explains.

'Well fucking stop it.'

Lux stops, not wanting to be harassed in the confined space of the police van.

The door rattles.

'Take this,' says the man next to Lux, and stuffs something into his hand.

It is three diamond rings and a packet of something. The door swings open and some police look in.

Lux crams the looted rings and the packet into his mouth.

A policeman drags him out of the van.

'What you got sonny?' 'Mmmbgmm,' replies Lux, trying desperately to keep the rings hidden without swallowing them. He knows that it will be bad for his insides if he does.

The policeman looks in his bag. Seeing the toy robot, spare army trousers and Star Wars toothbrush he realises that Lux is not a very dangerous character and they need the space in the van for a very dangerous character they have just marrested.

'I caught him nicking a battery,' explains the arresting officer.

The packet Lux is hiding contains more cocaine and the paper starts to come apart in Lux's mouth, freezing his tongue till he can hardly feel the rings any more. I'm doomed, he thinks. I'll get thrown in prison as a drug dealer and looter and I'll never see Pearl again.

'What the fuck have you got on your hair?' says the sergeant to Lux. 'Piss off out of here. If I see you again, you're nicked.' And he gives Lux a shove. Lux scurries off and round a corner.

He spits out the rings but there is not much of the cocaine left to spit out and on top of his earlier dose Lux feels like he is walking somewhere between the clouds and Alpha Centauri.

Another stroke of luck, he muses. Let out of the police van with a free mouthful of cocaine. I must have had ounces of the stuff tonight and normally I can't even afford to buy a little line. He does stay firmly enough in reality to notice members of the Jane Austen Mercenaries lurking on the next corner and to hurry off in the opposite direction. He wonders what he should do with all the demo tapes. Possibly he could record some of his poetry on them and send it to radio stations. That seems like a good idea.

Regarding diamond rings as hopelessly tacky he throws them into a garden and starts trying to work his way round the now heavily police-fortified centre of Brixton.

He makes it through an estate and down towards Stockwell where he is jostled by some men with beercans.

Strange dreams filter into his mind. They frequently do. For some reason he finds himself thinking of bison stew, although as far as he knows he has never eaten a bison. In fact he would hate to eat a bison.

Some youths stand next to him. 'Nice night,' says Lux, politely. Two of them take hold of his arms and hold him while another searches him. Finding no money, they go away.

'I've just been searched. I'm meant to be searching for Pearl. Where is she? What the fuck were those people mugging me for? Do I look like I've got any money?' He talks out loud to himself, unable to hear his thoughts too well above the wailing of sirens and stamping angry feet.

'Lux, involved in one of history's great love affairs, scours the violent streets for Pearl Freedom Fighter. Refusing offer after offer to stop and read poems to television cameras he sticks single-mindedly to his task.'

Perhaps it wasn't such a good idea to get obsessed in a love affair. On the other hand it is probably necessary for a young poet. No doubt Milton never had a moment's peace from having affairs all the time. Lux, utterly determined now to find Pearl, resolves to let nothing stand in his path and marches on resolutely.

Sebastian is now chanting furiously, spending much more time on it than Maybeline's suggested fifteen minutes each day.

He is completely determined to have himself headhunted.

Also, he is completely determined to win Maybeline's heart, but he suspects that she may be starting some relationship with a successful public relations expert from the company next door.

He has heard more rumours that Ace and We Get Your Man have been continuing their discreet enquiries about him and now completely believes in the power of the mantra.

This, along with phone calls to Maybeline and careful study of mercenary magazines, takes up all his time so he is unable to do any accounting for Happy Science, but this is nothing to worry about for a man with a bright future as head of Coca Cola or General Motors.

Kalia lives through more lifetimes struggling with the world's evil, and with Yasmin.

She scores a notable success when she finds herself in the middle of a plague in fifth-century Nigeria and helps tend thousands of victims.

Whenever Yasmin comes near she is now able to predict his whereabouts and move on. Having lived for so long on Earth she has also picked up a fair amount of expertise in physical violence, always useful for defending your peasant community, but she never thinks of fighting with Yasmin because it would only count as a bad deed and deduct from her total. She is fighting an unfair battle but carries on determinedly. The plague is very widespread and there are victims for her to minister to everywhere.

In her next life, as a peasant in Peru, she has a hard time just staying alive. But soon after, whatever god is unfairly rigging her incarnations lets his attention slip for a moment and she is born as Queen Guinevere. Of course her life ends fairly sadly but while she is King Arthur's wife she does kindnesses by the score, always helping knights out with their problems and feeding the poor round the castle.

A wandering minstrel appears. It is Lux, dressed in colourful rags and carrying a lute. He asks permission to play the Knights of the Round Table a few songs and, since they are all hopelessly drunk after a day's jousting, he goes down reasonably well.

Staying in the castle he falls in love with a young princess, another in the endless series of impossible love affairs that Lux gets tangled up in through the ages.

Kalia does her best to help by way of introductions and message-carrying, but it is a hopeless proposition because the princess is not a music or poetry fan and Lux can't do anything else. Finally he is banished after being caught trying to climb a creeper into her bedroom.

Before being banished he pleads eloquently to King Arthur for clemency, saying that it was an affair of the heart and he was overcome by his passions, but when Sir Galahad, always a sneak, points out that it was in fact the wrong bedroom Lux was trying to climb into King Arthur gets the impression that possibly Lux is not too fussy which young princess he crawls into bed with, and tells him to leave the kingdom.

Kalia, as Guinevere, dies being regarded as a saint. She nearly always does. People are astonished at her tireless energy in doing good. Mind you, she is actually totally sick of it. Sometimes she feels like poisoning a well or massacring a few hundred innocents, but this, of course, will not get her back into Heaven.

Nicky is in shock. Already racked with guilt for killing her computer, the sight of the rape has pushed her into deep trauma.

Pearl hunts the area for her, hampered by prowling police cars that drive round the blocks and over the grass verges like panthers.

Finally she notices a familiar shoe.

'Nicky, come on, get out from behind that skip.'

Nicky lets herself be led out but doesn't say anything and her face stands out white in the night. Pearl, grasping Nicky and her film, hustles her along, feeling like she has been hustling them along for hours without making any progress, just as she has been making the film for months without making progress, just like everything else winding its way along, never coming to a satisfactory end.

Gerry eventually finds a phone outside the police station. The police are letting the press use it and he has a press card.

'Cancel the Mary Luxembourg retrospective,' he tells the magazine. 'There has been a major re-evaluation of her in critical circles.'

'But you only phoned up an hour ago.'

'Things move fast in the literary world.'

'Are you going to give us a report on the riot?'

'Shortly. Right now I am busy gathering exclusive material.' He puts the phone down and it is eagerly wrestled over by waiting pressmen. He goes back to where Mark is photographing the Jane Austen Mercenaries.

'That's right,' says Mark. 'Scowl.'

'Right Mark, we've got to find the manuscript.'

Now it exists and is recoverable, Gerry is once again in line for plaudits from Mary Luxembourg. Things are looking up, as long as he finds Nicky.

Personal Computer Services have not found it easy looking for Nicky because she has left few clues as to her whereabouts. Johnny does eventually track her to Pearl's house, but before he can do anything the riot starts and he loses them when the house burns down. Johnny is becoming increasingly mad about everything. He is just waiting for somebody to attack him and when they do then he is going to kill them.

* * *

Lux, previously indifferent to the riot, is starting to get a little fed up with it. It is keeping him from Pearl. If he doesn't see Pearl regularly he gets withdrawal symptoms.

'It's not, as I thought, that death creates love. More that love knows death.'

Walking on, Lux passes, in the space of one block of flats, from an area of calm to one of violent activity, where some policemen are struggling and fighting their way through heavy resistance to try and clear the estate of rioters, some of whom are up on the balconies throwing petrol bombs. Temporarily distracted, he forgets to look where he is going and bumps into a press photographer.

How fortuitous, thinks Lux.

'Take my picture?' he asks, polite as ever. The photographer ignores him, so Lux stands in front of the camera.

'Get out of the fucking way, kid,' says the photographer, hardened to troublesome onlookers.

'Why won't you take my picture? What's the matter, isn't my hair looking good?' He hunts around for his hand mirror.

By the children's play area a policeman with a bleeding face is wrestling with a man with a knife and five other policemen pile in. The photographer is trying for some action shots but Lux is persistent. 'I'm a local poet. I edit a music paper. I play in a thrash metal band. I'm a cult figure. Get me in your newspaper. Tell them to send down their literary editor for a few words.'

This sort of storytelling is nothing to Lux who one time phoned up the BBC World Service to ask if he could host their arts round-up programme.

'I'm here to photograph the riot.'

'I am a rioter. I've been rioting all evening. I'm just having a break.'

Finally the photographer is forced to move away and misses his action shots, although as what is happening now is the police are breaking the arm of the man with the knife, his editor wouldn't have printed them anyway.

Damn photographers, thinks Lux, outraged at not being photo'd when he is a lot better looking than any of the policemen around. Photographers should be tied up in sacks and drowned.

'You wouldn't know a good picture if it poked you in the eye!'

he shouts after the departing pressman.

'No wonder your paper is rubbish! Remember to mention me to the literary editor.'

'Lux!'

Hmm, thinks Lux, figures stampeding towards him. I'd forgotten all about the Jane Austen Mercenaries. He sprints off, looking for a wall to climb.

Pearl and Nicky, resting, are moved on by a policeman who suggests loudly to his colleague that they are whores waiting for niggers off the estate, a good and clever insult.

'No wonder the whole place is going up in smoke,' screams Pearl, and gets a violent push for her trouble.

Foolishly, she pushes back, which is enough to have her arrested and jailed by a magistrate for assaulting an officer, or maybe actual bodily harm if the officer is looking for some more serious offences to bolster up his arrest sheet.

A delicate position is reached where the officer ponders briefly whether or not to make the arrest. He is temporarily disadvantaged by Lux, scrambling blindly over a wall and landing on his head.

'Pearl!' he yells, delighted. 'I've found you.'

'You're all nicked,' gasps the policeman, disentangling himself from Lux and looking round for support. His patrol, however, is just now coming under heavy fire from a rooftop and cannot come to his aid, and his sergeant shouts for him to come and help.

Undecided, the policeman hesitates.

'Stop hanging around like a fool, Lux,' says Kalia, appearing over the wall.

She drags him away, followed by Pearl and Nicky, to some temporary refuge up on another, quieter balcony.

The police, having now broken up the fierce resistance around the estate, are picking up everyone they can fit into their vans.

There seems to be nowhere to go for safety.

* * *

Mr Socrates of the publicity department is, after the Chairman and Managing Director, the most powerful man in Happy Science. He is suspicious of Sebastian Flak. He does not know quite what is going on but he thinks that something is.

Sebastian is inducing suspicion of himself by continually making phone calls and slamming down the phone if anyone else enters the room. Or else he disappears from his office for long periods.

What he is doing when he disappears, though, is reading *Soldier of Fortune* or chanting, something he now does in the executive toilet.

Maybeline seems more willing to meet him for lunch these days.

CHAPTER TWELVE

Lux, Kalia, Pearl and Nicky find a landing in the block of flats that is relatively free from urine, dog shit and rubbish the spews out from the hopelessly inadequate garbage disposal chutes. They settle down for a rest. Down below some rioting is still going on.

'Pearl,' says Lux, gripping her arm, overcome with emotion and finding it difficult to speak.

'Hello Lux,' says Pearl, prising loose his fingers and making some comment about limpets. Lux's voice returns.

'I've been looking all over for you. I was worried you might have been burned to death in the fire or killed in the riot or arrested.'

'You just about got us arrested, falling all over that policeman.'

'I saved you.'

'No you didn't, we were leaving safely when you almost ruined it.'

Lux ignores this.

'I've written you a new poem.' He scrabbles round in his carrier bag looking for the piece of paper with the poem on it.

Pearl is intent on comforting Nicky who is staring out into space, wild and deranged, but Lux is too insistent in his passion to notice anything like this and rambles on and on about what he has been doing that night and how many poems he has read to televsion cameras and how he has told some important media people all about Pearl's film so she can be famous as well as him and sits so close to Pearl that he is practically on top of her and asks her what she is doing tonight and would she like to pay him into a nightclub if she has any spare money because his hair is looking particuarly good with his new KY jelly and sugar setting gel and he figures he should show it off to the public, forgetting that what they are all doing is hiding from a riot.

'Be quiet Lux,' she says, eventually.

Lux smiles at her, his best smile, capable of melting the most unfriendly heart.

'You've been practising your smile in front of the mirror again,' she says.

Lux looks hurt. He starts to sniffle.

'Don't bother,' says Pearl. 'I know you practise crying as well.'

'She is horrible to me,' complains Lux to Kalia, but immediately turns back to Pearl, not really insulted because he knows that deep inside Pearl is crazy about him.

'Did I introduce you to Kalia? She has been exiled from Heaven for three thousaand years.'

'Lux, have you been fucking someone for cocaine again?'

'The last lot of photos were shit,' moans the drummer to his fellow Mercenaries. 'You couldn't hardly see me at all. I got fans too, you know.'

'Stop whining about the damn photos,' says Grub. 'We still got to find Lux.'

'I'm going to kill him.'

'Me too.'

'And me.'

'And me. I just don't wanna be obscured in the photos again.'

'Where we gonna look now?'

There doesn't seem any logical way of searching so they just carry on walking the streets.

With the twelfth-century Japanese incarnation of Lux on their side, the Yamamoto family massacre the opposition in the first round of the contest. Saki flows freely in the victory celebration.

'Chang Kwai Lux,' says Lord Yamamoto, 'you were sensational. All the most obscure perfumes from the far-flung corners of the world and you named every one, no trouble. The whole town is proud of you.'

Lux, completely wrecked on saki, accepts the thanks graciously and carries on composing a poem he is writing to the eldest daughter of the household, with whom he is smitten. She is pledged to be married to the Emperor's nephew but this does not worry Lux overmuch as he has heard that the Emperor's nephew is a dolt who spends all his time practising swordplay and planning to invade China. No doubt Lux will be able to win her heart.

Kalia congratulates him later.

'You finally did something successfully after a thousand years of trying,' she tells him.

'Yes, the contest did seem to take a thousand years,' replies Lux, not understanding what she means.

'Will you take this poem to Shimono for me? Stuff it under her door tonight and tomorrow tell her it's from a secret admirer. Insinuate the admirer is me but don't come right out with it.' 'It will come to no good.'

Lux shrugs.

In the guest room the beaten opponents are furious, particularly Lord Yasmin. He plots something for the following day. No one is going to humiliate his perfume-guessing team.

Sebastian's day starts off well when he puts on an Australian accent and phones Ace Headhunters on behalf of Rio Tinto Zinc to ask if they have any information on the talented accountant Sebastian Flak and Ace Headhunters say they are at that moment trying to contact him, but it worsens with a troubling experience while he is quietly chanting in the executive toilet.

A vision of Lux floats into his head. He sees the small ragged figure again standing outside the Happy Science building trying to persuade people that he is a genius. This vision worries him because he is still attracted to the figure. Worse, Sebastian starts being carried back in time so that he imagines himself as a knight in a castle somewhere, and Lux is still hanging around, playing a lute and causing general distress.

Unhappy about having visions thrust upon him when all he wants is a powerful position somewhere and no problems, Sebastian wonders if he should stop his chanting for a while because, after all, success seems to be headed his way already.

But he needs to carry on. He believes it is helping him with Maybeline. If he stops he might lose out to the public relations expert in the company next door. Sebastian has started to hate public relations experts. When Mr Socrates comes around he no longer speaks to him.

With Lux monopolising Pearl, Kalia, noticing that Nicky is in a bad way, draws her into a conversation. Normally this would not be possible for anyone except Pearl as Nicky is now appalled at the whole world, but Kalia, three thousand years of kindness behind her, is capable of most things.

Nicky starts to tell her about her grim experiences at Happy Science.

'As a compromise between the scientific laboratories and the publicity department Dr Carlson told me I had to enter the beauty contest and be mother to some genius babies. When I asked why me he said I was clever and quite nice looking. Mr Socrates thought I wouldn't look too bad on television although he would still have preferred a professional model.'

'What did you do?' asks Kalia, deeply sympathetic.

'I refused. I told them it was stupid and degrading. Then Dr

Carlson said he would sack me if I didn't.'

'And then?'

'I had a nervous breakdown, killed my computer, stole the genetic programme and fled.'

She buries her face in her hands. Her hands are filthy from hiding behind the skip.

'Well,' says Mr Socrates, later, 'I told you we should have got a professional model. We'll just have to hope this doesn't reach the papers.'

'My genetic programme is gone,' mumbles Dr Carlson, ashen. 'The work is ruined. I was to be nominated for a Nobel prize...'

'Well can't you just get another copy?'

'No. She wiped them all. Fifteen year's work, all gone.'

'Don't worry. I'll get Personal Computer Services onto her. They won't muck about. What about the new toothpaste?'

Lux is holding Pearl's hand. This is enough to make him happy. Content with the world, he stops talking. Pearl, still holding her film, is relieved that it is still in existence. Nicky, comforted by Kalia, seems a little less manic.

For a while, peace reigns.

Mr Socrates suspects that Sebastian has had something to do with the theft of the genetic programme because he has noticed how disloyal to the company he has become. He starts keeping an eye on him and taps his phone calls and so learns that some big headhunting operation is under way.

That's odd, he thinks. Why would General Motors be interested in Sebastian Flak? Everyone knows he is no good for anything. Also he hears Sebastian on the phone to Maybeline, talking about chanting. He finds this very suspicious and assumes that he is talking to an American accomplice in code.

It seems like further proof that the accountant had a hand in the theft. Perhaps he is bribing a new company to take him by supplying them with stolen details of the research.

He has him carefully watched.

Patrick, watching television, sees Mike approaching and entering the Enterprise Centre, an old department store recently converted.

'Damn Liberation Computers,' he mutters. He blames them for taking up all of Mike's time. They are as much to blame for the rift in their relationship as the awful Lux.

Lying with a Friend under a Burnt-out Truck

'Is the riot still going on?'

'I think so.'

'It's quite peaceful under this truck. Look, there's a beetle. I quite like beetles. I squatted in a basement with some beetles. Several times. They are much misunderstood. So am I. Did I ever tell you about my parents throwing me out of the house?'

'Yes Lux.'

'It was the day after they caught me in bed with my sister. I got flung out with a plastic bag full of clothes and twenty pence I'd stolen from the telephone box. A bit harsh, I always thought. It was only my second offence. Well, only the second one they could prove. I always got blamed for everything. My father used to say no one with any morals ever came out of a test tube.'

'What happened to your sister?'

'She went to work on an oil rig. She was pretty tough. I never hear from her any more.'

There is a small, sad pause.

'I remember when I had to go naked into battle. It was in the Trojan War. I got sent out with a sword and a shield and nothing else.'

'Lux, you're rambling.'

'No I'm not. It's true. I got killed. A man is supple and weak when living, but hard and stiff when dead, as Lao Tzu said. I feel funny.'

CHAPTER THIRTEEN

Sebastian's efforts at marketing himself, given strength by the huge amounts of psychic energy he was putting into it, began to show some powerful results.

Happy Science starts to crawl with operatives from all London's headhunting companies, each of them trying to organise a secret meeting with the now sought-after accountant.

Disguised as window cleaners and firms of healthy sandwich makers they trample the carpeted corridors of the executive block with contracts bulging in their pockets, all eager to get hold of the man who is fast becoming the sensation of the business world.

Furthermore, managing directors around the country, hearing rumours at their golfing clubs, start thinking that if Sebastian Flak is getting all this attention then he really must be hot property.

'IBM is on the point of stealing one of the country's leading executives,' they say to their subordinates, 'Why have we made no attempt to secure the services of this man?' So genuine enquiries start being made and the whole process escalates till it becomes the most talked-about business in the City.

Sebastian, however, keen to push up his market value, spends most of his time reading *Soldier of Fortune* in the toilet, holding out against accepting an offer too soon, although when he mentions to Maybeline at lunch that everyone is after him to offer him a new job she is of the opinion that he should get on and take one, because Maybeline is a practical sort of person. Always keen to take her advice, Sebastian arranges a meeting.

Over the main course Maybeline tells him how much she admires Britain's new determination to go with the free market economy and over dessert she mentions how much she dislikes homosexuals. Brought up in a conservative family she finds them disgusting.

'Would you like to spend another day in the country with me?' asks Lux, on the landing with the others.

'No,' replies Pearl.

'Why not?'

'Because last time you tried riding on a sheep and I had to bandage your ankle and help you to the bus stop. And before that you insisted on going into that barn and bawling out your poem about having sex with sharks. I've never had to run so fast in my life.'

'No,' admits Lux. 'Faced with forty panicstricken cows we didn't have much choice. But I enjoyed it.'

Pearl gives him an evil look.

'It is quiet down below,' says Kalia. 'I have a friend who lives a few blocks away. If we go there she will make us some tea.'

Everyone is dying for a cup of tea, so they set off.

Johnny receives a call from Mr Socrates on his portable phone. He reports that so far they have had no positive results, despite sighting their quarry. It proved impossible to keep track of her in the chaos of rioting, police cars and fire engines.

'Is there any sign of Sebastian Flak down there?'

'No. Should there be?'

'Possibly. I intercepted a call to his office. He has arranged a meeting with Coca Cola somewhere in the vicinity, presumably thinking it would be an unobtrusive spot for a rendezvous. Now he's in the thick of a riot. Keep your eyes open, you know we suspect him of being mixed up in this whole business.'

'Right,' says Johnny.

He likes his work. He likes tracking people down and having them arrested. He likes doing anything that will frustrate people's dreams. He always has, in every life.

He is Yasmin, and dreadfully evil.

Walking through the now empty courtyards, Pearl holds Nicky's hand to comfort her. Lux becomes dimly aware that he is not number one in Pearl's affections.

Momentarily sad, he remembers that Pearl is only being kind to Nicky, who is of course a candidate for an asylum. An understanding sort of person, Lux can accept this. No doubt Pearl will soon have more time for him.

He is warmly glowing from his gigantic dose of cocaine, slightly bleeding from his head, and still clutching his carrier bag full of possessions. As is Pearl. While Lux has his Star Wars toothbrush and spare army trousers, she has her film.

'I left my cap behind when I was evicted,' announces Lux, for no apparent reason. 'I miss it terribly. I used to look good in it, in fact I looked sensational. It used to stop traffic. People sometimes came up to me in the street and said what a nice hat it was. It was brilliant. It was the world's best hat. I used to look sensational in it. People in clubs used to stop me and ask where I got it. My hat was – '

'Lux.'

' – a masterpiece of headwear. It used to set off my hair to perfection. I used to organise my make-up around it. One time a woman stopped me in the street and wanted to take my picture. She said that my features were striking, and so was the hat. She said – '

'Lux, will you shut up about your damn hat?' says Pearl.

Lux manages to stay silent for a few seconds.

'Jane Russell wore a hat quite like it in a film one time,' he says, defiantly.

The riot being a flexible thing, it suddenly reappears as they reach the main road.

Used to it by now, none of them reacts much as a crowd of rioters flee round a corner towards them, pursued by the police, because they are all looking forward to a nice cup of tea and not much concerned with anything else, but as well as being engulfed by more fighting they are sudenly engulfed by a fire engine which mounts the pavement out of control and explodes in flames all around them, creating terrible confusion. The police and rioters pause briefly to wonder if they should carry on fighting or run away from the explosion or help the crew or throw stones at them or just stand by and watch. Standing by to watch, Lux, Kalia, Pearl and Nicky are engulfed by a further explosion which renders Lux unconscious.

'Well,' says the Chairman to Dr Carlson, 'it's all very well you complaining to me about the publicity department ruining your project but from what I understand it was your fault that the genetic programme went missing. Apparently the woman who stole it was your selection for the mothers' contest.'

This is true. Dr Carlson shifts around uncomfortably.

'And I understand she caused a considerable amount of damage. Very bad for our image, one of our employees doing a thing like that. Do we have any idea why she did it?'

'Only the note she left.'

'What did it say?'

The Doctor pulls a copy out from his well-worn lab coat. It is his lucky lab coat. He has resolved never to change it until he wins a Nobel Prize.

'Dear Happy Science Scumbags,

I am sick to death of your ridiculous fascist artificial breeding programme. I am sick to death of your utterly insulting and oppressive competition to find a suitable mother for the genius babies. I am disgusted at Dr Carlson trying to make me, a prize-winning biologist, enter the competition. I am sick of not being able to walk along the corridor without some fucking moron staring at my tits or commenting on my legs. I hate you all. I have pictures of your illegal genetic experiments which will shortly be appearing in a film. I intend to destroy the project and hope the company goes bankrupt.'

This was not the cleverest thing that Nicky could have done, giving her hand away but, already upset by the sight of her computer plunging eight storeys to a terrible death she was not thinking clearly at the time.

'The ravings of a madwoman.'

Along the corridor Sebastian reels out of the executive toilet. He has just had a terrible experience while chanting, a powerful and sustained vision of himself as a rich landowner in eighteenth-century Scotland, turning peasants off the land to make way for sheep. The sheep would make money and the peasants could do what they liked, which was mainly to starve.

CHAPTER FOURTEEN

Lux dreams again of going into a battle with only a sword and a shield and then dreams of being in Heaven but when he wakes up in a bathroom with two-tone fleck paint on the walls he knows he is not in Heaven but in a hard-to-let council flat in Lambeth because all hard-to-let council flats in Lambeth have two-tone fleck on the bathroom walls, and in the kitchen.

Kalia is dabbing his head with a cloth.

'Careful with my make-up,' says Lux, slightly weak. 'What happened?'

'You got knocked out by an exploding fire engine.'

'Where's Pearl?'

'She went to hospital with Nicky in an ambulance. They got hit by debris. They'll be all right.'

Lux leaps to his feet, howling. It is almost too much to bear. He has found the love of his life only to see her kidnapped by a doctor.

'What's wrong with these people?' he demands. 'Don't they have any sensitivity at all? You hunt for hours in a riot looking for your girlfriend and first thing they do is throw her in an ambulance. I got to find her.'

Kalia pushes him back in the chair.

'You should rest. You've been unconscious twice tonight.'

'I feel alright. But depressed. Pearl's been stolen. Why didn't you put me in the ambulance with her?'

'I was too busy hiding you under a bush from an irate bunch of musicians.'

'Oh.'

Lux looks glum. Pearl has been stolen.

'I just can't stand it,' he says sincerely.

'Cheer up,' says Kalia kindly. 'After all, at least you know Pearl is safe now. And she'll just stay in the hospital till the riot is over and then you can go and visit her.'

Lux brightens up.

'That's true. She is bound to stay there with Nicky. Did you notice what a sicko Nicky is? I am as sympathetic as anyone to sickos, in fact probably more so, but Pearl would be a lot better off with me. When she was getting carried into the ambulance did she call my name?'

'No.'

'Are you sure?'

'Yes.'

'Maybe just muttered it softly?'

'No.'

Maybe there is something wrong with your hearing. Or possibly you couldn't make it out over the riot. Anyway, she was probably thinking it.' Optimism floods into him. 'Did you notice how keen she was to hold my hand? Just about mangled my fingers. And we arranged a day in the country. In fact this has not been a bad night, I got to hold hands with Pearl and I got stuffed full of cocaine.'

'You got thrown out of your home.'

'I'll find another one.'

'You got hit with a brick and mugged.'

'It happens.'

Lux sniffs, nose still congested.

'Why do you take drugs?'

'Why not?'

'Well that's as good a logical answer as I've heard in three thousand years.'

In the entrance hall of the Enterprise Centre newsman after newsman dictates reports about valiant police battling against bestial black rioters.

Outside a TV crew is interviewing a young black woman.

'I've been for thirty-two interviews and can't get a job, ' she tells them.

The winter in Gdansk in 1792 is particularly harsh and everywhere children and the elderly are dying, succumbing helplessly to the elements that bite through their clothes and eat away their bones.

It is bitterly cold and the frozen poor huddle pathetically in their slums without firewood for heat or food for sustenance. 'What do you want?' demands a rich moneylender, annoyed at being called away from his blazing, roaring, forest-consuming fire by a woman garbed as a nun but much too insistent for his liking.

'The water comes through the roof of my flat and the council haven't got anyone to fix the water tank upstairs so the walls are all damp and the baby's sick,' says the woman, continuing the interview. 'I got struck off the social security because I was three minutes late for my re-start interview and it took five weeks to get my benefit sorted out.'

'I'd like a little more time for the families round my abbey to pay you back,' says the nun. 'They have no money for food or firewood.'

'Well they should have thought of that before they borrowed money off me,' replies Sebastian, who is the moneylender, motioning for one of his servants to show her the door.

'And tell them if they don't meet the payments I'll repossess their houses.'

'It could lead to trouble.'

'Then they will all be thrown in jail.'

'I go out to a social club once a month and last time I was there the police came in and separated all the blacks from the whites and searched the blacks.'

'Is this any reason to riot?' asks the reporter.

The woman shrugs and goes away to try and reclaim her baby from the babysitter somewhere across town.

The interview is shown on television but along with all the other reports it soon becomes either lost or meaningless, not being dramatic enough to grab anyone's attention.

The nun leaves. The moneylender settles down to some wine. Sebastian comes back to his senses with a sudden jolt, finding himself in the executive toilet. Outside his cubicle he can hear some directors discussing last night's football.

'Another one,' he mutters. 'I'm getting fed up with these visions of past lives. I don't even believe in past lives. What is causing them? And why am I always so horrible in them? At least that brat with the yellow hair wasn't in this one.'

Really he knows what is causing them. It is the religious chanting causing disruptions in his psyche. His psyche, previously concerned only with being rich and powerful, cannot cope with this new burst of spiritualism.

However he cannot give it up because of the success it is bringing him. And Maybeline wouldn't like it.

'There is something wrong,' says Lux. 'Everyone is rioting.'

'Very astute, Lux,' says Kalia. 'Now keep still while I bandage your head.'

Pearl, knocked unconscious by the exploding fire engine and Nicky, uninjured but comatose, moan, struggle and dream of each other as the ambulance crawls its way through the chaos to hospital.

'Do you think I should be out rioting?' muses Lux.

'I don't think you'd fit in too well.'

Lux quotes Kalia the four lines he made up in the police van and then makes up a second verse.

'Very nice,' says Kalia, still bandaging his head. 'What does it mean?'

'I haven't decided yet. I think I'll write a third verse about Pearl, then it can be about her.'

'I was a writer too,' she tells him. 'In one of my lives. I wrote an ethical tract on the problem of good and evil as seen from different points of view. Unfortunately no one would publish a philosophy book by a woman in the eighteenth century.

'You know, Lux, you always did look a little strange but in this life you've excelled yourself. I see you were created for the day colourful hair dye was invented.'

She goes off to help make a cup of tea with her friend, whose flat it is.

Lux looks in the mirror to see if the bandage matches his hair. He is quite pleased with it. Sort of piratical. He kicks his legs around, looking for something to do. Rummaging around in his carrier bag he finds the robot and the battery but when he sets it up it still doesn't work.

'Some major malfunction in the circuitry,' he mutters, displeased, imagining himself briefly as an important local expert on robotics. A copy of the demo tape falls into his fingers and he chuckles. This demo tape will never see the light of day if he can help it. Ignorant, unartistic, thrashing motherfuckers.

He notices that his nail varnish is chipped.

'Another indignity,' says Lux to Kalia, who brings him some tea. 'I know for a fact that Chaucer had a personal manicurist to make sure his nails were in perfect condition before he sat down to write *The Canterbury Tales.*'

'Stop rambling, Lux.'

Lux stops rambling and finds the Mary Luxembourg manuscript in his carrier bag. He doesn't know how it got there. He must have absent-mindedly pocketed it some time when he was around Nicky. He pulls it out for a read.

'What a bunch of garbage,' he decides, half-way through the first page, and hunts for his crayon to make some much-needed alterations.

'I killed my computer, I killed my computer,' mumbles Nicky hopelessly, in the ambulance. 'I killed my computer. It's haunting me. They're trying to artificially inseminate me. The country's full of rapists trying to get at me.'

Pearl wakes.

'Where's my film?' she asks immediately.

Nicky shakes her head hopelessly. 'It got lost somewhere along with the burning fire engine.'

'Oh for fuck's sake,' explodes Pearl. 'Let me out of this ambulance.'

'When I find Lux,' rasps Grub to Eugene, 'I am going to kill him. No messing about, I'm going to tear his fucking head off.'

'Maybe if we tear it off soon we can get some of our coke back.'

'Yeah. I'll teach him to fuck around with the Jane Austen Mercenaries.'

'The Jane Austen Mercenaries?' thinks Johnny, who is hiding round the corner with a sophisticated listening device. Who are they?

'Fucking hell, this is grim,' says Lux, appalled at Mary Luxembourg's novel. 'Whoever wrote this wants to be rolled around in barbed wire.'

He starts ripping pieces out of the manuscript, pencilling through lines and adding his own, writing poems in the margins and editorial comments all over the place that completely obscure the script. By the time I finish this will be a masterpiece, he thinks, busily scribbling away.

Kalia glances out of the kitchen window. Down below she catches a glimpse of someone who looks very much like a descendant of Heaven hurrying by.

CHAPTER FIFTEEN

In the fifteenth century Kalia has the misfortune to be born in the middle of a rash of terrible witch hunts.

As a servant of the Witchfinder she is expected to take notes on witches prior to them being burned at the stake.

Unable to do this, she tries to help them escape.

'You will never get back into Heaven this way,' says the voice of god to her, in a dream. You are meant to be doing good, not breaking the law.'

'I am doing good. I'm helping people escape when they are about to be horribly killed.'

'But you are still breaking the law. And you are being disloyal to your employer who is, after all, doing good, in his opinion.'

'Well every good deed could be interpreted two ways if you are going to look at it like that,' protests the dreaming Kalia.

'True.'

'So how am I meant to know what acts of kindness are actually kindnesses?'

'It's a difficult problem,' says god.

We Get Your Man Personnel and Ace Headhunters are now both competing madly for Sebastian Flak. With queries pouring in about him all the time they know he must be something special. Neither of them has ever heard of him before but there have been so many requests for his services that they figure he must be an accounting genius.

'Get me Flak at any cost,' demands the head of Ace Headhunters. 'He is becoming one of the most sought-after men in the business. I pay you to keep up with affairs, not provide me with a lot of third-raters while the big fish slip through the net. Now go out and make contact.'

'Maybeline,' says Sebastian, on the phone, 'about this chanting. It's starting to make me feel funny. I'm getting visions.'

'Nonsense,' says Maybeline endearingly. 'I don't get any visions.'

'Right,' agrees Sebastian. 'Neither do I.'

The ambulance carrying Pearl and Nicky comes to a temporary halt, unable to pass a burnt-out bus in the middle of the road.

Now's my chance, thinks Pearl. I'll make a run for it.

Beside her Nicky has gone quiet.

On the other hand, thinks Pearl, maybe I should stay here with Nicky. She should be in hospital. If I go and try to find my film she is bound to follow me. The humane thing would definitely be to stay here with Nicky and go to the hospital.

The ambulance door opens and a policeman's head appears. To hell with the humane thing, thinks Pearl, and sprints out the back.

'I'm feeling better,' she calls over her shoulder. Nicky runs after her, unable to face going to a hospital on her own.

There is rioting going on in this street and they have to duck their way through some flying stones and then round a huge circular rubbish skip that has been set alight and pushed into the road.

Kalia has finished bandaging Lux's head and talks to her friend Marion.

'It must be bad for you living here with a riot going on, especially as the hospital placed you here to help you work your way back into normal community life.'

Marion shrugs.

'Noise, violence, police cars roaming about, broken windows. Much the same as usual.'

'*What are you doing here, ghost among these urns, these film wrapped sandwiches and help yourself biscuits,*' says Lux. 'Or how did you get this flat?' He looks up briefly at the boarded windows.

'Special housing needs,' says Marion. 'The council gave it to me when I came out of the mental hospital. It is meant to be good for me, running my own home, although as I'm not much good at plumbing and the repair men have taken seven months to fix the hot water I'm finding it a bit difficult. Still, you could say I'm back to normal life.'

Sebastian, meeting with We Get Your Man Personnel all arranged, slips incognito onto a 159 bus which will take him from his home in St Johns Wood down to Brixton, a highly suitable area for a meeting because there he will be unrecognised. He understands that secrecy is essential.

* * *

'What are you doing?' asks Kalia, bringing Lux a sandwich.

'Revising my novel. Thank you for the sandwich.'

She looks at him. 'Well, someone else's novel,' he admits. 'But I am doing them a favour, it is a dreadful novel. The author has the soul of a pterodactyl.'

Kalia laughs and cuts up some more sandwiches.

She has a slightly disquieting habit of appearing to do some internal calculation whenever she does anything for anyone, but apart from that Kalia exudes wisdom.

'Pearl would like it now. I've put in some poems about her.'

'That reminds me of the perfume-guessing contest,' she says.

'What?'

'Something you were involved in in a previous life. Do you think I am rambling stupidly?'

'Certainly not,' replies Lux, politely accepting another sandwich and waiting a second while Kalia does some brief mental arithmetic 'If you say you met me in the past, I believe it. What happened?'

'I can't go on,' moans Nicky, and sits down on the pavement.

'What d'you mean you can't go on?' demands Pearl. 'We have to find my film.'

'I hurt. I can't go on.' With some difficulty Pearl checks back a flood of abuse. Given a choice between her lover dying in the middle of the riot and recovering her film she is not entirely sure which she would take.

'Have you seen Lux?' demands Eugene, appearing through some smoke.

'Go fuck yourself,' snarls Pearl, having more important things to think about.

The veins and tendons stand out in her neck, as they do when she is angry.

'So,' says Kalia to Lux,'after you helped win the first round of the perfume-guessing contest you were the hero of the moment.

The family stuffed you full of so much rice, fish and saki you looked like you might burst. Of course you had been wandering around starving for years so this was understandable.

'But you, fairly stupidly, insisted on trying to win the hand of the eldest daughter of the household, Shimono, and she was already betrothed to the Emperor's nephew.'

Lux, sitting beside Kalia as she speaks, is enthralled at hearing a story about himself.

'Also, there were problems brewing. The head of the opposing forces was Yasmin. He was lord of the next hamlet and sort of non-playing captain of their team. Not only was he determined to thwart any act of kindness I could commit, he was continually obsessed with making any life he had as successful as possible so he wasn't going to let you get away with beating his perfume squad. It was his intention to make his team the most famous in all Japan, thereby coming to the attention of the Emperor and gaining an appointment as chief perfume coach in Tokyo, a highly prestigious position.

'The next day he put poison in one of the perfume vials before it was passed to you – some Ethiopian musk, if I remember correctly. But fortunately I had predicted this very event and was able to divert the bowl away from you. And after this you went on to guess every single aroma correctly again and won the next round of the contest.

'Yasmin was furious, although formal etiquette prevented him from showing it. Worse, Shimono, always a woman of poor taste, began to be attracted to you because of the heartbreakingly romantic poems you kept getting me to stuff under her door every night...'

Sebastian, unused to travelling by bus, does not enjoy the journey very much but cheers himself up with thoughts of the telling-off he gave the Chief Accountant the previous day after being warned that his work was no longer up to scratch.

'Oh yes?' he had said. 'Well, let me tell you, Mr so-called Chief Accountant, that I am the one person in this company with any future, possibly excepting some of the sperm in the scientific department. Soon I won't need to bother about you or your damn company.'

And with that he buried his head in *Soldier of Fortune* magazine, no longer bothering to hide it inside a *Financial Times*, so confident was he of being headhunted at any moment and whisked off into the major league of company directors, where it is quite possible to award yourself a pay rise that gives you in one year more money than is taken home in a lifetime by one of your employees.

Over at the scientific department gloom has set in. Despite Mr Socrates pressing ahead with the arrangements for the beauty contest, trapped now in his own publicity, there is no way that the grand artificial insemination ceremony can go ahead without the genetic programme.

'Couldn't we fake it?' he suggests. Dr Carlson is not enthusiastic. As a scientist he has strong ethical objections to faking things.

CHAPTER SIXTEEN

Lux, slumped thoughtfully in a chair, sits upright, eyes widening so violently that he flakes off a few pieces of mascara.

'Pearl is somewhere close.'

'She can't be. She has gone away to hospital.'

'No,' says Lux frantically. 'I can smell her organic moisturising cream. She must have come back to look for me.'

He stands, gathering his coat about him.

'I'm really enjoying your story. But I must get out and look for Pearl.'

'You are obsessed with her.'

'Yes.'

'She doesn't seem all that keen on you.'

'Yes she does. She resents me a little because I am so good looking and I improved her film and I wasn't sympathetic enough when she told me she was sad about all the witches being burned in the fifteenth century. She spends a lot of time thinking about that. Did you know they used to burn witches?'

'I'd heard about it.'

'And of course she is busy chaperoning a manic depressive companion around, but I think I'm winning her over. Good looks are bound to win out against sick friends.'

'You keep insulting Nicky.'

'She's sick.'

'Maybe. But it was quite heroic of her, half destroying the company like that.'

Lux shrugs, not impressed by heroism if it comes from his rival.

'Shouldn't you stay here in safety?'

'It's all right. I'll be fine. Riots are no problem unless you happen to be a victim and I was born too lucky to be a victim. Pearl needs me. Thanks for bandaging up my head. Does the bandage suit me?'

'Perfectly,' smiles Kalia, who has long knowledge of Lux's incredible vanity and a fair idea of why Pearl may not be falling all over him. Still, she likes him. She always did and she is pleased to meet him again. Throughout all her lifetimes she has bumped into him often and he is always the same, never doing anything except wandering around on his own singing or writing poetry and trying to convince people of his huge talent, always in vain.

She laughs out loud, remembering the occasion when Lux panicked a field full of saffron-robed monks chanting sutras in the presence of the Buddha by trying out a few free-form variations of his own at maximum volume. Some people said afterwards that it was the only time since his enlightenment that the colour actually drained from the Buddha's cheeks, but this was probably an exaggeration.

'I'll come with you,' she says, getting her coat. 'You need someone to look after you. Also you are a prime candidate for receiving acts of kindness. Helping you out a few more times might get me back into Heaven. And I'm anxious to learn something about this heavenly descendant.'

'The one the birds told you about?'

'That's right.'

'I talk to birds too, sometimes. They seem like quite sensible creatures, just flying around enjoying themselves all the time. Do you think you'll meet this heavenly descendant?'

'I've already seen him. Out of the kitchen window.'

They head for the door.

'Put back everything you've stolen,' says Kalia.

'Right,' says Lux, emptying his pockets of Marion's pearl earrings and a few other trinkets.

Outside he sniffs the air.

'This way,' he says.

Pearl drags Nicky on.

'It's no use,' says Nicky, who can't hunt any more. Driven by desperation to lying, she tells Pearl that she saw her film consumed by a piece of burning fire engine.

Pearl, depressed, slumps against a wall.

They stay there for a while, both bleeding slightly from their cuts, ignoring the still active crowds walking up and down the broken pavements.

Mike appears. He has come out of Liberation Computers to see if the riot is still raging.

Seeing Pearl and Nicky standing forlornly by the wall, he offers them some shelter in the Enterprise Centre, which they accept.

'Look,' says Lux, halting close to where the fire engine is still smouldering.

'A carrier bag. I like carrier bags, I used to collect them.' He starts rummaging around in it, emptying it out so that rolls of paper start tangling round his legs. Always sensitive about any stray body harming his legs, he reaches down to free them.

'What's this?' Unravelling it reveals the paper to be some sort of computer programme. Underneath is a roll of film in a can.

'Look, Kalia, it's Pearl's film. It must've got left here when she got took off in the ambulance.'

The film, along with Nicky's bag, has survived the heat from the burning fire engine, protected by a sheet of asbestos removed from the roof of the flats by a sub-contractor and illegally dumped in the skip.

'So,' growls Patrick, watching on television as an incident-seeking camera swings round to show Mike helping Pearl and Nicky inside the Enterprise Centre. 'He's picking up women in the street now. First Lux and now this. The man is disgusting. It wouldn't surprise me if he was a closet heterosexual.'

Lux is overjoyed.

Now he can take the film to Pearl and she will practically fall all over him with gratitude because it is her most treasured possession.

The film is quite precious to Lux as well because he liked playing the part of the scarecrow and imagines that when people see it they will bombard him with offers to come and read them some poetry. Possibly he will be spotted by Hollywood.

'Few great poets have gone to Hollywood. I will be a sensation.'

He is already sensational as the scarecrow, or so he tells everyone. He wrote a special scarecrow poem for it which Pearl wouldn't let him use, but he is still sensational.

Kalia crosses the street to help a man who is trying to fix his front door back on its hinges and Lux takes the opportunity to examine the rest of Nicky's bag. The genetic programme is all written in scientific data and means nothing to him. Then there is a diary, some tampons, a book, a few pens and finally a memo on Happy Science notepaper. Finding nothing worth pocketing, Lux is a little disappointed. He reads the memo.

To: the Chairman
From: Dr Carlson
Please ensure that Sebastian Flak does not come anywhere near my laboratory any more. He may for all I know be a great accountant but he is interfering with our work.

Nicky had gathered up the memo by accident in her rush to leave Happy Science with the programme.

Kalia returns.

'Why are these musicians chasing you?' she asks.

'What musicians?'

'The ones I hid you under a bush from. The ones coming round that corner.'

Sebastian walks round the corner from the centre of Brixton to the slightly upmarket restaurant in Acre Lane and waits for his rendezvous. To his surprise and consternation, a riot starts outside.

Mike and Marcus of Liberation Computers make Pearl and Nicky welcome, in between standing guard with a hosepipe inside their small office in the Enterprise Centre. They are determined that, come what may, Liberation Computers will not be burned to the ground.

While they are drinking tea Gerry and Mark appear. Gerry has come to see how Liberation Computers are coping with the riot. He knows about them from an article he did in *Uptown* on left-wing computer groups. Actually Liberation Computers was the only one in existence but he managed to make it sound better by exaggerating a bit.

'Nicky,' he cries ecstatically, 'I've been looking for you all over.'

'I still won't go out with you,' Nicky tells him, staring at the floor.

'The manuscript,'says Gerry, ignoring this. 'Mary Luxembourg's book. I left it at your house. Can I have it back?'

Nicky doesn't reply. She is plunging in and out of a walking nightmare about dead computers and living rapists.

'It's gone,' Pearl tells him. 'Burned up by a blazing fire engine down in Stockwell. And my film.'

'Have you come to report on Liberation Computers again?' enquires Marcus in the friendly manner people put on when a reporter comes to say something nice about them.

'Later,' replies Gerry. 'Right now I have to find a phone.'

The Jane Austen Mercenaries appearing in the middle distance, Lux and Kalia quickly disappear back into the estate. A huge rabbit warren, the estate is good to hide in, good to get attacked in, good to make TV programmes about, good to discuss from a distance, good to riot in, good to do everything in except live.

'What a disgusting place,' says Kalia. 'Whatever induced anyone to build it?'

'A modern red-brick metropolis of urine-soaked walkways and concrete play areas,' says Lux, adapting freely from one of his poems. 'I wish I had a drink,' he continues, a little unsteadily now as his mind becomes slightly detached.

'Excuse me a second. I'm just going down there to help that person who is limping.' Kalia disappears.

'What are you doing here?' demands a voice.

It is Johnny and his patrol, scouting the area.

'I am here on private business,' replies Lux.

'You don't look like a businessman.'

'I am an associate of Sebastian Flak, a well known and talented accountant,' claims Lux, mind fixing onto the memo he has just read.

'I am putting him in touch with the Jane Austen Mercenaries, a local thrash metal band who I believe need some tax advice after reaching number one with their new record following some favourable reviews from Lux, the big music critic.'

'Really,' says Johnny.

Lux, seeing that he has gained an interested audience, makes up a little more. 'Of course, the whole thing could be a cover story for something different. I believe the Jane Austen Mercenaries are being hunted by the police for some reason. Possibly they are criminals. I know for a fact that Eugene used to be a thief before moving into industrial espionage. This conflict of interests is the reason they produce such fascinating music, along with the fact that Lux the Poet writes all their lyrics. He was voted top lyricist last year by four music papers. Would you like to hear an example of his work?'

'Not right now,' says Johnny, and leads his men off round the corner where he calls Mr Socrates on his mobile phone.

'You were right,' he tells him. 'There is a Sebastian Flak connection. I've just met his associate. I'll tail him. Can you see if you can find me any information about the Jane Austen Mercenaries? That is the code name being used by the other people involved. It seems to be a sizeable organisation. It sounds to me like they must have the genetic programme.'

'I just met someone interesting,' says Lux as Kalia returns.

'So did I.'

'Who?'

'Menelaus.'

'Who's that?'

'The descendant of Heaven.'

'What was he doing?'

'Limping. I helped him.'

'Where is he now?'

'He limped off. He wouldn't let me help him any more. I'll try and watch out for him as long as he is around.'

Kalia is close by, Johnny, or Yasmin, realises. He could sense it. He laughs unpleasantly.

He also knows that Kalia thinks she is close to one million acts of kindness. He also knows that she has in fact passed one million some lifetimes ago. But she is not getting back into Heaven. Ever. His master, the evil prince, is forging the figures. She will never make her total, no matter how long she tries.

* * *

'What is it Nicky keeps mumbling?' asks Mike.

'Computer police,' Pearl tells him. 'According to her we are being pursued by some organisation called Personal Computer Services.'

Mike and Marcus gather round eagerly.

'You're actually being pursued by the Personal Computer Services? The computer police? Don't worry, we'll help you. They are our arch enemies. We've been waiting for an opportunity to fight them.'

Mike starts programming something into a terminal.

'Incidentally,' he calls over his shoulder. 'Haven't I seen you round with Lux?'

'Only when I couldn't escape in time,' says Pearl. 'Why?'

'Oh, nothing. He just stole all my personal belongings and ruined my relationship with my boyfriend, that's all.'

'I can well believe it. The only reason he doesn't have everything I owned is because my house burned down before he could carry it away. I caught him one time sneaking out in my best leather jacket with the pockets crammed full of everything I hadn't nailed down. He claimed he was only taking my aspirins because he had a headache but I knew he was going to mash them up with my soap and set his hair with it. There is nothing that Lux won't try setting his hair with.'

'Too right,' says Mike, glumly. 'I now know that with KY jelly you can make a spike two feet long and it stays in position perfectly.'

Mike was exaggerating. Lux's hair currently stands around eighteen inches in all directions.

'Kalia. Seeing as you can predict the future, can't you just lead me right to Pearl?'

'I'm afraid not, Lux. Something is interfering. I can't see clearly at all. It has never happened before. I wonder if it might be Yasmin's doing. I feel he is somewhere around. Unless it is a sign that I am close to returning to Heaven.'

'Is Heaven nice?'

'It's better than Brixton. And Camberwell.'

'I stopped believing in god when I got a spot. I figured no divine being could be so cruel as to give me acne.' He looks slightly worried. 'Don't ever mention to anyone I had a spot, will you? It was only one and it went quickly.'

'I won't.'

'Promise?'

'Promise.'

Lux relaxes. He trusts Kalia.

'Tell me more about Menelaus.'

'He was the husband of Helen of Troy and Agamemnon's brother. This life he has come back as an accountant.'

'What's he like?'

'Horrible. You met him before.'

'When?'

'At the siege of Troy.'

'Was I a hero?'

'Not exactly. As a foot soldier you went into the battle naked with only a sword and a shield and some greaves. You quite liked that, being vain, but when the Trojans attacked you tried running off the battlefield. You still got hacked up into little pieces.'

'Oh.'

'I think it was that which made you stop being normal.'

'Sounds reasonable. Who wants to get chopped up on a battlefield? So after that I spent three thousand years wandering around being a poet?'

'Yes. As well as never doing any work and having hopeless love affairs.'

'Sounds to me like a series of solid achievements.'

Somewhere nearby a car alarm goes off. The alarm will wail for twenty minutes, but with sirens everywhere, it will not deter anyone from removing the in-car entertainment, and maybe the engine.

Lux wonders about something for a little while.

'Does everyone go through all their lives being the same?'

'No. You are an exception. Other people are always different. It depends on what sort of place they are born in, mainly. Right now there is an accountant wandering around the area whose main concern is to be a bigger accountant, and he used to be Menelaus,

King of Sparta. Lux, why are you crawling on your hands and knees?'

'So the person that lives up there doesn't see me.'

'Why not?'

'She got upset when she found out I was sleeping with everyone else she knew. Insanely possessive. I was lucky to escape with my life.'

'What happened?'

'I got backed into a corner and had to escape out the window. Fortunately there was a creeper outside and I shinned down it in safety. But it was very lucky. As far as I know it's the only creeper in Brixton. What happened next in the perfume contest?'

Gerry gets through to the editor of *Uptown* where everyone is in the office preparing for the riot edition.

'Re-run my Mary Luxembourg retrospective,' he tells him.

'We're busy doing a special riot edition. What's the idea of constantly phoning up with your changing literary obsessions?'

'It is highly relevant to tonight's events,' claims Gerry. 'It is books like Mary Luxembourg's that cause riots. Now be sure and print it or I'll tell everyone all about the way you treat your girlfriend.'

CHAPTER SEVENTEEN

Johnny is finding the situation difficult. They are meant to be a secret organisation but in the riot you walk down one street and you get a brick over your head, then in the next you're being photographed by a hundred newsmen. They can't afford to have their pictures in the newspapers. They might end up as highly publicised as the SAS.

'I think it's time to take action, men. We can't hang around here all night. If some nigger attacks me with a petrol bomb I'll shoot him dead and that will be bad publicity for us. I think the key to the problem is this bunch calling themselves the Jane Austen Mercenaries. Have you noticed how they all have utterly filthy leather jackets but speak with Oxford accents? They are obviously frauds. And from the information I tricked out of that associate of Flak it seems likely that they have the programme and probably know the whereabouts of the computer killer. So let's get them.'

He tries phoning in another report but finds that his line to Happy Science is no longer operative.

'What you doing?' asks Pearl.

'Interfering with the computer police line to headquarters,' says Mike, dialling some numbers and placing his computer phone in its modem. 'Ought to cause them some problems.'

He expects that this will cheer Pearl up. She bursts into tears.

'What's wrong?'

'Everything. Nicky in a coma. People being raped. And I've lost my film.'

'Can't you make another?' enquires Mike kindly.

'No I cannot make another,' screams Pearl. 'Don't be so fucking stupid. I'm still a thousand pounds short of finishing this one. It has been awful. My backer has fucked me around, the cameraman didn't take me seriously and ended up spoiling some film and Lux pestered me for three months to let him into the act. I admit he wasn't bad in it but he kept spouting poetry when he was meant to be dead.

'In the final dramatic scene he was carried in as a corpse and, no warning given, valuable film running, he sat up and started quoting *Paradise Lost*. He was up to line sixty-seven before I could shut him up.' The memory is too painful and her voice trails off.

'What did you do?'

'Clapped him round the head. He said he was just trying to show me he actually knew it.'

The Jane Austen Mercenaries prowl the streets, as far as it is possible to prowl with a riot going on. Sometimes they are forced to run and sometimes they are held up by a roadblock.

On their travels they meet some members from another band who tell them that they are just out gathering material for lyrics for a song they plan to record first thing in the morning, unless the cheap-rate recording studio for the unemployed has been burned down.

Spurred on by this disastrous news they search even more frantically, but are interrupted suddenly by the arrival of Personal Computer Services.

'I'd like a word with you,' says Johnny.

'No time,' they say, and try to pass.

'I know you have the programme. You think I'm bluffing? I received the news from Flak's confederate. The one with red and yellow hair and a disgustingly effeminate face.'

'Lux?'

'C'mon,' says Grub. 'We don't have time for this.'

'Search these men,' orders Johnny.

A fight ensues.

The Jane Austen Mercenaries put up good resistance but they are no match for the computer police, who are all trained for this sort of thing.

Sebastian wants to hide in the restaurant but it closes and all the customers have to leave and then the tube station shuts and the roads get blocked so he can't get on a bus and with the riot growing in ferocity he starts to panic.

* * *

'Yasmin set out to bribe the judges,' continues Kalia to Lux as they walk through the estate. 'He paid them to say that your guesses were incorrect when really they were right. I was powerless to help although I knew what was going on. As a result they pulled even in the contest.

'The Yamamoto family were distraught. They suspected cheating as well, but nothing could be proved. You were also distraught because you thought, fairly stupidly, that Shimono wouldn't like you so much if you didn't win the contest. You needn't have worried. Though she had poor taste in lovers, she was much too sensible a woman to bother about who won a perfume-guessing contest—'

'Now we've got you!' screams Eugene, appearing from an ambush round the corner. 'Prepare to die.'

Having been beaten up and searched by Johnny's men, the band are in an even more foul temper.

There is nowhere for Lux to run. He is surrounded.

'Well, hello,' he says, blithely. 'I've been looking all over for you. Where have you been?'

'Give us back our demo tapes.'

'That is just what I wanted to see you about. While I was in your flat, saving you all from being arrested for possessing cocaine, at some risk to myself, there was a phone call from a record producer. He was frantic to put out your record and wanted the demo tape right away. I was just about to bring it to him when some desperate PR men from a rival company burst in through the door, demanding the tape. They claimed they had first rights on it. Of course I put them off because I could see they were criminals and then when I went out to take your tape to the real record executive I scrawled a fake message on the wall in case the criminals came back.'

He beams at them.

'Unfortunately the riot prevented me making the rendezvous. I kept looking for you to give me some help but you were nowhere around. You're going to have to be a lot more dedicated if you want to make it in the music industry, you know. It's no good running around enjoying yourselves all the time when people are working hard to help your careers.'

'I don't believe a word of it,' protests Grub. 'Where are the tapes now?'

'I was coming to that. The bad PR men caught up with me just outside Kalia's flat. Isn't that true?'

Kalia nods.

'They stole all the tapes. They claim you have a contract with them.'

'We don't have a contract with anyone.'

'Some record companies will stop at nothing.'

'What were they like?'

Lux describes Johnny and his men.

'We did meet some people like that,' says the drummer.

'I'm going to search you anyway,' says Eugene. 'And if I find the tape in that bag I'm going to rip your throat out.'

Very fortunately, at that moment, a transit van full of police pulls up.

'What's going on here?' demands the driver, leaning out of the door.

'Nothing,' replies Lux, pulling out the genetic programme from his bag. 'I am just checking the riot damage on this estate against these plans here. I am a surveyor from Lambeth Council.'

The police look at him doubtfully. He doesn't look like a surveyor. Still, Lambeth council is notorious for employing all sorts of strange people and he might have sneaked in under their equal opportunities policy.

Two policemen leave the van and order them up against a wall where they are searched in case they are looters. Finished with before the musicians, Lux slips the tapes to Kalia.

An urgent message on the radio draws the police away.

'So you see,' says Lux, opening his carrier bag wide, 'I no longer have the tapes. They were stolen, despite my heroic attempts to save them.'

'What's going on?' says the leader of a police foot patrol, appearing in the wake of the van. The area is now crawling with policemen.

'Nothing,' says Lux, sidling round the corner with Kalia.

They flee.

'Lux, you are the most terrible liar.'

'Yes,' agrees Lux. 'It's because I'm a poet. All poets are liars.'

'I'd agree with that. I have met a lot through the ages.'

'It must've been interesting, living for thousands of years. Have you met any famous people?'

'A few. Mostly I was a peasant. I did meet Genghis Khan and Plato and Catherine the Great and some Incas and Aborigines you wouldn't have heard of, Confucius and St Augustine, both prigs, Wild Bill Hickock, Mary Queen of Scots, Betty Grable...'

'What?' explodes Lux, finding this hard to believe. 'You're actually telling me you met Betty Grable?'

'Certainly. I was a make-up artist for Twentieth Century-Fox'

Lux comes to a halt, gaping.

'Stop standing there with your mouth open,' says his companion. 'We should be moving along.'

Nicky comes briefly out of her coma.

'Pearl, I never mentioned it before but the stills I took for you from Happy Science for your film were pictures of illegal genetic experiments on cells and foetuses. They'll probably kill you to get them back.'

She sinks back into a trance.

'Wonderful,' grunts Pearl. 'This is just what I need.'

'Where is the film now?' asks Mike, taking a break from trying to penetrate the computer police main frame and wipe their memory banks.

'Burned.'

'Never mind. We will at least put Personal Computer Services off the trail.'

In this Mike is being a little optimistic. Liberation Computers are more used to doing things like running up mailing lists for Nicaraguan support groups and telling people how to break into banking systems than actually trying to fight anyone, and while they are doing their best by way of fouling up the computer police's links to HQ and sending out signals to wipe their memory banks, Mike has a definite notion that this is as far as the conflict will go—each side vying with the other in computer expertise.

The computer police, however, are only interested in technical expertise to a certain extent. They are more interested in hitting people and if they catch up with Liberation Computers and find them sheltering Nicky and Pearl then they will be quite prepared to tear them into bite-sized pieces.

Sebastian can't believe he has got caught up in a riot and he can't understand why the police are unable to quell it immediately and he doesn't know where to go for safety.

Mercifully, in order to remain incognito, he has worn some old clothes instead of an expensive suit. He imagines that anyone coming to Brixton in an expensive suit would be torn to pieces.

He tries leaving the area but every time he turns a corner he seems to find himself facing a platoon of policemen and he is soon lost and confused.

CHAPTER EIGHTEEN

In the Happy Science Laboratories gloom still reigns.

'We hear rumours of some problems,' says a journalist on the phone to Dr Carlson. 'Is it true that you tried to force one of your employees to be artificially inseminated and she went crazy and smashed the place up? And isn't this cheating? Wasn't there meant to be a contest to find a mother?'

'It is all lies,' barks the Doctor and raps the phone down. On his knee is a roughed-out genetic chart but he knows in his heart that it is useless. He can never make another one in time.

Anyway, you can't really rough out a genetic chart. Certainly not to Nobel prize-winning standards.

* * *

The riot grumbles on, although in most places the police are starting to get the upper hand as reinforcements from all over London and the surrounding counties succeed in completely isolating Brixton from the rest of the world and dragging more people away into vans where they are shuttled off to holding cells in police stations all over the capital.

But they later protest that what they really need to deal with the riot effectively is a law that allows them to drag absolutely everyone away and would the government mind passing one as soon as possible, and this is only sensible, of course, because if the whole population of Brixton is dragged away to prison then there certainly won't be any more riots.

The Enterprise Centre is a refurbished department store full of small shops in the front and small offices upstairs, including Liberation Computers, where Gerry now returns after making his call to *Uptown*.

Mike engages him in conversation. He has found it difficult getting much conversation out of Pearl or any at all out of Nicky.

'What've you been doing since I last saw you?'

'Oh, working, doing reviews, that sort of thing. I'm assistant editor of *Uptown* now. It's no easy life, you know, you wouldn't believe the amount of garbage I have to come into contact with. Last week I reviewed twenty-five novels.'

'Incredible,' says Mike. 'How do you manage it?'

'I only read every third page.'

'Doesn't that make it difficult?'

'Not really. Sometimes I don't read them at all. You can generally get a pretty good idea of what they're about from the cover and maybe someone in the office knows something about them ... Pretty good riot, eh?'

'I suppose so,' says Mike, worried about his computers. 'But I'm scared someone might smash up this place and ruin all our work.'

'Most unlikely,' Gerry reassures him. 'After all, you are not oppressors. No one engaged in a riot against government brutality is going to harm a left-wing gay-orientated computer firm, are they?'

* * *

'So,' says Grub, sweating from the exertions of the night.'Who does have the demo tape?'

No one is sure. Time is running out. If they can't deliver it to the record executive the next day he will find another Brixton band and have them put out the fashionable single.

'It's all your fault.'

'What d'you mean it's my fault?' protests Eugene.

'You left him alone in the house.'

'Well how come I was responsible for all the demo tapes?'

'You wanted to be. No doubt so you could show off your singing. Not that anyone cares much about the singing in a thrash metal band.'

'Shut up,' says Eugene, wearily. 'God, I'm fed up with this fucking riot.'

'We've got some good publicity shots.'

'True.'

'Look.' Eugene points past the wreckage of a customised fifties Ford that was once somebody's pride and joy. 'There are the people that attacked us. Did you notice how Lux knew exactly what they looked like?'

'They look horrible.'

'They could well be from a record company.'

'I'm going to have a word with them,' says Eugene bravely.

A police car screeches past Lux and Kalia, siren wailing, driver looking grim-faced and important.

'*What mad pursuit? What struggle to escape?*
What pipes and timbrels? What wild ecstacy?

'That's Keats,' he tells his companion. 'A good poem, though I have no idea what a timbrel is. Possibly it was something he just made up for effect. Did you really know Betty Grable?'

'Yes.'

Having been a make-up artist for Twentieth Century-Fox, Kalia is now Lux's hero.

'Was she nice?'

'Yes. Very. But generally the nicest people were the peasants.

I didn't really like many of the famous ones.'

They walk on in silence for a while, but Lux has an urge to talk.

'Brixton is in chaos,' he says out loud to the whole world. 'All around buildings burn whilst police and rioters battle it out. Somewhere in the darkness a hell-spawned band of heavy metal thrashers are trying to inflict their dire music on an innocent public. Only Lux can stop them. Elsewhere unknown forces claiming to be computer police pursue their own nefarious ends and men in vans try to stuff diamond rings down the throats of harmless onlookers.'

His voice gets louder. 'Meanwhile Pearl is sinking in a swamp of utter helplessness, partly of her own making, obstinately refusing the help of Lux, the only person standing in the way of total disaster, striding gamely through every trouble that life throws at him and laughing in the face of adversity. Lux, hero of film and poetry notebook, shining spirit, guardian of àrtistic sensibilities, fearless pursuer after...'

'Shut up Lux,' says Kalia, and stoops to help a young child back onto her bycicle.

'I can't help it. I'm bored.'

'We're in the middle of a riot.'

'I'm bored with the riot.'

'People are suffering.'

'I'm bored with people suffering. Anyway none of them like my poetry. They deserve to suffer. Look, a kebab shop. It's burning. Good.'

They observe the smouldering remains for a while.

'Always seemed like a strange idea to me,' says Lux. 'Cutting up a harmless sheep then cramming it into a bit of bread with a few tomatoes and onions. I hate the thought of all these sheep getting made into kebabs. Completely barbaric. Where is Pearl? I'm desperate to find her.'

He stumbles. Kalia looks at him, concerned. Blood is seeping out of his head wound.

'Did you meet Lana Turner?'

'Yes.'

'I look like her. Tell me more of the perfume story.'

* * *

Sebastian shakes his head to clear it of the smoke and flames and hallucinations. He is chanting to make things better but it is sending him into dreadful visions of past lives and this is no help at all while trying to dodge flying bricks.

'I'm going to scout the area,' says Mike. 'See if any of the computer investigators are about.'

He leaves the Enterprise Centre. The main street is a total shambles. Piles and piles of broken glass lie among burning rags and smouldering tyres and shattered shop-fronts and everywhere there are bricks, stones or shards of pavement that have been used as missiles. Every shop has had its metal shuttering wrenched off and inside, on the stripped counters, there remain only a few mangy items too unpleasant for anyone to even steal, like novelty watches or packets of instant noodles.

Down a sidestreet some firemen have to stand back as the front of a hi-fi shop crashes to the ground in flames sending sparks and fragments of hi-fi equipment bouncing around on the pavement, a pavement recently re-tiled by the council in a futile attempt to improve the area. Unable to provide any jobs for the inhabitants, the nice new pink pavement is a gesture that receives little thanks.

Groups of people still walk around, as they do all night. The police are eventually able to control the riot but unable to completely clear the streets, even with their huge numbers, because the riot involves not just a few but a large part of the community, all the poor and dissatisfied who have long since given up hope of attracting any sort of attention to their plight and see the riot as an opportunity to do something positive.

Everyone is pleased at fighting back. Mike catches the violent community spirit and, walking along, he plans a special riot edition of the Liberation Computers Monthly Newsletter.

Round the corner in Acre Lane he is singled out from a group of people and robbed at knifepoint. He is only able to pull two pound coins out of his pocket and the muggers look fairly disgusted but take the two pounds anyway and after this Mike goes back to the Enterprise Centre a little confused and bitter because it seems to him that he was singled out because he was white and as a white socialist this is very hard to cope with.

What's more, when he gets back to Liberation Computers he is too embarrassed to mention it to his partner Marcus because Marcus is black and Mike thinks that Marcus might think he is getting at him in some way so he ends up by being extra friendly and acting like a fool.

A little reasoned discussion between Eugene and Johnny leaves everyone still suspicious of each other but fairly sure that Lux has been lying.

The Jane Austen Mercenaries resume their search, now quite seriously intending to murder him. Personal Computer Services slink back into the darkness to consider their next move.

'So,' says Johnny to his men. 'Everything points to this Lux person. He must know where the genetic programme is. Putting us onto these musicians was just a ploy. Let's get him.'

Johnny is enjoying the riot. He always likes scenes of violence. As Yasmin, in every life he has four aims: to frustrate Kalia's good intentions, to frustrate everyone else's good intentions, to make himself as important as possible, and to participate in scenes of violence. He has no real desire to return to Heaven.

'The day before the final round of the perfume-guessing contest Shimono sent you a poem. You thought it was a terrible poem but, shamelessly hypocritical to the last, you told her it was a work of genius when you met her next day in the ceremonial garden.'

'Sounds like the only thing to do,' Lux interjects. 'If you're in love with someone and they suddenly send you a poem you can hardly tell them it is rubbish, can you?'

'No, not unless you are honest. Anyway, at noon you all assembled for the final. By this time your nose was so finely trained you could spot a perfume in the next county. I have no idea why in all your lifetimes the only supreme ability you ever had was the ability to identify perfumes, but there you are. The ways of the gods are strange.'

'It doesn't sound so bad. Better than going to war and cutting people up with a meat cleaver.'

'True. Anyway, I tried to attend the final but Yasmin bribed a maid to smash some valuable dishes and then had me blamed for it. I was banished to my room. It was a terrible time. Just the day before I had been trying to help an old man across a stream and Yasmin leapt out and frightened us and the old man was drowned. So instead of an act of kindness to my credit I had a murder on my slate.'

'Surely not. It wasn't your fault the man was killed. You still meant well.'

'Not according to Yasmin. He claimed the old man was a fugitive from justice and I was helping him escape. No doubt the gods supported him in this. He was always more influential than me. Now stop interrupting. I was telling you about the final day of the perfume contest—'

'Lux!' comes a scream that is loud even by the standards of the night.'Give us the demo tape. I'm going to wrap my bicycle chain round your neck.'

Lux, as keen on his neck as he is on the rest of him, looks for a wall to shin over.

No wall coming into view, he is forced to climb a tree, a sturdy nondescript type of tree planted in between housing blocks in the estate. Lux is not sure if he likes trees. He has a feeling that poets probably should but really he prefers concrete. Still, it serves a useful purpose now. Persistently vandalised, it has no branches near ground level and a smooth trunk that only someone as nimble as Lux could scale. While the Jane Austen Mercenaries gather round at the foot of the tree, unable to pursue him, Lux hardly notices the ascent.

Down below, not wanting to get into a fight with the band, Kalia slips unnoticed into a play area.

Lux finds a comfortable branch and glares down at his pursuers. A squirrel, cut off from its home in the park, frightened by the riot, hops over and joins him.

Amazing, thinks Lux. I am practically god-like. Even squirrels come to play with me, and squirrels are notably shy animals. Virtually a modern-day St Francis of Assisi.

Lux is noted for the way animals tend to flock around him, though no one generally goes as far as comparing him to St Francis of Assisi.

'*It is a being of warmth, I think,*' he says to the squirrel. 'That's a line from Stevie Smith. Do you like Stevie Smith? Yes? Good.'

He hunts through his memory for a nice squirrel poem. Unable to find one he quotes it a few lines of Kathy Acker.

> *'for you my love and me a few brief hours of sun*
> *then no consciousness blackness perpetually*
> *take it kiss me do it grab me*
> *grab my arm grab my ankles grab my cunt hairs—'*

He looks up to check if the squirrel is paying attention. It is rapt.

Good, thinks Lux, obviously an animal of taste, and gets ready to quote the rest.

'Lux!'

The shout from below interrupts him. He looks down quizzically, having forgotten that the Jane Austen Mercenaries are at present clustered around the bottom of the tree, waiting for his blood.

'Give us back the tape. If you give us it back now we'll let you live.'

'No chance,' screams Lux. 'You will only inflict it on people too weak to resist.'

'Well what the fuck does it have to do with you what we do with it?'

'Someone has to protect the innocent. Your music is an abomination. I hate it. Worse, Pearl hates it. She thinks you are pigfuckers and no one that Pearl thinks is a pigfucker is going to get a demo tape back from me. Now leave me alone, I'm busy with a squirrel.'

'He is stoned,' mutters Eugene. 'With all that coke inside him he's lost his mind. We'll just have to go and get it.'

They start standing on each other's shoulders, trying to lay a hand on the nearest branch.

'One move closer and I'll feed your tape to the squirrel,' bawls Lux, brandishing a copy. 'And he's looking pretty hungry.'

It is an impasse. The band settle down to starve him out. Round the corner the computer police watch, unsure of what is going on.

Lux gets back to discussing poetry with his friend. Everyone is away rioting somewhere else and it is peaceful here, in the tree, apart from the distant drone of helicopters and the occasional thud of a sound system far over on the next block where an MC relentlessly ignores everything that is going on around him and practises his rapping through the night, too involved in it to even notice the riot, or the neighbours going crazy upstairs.

Chapter Nineteen

A police Transit van draws up beside a pub, the landlord unbolts his door and brings out a crate of beer bottles and the police sergeant thanks him, loads up the beer bottles and drives off.

Outside, Sebastian watches. Some youths brush past him. Did they jostle me deliberately, he wonders, scared.

There is an alleyway beside the pub so he creeps down it to think in peace but it goes wrong when what he thinks about is chanting his mantra to see if that will make things better and his fear and confusion make him plunge immediately into a terrible reincarnation memory where his job is to count the money left over from heretics after they have been burned and distribute the profits evenly between the inquisitors and himself. The character with yellow hair is about to be burned for spouting heretical poetry.

'I didn't know it was heretical,' protests the figure, inglorious in death. 'It was an accident, I won't do it again.'

The same woman who figured as a nun in a previous vision comes to him and says she is going to help the poet to escape but needs a hundred gold doubloons to bribe the guards but Sebastian won't lend it to her so the poet is burned and afterwards Sebastian is mortified because he realises that the reason he would not help to save him was because he was attracted to him and if he was found out being attracted to a heretical male poet then burning would be the least he could expect.

He desperately shakes all this out of his head and tries to think what to do.

'It is hard being unappreciated,' says Lux, to the squirrel. 'And I am very unappreciated. No one likes my poems and Pearl won't fall in love with me. Never mind, soon I will be world champion poet and then they'll all be sorry.'

He goes off into a daydream about a new carrier-bag collection. The squirrel goes to sleep.

Down below, Grub, now driven almost completely crazy with rage and frustration, refuses to wait any longer.

'I'm going to burn him out,' he declares forcefully, and hunts around for something suitable to start a blaze.

On the far side of the small play area wall is an unignited petrol bomb.

'Is this wise?' says Eugene.

'I can't wait any longer. We need the demo tape. It could change our whole lives. I'm not letting stardom escape just because Lux decides to keep it. I'll have him out of there before he has time to destroy all the tapes.'

Grub smashes the milk bottle around the base of the tree and the petrol soaks into the bark. He lights it.

Hm, thinks Lux, tree burning under him. An awkward situation, but no doubt I will be rescued soon.

Sure enough some police and firemen appear, fresh from combatting a terrible blaze in the next street. The firemen run over with a net and shout for him to jump. More importantly, a man with a TV camera on his shoulder is in close attendance.

Lux is pleased. He is bound to be on television now.

'Don't worry,' he says to the squirrel, knowing that animals are scared of fire, 'I'll save us.'

He jumps down into the net, coat flowing up over his head and squirrel on his shoulder.

'Are you alright?' say the firemen, picking him out of the net.

'Fine, thank you,' replies Lux, polite even in a crisis, and hurries over to the TV camera.

'Did you get some good pictures? I tried turning my best profile to the camera though it was a bit difficult with the tree burning and everything.'

'Yes, we got some good pictures,' says the cameraman. 'Although you needn't have worried about your best profile because the squirrel's tail was covering up your face.'

'What?'

Lux is outraged. He aims a kick at the animal but it is now out of range, heading for safety in the park.

'Two-timing little monster,' he mutters, and stomps off, hands sunk deep into his pockets in disapproval.

The Jane Austen Mercenaries, meanwhile, have all been arrested for setting fire to a tree and are driven off in a Transit van.

Passing the flat where the sound system is still pumping it out, Lux directs a fierce scowl at the windows. Reggae sound systems are well down on the artistic approval list as far as he is concerned.

Johnny watches the arrest of the band with approval. It was him who brought the police here so quickly, calling them on his radio. He loves to see things going badly for people.

'Do you have anything to drink?'

Pearl feels like she needs something to cheer her up and calm her down. She has a sinking feeling in her stomach because she has lost the film, and with it eighteen months' work, in addition to all her possessions, which went up uninsured in her house. And also there is the matter of Happy Science apparently hot on her trail by way of Personal Computer Services, although she is still not entirely sure if she believes all this as Nicky is no longer a person you can really rely on, being either maniacally depressed or comatose.

'Yes,' replies Mike. 'We have a Liberation Computers emergency bottle of brandy. I'll get you some.'

He offers some to Pearl in a cup.

'You want some, Marcus?'

'No thanks,'

Marcus is busy working a computer.

'Go on, have some.'

'No thanks.'

'It's good brandy.'

'I don't want it.'

'Please have some brandy.'

'What's the matter with you?' demands Marcus, exasperated, forced to turn round from his console where he was filling in time making up a new computer game.

'Nothing, nothing at all,' cries Mike. 'Why, was I acting like there was something the matter with me? I'm not acting any different than normal towards you, am I?'

Marcus wrinkles his face and turns back to his work. The game he is making is called 'Together We Can Fight Imperialism!' and is a role-playing adventure centred on outwitting the CIA in Central America.

So far Liberation Computers adventure games have not been selling too well but home computer fans are notoriously indifferent to Trotskyism. 'Re-live the Fourth International' lost them a terrible amount of money but they are still hopeful of breaking through.

Pearl abandons the cup for the bottle and starts pouring brandy down her throat.

Kalia observes Lux's rescue and is about to follow him when she is suddenly attacked by a dreadful wave of nausea. Forced to retreat into a shop doorway, she slumps to the ground. Her head is pounding.

What is causing it? She has never felt anything like it before. It feels as if someone is inside her skull, kicking.

Johnny phones in a report to Happy Science, although to do this he has to show some credentials to the police and use one of their telephones because his direct link has been cut off by Liberation Computers. They have lost Nicky and Pearl but are continuing to follow Lux, having meanwhile skirmished briefly with rioters and the Jane Austen Mercenaries.

'Any further progress?' asks Dr Carlson, eagerly.

'Not really,' Johnny tells him.

'Get me my genetic programme,' snaps the Doctor, nerves starting to go, Nobel prize for Science starting to fade from view.

'All right, don't shout,' retorts Johnny, who is developing a headache.

There is a knock on the door. A cleaner comes in.

'Is this Mr Sebastian Flak's office?'

'No it is not.'

She leaves.

Odd, thinks Dr Carlson. This is the third cleaner this evening who has been looking for Flak's office.

I need something to take my mind off things, he thinks, and gets on with some foetus experiments to calm himself down.

A young girl leans over a balcony. Maybe four years old when the Sex Pistols first rehearsed, she is wearing full punk regalia.

Lux wanders by.

'Hey,' she calls, seeing him pass. 'Whatya doing? Come on up.'

* * *

Kalia's head clears slowly. Ignored by the people walking by, her thoughts begin to take shape. She can only assume that it is Yasmin's doing. He must have developed some way to attack her psychically, as well as blocking out her ability to see into the future. She knows that he is nearby.

She thinks about Heaven. I must be close to my total now. Very close. I hope so, I can't stand much more of it, and my incarnations are getting worse.

She could just about take the endless peasant lifetimes but the bedsit in Camberwell has really got to her. She fights off another wave of nausea and presses on.

It is Sebastian who is responsible for Kalia's sickness. His subsonscious mind altered by continual chanting and his conscious mind now full of fear, he is unwittingly sending out dreadful waves of psychic disturbance.

Finely attuned to psychic disturbances, both Kalia and Yasmin are now suffering badly.

The young punk is attracted by Lux's spectacular looks, something Lux knows by instinct.

She makes him some tea.

'Have you seen Pearl?'

'Pearl who?'

Lux shrugs. 'You wanna help me look for her?'

'No. What happened to your head?'

Lux can't remember.

The living room contains a modern sofa, an ashtray and nothing else. The sofa, a remnant of some previous tenants' abortive attempt to make the place comfortable, is now an unlovely affair of dented tubular metal and coffee-stained canvas.

The ashtray is a paint tin, another leftover from home improvements that came to a halt when the decorating grant from the social security was diverted into more enjoyable pursuits.

* * *

'We have done all we can,' said Lord Yamamoto. 'I have managed to change the judges for the contest. There will no longer be any biased decisions. It is now up to you, Chang Kwai Lux. The honour of the village rests in your hands.'

The contestants file in amid formal ceremony, bowing to each other, accepting small bowls of tea laid out on the beautifully carved table that is the centrepiece of the room, the splendid showpiece room where Lord Yamamoto entertains his guests.

Lux discovers that the girl's name is Jean, she comes from Scotland, she is lonely in London and she doesn't want to hear any of his poems, despite finding him irresistibly attractive. She wipes some damp blood from his cheek, kisses him, and they start fucking on the couch, adding a few more stains.

The perfumes are sent for. Everyone knows that today will be the most difficult of all, with scents gathered from all lands known to man.

'Greetings, Chang Kwai Lux,' says Yasmin. 'May you have the best of fortune in today's contest.'

Lux makes his formally polite reply. He is not worried about the contest. He has the best sense of smell in the country.

'I would like to bring one thing to your attention,' continues Yasmin, speaking softly so only Lux can hear. 'I have in my possession three poems you have sent to Shimono, eldest daughter of the household. They are of a very intimate nature, as was her reply. Unless you lose the contest I will show them to Lord Yamamoto. His daughter being engaged to the Emperor's nephew, you will be lucky to escape with your head. If Shimono speaks up for you she will be banished to a monastery in the mountains. Here are the perfumes. Good luck in the contest.'

Lux lies on the couch, body drained but mind still active with cocaine, pleased that Jean likes him.

She makes him some tea. Pearl always demands that he makes the tea.

'Not that I mind making tea of course,' he mumbles.'I agree that tea making should be shared. I will do anything for Pearl.'

'Are you in love with this person?' asks Jean, dressing.

'Yes.'

'Would she mind you fucking someone else?'

'No. She wouldn't care. Anyway she is probably fucking her girlfriend at this very moment.'

'Can two girls fuck?'

'I'm not sure. I may have chosen the wrong verb. But anyway, you know what I mean.'

The riot has not reached up to this second-floor flat, and Jean has been unaffected by it, other than the sounds and smells that have made their way into her home, and Lux.

He is disappointed that she doesn't want to hear any of his poems.

Sebastian wanders blindly, dreadful visions pouring in and out of his head, weakly wishing that Maybeline was here to protect him in between running from attackers and pursuers, generally imagined. Despite his constant fear, he never actually meets anyone in the riot who wants to do him any harm, and his only injury is a twisted ankle that he inflicts on himself while running around in a panic.

But when he finds himself close to an exploding fire engine and a violent melee he runs off again in terror and haunts the walkways of an estate, hunting desperately for sanctuary.

Gerry leaves Liberation Computers to gather some more information for his riot article, making his way down towards Kennington where fighting is still going on.

He sees a young woman being punched in the stomach as she

is arrested and some people with scarfs round their faces making a last stand with stones and petrol bombs before being dispersed. The helicopter flies overhead, as it has done all night.

A police van tears past but is forced to halt in the distance where the road is partially blocked by an overturned car and more police try to shepherd it through, although this is difficult as the group of rioters is still throwing missiles, some of which batter off the sides of the van.

Inside the van the Jane Austen Mercenaries sit in furious silence, each of them hating all the others, particularly Grub, whose idea it was to burn down the tree.

There is a brief thump on the door.

Jean looks through the spyhole to see what it is. Opening the door, she finds Sebastian slumped on the concrete.

He looks up, about to ask for shelter but, seeing the naked Lux in the background, a figure out of his nightmares, he moans dreadfully and passes out.

'That's funny,' says Jean. 'He looked at you and fainted.'

'I often have this effect on people. Do you think we should help him?'

CHAPTER TWENTY

In the centuries following Kalia's life with the Witchmaster, she becomes less and less sure about what she is doing. Half the times she does some act of kindness it seems to her that maybe from someone else's point of view it is no kindness at all and sometimes in her dreams she has more converstions with Heaven and really they are no help whatsoever.

But, having no alternative, she carries on as best she can so that when she is born a Maori in New Zealand she tries helping all the sick Maoris who are dying of white men's diseases and then when she is a Tibetan priest she stays up all night saying extra prayers for the souls of the dead and during the industrial revolution in Britain she travels the country giving bread to all the people who have been dispossessed of their land and are starving in the new cities.

'It's all very well you giving them bread,' a factory owner tells her, 'but you are not helping anyone. If you give them free bread then they won't have to work. They'll sit around drinking all the time and the country will not become great.'

Not convinced by this argument, Kalia keeps on handing out bread till she is thrown in prison as a subversive and transported to Australia, where she tries helping all the Aborigines who are dying of white men's diseases.

Jean is not all that keen on having a stranger in her flat and neither is Lux, who despite having met Sebastian at Happy Science does not recognise him. But after a while they decide that probably it will be all right if they give him a cup of tea, providing he wakes up.

Lux dresses.

'More tea?' asks Jean.

'Yes please.'

'I'd make you a sandwich but next door borrowed my only knife for cutting up some smack and they haven't brought it back yet. I could get you some heroin if you want?'

'No thank you,' says Lux. 'I hate putting brown things up my nose.'

Sebastian wakes from a dreadful nightmare, looks fearfully at Lux but more fearfully at the outside world, refuses a cup of tea and asks Jean, without much hope, if she has a phone.

She dredges a phone out from under the sofa.

'This is private,' he says.

'Well go somewhere else then,' says Jean.

Sebastian glowers at them but makes his call. Lux's eyes glaze again and he starts mumbling some poems.

Kalia walks up through Brixton. The police let her through, deeming her harmless. The riot is quietening down, but her nausea is washing back and forward.

She halts. Johnny is in front of her, holding his head.

'Hello Yasmin,' says Kalia.

'Is this your doing?' demands Johnny, eyes wild with sickness. They are both suffering at the hands, or mind, of Sebastian.

Well, muses Chang Kwai Lux, perfume being passed towards him in unmarked porcelain bowls. What is to be done? If I win the contest Yasmin will expose my relationship with Shimono.

But when he thinks about it the situation does not seem too bad. So what if everybody knows? Once Lux has won the perfume-guessing competition he will be the hero of the hour. Lord Yamamoto will be pleased to marry Shimono to him after he brings triumph to the hamlet. He can settle down to write poetry and eat rice in comfort. Possibly he can still do a little travelling.

For a poetic spirit there is only one thing to do and that is press on with the love affair. So he shoots a haughty glance at Yasmin, sitting regally behind his players, and starts reeling off the correct names of the perfumes.

'This one,' he says, nonchalantly, 'is Kubri, a distillation of flowers from the uncharted lands north of Tibet.'

The crowd applaud. Lux bows gracefully.

While Sebastian is on the phone Lux suffers an unpleasant hallucination of going naked into battle. Fatigued, he sits on the floor.

'I have to hunt for Pearl. But I'm tired.'

'I got some blues,' says Jean. 'Do you mind blue drugs?'

'No. Blue drugs are fine.'

Lux swallows the tablets.

'I couldn't make the rendezvous,' Sebastian explains on the phone. 'I got caught up in the riot.'

'You are close to Heaven, Kalia.'

'I know.'

'But I'll keep you on Earth for a while.'

'You will not.'

'I will. I have already delayed your return by hundreds of years. Fool. Wandering around doing acts of kindness.' Yasmin laughs.

But the confrontation is hampered by the pain and sickness that both of them are feeling, and Johnny's men, not knowing what is happening, help their leader away, leaving Kalia standing confused in the street.

'I was just arranging a business meeting,' says Sebastian, feeling some need to explain. 'I am being hunted by some big American companies for my accounting skills.'

'I've met you before,' says Lux, mind invigorated by the blues. 'I remember, outside Happy Science. You weren't no help to me getting in the genius project. How about if I read you some of my poems now? I'm an even better poet than I was two months ago, I got lots of great new material, all night I've been giving interviews for television. They're practically fighting each other to give me my own programme. Any chance of putting in a good word for me?'

'I'll do my best,' lies Sebastian, still horrified to meet the figure who has appeared in his nightmare visions. Only his massive desire to be recruited by Coca Cola is keeping him going.

'Where is the Enterprise Centre? I have arranged to meet my contact there.'

'I'll show you. I have to get out and look for Pearl. You wanna help me?'

'I'm too busy.'

'How about you?' He turns to Jean. She shakes her head, not all that interested in helping someone she has just fucked find his girlfriend. Lux gathers up his belongings, making sure that his treasures are in his plastic bag along with Pearl's reel of film.

Inside the small Liberation Computers office Pearl is drunk on brandy and Nicky is sitting staring at the wall and Mike is still trying to be extra pleasant to Marcus.

'Have some brandy. A cup of tea? That's a good game you're making, I could never make one that good, yep, you certainly are a genius when it comes to making computer games, I wish I had your skill, are you sure you wouldn't like some brandy?'

Marcus stands up.

'Mike. I am sick of you being nice to me. At a rough guess I would say you had some bad experience at the hands of some blacks.'

'Yes,' screams Mike. 'But it doesn't make me think any the worse of you! How did you know?'

'Because any time something like this happens you spend hours feeling guilty in case you are thinking some politically bad thoughts and try and make up for it by being extra nice to me. What happened?'

Mike hangs his head.

'I was singled out from a crowd and mugged.'

'Wow.' says Marcus. 'What a surprise. And now, having a sneaking, tiny, minute feeling at the back of your head that just maybe the racists are right because you have been mugged, you are unable to cope.'

Lord Yasmin's team stays level with Lux all through the final encounter. Perfumes from all around the world are brought in, aromas so obscure that none but the finest perfume-guessers in Japan could hope to name them.

When the last porcelain bowl arrives the watching crowd is deathly silent.

'Well?' enquires the judge, after a while.

Sweating with mental exertion, Yasmin's man opens his mouth.

'Quatrino, from Indonesia,' he says.

'Wrong,' says the judge, dramatically. 'Chang Kwai Lux?'

Lux looks over at Yasmin. Yasmin edges out a piece of parchment with Lux's poem on it, threateningly. The poet ignores the threat.

'Gujidana, from the unmapped lands of the Western Red Men,' pronounces Lux. 'Much used, I believe, as a natural skin toner and moisturiser.'

'Correct,' says the Judge.

Lux has won. The audience applaud wildly, in a polite restrained sort of way.

I absolutely can't stand any more of this, thinks Kalia, working her way weakly through Brixton. I will lose my mind if I am reincarnated on this Earth again. I used to be able to ignore much of the stupidity, ignorance, brutality, prejudice, exploitation, violence, evil and everything else. Now I have to watch it every day on television. And then there's the adverts as well.

I will do anything to reach my total and return to the heavenly palace. Where has this heavenly descendant got to?

To much ceremonial flag waving, Lux has led his team to triumphant victory. Never again will the neighbouring hamlet be able to sneer at them.

Lord Yamamoto personally congratulates him. Shimono throws her arms around him. Loved, the centre of attention, Lux is blissfully happy.

Yasmin concedes defeat politely before taking Lord Yamamoto

aside for a quiet word.

Kalia, released from her room to join in the general celebration, wrestles her way in between Lux and Shimono.

'Leave now,' she hisses. 'There is going to be trouble.'

'What trouble?' says Lux. 'I am the hero of the hour. Have some saki.'

Back in Liberation Computers, Marcus continues lecturing the guilty Mike.

'No doubt at this very minute a thousand racist acts are being committed by whites against blacks which will all go totally unreported anywhere. You, however, somehow expecting blacks to be perfect so as to fit in with your politics, cannot cope with a racist attack yourself. Kindly take your guilt feelings somewhere else and leave me to finish my Nicaragua computer game.'

There is an awkward silence.

Lord Yamamoto thunders back into the room and has it cleared by his bodyguards.

'Is this true?' he demands, brandishing Lux's romantic poems.

'Yes,' beams Lux. 'You don't mind, do you? Everyone knows the Emperor's nephew is a moron, it would be a tragedy to marry Shimono off to him. They wouldn't have a thing to talk about.'

Lux is taken outside. There is a brief ceremony before he is beheaded with the family sword which is kept sharp specially for this sort of occasion.

Idiot, thinks Kalia later, supervising his funeral. You just have no idea, do you?

'Come on,' says Lux, walking up the road with Sebastian. 'I'll show you where the Enterprise Centre is. Don't worry, the riot isn't so bad now.'

'Is it always like this?' asks Sebastian, ashen-faced, clambering over some burnt-out rubbish bins.

'I don't think so,' replies Lux. 'Though I don't generally take much notice. I'm always too busy writing poetry and looking for Pearl.'

I don't believe this, thinks Sebastian. I'm an accountant. I'm not the sort of person who has to cope with inner-city disturbances. He is rapidly going off the idea of sorting out a trouble spot for Coca Cola. He will ask them to send him somewhere quiet.

And nor am I the sort of person who keeps plunging into homoerotic fantasies of past lives, he continues, the filthy streets in front of him alternating with guilt-inducing thoughts of Lux and longing for Maybeline.

'Are you a crooked accountant?' asks Lux, making conversation.

'Certainly not.'

'You want some blues? I pocketed a few.'

'No.'

'They'll give you energy.'

'I don't take drugs.'

'What do you do?'

'I'm an accountant.'

'What for?'

'What do you mean what for?'

'What are you an accountant for?'

'I'm not an accountant for anything.'

'What do accountants do?'

'Accounts.'

'What accounts?'

'Business accounts.'

'What for?'

Sebastian clutches his head. He is having erotic fantasies about an imbecile.

Johnny stumbles into view. 'There he is,' he screams, pointing at Lux. 'Get him.'

Lux, not knowing what Johnny is wanting but not willing to find out, heads for a wall, full speed.

* * *

'I will kill Lux,' snarls Grub, crammed in a crowded police cell.

'Ha!' snorts Eugene. 'Big talk. You are full of big talk.'

'Shut up.'

'Shut up yourself. And next time you want to burn down a tree try doing it when there isn't a van-load of policemen about. You must be the thickest person I know.'

'Oh yeah?' retorts Grub. 'Well who was it got a first in astrophysics from Cambridge? You or me?'

CHAPTER TWENTY-ONE

Lux, not realising that Johnny is after the genetic programme in his carrier bag, assumes he is just some madman, unless he is a poetry critic.

Lux knows that his poetry is too modern for some people's taste. His radical version of *I wandered lonely as a cloud* suffered terrible criticism one night from an intellectual friend of Mike's who claimed it was not possible that Wordsworth was feeling guilty about murdering babies when he wrote it.

'How do you know he never murdered any babies?' demanded Lux. 'The daffodils could well be child substitutes.'

'Well if he did it never made it into any biography I've read.'

'It could have been hushed up. Any close reading of Wordsworth reveals him to be a total psychopath. He must have been guilty about something. Why else did he keep wandering around in fields? I suspect he was a cannibal.'

Jumping down from the wall jars Lux and makes him reel. The drugs speed up his metabolism and speed up his mind and he is gripped with a terrible passion to find Pearl and give her the film and make everything all right.

But blood loss from his head wound along with huge drug abuse is starting to take its toll. Even Lux's healthy system cannot entirely cope and he starts to stumble along.

Some passers by, heading home as the riot quietens, help him to his feet. He clutches determinedly onto his carrier bag and walks on but trips over a chewing-gum machine, unfilled for years but left in place on the street till knocked over by a surging mob.

An ambulance pulls up.

'Looks like we reached you just in time,' says the friendly ambulance driver and bundles him into the back.

'No,' wails Lux, desperate not to be taken away to hospital when Pearl needs him, but his protests are useless and they start driving off, lights flashing.

'I'm perfectly healthy, I must find Pearl before the computer police get to her,' he says, and starts to struggle.

'Drive fast,' shouts the attendant to the driver. 'His mind is starting to go.'

'My mind is not starting to go,' protests Lux. 'I'm perfectly alright. Listen, I'll prove it.' He launches into a poem, to his mind a very sane thing to do.

'Where is your fabled Doric beauty?
The fringe of your towers, Corinth, your ancient properties,
The temples of Gods and men's homes,
The women of the city of Sisyphus...

'See? I'm fine. Would you like to hear the next verse?' The attendant starts holding him down and mopping his head with a damp cloth.

'Stop for nothing,' he yells at the driver. 'This is serious.'

Some people from the street outside enter the Enterprise Centre, push past the doorman and wander around looking for some way to carry on the excitement of the night.

Everywhere is locked except Liberation Computers, which they enter. There they intimidate Mike, Marcus, Nicky and Pearl, smiling at them, walking around pushing buttons on the computers, taking some brandy, sitting down beside the two women, talking about the violence they have done tonight, fingering pockets that may contain knives.

Intimidating other people is a good way to carry on your excitement.

Kalia meets Sebastian again. The meeting causes her more nausea and headache although she still does not realise that it is Sebastian's doing.

The accountant is reeling up the street.

She doesn't really like him, but supposes she should help. After all, the birds did say he was heading for serious trouble. And helping him then might be her ticket back into Heaven.

Lux resigns himself to being taken to hospital. When he arrives he will just have to slip out of a side exit and walk back to Brixton.

Normally he might be pleased at the opportunity of lying around in hospital for a while with hordes of doctors and nurses all looking after him while he lies in bed eating grapes and writing poetry. In fact he imagines it would be quite a nice life with no people from the social security dropping hints that he should try getting a job and maybe the whole ward full of patients flocking round to listen to his poems and nurses being nice to him and helping him fix his hair but of course at this moment he has more important things to do.

The ambulance comes to a halt.

'Are we there?'

Stones start to crash around the sides of the vehicle. Unable to pass an overturned car, it is a sitting target.

'The animals,' says the attendant, temporarily releasing his grip on Lux. 'Have they no respect for the medical profession?'

What a stroke of luck, thinks Lux, and waits for his chance.

There is a knock on the door and the helmeted and visored face of a policeman appears.

'You can't get through this way,' he says, his riot shield protecting him from the hail of rocks. 'You'll have to go back.'

'But we have a very sick patient in here.'

'I'm feeling much better now,' says Lux, sprinting for freedom.

'Damn,' says the ambulanceman. 'I never saw anyone escape from an ambulance before. That's the second one tonight.'

'He doesn't look very sick to me,' comments the policeman, looking at Lux's quickly departing figure.

He gets back on the job, not having time to stand around chatting with medical crews. He has a riot to control and later he will have to make out a report on the desperate criminals he arrested earlier in the evening for burning down a tree, just one of many senseless acts of vandalism he has witnessed that night.

Inside Liberation Computers it is tense. Mike trys to defuse the situation by being friendly.

'We are a socialist computer co-operative,' he says weakly, as on of the invaders pockets some electrical leads and picks up a keyboard, looking as if he may steal it as well. Mike is disturbed. He feels that a socialist computer co-operative should not be suffering at the hands of rioters.

'Yes,' continues Marcus. 'Good riot.'

The gang carry on pocketing things, not very interested that Liberation Computers thought it was a good riot.

'Are you queer?' demands one of them, aggressively, noticing Mike's Gay Pride badge.

'What the fuck do you think you're doing?' demands Pearl, standing up, as someone touches her.

Lux, excited and triumphant, scrambles his way back into Brixton by way of the rows of gardens in the sidestreets, arriving finally at the centre, where assorted newsmen are now drinking tea in plastic cups, including one newsman who has a cut face with blood matted down his cheek but is still sticking to his task.

'Hello,' says Lux, brandishing the can containing Pearl's film. 'I am Lux, a big film-maker. I've just been out in the thick of it, the rioters attacked my camera crew and killed them all but I managed to fight them off and save this roll of film, probably it will win me a prize when the next journalists' award ceremony rolls around. Apart from the scenes of carnage, the most interesting thing I filmed was Lux the Poet, a young genius who lives in these parts.'

'Lux the film-maker and Lux the Poet?'

'Many talented people are called Lux. This one was thrilling the rioters with a series of liberation poems. What have you all been doing? Hanging round here in safety? It's no good hiding, you know, you have to get out where the action is if you want to be a success in this business.'

Everyone stares. Lux by this time is no longer the perfectly made-up creature who set out earlier in the evening. The jagged forest of his hair is now mangled around his head, with blood, setting gel, soap, sugar, hairspray, squirrel fur and some assorted riot debris all oozing out to dribble down his neck and collar. His coat, a shabby affair at the best of times, is ripped in three places and his left foot is sticking out of his baseball boot. Most of his skin is filthy from the smoke and the crawling round in gardens and those bits of his face that aren't dirty are smeared with cocaine, lipstick and mascara. The general effect is something like Lana Turner through a mincing machine.

Lux, not realising there is anything unusual about his appearance, thinks he has an attentive audience and is about to launch into a poem or continue his story when something diverts his attention.There is a scent in the air he recognises. The air is still thick with smoke but Lux knows he can distinguish something.

Of course. It is the distinctive smell of Pearl's organic moisturiser. Bought from the local health-food store, it smells like nothing else.

She is somewhere close. His eyes blaze with happiness and he pushes his way through the reporters.

'There is the Enterprise Centre.'

Kalia points.

'Thank you,' says Sebastian. 'You have been very helpful. Tonight has been terrible. I've been chased around by rioters and harangued by an imbecile with red and yellow hair. This place is disgusting. Everyone here makes me sick.'

He leaves and Kalia wanders on, not knowing any more what she is meant to be doing.

Lying With a Friend under a Burnt-out Truck

'I'm cold,' says Lux, shivering.

CHAPTER TWENTY-TWO

The Jane Austen Mercenaries spend the night and part of the next morning in police cells before being released without any charges being made because there is so much confusion and so many charges to be laid against other people that they are not worth bothering about. But with no demo tape to play the record producer, they never do get to make the record.

* * *

'Kalia!' Lux shouts across the street, and hurries across, smiling wildly.

'What've you been doing? I've been talking to a squirrel and jumping out of burning trees and being filmed by TV cameras then I got forced into bed by a girl called Jean and I helped out this strange accountant then I got kidnapped by an ambulance and driven for miles so I had to break free and make a run for it before they done an operation on me or something then I crawled through gardens for miles till I picked up Pearl's scent and now I'm gonna take her the film then I saw you across the street.'

'Lux, you are a terrible liar.'

'It's all true. How about you? What've you been doing?'

'Oh, walking around, helping people. What were you doing to that accountant?'

'Nothing. I was friendly.'

'Well he certainly doesn't like you.'

'I expect he is wrapped up in guilt feelings because he is madly attracted to me. It happens all the time.'

'How do you know he is madly attracted to you?'

'I can always tell. No doubt he has a girlfriend somewhere who wouldn't approve. I didn't really like him.'

'Neither did I. As a descendant of Heaven he is a big disappointment.'

'It was him?'

'Yes.'

'Oh. He seemed a little strange. How did he manage as King of Sparta?'

'Fairly well, in the end.'

Pearl picks up the phone.

'Security?' she says. 'Get up to Liberation Computers and help us out. We're being harassed by a mob.'

'Hey, bitch, what did you do that for?'

There is a pause while the gang contemplate some violence against Pearl, who stands protectively in front of Nicky.

Two security men arrive.

'We've called the police,' they say. 'They're downstairs now.' The gang leave.

Afterwards Mike tells Pearl he doesn't think she should have done that because he does not really approve of calling the police on people and maybe getting them arrested, and Pearl says this is fine in theory but what else are you meant to do when someone is harassing you or about to attack you, and Mike has to agree that it is a difficult problem. And he finds the fact that some people in a riot against oppression were quite happy to oppress him for being gay another difficult problem.

Lux, still unaware of Pearl's exact whereabouts but knowing she is close, is stopped only yards away by a police cordon. He and Kalia are forced to turn back.

'Don't worry,' says Kalia. 'We'll work our way round.'

'The street was closing, the city was closing,
would we be the lucky ones to make it?' mumbles Lux.

A van draws up.

'Want a lift?' says the driver, a woman in overalls. On the side of the van it says Stockwell Women's Lift Service.

'We are out looking for people in trouble,' says a woman in the back to them, as the van drives off.

'Thank you,' says Lux. 'Drop us near the Enterprise Centre.'

'One moment,' says the woman. 'Are you female?'

'Not exactly,' replies Lux. 'Although I do get a lot of harassment from men on scaffolding.'

The van draws to a halt and Lux is bundled out.

'Don't expect a big contribution from me when my royalties start pouring in,' bawls Lux as it drives away.

'You should have told them you were having a sex change,' says Kalia, who has loyally left the van with him.

'I never thought of that. Oh well. Let's keep looking.'

Sebastian never makes it to his rendezvous. He is spotted by Johnny and arrested on suspicion of stealing the genetic programme.

Kalia and Lux, approaching, see it happen.

'Aren't you going to help?' whispers Lux, hiding round a corner so as Johnny doesn't see him.

'No.'

'But he's the descendant of Heaven. It might be the important good deed that gets you back.'

'I don't care. I'm sick of it. I don't want to help people I don't like any more. If a famous mythological figure turns up in this century as a power hungry accountant who harasses his secretaries he isn't going to get any assistance from me.'

'How do you know he harasses his secretaries?'

'My powers are returning.'

They walk on.

'Did I ever meet Helen of Troy?'

'Fortunately, no.'

'Did I ever settle down happily with anyone?'

'Yes,' lies Kalia.

'Do you think Pearl will fall in love with me?'

'Yes,' says Kalia, lying again.

She is sad. She is beginning to think that she will never reach her total.

Happy Science has to abandon the genetic programme. Dr Carlson retires a twisted and broken man, spending the rest of his life rambling about how he was unfairly denied a Nobel prize.

The company stays successful, however, led by Mr Socrates into new profitable areas of fast food research and better video cassettes.

'Hello Gerry,' says Lux, as they meet. 'What are you doing still wandering around?'

'Nothing much. I've lost a manuscript.'

'Have this one,' says Lux kindly.

'Where did you get this?' screams Gerry, recognising it as Mary

Luxembourg's.

'I can't remember. Is it important? I'm looking for Pearl. I know she's close.'

'She's in the Enterprise Centre.'

'Brilliant,' says Lux. 'Did she mention me? Did she imply she was falling in love with me?'

'No.'

'Did she mention anything about wanting to fuck me?'

'You disgust me,' says Gerry. 'There is more to relationships than having sex.'

'We've been through all the other bits. We've been through sex as well. But I'm still enthusiastic.'

Gerry gives him a look of contempt but the three of them head for the Enterprise Centre together.

'Look,' says Lux, 'a fox.'

They watch as a fox runs out of some bins and along an alleyway, then they witness one of the most violent sights that any of them see the entire night, a last battle by some particularly determined rioters with some police who have been tracking them over the rooftops with the aid of the helicopter spotlight. Determined not to be arrested, two men and a woman clamber down a drainpipe and make a run for it.

Two policemen set their dogs after them. The dogs run, jaws open, vicious and angered by the noise and confusion of the night.

'Here doggies,' says Lux.

The dogs stop to lick his face.

'What's the idea?' demand the policemen.

'I can't help it. Animals love me.'

He pats them on the head.

The three making the getaway have no chance. Despite Lux diverting the dogs, they are surrounded but, unusually determined, they fight furiously so that more and more policemen have to pile in and it becomes a bloody and one-sided mêlée of boots and truncheons and hate-filled yells.

'Stop hitting them,' says Gerry, but no one takes any notice.

The bodies are carried away face down.

'Pigs,' snorts Gerry. 'They are disgusting.'

'Fancy seeing a fox here,' says Lux. 'It is good the way they are starting to live in cities. What happened next in the perfume contest, Kalia?'

Sebastian is led off as a suspect in the Happy Science scandal. He is later cleared of complicity in the affair, but, missing his rendezvous with Ace Headhunters, does not make it to a position of wealth in Coca Cola. Maybeline is not impressed.

However, he is still a sought-after person, and may yet end up as something important.

But it will take him a very long time to get over the sight of the naked Lux.

Before Kalia has to face telling Lux that what happened next in the perfume-guessing contest was that he was beheaded, Lux grabs her arm.

'There's that man again. The one that arrested the accountant. He's after me as well.'

'Why?'

'I don't know. Some spurious reason, I expect. Unless he wants my autograph. No doubt I could put him off with some well-constructed story but I'm anxious to reach Pearl and give her the film.'

Kalia is starting to feel better now that Sebastian is out of the area and no longer broadcasting psychic disturbance.

'You carry on,' she says. 'I'll divert him. That man is head of the computer police. But he is also Yasmin, and totally evil. You might find it hard to put him off.'

Patrick, watching a specially extended late-night news bulletin, sees Lux approaching the Enterprise Centre, where, by coincidence, he meets Mike, out for another breath of fresh air.

'I don't believe it!' explodes Patrick, worst suspicions confirmed.

'They've arranged a secret meeting in the middle of the riot!'

I'm not standing for this, he thinks, and puts on his coat.

Lux and Gerry enter the building. Gerry goes to use the phone while Lux rushes upstairs.

Too excited to control himself, he bursts into Liberation Computers and throws himnself into Pearl's lap. Drunk, she overbalances and they collapse in a struggling heap onto the floor.

'Hello Pearl,' he bawls, 'I've saved your film.'

Pearl is elated at getting her film back. She kisses Lux. Lux is elated at this and happiness prevails.

Kalia stands in front of Yasmin.

'Hello again,' he says. 'I have been having a very entertaining night. I love all troubles. I love to see people squirm. And I love to keep you here on Earth.

'You can't keep me here on Earth.'

'Can't I? I know you hoped to save the heavenly descendant, Menelaus, King of Sparta, reborn as a power-hungry accountant. Well I have had him thrown in jail. So much for your good deeds.'

'There will be plenty more opportunities.'

'None that I cannot prevent.'

Kalia bites her lip.

Yasmin grins, knowing he is getting to her.

'Later tonight I am going to arrest the small one with red and yellow hair. The effeminate one. I know you like him. I will also have his friends arrested. They are all implicated in robbing Happy Science.'

'I'll prevent you.'

'I doubt it. And if you did, would it count as an act of kindness? To you, yes, but to Heaven? Probably not.'

'And,' he adds maliciously, 'even if it did count it wouldn't help you. You can't get back into Heaven. No one is keeping track of your good deeds any more. My master saw to that. You passed one million long ago. You are never going back.'

'A woman made this film
against

the law
of gravity,'

says Lux, on the floor in a heap with Pearl and the can of film.

'What?' says Pearl.

'A poem by Adrienne Rich. And very appropriate. I love you.'

The general happiness is interrupted by Nicky bursting into tears.

No one can cheer her up. Pearl tries being supportive and Lux gets in the way and Marcus has to stop programming his computer game.

'Can nobody help?'

'It's a difficult case,' says Mike, sagely. 'Deep trauma from killing her computer. She may never recover.'

'Surely there must be some cure?'

'Not much research has been done on it yet. It's a comparatively new disease.'

Pearl puts her arm round Nicky, though she still grasps her film tightly and allows Lux to hold her arm, or the only bit of her arm he can get hold of.

'When I was young,' says Lux. 'I suffered a similar sort of thing when my pet dog fell under the lawnmower. We had a terible time with lawnmowers in my family. Anyway I was distraught but as soon as I got a new puppy I felt much better.'

'So?'

'So give Nicky a new computer. It is bound to help. I was a new person when I got my new puppy. It completely restored me, while I still had it.'

'What happened to it?'

'It got eaten by an alligator when I took it to the zoo. I was never very lucky with my pets. Still, a new computer substitute is bound to help.'

Lux is being cunning as well as helpful, thinking that possibly if Nicky is wrapped up in a new computer then Pearl will have more time for him.

Mike goes and drags something out of a cupboard.

'Here,' he says to Nicky. 'Take this. It's a new model we haven't started to use yet.'

Nicky takes the computer and looks at it. She smiles.

'Lux saves the day again,' says Lux. 'Thwarting the Jane Austen Mercenaries, saving Pearl's film, solving Nicky's problems, talking to TV cameras, guarding squirrels, saving rioters from police dogs...'

'You didn't save them,' says Gerry, fresh from reporting to *Uptown* that both Mary Luxembourg and the riot are fine.

'Saving rioters from police dogs,'continues Lux, ignoring the interruption, 'escaping from ambulances, leaping from burning trees, writing poems, there seems to be nothing I can't do. Good prevails all round.'

'No it doesn't,' protests Gerry. 'Outside there is the remains of a riot and the whole area is totally depressed. I don't see you doing any good in that direction.'

Lux goes to the window.

'The riot was all my fault,' he yells. 'I started it. I am responsible. Now everyone stop rioting and go home.' He pauses. 'Which direction is the Houses of Parliament?'

'Over there.'

Lux points his head in the vague direction of Parliament. 'Give everybody a job and make things better! Pump money into the local economy. Do I make myself clear?'

He leaves the window. 'There. I've done my best. Would anyone like to hear a poem I made up while I was hiding up the tree?'

No one volunteers to listen to the poem.

'Stop ignoring me,' says Nicky to Pearl.

'What?'

'Stop ignoring me. Since Lux brought the film back you've been hugging it like I don't exist.'

Pearl is a little exasperated.

'Well you're too busy with your new computer to pay me any attention. All night I've been keeping you safe and all you're grateful for is a new computer.'

'Well no wonder I need a computer when you're always too busy with your film to pay me any attention. All you've done for months is to make that damn film.'

Slightly drunk, the two women argue.

Ha, thinks Lux, pleased. The new computer plan was a masterstroke. Soon they'll never speak to each other again.

Suddenly catching sight of his reflection in the window, he realises what a shambles he is. He has temporarily forgotten his vanity in the excitement of meeting Pearl. Figuring that he ought to make himself look nice for her he goes to hunt for a toilet to make himself look presentable.

In the corridor he meets Kalia.

'Hi Kalia,' he says cheerfully, 'Pearl and Nicky are having a terrible argument. Soon they'll never speak to each other again. Pearl is bound to fall in love with me.'

He stops.

'What's wrong,' he asks, finally noticing that she is looking immensely sad.

Kalia tells him about her never getting back into Heaven.

So that is where they got to, thinks Johnny, passing by outside with his computer police squad, and hearing Lux's voice.

'Listen,' says Kalia, entering Liberation Computers. 'Johnny and his squad of computer police are still hunting for you.' Her powers of foreknowledge are returning, and despite her own problems she wishes to be helpful. 'I think they will be here soon.'

'What'll we do?' says Pearl. 'They're after Nicky and me. We'd better run.'

'Too late,' says Kalia. 'I can feel them coming. Lock the door and keep silent. We'll hide till we can think of something better.'

* * *

Outside it is now quiet. The police are in control and will continue to patrol the streets in numbers for months to come. Round corners they will sit in rows in their green buses, waiting for trouble.

There will be an inquiry into the riot, like there was an inquiry into the last one.

Newspapers will condemn it as violent hooliganism, and call for wider police powers. They may mention that both blacks and whites were involved, but will be sure to put a picture on the front page of a young black throwing a petrol bomb. They will give a cursory mention to the bad conditions in the area.

Uptown will support it as a justified action against oppression. They will give a cursory mention to all the poor people who got robbed and the women who got raped.

The government will announce a new programme for helping the inner cities. The new pink pavement will be cleaned up and the job centre will get a facelift.

Johnny prowls the corridors with his four men. To an outsider the building is a little confusing with small rooms and corridors everywhere, and they spend a long time searching without finding anything.

'Perhaps they're not here,' suggests one of his men. They are all tired and want to go home.

Johnny considers it. They have been all over the building and found no trace. Perhaps they should abandon the hunt for the night. After all, they have already arrested one major conspirator.

For a brief second it seems that Liberation Computers may escape.

Patrick appears. He has come to give Mike a piece of his mind about the secret meeting with Lux.

'Security,' says Yasmin. 'Do you mind stating your business?'

'I'm just calling in to Liberation Computers on the next floor,' says Patrick.

* * *

Everyone at Liberation Computers is becoming drunk as more emergency brandy is passed around.

'He saved my film,' says Pearl to Kalia. 'He told me all about leaping into the blazing inferno. I guess he is not so useless.'

Kalia is looking thoughtful.

'Right Mike,' shouts Patrick, unlocking the door and bursting in. 'What's the idea of walking out on me and then carrying on with floozies in the street? And what about the secret rendezvous with Lux? Don't deny it, I saw it on television.'

'You're all under arrest,' says Johnny, appearing behind him, 'for complicity in the theft of a secret genetic programme. And wrecking Happy Science property, stealing the programme and interfering with legitimate police business. And I will have to confiscate this film which contains classified material from Happy Science, illegally gained.'

In the toilet, Lux, fixing his make-up, is thoughtful. He is thinking about Kalia and thinking about everything else.

Pearl, film threatened, tries to hit Johnny with the brandy bottle but he blocks the blow and a fight ensues, a fight in which Pearl and the rest have little chance and Liberation Computers suffers more damage.

'Excuse me,' says Lux very loudly, reappearing in the room, face shining. The fight stops.

'I am aware that you do not take me or my poetry seriously. Nevertheless, I am now going to read a poem. I have just written it. It is about my friend Kalia, and me. It's called *On being exiled from Heaven for three thousand years, on being exiled from Pearl for ever.*'

He pulls out a sheet of paper from his carrier bag.

* * *

Outside in the blackness of the night firemen dampen down some remaining flames and the newsmen go home to bed.

Lux's poem is heart-rendingly beautiful. It talks of Kalia's misery in eternal exile and Lux's misery in eternal loneliness. Everyone in the room forgets everything else and listens.

Lux, so eager to write the poem that he didn't finish his eye make-up, reads it out, a steady voice in the silence.

His voice sucks in the onlookers. The poem makes their hearts ache. Every sad and lonely feeling ever felt between Heaven and Earth haunts each line, every hopeless defeat ever suffered by humanity is contained in its words.

He finishes. People are wiping away tears.

Yasmin sniffs loudly before turning abruptly and leaving.

Confused, his men follow.

CHAPTER TWENTY THREE

In the silence of Yasmin's departure, nobody speaks.

Lux, having finally had a dramatic effect on the real world, is a little embarrassed, and stares at his feet.

Kalia slips out quietly.

Pearl and Nicky sit holding hands and staring into each other's eyes while Mike and Patrick huddle in a corner, all relationships reconciled after listening to the poem.

Liberation Computers is a wreck after the fight. Another failure for the social security's start-your-own-business scheme. Marcus starts tidying up.

* * *

Outside Kalia meets Yasmin.

He tells her that Lux's poem has made him cry for the first time in three thousand years. He is going to abandon his persecution of Kalia and inform the proper authorities in Heaven that her sentence is completed.

He leaves. His men, not understanding, hang around. Kalia, unsure whether to believe him or not, wanders back inside. There is little of the riot left anywhere.

Suddenly her ability to read the future returns in full and she starts running up the stairs.

With Marcus busy clearing up, Mike and Patrick in a corner, and Pearl, Nicky, Pearl's film and the new computer in a close embrace, there is no one for Lux to talk to. For the first time in his life he feels awkward.

'Well,' he says. 'I'm going to look for a TV camera.'

'Lux,' says Pearl.

'What?'

'Nothing.'

Lux crosses to the window and peers out.

'A film crew,' he says, excited, returning somewhat to his normal state. 'There's a film crew out there. They're filming the mopping-up operations. Hey! Look up here! It's me, Lux the Poet!'

He leans out of the window and starts shouting out some of his favourite lines.

'Be careful Lux,' says Pearl, seeing that he is a little unsteady. 'You're not well.'

'Of course I'm well,' says Lux. 'I'm an important local poet. How well can you get?'

He climbs onto the window sill, waves to the camera, faints from loss of blood and falls to the ground outside.

Gerry is on his way back to personally deliver his riot report to the all-night emergency editorial meeting at the offices of *Uptown*.

When he arrives he finds Mary Luxembourg sitting in.

'Hi,' he says. 'I've brought your manuscript.'

'What's this I hear about a retrospective?'

'What retrospective? Nothing to do with me.'

Pearl rushes downstairs, barges past Kalia and runs out into the street in time to see Lux picking himself up off the pavement.

'Lux, you idiot. You trying to kill yourself?'

It seems miraculous that he is unhurt. But, stunned by the fall, Lux no longer quite realises what is happening. Seeing the remains of the computer police in the distance, Johnny's men now standing leaderless, he thinks that Pearl is still in danger. He grabs her arm and runs. Pearl runs with him.

Round a corner he dives under a burnt-out truck.

'We'll hide here for a while,' he says.

Sebastian is released from the police station, freed pending further investigation. The Jane Austen Mercenaries walk out at the same time, silently depressed.

Sebastian phones Maybeline, but she isn't home.

'What the hell is this?' demands Mary Luxembourg, brandishing her novel, the only copy of which is now covered in Lux's poems, scrawls and alterations.

'Your novel,' replies Gerry. Not actually having read it, he doesn't realise there is anything wrong with it.

'Don't count on any endorsements from me,' says the author, a little upset.

'It wasn't such a bad night,' says Lux under the truck. 'I get stuffed full of cocaine, I write a good poem, I meet a nice woman from Scotland and a nice woman from Heaven. And I end up lying under a truck with you, which is best. We can leave when the riot finishes.'

'The riot is finished.'

'Can't be,' says Lux. 'I can still hear all the shouting.'

'That was a good poem,' says Pearl.

'Thank you.' Lux shivers and pulls his coat tighter around him. 'I'm pleased you're getting on well with Nicky,' he says.

Blood loss and huge internal injuries from the fall get the better of him. He coughs, sighs, and dies.

'Lux?' says Pearl. 'Lux?'

She twists her head round and stares into the small dark space beneath the truck, expecting him at any minute to sit up and start quoting *Paradise Lost*, just to prove he knows it. Lux, however, is too dead to quote any more poetry.

Kalia apears with Nicky, and helps Pearl out from under the vehicle.

'You go home,' she says. 'I'll wait here for an ambulance.'

The night is busy with patrolling policemen but still and quiet in Kalia's soul.

Waiting for the ambulance she has the sudden conviction that a good turn she can do for Lux will be the one that gets her back into Heaven. So she cleans his face and arranges his hair a little, knowing he would like to look his best.

Nothing happens. She is not returned to Heaven.

The ambulance arrives and takes Lux away and Kalia walks off into the night.

'Goodbye Lux,' she says, without emotion. 'You never managed to fit in anywhere, did you?'

Round the corner she comes across a tramp, shivering because someone has stolen his coat.

Kalia takes off her own coat and gives it to him. She tingles slightly, and de-materialises, saved from any more suffering on Earth.

Also available in Fourth Estate Paperbacks
by Martin Millar

Dreams of Sex & Stage Diving

Elfish, a woman who rarely eats and never washes, is governed by twin obsessions: her thrash metal band and Queen Mab, Shakespeare's dream fairy from *Romeo and Juliet*. To feed her dreams Elfish is obliged to lie, cheat and steal. Happily, Elfish is a compulsive liar, and fond of cheating and stealing . . .

This novel finds Martin Millar on sparkling form, racing through an urban landscape that is both as real as concrete and as ethereal as stardust.

ISBN: 1 85702 213 0 £5.99

Milk, Sulphate & Alby Starvation

'What's allergic to milk, collects comics, sells speed, likes The Fall and lives in Brixton? Alby Starvation, the first true British anti-hero of the Giro generation. *Milk, Sulphate & Alby Starvation* is a strange and wonderful story . . . I've yet to come across someone who has not enjoyed it.' – *New Statesman*

ISBN: 1 85702 214 9 £5.99

All Fourth Estate books are available at your local bookshop or newsagent, or can be ordered direct from the publisher.

Indicate the number of copies required and quote the author and title.

Send cheque/eurocheque/postal order (Sterling only), made payable to Book Service by Post, to:

Fourth Estate Books
Book Service By Post
PO Box 29, Douglas
I-O-M, IM99 1BQ.

Or phone: 01624 675137

Or fax: 01624 670923

Or e-mail: bookshop@enterprise.net

Alternatively pay by Acces, Visa or Mastercard

Card number: □□□□□□□□□□□□□□□□

Exprity date ....

Signature ....

Post and packing is free in the UK. Overseas customers please allow £1.00 per book for post and packing.

Name ....

Address ....

....

....

Please allow 28 days for delivery. Please tick the box if you do not wish to receive any additional information. □

Prices and availability subject to change without notice.